Pat,

ON CLIPPED WINGS

Where else, but in books,
can we capture the souls of
mankind with whom we
cannot always connect...?

Jameela

6/7/15

ON CLIPPED WINGS

Where else, but in books,
can we capture the
souls of mankind with whom
we cannot always connect...?

JAMEELA ALTER

To order additional copies of this book, contact:
Xlibris Corporation
1-888-795-4274
www.Xlibris.com
Orders@Xlibris.com
32402

DEDICATION

To Pappa and Mamma who graciously served the noble Dawoodi Bohra community for as long as I can remember.

To my husband, Steve, and to my daughters, Yasmin and Shirin—For making my life complete.

ACKNOWLEDGEMENTS

No man is an island. Therefore, it goes without saying that without the invaluable help of my family and friends this book would never have been completed. My deepest thanks goes to:

My ever-loving husband, Steven Alter—without you it would have been impossible for me to arrive at this point. Thank you for laboring with me; for putting up with my flaky ways; for your love, your support, and your patience.

Dr. Julia Elam—thank you for playing the organ, playing the piano, treating me to snacks, and then going through page after page after page of my manuscript! What great memories to carry to my rocking chair! Thank you for your encouragement.

Patti Euler—the catalyst—my bottomless thanks for your faith and encouragement. Without you I may never have come this far!

Dr. Virginia Guilford—thank you for opening the doors of the English department at Bowie State University. The encouragement I received simply rekindled my dormant passion to write. Thank you for going through my manuscript; for guiding me, and encouraging me.

Nutan Jai—thank you for smiling even as I rushed you to guide me within unreasonable time frames; thank you for your invaluable insights and corrections; thank you for allowing me to breeze in and out of your home as and when I needed to.

Patti Price—thank you for reading my manuscript; for pointing out mistakes that I happily corrected; thank you for your faith and encouragement.

CONTENTS

CHAPTER 1

INNOCENCE

Komli's one pleasure in life was to get drenched in the rain. Sitting cross-legged on the side-walk, with a parched face and one spindly hand turned skyward in total abandon, she gorged on every droplet that came her way. Her gritty skin began to glisten like desert sand. Her eyes sparkled with excitement. Watching her, one would think Santa Claus was wafting towards her on bulging black clouds filled with gifts. The puddle of water around her slowly turned muddy brown, while what usually looked like knots of coarse rope on her head gradually turned to multitudinous black curls not quite able to tumble down her slender shoulders because her hair had never been combed. Suddenly that horrible itching was gone, for a few hours at least. Thank goodness it rained quite often in Calcutta because that was the only time the beggar girl and her one and only threadbare dress had some reprieve from the soot and grime of the city. Not that Komli cared one way or another about her body. As far as she was concerned, it was just an uncollapsable frame that housed one, singular desire—to milk a handful of pennies from the wealthy by showing them her butchered left hand. People responded well to Komli; she had a stump for left hand, an engaging smile, no trace of self-pity, and large hazel eyes that bore no signs of becoming dulled, even though she was always hovering on the brink of starvation.

The earth had circled around the sun only seven times since Komli was born. All Komli had learned during those first seven revolutionary years was that her role in life was to beg and beg and beg, day in and day out. There were no lunch breaks, no weekends, no holidays. Like the stray dogs and cats of Calcutta, with some of whom she had made friends, she was oblivious of the arbitrary division of time into weeks, months and years. She had some sense of the passage of time from the rising and setting of the sun and from the waning and waxing of the moon. She had some sense of the only change in season she knew, when her body shivered during the somewhat colder winter months. Fortunately, winter was short and summer long. Heat and humidity did not bother her as much as the cold. Like her stray animal friends, she was content to let the sun and the stars dictate when she should grapple for food from trash cans and when she should sleep. Instinctively, she knew she must live and let live in order to survive, so she always shared her loot with her animal friends, happy in the knowledge that, unlike inferior quadrupeds, she had the intelligence at least to charm people out of a few precious pennies. Pennies which she handed over to her mother who, in turn, handed the money over to Rana.

Rana was the only *animal* Komli disliked.

"Look, Ma, even the dogs and cats scurry away when he comes skulking around," Komli remarked once.

"Shhh, little one. He'll hear you!" Ma reprimanded gently, while she wished in her heart of hearts that she, too, could scurry away when Rana slithered in with his crocodile smile and shifty eyes that were more often than not concealed behind cheap, black sunglasses. The words from his forked tongue were always poison to her ears.

"So how much did my girls make today?" he asked perfunctorily. If the pennies weighted his hands down more than usual he would smile at Ma's older daughter, Roshni. "It won't be too long before I'll give you a room of your own."

Yes, yes, I know, Roshni always wanted to scream back as she stared at him with dulled eyes. You'll give me a room, and a huge bed, and beautiful saris, and plenty of cosmetics, and a mirror, if you please. And all the begging will come to an end because we'll prosper on the mangy commission you'll allow me, you bastard of a niggardly pimp!

"You're not listening to me are you?! Come, let's go. You still need lots of training." Go she did, without any resistance. She had learned long ago that to resist meant causing her beloved Ma unnecessary anguish. To make matters worse, her precious little sister was at that questioning age. And even unschooled Roshni understood that there was no way one could explain to a seven year old that the streets of Calcutta were littered with women who quietly allowed their bodies to be abused so loved ones could survive.

Silence became Roshni's armor; it was with silence that she swathed emotions on the verge of erupting; it was in silence that she swallowed her tears, like an iceberg that never drips; and it was in silence that she wished her untainted heart and soul could detach itself from her defiled body. But, like an athlete in training, she was tough; she could will her body to do whatever her horrendously demanding *coach* asked of her in order that she could become pick number one among women accomplished in the arts of pleasing men. She knew that if she failed, all hope would be lost for her ailing Ma and beloved little sister. So Roshni went through life with the somewhat serene disposition of a nun, hoping that a better life awaited her, hoping that the hell she went through each night was but a pathway to heaven, if not for her, at least for the only two people that mattered in her otherwise cold and callous world.

For Ma, Rana was a nocturnal nightmare who probably tormented more women each day than the pennies she earned and whose veins probably carried more alcohol than blood. She hated the occasions when Rana forgot to put on his sunglasses because she couldn't bear to look into his evil, blotchy, bloodshot eyes. Being the kind of brute who got a perverse pleasure out of forcing people to do what they hated, he often grabbed Ma by the chin and yanked it upwards so she was forced to look into his evil eyes. Of him, Ma had once simply remarked, "The mighty sun must be happy it doesn't have to waste its rays on a creature so foul!"

Rain water was for free, thank heavens! Especially good were the times when it seemed that the sky had opened up its entire vault so rain could come pouring down like one massive, musical, gray sheet through which it was impossible to see anything. While Komli reveled in the rain as children do universally, those were the times when Roshni cried with abandon, knowing that neither her Ma nor her sister would be able to tell that some of the water coursing down her face was salty. Ma accepted the rain wordlessly, as she did her hapless fate, wishing that rain water would cleanse her soul as it did her body.

Although it was yet to make it on the stock market, begging was one of the thriving industries of Calcutta. It was over twenty years ago that Rana had been inducted into that world:

"I've watched you pick-pocketing rich men, young lad. You're pretty impressive!"

"Oh yeah?!" Rana had responded warily, wondering if the stranger was a policeman dressed in plain clothes. His gut feeling had been to the contrary though; the man was dressed in black; he was a little too sleek; something about him did not smell right.

"Got family?" the stranger had asked.

"It's none of your business!"

"Well, I'll tell you what my business is; then maybe you'll tell me. I hire handsome, single, cunning, young lads like you to bring me young beggar women and their children. I pay my men about ten times what you can make picking pockets, and I can guarantee that the police will never bother you. I give you a room to live in and as many women as you want as many nights as you want."

"What do I have to do?" Rana had asked cagily.

"Got family?" the stranger asked, tongue in cheek.

"No."

"That's what I thought."

"How do you know?"

"Let's see, in the last three days you've successfully robbed nine people, three men, two women, three old ladies, and an innocent young school kid: two on Park Street, one in Chandni Chawk, two in . . . ."

"Why have you been following me?"

"Not me. Let's just say that I own the streets of Calcutta. My men have been observing you. I'm told you will do well with us. They tell me you are hungry for money and ready for women. Is that right?"

Dumbfounded, all Rana could do was to stare at the stranger.

"And you do not have a home?"

"I used to live with my uncle. He beat me and his kids during the day and his wife at night. One day I decided to run away. They don't miss me. One less mouth to feed!"

Perfect catch, thought the stranger to himself as he delved into his pocket, "Look, here's five hundred rupees in advance. Bring me a beggar woman with a young child, preferably an infant. Entice them in any way you wish. You have till this time tomorrow. If you are successful, I will pay you three times five hundred."

"Is this what . . . ."

"No more questions. I hire those who can carry out orders. If you are successful, I will explain fully. Go!"

"What if I run away with your money?"

"My men deal with those who don't show up," the stranger replied smoothly and stalked off.

Rana returned the following afternoon, catch in hand.

"Good job! the stranger remarked without so much as looking at the teenage girl with the infant in her arms. "Watch the bitch. I will return with the infant in a few hours. By the way, what is your name?"

"Rana."

Rana spent the night trying to drown out with alcohol the horror he had witnessed that afternoon. As promised, the infant had been returned to the teen-aged mother. Two soggy, bloody rags swaddled whatever was left above his knees. The unconscious child looked like a legless stump. The teenage mother shrieked and wailed and pounded with all her might upon Rana's chest. The infant was motionless, Rana deathly pale, while the stranger simply waited for the furor to abate, as he knew it inevitably would. When the wailing stopped, the stranger turned to Rana and said matter-of-factly, "They howl like animals, eat like animals, and procreate like animals! She's yours now. Screw the bitch when you wish but, above all, train her to screw well. Rich men pay good money for a good whore."

"What if she refuses?"

"Refuse?! A homeless bitch with a maimed, bastard child? Tomorrow my men will teach you how to dangle the right carrots in front of her so she does not refuse!" He turned to the whimpering mother and addressed her next, "Ask and you shall receive, god's men preach. You will be amazed what you will receive now when you beg. Just make sure you hold up your baby so people can see he's crippled. Rana here will visit you each night and give you an allowance from what you earn. If you're good, you'll sleep in his shelter at night. As for you, Rana, go get a drink! It's what makes the world go round. I'll see you tomorrow."

"What if she goes to the police?" Rana whispered.

"Have you ever seen an animal go to the police?" the stranger asked coolly.

And I suppose the police have no time for the thousands of homeless animals that wander the streets, Rana thought to himself as he walked in the direction of the nearest liquor house.

"My men call me Captain," the stranger had informed Rana the following morning. "The more women and infants you bring to me, the more you make. In time you'll find it's not a bad life at all—women, wine, cigarettes, cards, dice, get up when you want, sleep when you want. Here are a couple of rules you must follow: those beggars must remain illiterate, and, above all, the little voice that drums inside each wretched beggar must drum one message alone—*I'm hungry, I'm hungry, I'm hungry.* Never leave them enough money to have too much food. Now, let me introduce you to the guy who will show you your room and whatever you need to know. If things run smoothly, we may never meet again. So long."

Within a few months, Rana became an expert at training his squad of beggars: *The first thing you do, before you go up to beg is to determine whether the man or woman is a Muslim, Hindu, or Christian. Muslim men often have beards, their women might be in purdah; Hindu women wear saris, they have tikas on their foreheads; Christians are of fairer skin; their women wear dresses. So, say you've determined the woman is a Muslim, tell her you're starving, show her your handicapped child, tell her he hasn't eaten for days and, above all, make sure you tell her Allah will bless her children. You must know the names of their deities. Muslims pray to Allah. Hindus to Bhagvaan and Christians to Jesus. Invoke the name of the right deity. Make them remember their own children who are not as unfortunate as you are. Nine times out of ten, they will relent. Sometimes there will be no giveaway signs, but with the precious few items of knowledge rattling around in your empty brains, you should be able to make an educated guess! Of course, like any other game, you'll win some and lose some. And you must know the colors on the traffic lights. Red means GO. Go scurry up to the rich, make sure they see deformities. Milk their pitying hearts. Beg and beg and beg, until they relent, or the light turns green. That's when you STOP. Yellow must be ignored; it is for the cowardly!*

Invariably the lessons worked wonders. Unlike athletes who are told that it is more important to participate than to win, these beggars were taught the opposite: *It is crucial to win! Your lives depend upon it. Even if the glass in the car is rolled up and the passenger inside is looking the other way, shove your deformity up on the glass, keep putting your hand to your mouth, rub your belly to show you are starving, look up to Heaven. Sooner or later the donor will feel sorry for you. Just never give up. If he is walking, keep walking beside him, pester him and pester him. Keep repeating the motions you have been taught until he relents.*

Captain had been right; in time Rana simply accepted that aberrations like a hole for a nose, no eyeball in one socket, or a castrated limb here and there were just a part and parcel of the baggage carried by the beggars of Calcutta. Ironically, the educated masses of Calcutta contributed to the success of the begging industry because somewhere between shuffling in and out of schools and colleges, they had learnt that the poor and the meek are the apples of god's eyes; that theirs is the kingdom of heaven. It was not difficult for the literate to deduce, therefore, that every time one gave alms to the poor, God would look down on one, too, with kindly eyes.

In time, Roshni became Rana's most prized victim. The fact that Roshni had both an ailing mother and an infant sister to feed made it easier for him to manipulate her as he willed.

"Come on, Tusneem darling, please finish your chocolate milk. You'll be late for school."

"I'm full, Mamma. I keep telling you, ayah fills up the glass too high."

"And I keep telling you, eat less toast and honey. You don't have to finish your egg, but you must finish your milk. What is it good for?"

"My two hundred and six bones, I know, I know," Tusneem said with good humor as she raised the glass to her mouth and downed the rest of the milk. She loved learning and, in spite of the long drawn-out breakfast ritual, she always made it to school on time, thanks to ayah, her doting maidservant, and to her chauffeur who somehow managed to honk his way through Calcutta's countless jaywalkers, traffic jams, and fearless rickshaw-wallahs tearing through the streets like two-legged Roadrunners, not to mention confused cows squatting on the asphalt, wondering where all the green meadows had gone.

"I keep telling you Sahib (sir), you need to have more children so Memsahib (madam) can stop doting on her one and only. I can't remember Burrasahib (big sir) ever worrying about what you or your brothers and sisters ate. And in the fifty years I've served your family, I never saw one broken bone! Nor did I have one white hair until you got married, Sahib!"

"That will be all, Abdul, clear the breakfast," Zenub said as politely as she could.

"I wish you would not allow Abdul to take so many liberties, Rashid!" Zenub told her husband as soon as Abdul had disappeared. "How many times do I have to tell you that it does not bode well for the rest of the servants that Abdul gets away with all his cheekiness?"

"He means well, Zenub. You know it. I'll talk to him privately, if you insist, but don't forget he was there when all my brothers and sisters were born. For some reason, he doted on me."

"Too bad there were no more siblings after you!" Zenub retorted with a half smile.

"Pappa and Mamma had so many social commitments that I saw Abdul more than I saw my parents. Except perhaps on Sundays. Do you know, neither Pappa nor Mamma ever raised a hand to me but . . ."

"Abdul did, I bet!"

"Yup!" Rashid said with a laugh. I was probably five or six years old. Abdul knew how much I loved to see the cows being milked. So every morning, about the time the sun came up, Abdul woke me up. Down we went, hand in hand, to greet the milk man coming down the lane with his big fat white cow. Abdul would hand the milk man the same old pail. We watched the milkman squeeze and pull and squeeze on the cow's pink udders. It was magical to watch! Sometimes he would shout at the poor milkman and accuse him of giving us milk adulterated with water!"

"Hasn't changed much, has he!"

"Well, one day, I managed to wiggle away from Abdul and got right under the cow's belly. I actually managed to squeeze its udders a couple of times before I felt my bottom being spanked with quite a whollop! 'You get kicked by this cow and I get kicked out of a job,' Abdul hollered. He yanked me by the ear and made sure I stood well out of reach of that cow."

"Was that the last of the cow milking you saw?"

"Oh no. I think Abdul loved taking me as much as I loved watching the milk come oozing out into the bucket."

Zenub looked at Rashid with loving eyes, "Calcutta's famous judge Rashid is just a sweet country boy at heart. I wonder how many people know that."

"What others think and what others know is of little consequence to me, as long as you understand me, Zenub. No one is as precious to me as you and our Tusneem."

"And Abdul?"

"And Abdul, but in a different kind of way, Zenub. I care for him deeply because I'm old enough and smart enough to know that in this day and age we will never be able to get a servant who will look after our household like Abdul does. You do know that he would willingly give his life for us, don't you?"

"Go on," Zenub said softly, You always find such wonderful qualities in people."

"Abdul sees his family about four times a year . . ."

"Thanks to your indulgence. Most servants go to their village twice a year, if that."

"And you think he loves his wife any less than I love you? His children any less than I love Tusneem? He is a warm, loving, noble servant who pours all his pent up love on us 'cause he's away so much from his family. We, who lack in nothing, are so lucky to have Abdul even though I know he oversteps the limit sometimes."

"And I am so lucky to have such a kind, wise, doting husband."

"I think Abdul's right about us trying to have more children. Shall we, before I go to work?"

"Yeah, right, to have Abdul walk in on us because it's time for him to dust and polish and re-polish your dresser, and rocker, and fountain-pen for all I know!"

"Then I'll take a rain-check for tonight, alright?"

"Maybe."

"What are you doing this morning?"

"Having lunch with my old school friend, Neelum. Now don't go telling Abdul," Zenub quipped sarcastically, "Otherwise I'll have to cleanse myself for being defiled by Hindus!"

"Sarcasm doesn't behoove you, Zenub! Enjoy your lunch. I better go get dressed for court."

"It's Friday, Rashid, don't forget to give Abdul alms for the beggars."

"Come, Roshni, come, Ma," Komli said excitedly, "We have to be in front of the line. It's the day for alms-giving at the rich peoples' house."

"Are you sure? Do you have your seven petals?" Ma asked with a smile.

"Yup! Let's line up."

Cascading boughs of bright magenta, tissue-like bougainvillea leaves adorned the wrought iron gates to the Khan household. Every time the gates opened, the leaves fluttered gently, as if to say, come get what you can while someone wealthy is passing through. It hadn't taken Komli long to figure out that it was tradition in the Khan household to start every seventh day with a donation of alms for people like her. Not only did she make sure she was first in line, she also pulled off a bougainvillea leaf each day in order to keep track of when it was time to line up again.

And the line was always long. Early in the morning, one of the servants stepped outside with a huge copper bowl filled with pennies. Always, there were more beggars than pennies in the bowl, pennies that the servants handed out condescendingly, knowing that for a short while in their dutiful lives they were superior beings—superior to those that groveled shamelessly for but a few pennies.

"It's so good to live on the street outside this mansion," Komli exclaimed from time to time. Her seven-year-old brain had also figured out that when a lot of cars went through the gates, sooner or later someone was sure to come out with the most exquisite leftovers— leftovers that even the servants deemed unfit to eat—bones devoid of meat and rice swimming in mustard puddles of unfinished curries. One of the kindlier servants brought it out on a 'platter' of soggy white rotlees (unleavened bread), which would have definitely disintegrated had they not been wolfed down as soon as they touched the untouchable hands of beggars.

After licking the bones to a polish, Komli cracked them open, as effortlessly as a dog. Every bit of marrow and juice wound its way down to her growling, appreciative stomach. The cracked, sharp, ivory bones that were finally relinquished rarely hurt a shoeless pedestrian because the bones were immediately whisked away by other starving scavengers scouting the streets of Calcutta, scavengers who had their own assigned rung on the hierarchy of street dwellers. Sometimes it was hard to tell who was way down at the bottom—the rat, the cockroach, the fly, the little ant or the minute little fleas who seemed to believe that safety lay in numbers.

It was hard to tell who appreciated a particular food the most—those that had it piping hot, served on polished platters of silver and bone china, or the less civilized animal kingdom that fought for it like spectators at a baseball game scrambling for the ball that comes flying out to the stands.

Hunger pangs rarely assailed Roshni. Being the first-born child, she paid close attention to Ma's advice. "Eat less than you get; that way your stomach will shrink to a point where it will feel full quickly. Without a full stomach, you can never be powerful. Besides, your little sister is always hungry. Little children need more food to grow. Give her some of your share if you can."

Komli was the only doll Roshni had ever played with; Komli was the only loving reprieve Roshni had from the men who abused her. Without begrudging her anything, Roshni happily indulged her spirited sister who, in turn, seemed to have an insatiable appetite not just for food but for learning as well. And the streets were such a storehouse for learning. Komli inspected everything she could lay her hands on—sticks, stones, bottles, pictures on discarded papers, a spider, a dog, wheels on cars, peoples' expressions, their makeup, their million mannerisms. She had all the time to study the world in motion: in cars, in buses, in trams, and on the Herculean, but skinny legs of rickshaw-wallahs; masses going to school, to work, to shop, to worship, in shoes, in high heels, in low heels. Shoes too were fascinating to study, although Komli was yet to experience what it was like to have a cushion between the hardened, cracked soles of her feet and the hardened, cracked concrete of the city.

The luncheon with Neelum was a disaster in that it shattered Zenub's peace of mind to smithereens.

"You know, Zenub," Neelum asked in the course of conversation, "I heard the other day that you Bohra women are circumcised at the age of seven so you don't get too wild in bed, and it discourages infidelity in married women. Is that true?!"

"Whoever told you that?" Zenub asked with bated breath, while her thoughts flashed back like a bolt of lightning to that unmentionable of unmentionable day of childhood when something painful had been done to her between her legs. She recalled clearly how she had been taken to her grandmother's house, asked to lie down on the floor, legs astride, while Nargisboo Kaachwallah (glass lady) a woman with fiery red hair, had bent over her and hurt her between her legs. Next thing she remembered was that she had to lie in bed for a day and that it stung when she urinated.

"Someone from your community told me. Is it true? Neelum asked with a grimace.

"I wasn't!" Zenub replied, a little too sharply. No, she quickly decided, she wasn't going to share her personal trauma with a school friend she met but a handful of times a year. Besides, she was now a happily married woman who not only had everything money could buy, she also had to protect the reputation of her well-renowned family.

Although Neelum had a strong suspicion that Zenub was lying, she chose to drop the subject. They were both mothers with umpteen other topics of conversation with which to while away a couple of hours.

It was with mixed emotions that Zenub bade farewell to her friend. Her marriage to Rashid had been arranged by the mutual consent of both parents. While love had slowly crept into their marriage, especially after the birth of their baby girl, Tusneem, sex had yet to become an act of passion for Zenub. For some unknown reason, orgasms always escaped her. Sex, however, was not something to be discussed. It was an act of secrecy, to be performed within tightly closed doors of one's room and heart. So Zenub never let anyone know that she yearned to have an orgasm, even if just once in her life. She refused to ask anyone what might be wrong with her, not even her older sister, Sakina, with whom she shared most secrets. She simply resigned herself to what she had read in magazines— that she was but one among thousands of women who were not fated to experience sex to the fullest. Everyone had crosses to bear, she had learned from the nuns in school, and she was wise enough to realize that her cross was not that heavy a burden to bear compared to the beggars who lived outside her house. No, she would never, never, never tell anyone how much she yearned to have an orgasm that no amount of money could buy.

While on the one hand she felt curiously elated that perhaps the reason why she could not have orgasms was because of what had been done to her all those years ago as opposed to her lacking in some sort of sexual drive, on the other hand she felt like a panic-stricken lioness who knew that her cub, her precious, one and only daughter had just turned seven. All Zenub could think of was that she must protect her little one at all cost.

Zenub sat back in her car, allowing fear and painful memories to crisscross through her mind while her chauffeur mechanically wove her Mercedes in and out of the busy streets. The driver could tell that his Memsahib was deeply distressed. Not only was she kind and gracious, she always had a smile for him. He had never known her to slump into the back seat like a speechless ghost.

In the few seconds that it took for the gates to be opened, Komli managed to present herself, showing her maimed hand in the hope of getting her usual pennies. It was with a different eye that Zenub saw that maimed hand this time. "Please Allah, save my little one," was all she could say to herself as she fished out a ten rupee bill from her leather purse and handed it to Komli.

Zenub decided there and then that she would have to summon up the courage to ask Sakina about circumcision, as awkward a conversation as that might turn out to be. Circumcision was one of the very few subjects the two sisters had never discussed.

Komli turned the bill over a couple of times, wondering if paper money had the same value as coins.

"Woh! Who's your guardian angel?" asked a husky voice breathing down Komli's neck.

"None of your business! What are you doing here, Nuttoo?"

Nuttoo was the eight year old son of a rickshaw-wallah. Neither father nor son had ever been to school, but at least they did not have to beg in order to survive. The pittance the rickshaw-wallah earned each day pulling people around for as long as his body permitted went towards feeding his wife and three children. Komli loved meandering in and out of the shacks Calcutta's manual laborers set up at random on the sidewalks of Calcutta. These shanty dwellings, that the educated referred to as slums that they would never deign to step into, housed surprisingly happy, clean people who cared only for their fundamental needs and for their neighbors.

A poor cobbler hardly cared that each of the four precarious walls of his abode had been erected with different materials. At least the patchwork of discarded cardboard, bamboo, metal, and plastic provided him with a shelter. At least the tattered towels and bed sheets and worn-out clothing thrown over his walls provided him with a roof over his head. He never did have to worry about windows; there were always cracks and crevices between the un-cemented materials that allowed him to gaze into the outside world.

The original colors of each shack had long disappeared under the soot and grime of an industrialized city. Although no two shelters were ever alike, sooner or later all the shacks assumed the uniform look of a black-brown growth of fungus. But the fungus served as a black umbrella that protected the under-privileged from the less severe ravages of nature. And if the more severe floods and typhoons washed away their ingenious shelters, the good news was that not a single penny had been spent on building the shacks; they contained no belongings or precious artifacts the cobblers or fishermen could call their own. The poor simply let it go; it was but a whim of the gods. And since they had no money any way to pass away their time at the movies or on vacation, they never resented the fact that they would have to spend time rummaging for more discarded materials with which they could quickly prop up yet another shelter.

Because there were no schools in these slums, its nameless meandering alleyways were usually teeming with unattended, semi-naked children happily whiling away toy-less hours playing hopscotch or jumping rope on fleshless limbs supporting huge, pot-bellied stomachs. Because cooking indoors in such dwellings was a fire-hazard, most women cooked in the alleyways themselves, happy in the knowledge that from infancy their carefree, playful children had acquired the dexterity for dodging coal-burning clay stoves.

"Want to play? Or we could go buy some candy—I see you're rich today!" Nuttoo exclaimed.

"This money's for my sister. So we can have a room, like you."

"We can wait a little longer. I think you should go buy some candy," a soft voice behind her coaxed indulgently.

"I didn't see you! When did you get here, Roshni?"

"Crept up on you didn't I! Who gave you all that money?"

"The rich lady. But she didn't smile like always. Will this money help us to get a room a little sooner?"

"Perhaps," Roshni replied, gently stroking her sister on the head. Her dulled eyes sparkled with love for her trusting, naïve little sister. "Go buy Nuttoo a treat," Roshni urged. "Just come back with the change for Rana. It will be our secret." Roshni knew that it was to Nuttoo and to the more fortunate slum-dwellers that Komli often strayed when Ma decided to let her have a reprieve from begging. Komli loved playing with the other children and, if she was lucky, a kind mother sometimes shared a morsel of food with her. It was in these slums that Roshni had inadvertently picked up some tid-bits about the prehistoric art of cooking food. Komli's favorite treat, suttoo, came from Nuttoo's mother. Komli loved watching the woman knead a beautiful round ball with lentil-flour and water, to which she added salt, onions, and green chilies. Nuttoo's mother made sure her husband had this uncooked dough day in and day out because it was said to give one the kind of strength required to pull rickshaws from dawn to dusk. Knowing that the little girl's eyes turned almost as large as her ball of dough, Nuttoo's mother always threw Komli a sampling. Some mothers shooed Komli away like a fly but, like all flies, Komli seemed to take no offence, knowing that she was free to flit off to someone else.

"Let's go, Komli," Nuttoo said, dragging Komli by the hand, "it's about time you treated me!"

"Where's the candy store?"

"I'll show you. Let's go."

It was a day for unusual happenings. Nuttoo took a wrong turn. Instead of the candy store, the two landed up at the Calcutta zoo. Komli had no idea what lay inside. She simply stared in fascination at the turnstile.

"Can we go back and forth?"

"Looks like you need a ticket," Nuttoo replied.

A kindly gentleman with two children smiled down at them just then. A smile was a very good sign, Komli had learned a long time ago.

"What's inside, Sahib?" she asked, returning the smile.

"The zoo."

"What's in the zoo?" Komli persisted.

A deprived beggar, the gentleman realized as he looked at her more closely. "Would you like to go inside?

"And my friend?" Komli asked, beaming from cheek to cheek. Wow, she thought to herself, she had asked and she had received, without begging!

The gentleman even gave them money to buy nuts for the monkeys. Komli walked through the turnstile, feeling as important as a queen. As for the nuts, there was no way she was going to share that with monkeys!

"Where have you been?" Ma asked with anger and relief when Komli finally returned late that evening.

"I got a ticket to go to the zoo."

"You're not supposed to spend money on other things. If Rana hears we'll be in trouble!"

"I didn't spend any money. A kind man gave me the ticket. He also gave me money to feed the monkeys."

"And where's that money? I know no beggar alive who would spend money feeding other animals!" Komli handed Ma the ten rupee note she had received earlier.

Ma was speechless. "Just don't go off so far next time, Komli. Your sister and I were worried sick."

"Don't worry Ma. I know how to find my way back."

"You learn quickly, Komli," Ma said with a smile.

Komli decided not to tell Ma that she had, in fact, spent some money on nuts; that she had shared them with the monkeys because, in turn, she had been able to put her skinny hand through some of the bars and help herself to left-over carrots. She had even managed to sneak away with a delicious sugar-cane that was meant for the elephants. She did not tell Ma that she was planning to go there again; that she wanted to go on an elephant ride. Alas, one had to pay extra for elephant rides. Best of all had been the countless ice-cream sticks that she had been able to lick just by hovering around other children; as soon as she noticed that they were done, she offered to throw away their sticks or their cups. Luckily, rich young girls never scraped food to a polish. It was a happy Komli who had finally fallen asleep that night with the new-found realization that the world was a treasure chest; that one just had to be gutsy enough and step outside one's boundaries. And yes, before falling asleep that night, she had gazed at the stars and wondered what was better—being caged and fed or being free but starved.

Rana was livid that evening. Komli had failed to appear with her earnings of the day, Ma had been lying huddled on the streets, too sick to beg, and of late he had noticed that Roshni was becoming more and more silently uncooperative, as though she had realized that the promised room was but a dangling carrot, never to be attained.

"I cancelled two community meetings to have lunch with you! What's so important that it simply couldn't wait?" Sakina asked Zenub without bothering with the usual civilities.

"I don't recall saying I couldn't wait. You can never resist our exotic luncheons at the Calcutta Club! Admit it, Sakina, you came for the food," Zenub teased fondly, trying to appear calm.

"Of course I come for the food! Do you know any Indians who would refuse a meal at the hoity-toity Calcutta Club? Who doesn't want a peek at how the British once socialized at this place!"

"But you're the only one I know who misbehaved deliberately the first time we came here!"

"You'll never forget that, will you!" Sakina remarked with an impish giggle.

"Neither will the waiters or anyone else who saw you!"

"Stop exaggerating, Zenub. All I did was eat with my hands . . ."

"and sip soup like it was a cup of tea, and proclaim as loud as you could, 'Why must I sip tea from a cup and have soup with a spoon?'" Zenub said mimicking Sakina in a low voice.

"Well, the Brits no longer rule us. I hate the fact that they've left us with such an inferiority complex. We Bohras eat so beautifully with our hands. Come to the Calcutta Club and suddenly we have to pretend wielding knives and forks comes as easily to us as breathing! Some of their customs make about as much sense as their spelling and pronunciation!"

"You were always in trouble with the nuns when it came to English," Zenub quipped.

"Don't even remind me!"

"Well, here comes the waiter, to your rescue!"

As soon as the two ladies finished ordering, Sakina asked, "So why are we here? I can tell your mind's far away."

"Tusneem turned seven recently and I've been thinking . . ."

"Me, too. We have to make arrangements for Tusneem to be circumcised." Sakina charged forward like a speeding train that cannot be stopped until it reaches its destination, "I've already phoned Nemaboo Kaachwallah. She's the daughter of the lady who probably circumcised us. She's given me a few dates when she can do it. I will be there of course with you. Tusneem will have to take a couple of days off from school."

The religious head of the Bohra community was popularly known as Bawasahib (Bawa—father). Other than Bawasahib whose every word, no every syllable were like music to Sakina's ears, Sakina rarely allowed people to complete their sentences. She made a natural headmistress with whom no one dared back-chat, although those who got to know her well knew that her bark was much worse than her bite. She could be rude, she could be gutsy, she could be dictatorial, but her saving grace was that if someone in her family or in the Bohra community wanted to get something done, it was to Sakina they invariably turned, knowing that she cared deeply for the welfare of her people, and that she would do everything within her means to help, provided of course that it didn't conflict with the customs and traditions of her community. There were several reasons why Bohra women always listened to Sakina: unlike most of them, Sakina came from a family where the women had been to the best Catholic school in Calcutta. Not only did they speak English and read books and magazines that came all the way from England, they were also talented in feminine arts such as crocheting, embroidering, and flower arranging. Sakina was President of the Bohra Women's Association; she, and her sisters, always worked wonders with any projects they undertook. Sakina was also known to be among the few women who not only had private audiences with Bawasahib, rumor had it that she chatted with him quite informally, could even make him laugh, while most Bohras quaked in awe if they were lucky enough to have but a few seconds to do salaam (pay their respects with money) to Bawasahib.

"Sakina, do you know why we're circumcised?" Zenub asked after taking a deep breath.

"What?!"

"Why are Bohra women circumcised at seven?" Zenub asked, a little more deliberately. If Sakina thought the question would simply go away, she was sadly mistaken. Zenub was determined to discuss the undiscussed. Seeing that Sakina was still speechless, she continued in earnest, "I know that when our boys get circumcised they have their foreskin removed."

"That's right." Sakina said, feeling comfortable about discussing male circumcision.

"And what is the reason why we women are circumcised?" Zenub persisted.

"I don't know. We Bohras do it for a good reason that's in our religious books, I'm sure." Sakina couldn't even remember when it was that she had last admitted to anyone that she was unsure about something. She was just glad she was able to answer briefly but authoritatively.

So we can't enjoy sex, Zenub wanted to snap, but held back, knowing that she needed to keep her sister in good spirits. Zenub had always assumed that her sister had a great sexual relationship with her husband. She couldn't help wondering now if they were both in the same boat. If for Sakina, too, the cross had become somewhat lighter to bear as it got out-shadowed by the joys of raising children and becoming more and more involved in wonderful causes that enhanced the quality of the lives of the uneducated and poorer women of their community. Taking a deep breath, Zenub asked yet another preposterous question, "What if we don't circumcise Tusneem?"

"Are you out of your mind, Zenub? All seven year old girls in our community are circumcised. I've arranged countless dates with Nemaboo Kaachwallah. It only stings a little for a few hours. Tusneem will be in school in a couple of days and not even think about it!" Sakina claimed with calm assurance.

"Don't you ever think about it, Sakina?" Zenub asked in disbelief.

"I think about it all the time. Remember, I am the one who makes arrangements for so many mothers."

Realizing that Sakina would never admit to any negative effects of circumcision, Zenub asked, "What does this Nemaboo do to the girls?"

"I don't know. I don't watch! Tell me, Zenub, why do you suddenly want to defy tradition? I'm sure our mother and her mother and all our female ancestors were circumcised." For Sakina, the trinity of fundamental needs of human beings was not food, clothing and shelter; rather, it was religion, obeying Bawasahib, and performing all the rites and rituals her religion and Bawasahib prescribed. Her faith was as staunch as her noble forefathers; like them, she, too, could lay down her life for Bawasahib.

"I don't want her to go through the pain," Zenub said, unable to voice the real truth—that she wanted her daughter to enjoy sex when she got married.

"Pain?! I told you she would be up and about in no time. Tell me, Zenub, do you remember experiencing terrible pain? I've supervised countless circumcisions. I've yet to hear a girl howl in pain. Look, if it's so hard for you, don't come into the room with Tusneem. I'll stay with her." As far as Sakina was concerned, the matter was settled. She fished out a piece of paper and scribbled some numbers on it, "Take a look at these dates and tell me which one suits you best. The sooner we get it over with, the less you'll worry."

The waiter served their food just then. Zenub was thankful to be able to bend her head down into her plate to conceal her emotions. Her sister couldn't understand her anguish because she had no daughters, Zenub thought sadly. She knew in her heart of hearts though that even if Sakina did have daughters, she would not think twice about circumcising them. Although she loved Sakina dearly, she suddenly felt that her sister was like the race horses they often watched at the Turf Club of Calcutta—horses racing madly to the finishing line with blinkers on. With blinkers of religion on one side and tradition on the other, Sakina, too, raced through life convinced that heaven awaited her at the finishing line. It wasn't as if Zenub totally disregarded the notions of heaven and hell; she just wasn't as convinced as her older sister that heaven was just for the Bohras, much less that circumcision was a passport to heaven. If anything, it was a passport away from one heaven at least. While they were awaiting dessert, Zenub asked quietly, "What if I were to defy tradition and not have Tusneem circumcised?"

"The entire Bohra community looks up to our family," Sakina retorted with some signs of anger. "We follow our religion, and every directive given by Bawasahib. Have you ever considered what embarrassment, no, what shame, that would bring upon our family?"

"There is no ceremony or celebration after female circumcision. No one I know proclaims it to anyone. So how would it bring shame or embarrassment to us? I don't want to hurt my Tusneem!" Zenub exclaimed with tears welling up in her eyes. "It could damage her psychologically as well, Sakina," Zenub threw in as a last measure.

Sakina softened a little. She loved her sister. Besides, as authoritative as she could be, she hated seeing anyone in tears, least of all her youngest sister. She placed her hands over Zenub's and continued, "You read too many of those British magazines, you know. You must not take child psychology and all that British humbug so seriously! Those Brits think they know everything! But look at their youngsters who come drifting to India for peace. They go around half naked, nothing circumcised and everything pierced, dyeing their hair red and green like parrots, no traditions, no values, just doing as they please, without parental direction. Our teenagers are so much more civilized! Come on, give me a smile, Zenub. Normally you would be laughing." The two sisters quietly exchanged a smile. Sakina looked into Zenub's eyes, held her hands a little tighter and asked, "Are you suggesting that we don't circumcise Tusneem, but pretend that she is?"

"No! I'm not suggesting that we pretend for a minute! We simply don't do it to Tusneem and that's that. It's not like anybody's going to ask questions! Come to think of it, there may be many Bohra mothers who decide not to have their daughters circumcised. How would we ever know? Whom will we hurt, Sakina, if we don't circumcise Tusneem?"

"Your conscience, our honor, and our family. This is so unlike you, Zenub! I'm at a loss to figure out what's got into you!" Sakina declared in frustration. Tears started trickling down Zenub's cheeks. Sakina was not quite sure how to deal with that.

"Sakina, do you think you could ask Bawasahib for an exemption?"

"Have you gone crazy, Zenub? On what grounds would I dare ask Bawasahib for exemption? As outspoken as I may be, I don't think even I would have the courage to approach Bawasahib about such a delicate matter."

"You make it sound so shameful and embarrassing, the way you say it, Sakina." Zenub answered quietly. If it's so important and necessary to get it done, why is it such a hushed up matter? Why aren't there any explanations about why we do it?"

"I'm sure there are. But there's also such a thing as trusting the wisdom of our elders."

"I know, Sakina, and I do respect our elders. I just want to know why this is necessary."

"Zenub, I am the one who does a lot of asking. I refuse to take this upon my shoulder. You go and ask Bawasahib. I refuse to live with what he would think of me and our family if I were to approach him with such a request. And have you even thought of what Mother would go through, Zenub? She may be ill and bedridden, but she hasn't lost her senses yet. In fact, she asked me the other day about making arrangements for Tusneem. Are you going to lie to her during her last days?" There was no question that Sakina was the matriarchal head of the family. It was Sakina with whom her now-ailing parents lived. It was Sakina who shouldered responsibilities and made final decisions about what was good or bad for the welfare of their family at-large.

All Zenub could do was shake her head, while fear dried out any further tears of anguish. Zenub's silence had a greater effect on Sakina than her words. "Zenub," she whispered lovingly, "you've been circumcised, you have a loving husband and a wonderful daughter. Is there anything you lack? It will be the same for Tusneem, believe me."

"I believe you, Sakina. That's . . ."

"Then let's go to the movies. We need it!" Sakina interrupted.

. . . *that's exactly why I don't want her circumcised,* was what Zenub had wanted to say. Instead, she quietly replied, "I have a teacher's meeting. We'll go to the movies another day."

No! No! No! Zenub's inner voice had not stopped screaming at her ever since her luncheon with Neelum. She could not bow down to tradition or to her family and allow her precious daughter to be circumcised if, indeed, circumcision was the reason why sex was a passionless act for her. She owed it to her daughter to first find out at least what circumcision was about, what it entailed. But Sakina had provided no answers, other than big words with no reasoning—TRADITION, HONOR, CONSCIENCE . . .

When the sisters parted company, Zenub was thankful to be left alone so she could deal with the storm that was brewing inside her. She knew she could not hurt her beloved, noble mother. It was through her mother's gracious acts of devotion to her husband and to her children, and through her dignity and kindness towards everyone, including all the servants of the household, that Zenub had learned what grace and dignity and goodness were really about. Those lessons had not come from books and magazines; rather, like the oxygen she breathed, she carried them in her bloodstream without even knowing it. On the other hand, that very same love and devotion in her bloodstream were now urging her to defy tradition. Whom should she put first, she asked herself: her mother or her child? There had to be a way out of her dilemma.

She recalled asking her mother time and time again why she had to pray in Arabic when she did not understand a word of that language.

"It's just like taking medicine," her mother invariably replied. "Even though you don't understand why, it will do you good, later if not sooner." And to this Zenub never had an answer. Like all her sisters and brothers, she did what was asked of her.

She remembered clearly, when Mullasahib (religious instructor) had told her that man would never land on the moon and that if he did, he would renounce Islam. Man had landed on the moon; Mullasahib had not renounced Islam and was probably looking down on her from Heaven, she thought. After all, he was a good, well-meaning man and, as far as she was concerned, all good souls went to heaven, not just Bohras, as she had been led to believe.

All in all, she had very happy memories of her childhood, interspersed though they were with prayer and rigorous rituals. The only dark cloud in her otherwise clear blue sky of memories was that one day when she had been circumcised.

But Zenub was now a responsible, loving mother. She was faced with the question of saving or hurting her daughter. Was everything she had learned and obeyed about her religion right, she could not help but ask herself. If her daughter was not circumcised, would she go to hell? What was hell? And in seeking the heaven that was promised, should she passively allow that heaven in bed to elude her daughter as well? No one cared about that heaven it seemed. That was not a heaven to be discussed.

The car approached her home. In the few seconds that it took the durwaan to open the gates, Roshni scurried up to her, "Please can you spare something for my Ma? She's dying. Please Memsahib." Zenub delved into her purse and perfunctorily handed out some pennies. Zenub looked at her for a second and envied the beggar her freedom from custom and tradition. A death knoll is about to ring on my daughter's ability to blossom into full womanhood and I, her influential, wealthy mother have no honorable means to change that, Zenub thought to herself. And this beggar woman has a dying mother, but no means either to save her. At least suffering is fair, Zenub thought wryly. It has no eyes with which to differentiate between the rich and the poor. Her head reeled with the sudden sensation that the gates being closed behind her had changed to prison doors from which there was no escape.

That night both Zenub and Roshni approached their respective male mentors, hoping to find an answer to their dilemma.

"Rana," Roshni begged, "Ma is very sick. She's coughing up blood. She's in a lot of pain. Can I have some money to buy her medicine?"

"Oh yeah, chichree! You've hardly been bringing any money to me lately. Not as many of my clients ask for you these days. There was a time when even I couldn't have enough of you! You don't give, you don't get. It's how the world works."

"What do you mean, I don't give. Your people deliberately cut off my little sister's hand when she was born so we could milk on the sympathy of the rich! Isn't a human arm enough payment for you, you bastard?!"

Rana grabbed her viciously by the hand, "Don't you ever call me that, you mother-fucking whore. Go find another man and see if he'll pay you. Just remember, prostitutes like you who can't even read and write will always be at the mercy of men. We peel you like an orange, devour what's inside and chuck out the bitter, flattened rind!" He spat hard at her feet and thrust her away to demonstrate what he meant, before he continued, "You gotta give, chichree, otherwise you get nothing! Your illiterate sister will be next in line. Maybe I'll try her one of these days. She has more flesh on her body than you have!"

"I'll kill you before I let you touch my sister, you evil son of a bitch. If Ma dies I will pray on her dead body that you suffer the wrath of Shiva (God of Destruction)."

"You do that, chichree!" Rana replied with the air of an invincible monarch. Callously, he pushed her down to the ground and walked away.

Roshni despised the word 'chichree', but wondered suddenly if that was perhaps a more befitting name for her than the one her mother had given her. Chichree meant unwanted gristle.

While Roshni had pleaded her case in hell, Zenub spoke to her husband in the privacy of a heavenly, powder-blue bedroom. Not a speck of dust was to be found on the rosewood furniture Abdul polished lovingly each morning. Not a wrinkle was to be found on the bed-sheets or hand-embroidered floral bedspread that ayah laid out before Abdul came in. And the jamadaar who came each afternoon to sweep and clean their bathroom made sure the floors were polished to a shine.

Unfortunately, both women failed: one because her man was heartless; the other because her man claimed to be helpless. One knew nothing about honor and tradition; the other refused to fight honor and tradition. The end result was that both women, engulfed in a sense of helpless despair, felt miserable and desperate.

Zenub tossed and turned in bed that night, wondering how she would be able to cope with life after allowing her daughter to be . . . . no she would not allow even the thought to enter her head. She would find a way out. She could not live with such guilt festering in her soul, much less face her beloved daughter for the rest of her life. It was one thing, she told herself, for unschooled women to bow down to tradition; it was another for an educated lady to allow her own child to be maimed.

Strangely enough, it is often during times of grieving that one can be the most giving. When Zenub drove out the next morning, Roshni came up to her again with tears streaming down her face. Zenub took out a bundle of five one-hundred rupee notes and handed them to Roshni with a new-found empathy for the suffering woman. "Make sure your mother gets well," she said simply. Zenub's eyes were also blurred with tears, but her sunglasses screened them from the outside world.

On her return home, Zenub quietly said to her driver, "Ahmed, will you go find that beggar to whom I gave money this morning. Tell her I would like to see her in the garden as soon as possible." Ahmed was baffled, but he had yet to question Memsahib's orders.

"Sit down, please," Zenub said gently as Ahmed escorted a bewildered Roshni into the garden. "Were you able to get the medicine for your mother?"

"Yes, Memsahib. Allah will always bless you!"

"My name is Zenub. What's yours?"

"Roshni," the beggar replied, knowing that there was no way she could call this elegant, rich lady by her first name. Roshni could not help but notice the beautiful red rose bushes in front of her. "These flowers are so beautiful," she remarked simply while she wondered why she was accorded the honor of stepping inside the grounds of this *palace*.

"Smell them. Their fragrance is even more beautiful," Zenub said gently, wondering how many flowers this deprived woman had smelled in her life. Here they were, facing each other, filthy rich and filthy poor, yet how they felt inside could not be that different, Zenub thought. Her heart was beating fast. Dare she ask this vulnerable creature for the favor she wanted? She was desperate. She must try. But first she must offer her something to eat and drink. Such civilities came as naturally to her as gliding does to a seagull. "Would you like some tea and biscuits, Roshni?"

Roshni was dumbfounded. For as long as she could remember, no one had ever asked her if she wanted something to eat. She became suspicious. Maybe this angel of a lady was a female Rana! Taking the silence for an affirmative, Zenub beckoned the gardener, "Maali, go ask Abdul to bring us some tea and biscuits."

Roshni was momentarily distracted by a brilliantly striped butterfly that had stopped to hover around a cluster of fragile purple and yellow pansies. The butterfly collected what it needed and took flight. What a luxury it must be to quietly flit in and out of this haven whenever one pleases without being pushed and shoved and cursed, Roshni thought. She wished suddenly that she, too, could take flight. She had the uncanny premonition that even in this paradise, she was somehow trapped. Sensing Roshni's discomfort, Zenub decided to get down to business straight away. Besides, it wasn't as if there was a whole lot the two women had in common to converse about.

"I see you with your mother and another little girl, Roshni. Is she your daughter?"

"Oh no! She's my sister."

"How old is she?"

"Old?"

"It does not matter. What happened to her arm? Did she have an accident?"

"No, it was hacked off deliberately."

"Why?!"

Were the rich that blind, Roshni wondered. Did they really not see or know anything about the thousands of maimed beggars that loitered the streets of Calcutta? The horrors of life had long dried out any self-pity Roshni had once indulged in, so she said sarcastically, "We have bosses who think one arm can earn more money than two. So they cut off my sister's arm when she was new-born so people like you would take pity on us." Roshni recalled clearly how Ma had asked her to count her blessings when Rana had first come to get her.

"Go with him, Roshni. Otherwise he will hurt you, too," Ma had urged. "Count your blessings that your arm isn't cut off. These animals stop at nothing."

"Fortunate people like me," Roshni continued, "who have all parts intact are sold to rich people by the hour, or night, depending what they can pay. So though I count my blessings for having all my body parts, I often wish I was without the ability to see or smell or hear the lecherous, stinking men who demand the most beastly favors of me."

Zenub winced, visibly. She had heard about the *underground industry* Roshni was referring to. As her husband casually remarked sometimes after an unusually trying day at the courts, 'We should be really thankful that we have to deal with only a handful of sorrows in our lifetime, compared to the millions of tragedies that are metamorphosed into lifeless words that get buried in files.' For Zenub, until this moment, horrors such as concentration camps and Sati and the rape of rainforests were things that were delivered to her in books, for the advancement of knowledge. As uncomfortable as she felt, facing some semblance of real horror, she was relieved that Roshni was so cold and matter-of-fact. It made it easier for her to make her bizarre request.

"Roshni, I have something extremely difficult to ask of you. If you can help me out, I will give you all the money you need to live in a home where your mother can sleep on a bed, have a doctor come and visit her, eat what you want, and even send your little sister to school. No one in your family will ever have to beg again, I promise."

"What do you mean, Memsahib?" Roshni asked, warming up a little to the fact that the lady herself seemed to be distressed about something and, unlike callous Rana, she had the good grace to ask, instead of demand. "I have nothing," she continued, "How can I do anything for you?"

"I have a daughter who is about the same age as your sister. My daughter has to go through a custom I don't want her to go through. Would you let your sister go through the custom instead? No one but you and I will know about it. In exchange I will give you what I told you I would, and anything else you wish."

"What is the custom?" Roshni asked in amazement, unable to comprehend why anyone would part with so much wealth to avoid a custom.

"It involves making a little cut in the clitoris."

"Clitoris?"

This wasn't easy. Zenub decided to dig in her heels, be blunt, and get it over with as quickly as possible. "It's a small part between your legs. It gives you pleasure when you sleep with men. Girls in my community have to go through this ceremony."

"So they don't enjoy sleeping with men?" Roshni asked, wondering if she didn't have a clitoris after all.

"So they don't get too wild, someone told me. It was done to me when I was seven. From what I remember, it did not hurt much. You're lucky, Roshni, you are never forced into customs, are you?"

"No. But I still don't understand how a rich Memsahib like you can be forced to do anything."

"Life behind walls can be life behind walls, Roshni," Zenub said philosophically, more to soothe her aching soul than to help Roshni understand. "As wonderful as you may think my life is I, too, am facing a great dilemma right now. Would you . . . this is very hard . . . and I know it's very cruel to ask . . . but if I promise to give you any and everything money can buy, will you allow me to take your sister for a day and have her circumcised instead of my daughter?"

Roshni was speechless. So Zenub continued, "I know what I am asking is a sin. I know I will be punished, but I don't want my daughter to go through with it. I would never dream of asking you, but since you yourself are so desperate, maybe we can help each other. Maybe I can help all three of you to get off the streets, while you help my little daughter."

It was strange to see the rich lady begging, imploring, aching. If there was one thing Roshni understood, it was suffering. Zenub felt relieved; the worst was over. She had finished uttering the most cruel words of her life. Although she was normally fun-loving, thoughtful, and caring, at this point in her life all she cared about was saving her daughter, no matter what the cost. The little voices that had tormented, tortured and egged her on came back quickly to haunt her and soothe her. Like a pendulum, her conscience had swung from left to right, and from right to left:

> *How could you possibly ask another woman to put her loved one through something so barbaric?*
> *They go through so much worse, these beggars. You're actually helping them.*
> *No crime is ever looked upon as a form of help. Your husband's a judge; he'll tell you that!*
> *That little girl's choice would be prostitution, a few unwanted pregnancies and a litter of illiterate, starving children. You can change their lives for the better. Surely, under the circumstances, circumcision is not such a heinous crime.*
> *It's not for you to decide when a crime's not a crime.*
> *Then leave the choice to the beggar woman. There's no harm in asking. You're not forcing her!*

Well, she had done it. She had asked. All she had to do now was to hope and pray that Roshni would succumb.

Roshni, too, had to contend with little voices swinging hither and thither:

> *Isn't one cruel cut to your sister's arm enough punishment in one lifetime? How can you allow her to suffer again?*
> *What will Komli lose? The ability to enjoy sex? Aren't you already dreading the moment when lecherous Rana will take her away and sell her body to filthy animals in human guise? Worse still, can you bear the thought of Rana abusing Komli first, in the name of 'training'?*
> *What would Ma say?*
> *Save her! But from what? Rana, or a little cut? Ma's dying. She can hardly think! You have to think. You can save Ma, too.*
> *You can't hurt Komli! Maybe you should just let Komli run away somewhere to escape from all this evil.*
> *Remember what Rana said? Without schooling beggar girls have no choice but to prostitute themselves.*

"If I agree, will my sister be able to go to school?" Roshni asked desperately. It seemed that her shriveled stomach had turned into a bottomless pit for harboring fear.

"Yes, yes, and I can give you whatever else you want for yourself," Zenub replied.

Roshni's battle was over. The little voice that urged her to save Ma and her sister won easily.

"How can I be sure that you will give me everything you promise? And how will you pass off my sister as your daughter, Memsahib?"

Zenub heaved a sigh of relief. The voice she had succumbed to had been right. For the beggar girl, circumcision wasn't such a high price to pay. "No one but you and I and your sister will know. What's her name?"

"Komli."

"That means a tender bud."

"Oh! She's very tough though. But she can be tender sometimes," Roshni added with the glimmer of a smile. Memsahib, I know you are an honest lady, but I'm still wondering, what if you don't pay me? Who can I go to?"

"I could give it to you in writing. Would that mean anything to you?"

"No."

"Trust me Roshni. I am as desperate as you are. I can give you as much money as you need to go wherever you want to. If you don't want to stay in this city, I can put you on a train and help you start a new life somewhere else. Believe me, Roshni, I have more money than I need. I will help you. If my daughter were here, I would swear on her head that I will help you."

"If Rana finds out he will take everything you give me. Can I stay here and become a servant in your house?"

"No, that will not be possible. You will be happier starting out somewhere completely new. I can make sure you go to another city, if you wish." She did not have the heart to tell this unschooled woman that they only employed Muslims in their household; that, in fact, their loyal old servant, Abdul, who was just approaching them with a sparkling silver tray with tea and biscuits sitting elegantly on hand-crocheted white napkins, was probably having a heart attack because his Memsahib was entertaining two things vile, rolled into one—a Hindu, and a prostitute!

The two cups of tea did, in fact, experience a major tremor as Abdul staggered but for a second, seeing that his Memsahib was entertaining the untouchable street woman. Even though Muslims did not believe in the caste system of the Hindus, which divided the latter into four distinct classes, excluding the lowly, classless, untouchables, Abdul simply believed that all Hindus were untouchables, that all Hindus would be consigned to the ever-lasting fires of hell because they were idol worshippers and animal worshippers and, as rumor had it, they sometimes sprinkled the urine of their cow gods on their food! Given the choice, he would rather die than partake of their food. As far as Abdul was concerned, no decent Muslim family ever allowed Hindus to enter its household. Although his grown-up modern master, Rashid Sahib, had advised him not to believe everything he heard, Abdul would never take the risk of so much as smelling their food. As far as he was concerned, Islam was the only ticket to heaven; it was the only pure religion that believed in one god, Allah, the beneficent and the merciful.

Abdul usually took a two-week vacation during the Durga Puja festival of the Hindus, just in order to escape their loud music that blared from all street corners; just so he wouldn't have to look at their goddesses with ten arms or red tongues, or elephant heads. It was hard for austere, old Abdul to understand how human beings could worship things so inhuman. It infuriated him when they dared to come around for donations for the festival. Thank goodness, he never had to deal with them; he made sure the durwaan shooed them out at the gates itself.

However, other than innocuous verbal attacks, Abdul had never harmed a soul. For Abdul, Allah always came first. When Abdul prayed, no one dared to disturb him. The rest of his time Abdul was content to devote to the Khan household.

Abdul glared at his dear Sahib's modern wife with her so-called educated ways. She had dared to invite this sinful rag into their garden! Thank heavens only the outer walls of this noble household had been tainted, he thought. And, horror of all horrors, she actually expected him in his ripe old age to defile himself by serving the Hindu street woman. As though he was standing before Allah on the Day of Judgment, Abdul's entire life reeled before him. It seemed that it had suddenly become necessary for Abdul to stop and review his life so he could decide whether it was worth defiling himself by obeying Zenub Memsahib's orders or whether he should retrace his steps back into the kitchen.

Abdul first thought of his very own childhood in the village. That was a time when he saw his father for only four weeks in a year when the latter returned to the village for his annual vacation. He had been told that his father held the most prestigious job of head servant for the great Khans of Calcutta. Abdul lived with his sweet mother and brothers and sisters. Life was simple then. Either they tended the vegetables in the small patch of land around their thatched hut, or fed the goat and handful of chickens they owned. There was no school in their village. Their sweet mother had helped them to memorize enough Arabic to enable them to recite their prayers. From early childhood he had learned about the simple tasks all good Muslims must perform: pray five times a day; perform ablution before praying; fast for thirty days during the month of Ramadan; pay zakaat (religious tax); save, if possible, to perform the holy pilgrimage of Haj and, if necessary, fight for the cause of Islam. In his village there had never been a need to fight for anything. In fact, it had been easy and peaceful to be a good boy, a good farmer, and a good Muslim all rolled into one. The love he had felt for his father was a little strange—like loving and revering a holy man one rarely sees. The love he felt for his mother was like loving the earth itself; she was always there to nurture him.

Then there were the pre-teen years when Abdul's father had announced that Abdul had turned into a young man and must come work under him. He would be trained so that he, too, could one day enjoy the honor of being head servant at the Khans.

Then came Abdul, the man, who had outgrown his teen years, and his father had said that he must get married. Sex came first, children followed, and then, after several years, came true love. During those years he had mastered the art of working as a loyal, loving servant for little Rashid Sahib, the youngest son of Burrasahib. He had learned never to complain, never to let anyone know how much he longed to indulge in the day-to-day things his master and mistress took for granted—he, too, wanted to be with his devoted wife and six children tucked away in the village. For his sacrifice, devotion, and loyalty, Abdul was handsomely compensated. Not only did his wife and children have a roof over their heads and food in their bellies, but his children were also able to attend the village school which had been started in recent years.

Abdul had mixed feelings about sending his children to school. He wasn't exactly as impressed with schooled Zenub Memsahib, as he was with Zenub Memsahib's unschooled mother-in-law whom he had served when he was much younger. He blamed modern-day Zenub Memsahib for most of his frustrations. She had long abandoned the wearing of purdah; she painted the talons on her fingers and her toe nails; she did not always wear the traditional orna ghagra (skirt, blouse and sheer cloth to cover the head and chest) that all good Bohra women wore, and she even allowed her daughter to wear the garb of western women—dresses that showed her wobbly knees! What was wrong with the lovely jhabla, izaar and topi (tunic, slacks and cap) that young girls used to wear when he first came to work in this household, he had fearlessly asked on one occasion. And, to compound matters, this modern Memsahib sent their little Tusneem to a Catholic school. Ayah often taunted Abdul with tales she picked up from her little mistress about Jesus being the son of God and changing water into wine.

'Cheee cheee cheee cheee cheee!' Abdul had exclaimed in disgust. All his life he had been told that if someone threatened to kill him if he didn't eat pork, he should eat it. But kill yourself first, before you partake of any form of alcohol. First of all, there was only one god, Allah. God had no sons, everyone knew that! And how could God even dream of turning water into an alcoholic beverage? He shook his head silently and wondered about the wisdom of schooling a Muslim fledgling with Christian nonsense, or, indeed, about the wisdom of sending his own children to a village teacher. He didn't see anything wrong with his own home-schooling under his loving mother. But it seemed that just as he had succumbed to the pressures of his wife insisting that their children attend the village school, Rashid Sahib had succumbed to the pressures of his wife insisting that their daughter go to the so-called best Christian school in Calcutta. Alas! It was not his place to critique every little thing about the changing lifestyle of young modern-day couples who even chose to abandon the healthy tradition of living in joint families. Joint families with brothers and their wives and all their children living happily under the protective canopy of the wisdom and traditions of the old. Youngsters who were under the misconception that wisdom came from schools and books!

The older he got, the more fervently Abdul served his master. It was Abdul who personally washed and purified Sahib's special clothes for praying. Ayah was relegated the task of doing the same for Memsahib. In the beginning Abdul had fought with ayah for not purifying her mistress's clothes as carefully as he did his master's, but in time he realized that the aggravation it caused him in his old age was not worth it. He would simply serve his beloved Rashid Sahib as he had always done, and watch the rest of the world go by with their wishy washy, fast-paced, modern ways.

From behind the curtains as it were, Abdul had witnessed the grandeur and glory of the lives of the wealthy Khans. All Burrasahib's children were like little princes and princesses who did not lift so much as a bag or a book even when they went to school. If the family went to Surat for a wedding, Abdul was among the few privileged servants who accompanied them. Surat was Burrasahib's hometown. That was where the family always went for lavish weddings; weddings with glorious processions of elephants and horses splendidly attired in brocades of shimmering gold and silver; weddings with marching bands loudly heralding the arrival of bride and groom. After a few hectic weeks of lavish breakfasts, lunches, and dinners, the entourage always returned to Calcutta.

Abdul recalled how he had been both happy and sad when it was time for his Rashid Sahib to get married. For now it was his master's turn to acquire new passions. At first he had hated Zenub Memsahib and her modern ways. But there were those thoughtful things she did that helped him realize that she was not all nail polish and veneer. For it was Zenub Memsahib who had suggested that he should write to his wife and children, instead of just sending them his wages each month.

"But I don't read and write, Memsahib, how can I do that?"

"There are many people who dictate letters to those who can write it for them. I could do it for you. But if you would find that embarrassing, our driver could do it for you, he reads and writes."

"And who would read the letters to my wife, Memsahib? She cannot read or write either."

"There is probably a person in your village who can do that for her. Sometimes postmen will do it, too, for a small tip. What about your children? I know they can read and write."

"I'll think about it."

"If you looked up to me a little more, perhaps you wouldn't see just the nail polish on my toes, Abdul!" Memsahib had joked. Making changes in his lifestyle were not things that occurred to Abdul. Memsahib had touched his heart; he had softened a little and embarked upon communicating with his wife via the driver.

All the reminiscing came to a sudden halt. Here was another occasion when his mistress had deeply aggravated him. He had lived the life of a good pure Muslim for over sixty years. Why, Rashid Sahib had even granted him sufficient funds to enable him to fulfill his dreams and undertake the long and arduous journey to Mecca to perform the holy pilgrimage of Haj. He was a Haji; the only revered Haji in his village. No, there was no way he could taint his pure record and defile himself by serving a Hindu street woman. Abdul sometimes looked upon himself as a tree whose branches had witnessed several different lifestyles. Well, he said to himself, I am not a tree that is root bound or dead! Sooner or later I will accost Memsahib and leave, if necessary.

Abdul turned around and walked back into the kitchen, thankful that at least the woman had not defiled the inner sanctity of this noble household. He ordered one of the younger servants to take out the tray to their Memsahib. With the quiet dignity accorded to all guests, the younger servant set down the tray on the intricately-filigreed white wrought iron table. He waited quietly until he was dismissed by his mistress. Zenub was pleasantly surprised to see that Roshni nibbled at the biscuits and sipped at the tea. She had expected her to wolf it all down.

When Roshni was about to leave, Zenub plucked a rose and handed it to her. "They say this flower is the symbol of love. Take it with you Roshni, just to remind you that we are both acting out of love." Zenub looked deeply into Roshni's dark eyes, to assure her that there would be no foul play; she would be handsomely rewarded. Roshni clutched the rose and looked deeply into Zenub's eyes. Yes, she decided, she could trust this lady. There was something about her that smelled as good as the rose.

"I promise that I will not let you down," Zenub said quietly when Roshni got up to leave.

"I trust you, Memsahib." Roshni said before she walked out.

Later that afternoon, Abdul went up to his mistress and said simply, "This is your house, Memsahib. I know you can do as you please. But the next time I am asked to serve a Hindu, I will leave this household!" Zenub was tempted to ask him to leave there and then. It was one thing to allow a servant to speak his mind by virtue of the years of devoted service he and his father had rendered; it was quite another matter to allow a servant to push one into living in the Middle Ages, Zenub thought with anger. The only reason she held back was because she quickly realized that this was perhaps the worst time to antagonize anyone in her household, especially her husband. She had some serious plans to execute. So she said quietly to Abdul, "It will never happen again. I don't know what got into me. The beggar woman's mother is very sick. I was trying to help her."

'Didn't look like that to me,' Abdul said to himself as he quietly retreated.

Over and over in her mind Zenub went through every little detail of her plan. As strange as Sakina and Rashid thought Zenub's demands were, they indulged her, happy in the knowledge that she had at least succumbed to the demands of tradition and agreed to have Tusneem circumcised. They were magnanimous, religious, influential community leaders with reputations to uphold. If Zenub wanted to have Tusneem circumcised privately, with no one around, so be it. After all, circumcision was like one of those articles of clothing one acquires for a special occasion, after which it gets buried deep inside one's closet, never ever to be aired again. What mattered was that there was going to be no defiance, no dishonor.

Sakina contacted Nemaboo Kaachwallah. Unlike other such occasions, that was to be Sakina's only involvement. All servants in the Khan household, barring the gatekeeper and driver were released for two days. Two blessed, unexpected days to do as they pleased. As for Rashid, all he wanted was to have the unpleasant ceremony done and over with. The less they discussed it, the more comfortable he felt. So when Zenub suggested he plan one of his two-day business trips to Patna, he obliged, quite happily.

Zenub's plan was perfectly executed. While the driver went to pick up Nemaboo Kaachwallah, Zenub took a taxi and dropped off Tusneem at a friend's; a non-Bohra friend, she had made sure. She then asked Roshni and Komli who had been instructed to make sure they were standing by, to come in. Roshni had prepared Komli by telling her that she must not breathe a word to their sick mother. And she must not ask the lady any questions. That she would feel some pain between her legs but that if she cooperated and said nothing, her reward would be as much food as she wanted, every day, for the rest of her life; a home with a room for Ma and the two of them, and if she did absolutely everything right and made no mistakes, she might even be able to go to school. Komli was far smarter and larger at heart than her rags would lead one to believe. Actually, she would have obliged just to see Ma get well again. Ma had been told a half truth—that they were looking into a place where they could make more money and that they would be back to get her as quickly as possible.

Zenub realized that a dirty, unkempt child would rouse Nemaboo's suspicion. Unpleasant as the task was, she gave Komli a quick bath, too nervous to squirm about the caked dirt or brown suds that covered her hands. She fed the sisters, gave Komli a warm glass of milk with two sleeping pills after which she slipped Komli into a long-sleeved gown she had bought for the occasion. While Roshni waited in another room, Zenub tucked Komli in Tusneem's bed, making sure Nemaboo Kaachwallah would not see her arm. Even though the woman had no idea what Tusneem looked like, Zenub didn't want to take the risk of a handicap being mentioned inadvertently to Sakina. The bottom half of the bed-sheet was left untucked.

Zenub looked at the clock. Perfect! She still had about twenty more minutes before Nemaboo was expected. She decided to read to Komli. Deliberately, Zenub chose a long, dry, uninteresting story, in the hope that Komli would fall asleep. By the time she heard the doorbell, Komli was sound asleep.

After taking Roshni to her own bedroom, Zenub opened the door to Nemaboo. She looked a bit like a voodoo witch with bright, fiery-red hair. It was just as well that one never saw Nemaboo at the mosque or at community functions.

"Where's your daughter?" Nemaboo asked matter-of-factly. Zenub led her to the room, picked up the bottom half of the gown and deliberately laid it over Komli's face.

"Would you mind not saying anything to the little girl. She's extremely nervous," Zenub asked in a whisper.

"I never do. You may leave. I'll call you when I'm done," Nemaboo said without so much as casting a glance at what lay above the two legs.

Within fifteen minutes she was out again, smiling. "Your child will be alright," she assured Zenub. "She flinched a little, but seemed brave. It will sting when she goes to the bathroom. Keep her in bed today." Zenub offered her some tea, which was declined. Zenub heaved a sigh of relief and had the driver take her back.

The telephone rang just then. "Tusneem's asthma's bothering her badly, Zenub. She needs her inhaler," the voice on the other end said. "Would you like me to bring her back? What should I do?"

"I was just about to go out," Zenub lied, "I'll come and give it to her." With quick instructions to Roshni to sit beside Komli, Zenub rushed out.

While Komli was sleeping, Roshni sat and studied yet another incredibly beautiful room. Never in her wildest dreams could she have imagined that people could live in such luxury. Would Komli be lucky enough to have a bedroom like this, Roshni wondered as her eyes slowly took in her surroundings. The walls were a pale lemon with a deep blue ceiling studded with shimmering stars. In one corner of the ceiling there was a luminous crescent that seemed to be looking down on the bed like a guardian angel. Roshni noticed the book cases in one corner, hoping that Komli could have those at least. She wondered about the frilly, laced dolls staring back at her. She had never seen humans with big blue eyes, curly blonde hair, rose-bud lips, and pale pink skin.

Roshni decided suddenly that she would go to the garden to smell those flowers once more. It was in that bent position, smelling the flowers that he rarely stopped to smell, that Rashid first saw Roshni. From the day he was born, Rashid had always been treated with the greatest deference. In turn, he knew no other way but to return the favor to all of mankind, regardless of caste, class or creed.

"Excuse me, does Zenub know you're here?" he asked politely.

Shock and fear caused Roshni to lose her balance as she turned around and tried to stand up at the same time. As Rashid stepped closer to help her up, he could not help but notice how foul she smelled. A little voice told him suddenly that perhaps something fishy was going on under the still waters of this unusually quiet household.

"Tell me, what are you doing here? Did the durwaan let you in?"

"No, Sahib. Memsahib will be back soon. She can explain. Please don't call the police, Sahib, I have done nothing wrong," she pleaded.

"Was Memsahib's daughter with her?"

"No. But she went to give her some medicine."

"What do you mean, went to give her some medicine. They're supposed to be here."

"I don't know, Sahib. I heard a bell ring. Then Memsahib started talking. Then she just told me she would be back as quickly as she could."

Rashid did some quick thinking, although he was still at a loss to understand why his daughter was out when she was supposed to be in bed, resting. In a calm voice that belied his state of mind, Rashid asked, "Tell me why you're here. I promise you, you will get into no trouble at all if you tell me the truth."

"Sahib," Roshni muttered tremulously, "I am not here to steal anything. Memsahib said she would help my dying Ma and, may Allah bless her, she already has given me a lot of money. Please, Sahib, just don't call the police, because if the police find out about Rana, he will kill me, and there will be no one to look after Ma or my little Komli." Her rambling made little sense to Rashid, but his heart went out to her. What would he do, he wondered if his dear wife were in this kind of predicament. He had never had to worry about such things. It made him extremely uncomfortable.

"Why don't we go inside and wait for Memsahib."

"Oh no, Sahib, Komli is sleeping inside."

"Who's Komli?"

"My little sister."

Something told Rashid he must quickly get to the bottom of this, before his wife returned. He decided to frighten her. "Tell me what is going on. I promise you, if you tell me the truth nothing will happen to you or your family. But if my wife comes in and tells me something different, then I will know that one of you is lying. If it's you, I will call the police!" he added emphatically. He was astute enough to quickly realize that the chances of getting the truth out of a fear-filled, unsophisticated woman, to say the least, were far greater than getting the truth out of a wife who was smart, had countless people at her command, a husband who loved her dearly, and little to fear since he was a renowned judge to boot. It didn't take the judge in him long to realize with hindsight that all his wife's recent actions suggested that she was into something secretive. No wonder she wanted no one around! It was he who had insisted that the durwaan stay, to guard not just the house, but his precious wife and daughter.

Roshni looked down at the green grass. Rashid followed her eyes and had a glimpse of her filthy shoeless toes. Quickly he looked away and heard her out, "Memsahib wanted my sister to have a little cut done between her legs."

"Carry on, I need to sit down," Rashid whispered as he staggered down on the bench.

"She said no one would know except me and her. She promised me a place to stay and more money so I could save my dying Ma and my sister."

Like a freshly butchered, bloody wound, Rashid's heart throbbed with pain. But he sat still and stared into the void, thinking how clean were these woman's filthy toes compared to what his wife had done. Through one insane act, his wife had undone everything he believed in, everything their families upheld. One heinous act had cast an indelible stain on everything he loved more dearly than his very own life—his wife and child. Worse still, he was convinced that his innocent child and demented wife would have to suffer some consequences for this act of barbarism. Although he was not as old-fashioned as Abdul, Rashid was also a firm believer in Islam and accountability.

It was his turn to totter a little, before he managed somehow to stand in front of her. "I'm sorry," he said, holding her by both shoulders.

"Oh no, Sahib, I am an untouchable beggar. It is a sin for people of your caste to touch me."

He couldn't remember when he had been more touched in his life. "We Muslims don't belong to any caste," he said humbly, "but if we did, my family would now be the untouchables, I assure you." Although the caste system and untouchability had been legally abolished in India, he realized at that moment that the illiterate and the so-called untouchables were the last ones to hear about it. And even among the literate, he wondered how many knew that when the caste system had originally started in India, a person of the highest caste could be relegated to the bottom or be excommunicated if he violated certain rules or committed a sin. He said simply, "It is no longer a sin for anyone to touch anyone. You can come in with me or sit here if you wish. I will await Memsahib inside." He felt so estranged from his wife that he could not even bring himself to utter her name. He had judged thousands of innocent and guilty people over the years. With judges eyes he compared this pathetic piece of bedraggled humanity to his elegant, once-noble, wife. His family had been forever tainted, he thought with a heavy heart, while all he could see in this woman was her shining purity. He was blinded to the fact that actually both women had acted out of pure love. Suddenly, he envied the criminals that he sentenced to prison and to manual labor; at least, they could serve off some of their guilt, while he would have to live quietly with this horrendous, unforgivable sin for the rest of his life. It was an act that could never be undone, a deed that would putrefy in his soul and multiply like fungus because he could never expose it to the healing rays of the sun. His mind wandered to the harried mumbling of Shakespeare's Lady Macbeth. He had seen her on stage several times. But it was not until this moment that he truly understood the anguish behind the tormented woman's famous words, *out damned spot!*

"I want to go in and see my sister," Roshni said simply, marveling that the world did actually contain gentle, decent men like the one standing before her. Rashid followed her, like a mute shadow. What he saw looked like a shaggy brown bear usurping the bed of his beautiful Goldilocks. He walked away into the privacy of his bedroom, thankful for once that Abdul wasn't there with a piping-hot cup of tea. With forehead clasped between two hands, he spent a hellish eternity, awaiting his wife.

"Where is Tusneem? Is she alright?" Rashid asked as soon as Zenub walked in.

"I thought you were in Patna. What are you doing here?!"

"You didn't answer my question, is Tusneem alright?"

"Yes. You didn't disturb her, did you?"

"In this house there seem to be three disturbed people right now—that beggar woman, you and me. I met her in the garden when I came in. Please tell me what she told me is not true, Zenub. Please help me to understand what's going on," Rashid pleaded.

Zenub sat down on the bed. With her face in the palms of her hands, she managed, "You're never going to forgive me, I know . . . ."

"Just please tell me what's going on, Zenub, please."

"I could not bear the thought of Tusneem being circumcised. That beggar is desperately in need of money because her mother is sick. I offered her anything she wanted if she would let her sister take Tusneem's place."

"You could have saved her mother by just giving her money. When have we ever said no to charity? Using her as you did is a crime, Zenub! I cannot believe that something so diabolic would even occur to you!"

"I didn't think anyone would find out."

"And you could have lived with the burden of that guilt all by yourself, for the rest of your life?" Rashid asked, in sheer disbelief.

"What guilt?"

"Taking advantage of the destitute, to put it mildly!"

"Taking advantage?! That woman has a mother who is dying of TB, I think. She has no choice but to prostitute herself to earn money. The little girl in bed is the younger sister. She would follow in the older one's footsteps in but a matter of time. I have promised her a roof over her head and enough money to take care of their day to day needs. I didn't force her. I gave her the choice and she accepted quite readily. Her only question was, what if I didn't keep my part of the promise."

Rashid could only focus on the fact that everything he had stood for all his life, all the values he had cherished, were shattered by one senseless act. He had judged hundreds of cases over the years. Here was one, thank Allah, on which he didn't have to pronounce judgment in public. There would be no witnesses or juries to help him out either. He felt it was he who was being sentenced to lifetime imprisonment. After all, they had become one, in marriage. Therefore, he, too, would live with the shame and the guilt of having abused a vulnerable human being, and a child at that. To whom could he go and confess? It was a guilt that no hard labor, no harsh sentence could alleviate. He remembered his father's words, "Bad deeds are like boomerangs; sooner or later they come back to you." He prayed to Allah to spare his innocent daughter the consequences of the sins of her parents.

"Why is it so important to you that our daughter is not circumcised when all the ladies in our community have been through it? What's wrong with them? Look at you. I could not have asked for a better wife. Were you not circumcised? Am I not circumcised? Our parents and our parents' parents were all circumcised, and who knows how many people all the world over. Why is it so important that Tusneem be spared?"

"Everything is perfect in your eyes, Rashid! I, too, could not have asked for a better husband, or a better life, but there is something missing in my life."

"All you have to do is ask. You know I would give it to you."

"You can't, Rashid."

"I can't?" Rashid repeated with some hint of sarcasm.

"I was too embarrassed to mention it to you. All these years I thought it was a personal problem, until Neelum casually asked me the other day if Bohra women get circumcised to curb their sexual pleasure . . . ."

"What?!"

"Please don't interrupt me. I may never again have the courage to say this again. When we make love, Rashid, I come close to having a climax, but it always eludes me. When I realized that circumcision is probably the reason why I cannot enjoy sex to the fullest, I decided I would not put our daughter through the guillotine, for tradition, honor, or whatever the reason. I tried to find out the reasons, Rashid, but no one really knows." Zenub screamed and cried at the same time, "No one wants to talk about circumcision. All people care about is custom and tradition and honor. Is it such a crime, Rashid, for a mother, for a woman, to want her daughter to be a woman in the true sense of the word?

To enjoy sex and not just be a child-bearer?" Many a times you have said to me that there is nothing as wonderful in life as making love. If I could only experience that joy once, Rashid, I would be satisfied."

"How come you've never told me this all these years?" Rashid whispered, lifting her face tenderly so he cold look into her eyes.

"I couldn't Rashid. You and I hardly knew each other when we were married. We come from that generation when parents choose spouses for their children. Sex is not so much as mentioned by anyone. They couldn't have chosen a better man for me. You were so ecstatic when we first made love. I, too, felt excited and wonderful but the climax never came, like it did for you. At first I thought it was because I was a virgin. It would come. It didn't. I got pregnant. We grew to love each other more and more . . ."

"But why didn't you say something over all these years? You yourself said we grew to love each other more and more. How could you not communicate with the man who would do anything for you, Zenub?"

"We're not brought up to discuss such matters."

"So you just allowed the animal in me to be satisfied," Rashid said with new-found respect. He had often wondered why his wife never erupted like a volcano, as some books suggested.

"Please let me finish, Rashid. You want your daughter to have the best education, to be liberated. You don't want her to be a slave to her husband and all that. Would you like her to be deprived of that pleasure that you so often tell me is Allah's greatest gift to mankind? You always thank Allah for our five senses. Do you know, I can think of only two instances when we use all five senses at the same time—when we make love, and when an infant suckles on a woman's breast! Sex and an infant suckling—one resulting from the other. I want my Tusneem to live, in every sense of the word. And I did not force that beggar woman to do anything! I will hopefully enable her family to live a decent life, and for our child to live, too, to the fullest. Is that such a crime?" she asked quietly. She felt shaken and exhausted. Her dreams had turned into a nightmare.

"Zenub, what makes you so sure your friend's claims about circumcision are correct? There may be other deep-seated reasons, reasons that you and I have not bothered to research . . .

"If there are some wonderful, deep-seated reasons for circumcision of young girls, then what crime have I committed, Rashid? Perhaps I've done that beggar girl a favor!" Zenub dared, a shade cheekily.

"These are our beliefs. You cannot impose our beliefs on non-believers! Why, why, did you not take me into your confidence? You know I love Tusneem as much as you do. If necessary, I could have joined you in your fight . . ."

"I tried to find out. I tried talking to you . . ."

"But you were not candid enough, Zenub," Rashid interjected, thinking sadly that the lioness had, however, brazenly committed a crime. "And why did you rush into things? Waiting and thinking things out work wonders."

"In this case waiting and thinking was like being in some torture chamber. Sakina had already made tentative arrangements for Tusneem. To make matters worse, she asked me if I was willing to hurt our sick mother by defying tradition. I panicked, Rashid. Mothers will do anything to protect their children. Is that so hard to understand?"

"I need time. I'll try to understand. Right now, the judge in me is at a loss. Tell me, how do you propose to dispose of the beggar girls now?" Rashid asked with genuine concern.

"My plans were to house them in a different city because there's a man here that hounds them, give them a large sum of money and let them go. What would you like me to do, Rashid?"

Rashid had no immediate answers.

"You have a few thousand rupees always at your disposal. That would buy them some furniture maybe, but certainly not an apartment.

"I have already asked someone to appraise some of my jewelry. Half of it would probably house a few families!"

"You're going to sell the family jewelry?!" Rashid asked, aghast.

"Not what you gave me," Zenub said defensively, although she knew in her heart of hearts that if she had to, she would have sold that, too. As much as Zenub enjoyed her lavish lifestyle, her passion for precious gems and jewelry had been on the decline lately because Rashid and his family denied her nothing. She had lost count of the numerous occasions when she spent hours at her gracious in-laws and their jeweler. A whole morning would go by as the jeweler opened packet after packet of priceless gems wrapped up in tissue paper. Together they would arrange and re-arrange gems of her choice on the many different blank patterns the jeweler spread out, until everyone was satisfied as to what setting best suited the gems she had picked. And if for whatever reason Zenub disapproved of the final result when the jeweler returned, all she had to do was to ask him to re-set it. In her in-laws household she could pick jewels with as much abandon as picking shells on the seashore. As for hard cash, it did not grow on trees; for the Khans it simply gushed out like water that was unappreciated and taken for granted. Rashid had stacks and stacks of it just for petty cash, tucked away in a solid, steel safe which also contained the family jewelry. The safe was by no means as large as the wardrobes that contained her clothes, but it was at least twice the size of one of the free-standing ovens in the kitchen. It was stacked high with red and blue velvet boxes containing jewelry to match the countless clothes she had.

"Zenub, you cannot just hand illiterate people a large sum of money and expect them to go fend for themselves! Has it occurred to you that there is little one can do if one can't read or write? How are they going to sign a lease, write a check, or do the other one hundred and one things that involve reading and writing?"

"As rich and mighty and educated as we are, Rashid, I doubt if we would survive on the streets for more than a week. This wretched, illiterate family has survived the streets for years! Don't under-estimate them!"

"What if they decide to blackmail us?"

"Never! She's a good woman."

"I read once that there is an animal in every man and a man in every animal. I commend you for believing in the goodness of man. How long have you known this woman, Zenub? What do you know about her?"

"She's begged outside our streets for as long as I can remember."

"You know her about as well as the people on the trams and buses that pass us by daily." How amazing, he thought, that a woman, so naïve in many ways, had executed a near-perfect plan. Since the time of his great, great grandfathers, this house had never been drained of all its servants. She had vacuumed it clean, only to bring in a stain that no amount of servants or detergents could eradicate. The only thing he could do now to salvage their souls was to make sure the beggar and her family were properly looked after.

"What were your plans if I hadn't come in now?"

"Take them to a hotel in a few hours. In a couple of days I would have given them the money from the sale of my jewelry and put them on a train."

"When is Tusneem coming back? I want to see her."

"After the two girls have left."

"Didn't you think that I would ask Tusneem how she felt?"

"She would have said, fine. You would never discuss circumcision with her, I know. No one does!"

"What about your sister, Sakina, surely she will ask Tusneem questions?"

"I got her to promise that she would never embarrass Tusneem by bringing up the subject, to which Sakina laughed and said she never has before, so why would I think she would this time. You know, Rashid, we live in this great age of instant communication around the world, yet we cannot properly communicate within our own family and our own souls, can we?"

"No," Rashid agreed quietly, knowing that he would never tell his wife how deeply he would grieve for her sin, how deeply guilty he would feel from now on, knowing that sex was a one way act between them.

If there was anything Rashid had in greater abundance than material wealth, it was his sense of justice. He would make sure the beggars would get what was promised. But his wife was the foundation on which his child and his household survived; there was no way he was going to allow her to wade into unknown, dangerous territories such as dealing with the destitute and, by the sound of things, a hardened prostitute who was probably well trained in the art of milking sympathy. What if Zenub disappeared, or died? That would be even worse than dealing with the loss of self-respect, he realized. And although he knew countless people to whom he could have entrusted the task of rehabilitating the beggar girls, he stone refused to allow anyone into their dirty closet. He and his wife alone would have to live with it, he decided.

"Where is your daughter?" Rana hollered at Roshni's mother.

"She'll be back," Ma whispered with all the strength she could muster.

"But where has she gone? She's always here for me at this time!"

"She'll come back," Ma repeated, coughing violently between each word.

Rana was quite baffled, knowing that Roshni would never abandon her dying mother. "You tell her when she comes back that if she disappears on me again you'll be dead meat! I suppose that little one is with her, is she?"

Ma nodded her head, silently thanking Bhagvaan. There was no telling what he would have done to her little one, had she been around.

"She's never going to get that room!" Rana threatened loudly as he walked away. Rana's frustration stemmed from the fact that it was taking him much longer than he thought to acquire the sum of money he needed to get a visa and a work permit to work in the Middle East. Many of his acquaintances were amassing quite a fortune working under wealthy Arabs, he had heard. Of late, all he could do was to dream about making quick money in the oil world, although he had never done an honest day's work in his life.

Ma gazed peacefully at the stars that night, thankful that Calcutta was having one of its power outages. The hushed streets and midnight blue sky that blanketed the city warmed her lonely, beleaguered soul. Hai Bhagvaan, she prayed, you've never answered my prayers, but now that I'm dying, perhaps you will. Free my girls from the clutches of Rana. She missed her girls. On nights such as these she especially loved telling them stories. The little one loved her stories, especially about trees.

Some stories had been orally handed down to her; some she simply made up as she went along. Stories were for free, thank goodness. And thank goodness she had a great imagination because the girls were always hungry for stories, and her well of stories never ran dry. One day the tree was an ageless giant; another time, in its hollow it had protected a little boy from a demon, or it had borne golden fruit and changed the fortunes of a family; best of all were the stories of the golden age when the world was all green with wooded forests, when for every creature on earth Bhagvaan had created a special tree that satisfied all that person's needs. That was a time when there was no money and no begging and no starving and everyone was happy.

"What happened to that time, Ma?" Roshni had once asked.

"People started using trees for making paper. And paper makes some people very rich and other people very poor."

"How's that?"

"When you grow up, you'll understand."

And it was with the twigs of the Neem tree that the girls brushed their teeth. Twigs that helped generate juices in their otherwise dry mouths. When Komli had the measles, the leaves of the Neem tree had helped stop the itching. Then there were stories about the Banyan tree, the king of all trees, and the Bodhi tree under which Gautama Buddha had received Nirvana. Before long, the girls began to believe that trees were silent spirits that must be revered at all cost. Ma smiled lovingly as she thought of her innocent children. In peace, she shut her eyes.

So it was the unwilling, miserable conspirator, the prudent, practical, professional gentleman who accompanied the beggars under the pretext of yet another 'business trip' to Patna. Rashid's secretary had looked utterly baffled when he had said he wanted three third-class train tickets, instead of first class. He had explained that the tickets were for his servants.

Judging from the way the two girls gaped and gawked at everything, it was obvious they had never seen Howrah Station before. He realized within the space of a harrowing half hour, how helpless the two illiterate beggars really were. They had no clue about tickets, or platforms, or time.

Howrah Station was not just infested with hundreds of people, Howrah Station was like a bee-hive buzzing with busy creatures that never stood still. Night and day, seven days a week, Howrah Station witnessed people pouring in and out of its platforms, some on business trips, some on transfer, some on vacation, crying, laughing, rushing, like the mighty Ganges that cannot be stilled. And for every person that was coming or going, there were probably half a dozen friends and family members hovering around the passenger.

For every passenger that was coming or going, there were red-turbaned coolies hankering around to hand-carry their luggage. It was unheard of for passengers to travel with just one piece of luggage. Fortunately, the coolies of Howrah Station had metamorphosed into human trolleys that could easily walk with two or three suitcases precariously balanced on their red turbans. The soft, red turban seemed to play the dual role of alleviating some of the pressure and creating a flat surface that could balance several pieces of luggage on one human head; no, one turtle-head with neck retracted. The coolies always made sure they carried the heaviest suitcase in their right hand. The empty left hand was used either to straighten the bags that threatened to slide down from their heads from time to time, or to flail around in front of their fast-moving bodies, in order to carve out a pathway among the teeming throngs.

Then there were the countless hawkers who, too, were trying to eke out a living off men in transit. Some had stands, and they were easy to meander around. It was harder to avoid the wandering hawkers who knew exactly when to make a bee-line for a passenger. Their means of livelihood usually consisted of selling one item only, such as coffee, tea, candy, fruit or sodas. Indeed, it seemed that a supermarket was on the move at Howrah Station. Every second, a vendor somewhere, was drawing attention to his wares; some with rattles, some with vocal chords that seemed to suffice, some just clattered their cups and saucers, or their soda bottles. A stock market at its busiest would seem quiet compared to Howrah Station.

Rashid, understandably, was petrified that some small wave of humanity would sweep away the two helpless women; that, like animals, they would sniff their way back to his doorstep again. So he made sure he walked closely behind them. The coolies were somewhat like beggars, Roshni noticed. Some haggled for a little more money because the walk had been long, the baggage too heavy. Others simply begged to carry some luggage—

they had families to feed. Like beggars, they were treated like annoying pests that had to be shooed away.

Zenub had given Roshni a purse with some money in it. To that she clung on tightly. Roshni decided to tip their coolie handsomely. She did not need to, however. Rashid had tipped him so handsomely that the coolie thanked him three times before disappearing to scout for his next customer.

Rashid had deliberately chosen to travel by third class. In first class compartments there were always greedy conductors obeisantly attending to him, knowing that the handsome tip at the end would be well worth it. Many of the conductors knew him. He was a frequent, respectable passenger. He could not bear the thought of having them hover around him stoically, assuming all the while that he, too, had joined the club of wealthy men who enjoyed the favors of unscrupulous women. Rashid felt much more comfortable, lost in a compartment crammed with uncouth, loud passengers arguing about unreserved seats and excess baggage. The odor from their perspiration and even the stench of urine from a lavatory that was over-used, and whose doors were never shut for long, did not seem to bother him too much. It was a small price to pay for the luxury of traveling unrecognized.

Fortunately, his two companions didn't bother him much either. The younger one seemed preoccupied with the novelty of being transported by something other than her feet; of having a new dress with two pockets, one containing candy and the other a few rupees with which she could buy anything her little heart desired when the vendors came around! And as if that were not enough, the kind Memsahib had given her a back-pack containing a coloring book, a box with twelve crayons, and a pretty pink comb and brush. The pain between her legs had vanished into thin air and, better still, she had made friends with the young girl traveling beside her. Komli had never been more excited in her life. Rashid stared at her with a lump in his throat. How could a wretched girl with so little look so happy, he asked himself. And she seemed to be talking incessantly with the girl beside her. What could she possibly have to talk about? His thoughts jumped to his beloved daughter; Tusneem was a porcelain doll without a blemish, compared to this girl with parched, leathery-brown skin. Rashid loved to kiss his daughter on the tip of her slender nose each night, before Zenub took her to bed and read to her. Sometimes he read to her, too. He loved making his daughter laugh, just to see the deep dimples break into her cheeks. Tusneem was the envy of many of his teenage nieces who would give anything to have his daughter's soft, green eyes and creamy complexion. But it was not his daughter's looks that Rashid was proud of. Tusneem was a sensitive, loving child who rarely picked a fight. There was not a teacher in school who was not delighted with Tusneem's hardworking but gentle ways. And once the teachers met the Khans, it was easy for them to figure out why their student had such a lovely disposition herself.

What would Komli turn out like, Rashid wondered. Zenub had tried to turn her into a respectable young lady before she turned her over to Rashid. It seemed that her hair had rebelled, the way her curls shot out in every direction. Komli had a flat nose that bore no hint of anger or arrogance, although Rashid noticed that her nostrils were flared out like one who would not be afraid to do battle.

The older sister seemed oblivious of her surroundings, to anything terrestrial as a matter of fact. She was still trying to deal with the fact that her mother had vanished into thin air. According to Memsahib, whose husband had checked with the police on duty, a beggar woman had been found dead not far from their house. Since she had appeared to be homeless, nameless, and without family, her body had been quickly cremated. Fire had wiped away the stench of a body that some thought had been dead for two whole days when, in reality, the mother had died countless deaths over her daughters' sufferings. In the end, she had gone in peace, because when she had last seen Rana, he was desperately looking for the girls. They've escaped, she thought ecstatically, as she breathed her last.

Roshni was in a trance, unable to grasp the reality of her mother transformed into ashes floating away to unknown shores, even as she herself was being transported to an unknown world. Was this Bhagvaan's way of avenging her for sacrificing her little sister at the altar of money, she wondered. She looked sadly but lovingly at her little sister who seemed so excited. She resolved she would do everything within her means to ensure Komli's happiness. To the world she would pose as her mother, she decided, but to her sister she would be everything she needed—sister, mother, and slave, if necessary. No price would be enough compensation for the injustice her sister had suffered. Like a Rose that droops when it's dead, Roshni bent down her head into her hand and prayed—Hai Bhagvaan, look after my innocent sister. Let her learn well; let her be happily married; let her have lots of children. Forgive me. Guide me to give her what is best. She had the strange sensation that her thoughts were being transported in two different trains going in opposite directions—one going back to her mother and to the streets she had left behind, the other whistling forward through a cloud of smoke beyond which it was impossible to see anything.

Rashid unlocked the door to the apartment he had bought outright so that Roshni would not have to deal with rent or paper work of any kind. He stood on the threshold and smilingly beckoned to the girls to walk in. It was all theirs.

"Sahib!" Roshni exclaimed suddenly, "Ma always said to me that if ever Rana provided me with the room he kept promising, I must step into it with Ganesh in my hands. He is the god who removes obstacles from our way. I simply cannot enter in here without Ganesh in my hands. Do you know where I could get Ganesh?"

Rashid was exhausted. All he wanted to do was to show her the place, leave her with money, check into his hotel and go to sleep. He still had to enroll the little one in a school the next day. How would I know anything about your countless idols, he wanted to scream. But he was educated; he managed to restrain himself. Besides, he understood the human need to bless the home one is about to enter. His family had always done such things themselves. "Let's go find a taxi driver. I'm sure he'll be able to take us to the right place," he said, betraying little emotion.

Rashid took one look at Ganesh and wondered if Abdul was right after all about some of the coarse remarks he made about the senseless idols Hindus worshipped. Ganesh had the body of a man and the head of an elephant. He couldn't help but appreciate the laws of Islam—no images of Allah were allowed, in any form or shape. What was worse, there was a little mouse sitting beside the elephant god. Rashid's curiosity got the better of him. He doubted if this illiterate woman would be able to satisfy it but he went ahead and asked anyway, to bide the time in the taxi, if nothing else. "Why does Ganesh have an elephant head? And what is the mouse doing beside him?" Rashid asked, trying not to show his contempt for the idol.

"Ma used to tell us that goddess Parvati created him. Her husband, Shiva, was always away and they had no children. One day, when she was lonely and had nothing to do, she created a baby out of clay and water, and called it Ganesh. When Shiva came back, he smashed off the baby's head. Parvati could not be consoled. Shiva loved Parvati, but he could not understand why she was so upset over the loss of a clay baby. 'But for me he is not a clay baby. He is real!' Parvati sobbed. When Shiva asked her what he could do to make her happy again, she asked him to go to the jungle with the mighty sword that he always carried with him and bring her back the head of the first living creature he found . . . ."

"And Shiva found an elephant?"

"Yes. And he slew it and brought it back to Parvati. Parvati placed the head on her clay baby. Even though it was funny looking, she still loved it."

"And did Ma tell you why you worship Ganesh?"

"Oh yes. That is the most important part of the story. Ganesh may look fat and awkward but that is to teach us that outer beauty has nothing to do with inner beauty. And Ma used to say that the little mouse is to remind us that little animals are as important as big animals." There was no sarcasm in Roshni's voice. She simply looked up at him, as meek as a mouse. If Ganesh could have smiled then, he would have smiled. Rashid smiled instead. Quietly. He had been pleasantly surprised by the profound symbolism of her God. He had been taken aback by the sparkle in Roshni's huge, black eyes. Although he could not pinpoint why, she seemed very different from her younger sister. She seemed a little more refined, the younger one a little more streetwise. He would not call either of them beautiful, but the older one definitely had a softer, more sensitive air about her. For so many years, Rashid thought, their paths had crossed every day, literally, and yet they had been as interested in one another as passersby are in trees that they know exist, yet never truly see; neither family had stopped to think about the other's roots, or what it was that stirred them.

And so, with Ganesh at home to bless them, Roshni and Komli embarked upon a reincarnated stage of their lives. Rana had steered them through hell. Rashid had opened the doors to heaven.

CB80

CHAPTER 2

CONFUSION

"I'm sorry, Mr. Khan, I cannot accept Komli," the principal of St. Mary's convent stated politely.

"Why?!" Rashid asked, a little taken aback. As worldly and knowledgeable as he was, he had been naïve enough to make arrangements for Komli to be interviewed by the best Catholic school in Patna, confident that his standing in society would be the passport to Komli's acceptance there. "May I have some reasons, please?"

"You have no documents, no birth certificate. I can only guess by her build that she is seven or eight years old. Yet she does not recognize a single letter or number. Would it be fair to place her in a class of four year olds?"

"If you think that will work, it's fine with me. I would be happy to make a donation towards a project you might have in mind."

Mother Christina was a kind, understanding nun. She knew in her heart of hearts that the child of an illiterate mother would feel terribly out of place in her school. The fact that Roshni was illiterate did not surprise her at all. Millions of women in India lacked a formal education. She recalled how she herself had been inspired to come to India not only to educate the illiterate, but to enlighten the heathens who knew nothing about Jesus and who relegated their women to a life of domestic drudgery. "Mr. Khan, I would love to help you but the child would feel out of place and therefore miserable in this school. All our parents come from professional backgrounds. They are deeply committed to being involved with the school's many programs." Leaning forward, she whispered, "Rags and riches just don't go together. Believe me, Mr. Khan, you would be doing this girl a great disservice by enrolling her here. My conscience will not allow it. I do appreciate your offer to become one of the school's benefactors," she added with genuine appreciation.

Roshni overheard what Mother Christina had said. Komli is not in rags, she thought indignantly but remained quiet because Rashid had advised the girls to speak only when spoken to.

"Is there another good school you can recommend?" Rashid asked, "I came to your school because I wanted the best for this child."

The principal couldn't help but wonder why a man of his obvious standing was obligated to this unrelated, illiterate woman and child. She wondered if he had fathered the child, although he just didn't look the type. Perhaps he was trying to help out another man, some relation maybe. It wasn't as if these things didn't happen in her part of the world. She knew there were more secrets floating in the wind than there were stories written in books. She, too, had her secrets and, indeed, she was glad to be in a country where people never seemed to wonder what lay behind her black and white gown; or what she prayed for on the rosary that hugged her forty inch waist.

Because there was something so genuine about the man, Mother Christina responded with empathy, "I can ask Father Michael to get in touch with the two ladies immediately. He runs a Sunday school . . ."

"Mother Christina, I want the child to go to school full-time, not just on Sundays," Rashid said as politely as he could. He knew he could not well shout at the nun and say, *I'm not paying for her to become some Catholic convert!*

"You didn't let me finish. Father Michael belongs to a group of missionaries who take the destitute and the illiterate, and work with them for a while, not just on Sundays. They then send them to different schools, depending on their abilities." Mother Christina failed to mention that most of the children were rewarded with free milk just for attending; that it took the destitute as little as one glass of free milk a day to agree to convert to Catholics. "Those who show potential end up at an excellent Montessori school where children of different ages work well together. Believe me, Komli will be appropriately placed by caring, experienced people. I am sure something can be worked out, provided she co-operates and works hard. Would you like me to get in touch with Father Michael?"

Rashid had little choice and little time. He had to catch a train that afternoon.

If I leave you their address, will Father Michael definitely get in touch with them, Mother Christina?"

"I promise you he will," Mother Christina replied with a smile. Rashid felt he could trust her. Besides, he could always check on the girls the next time he was in Patna. A few weeks' delay would make little difference in Komli's education, he realized.

Roshni was relieved to get out of the pristine *cell*. It seemed that the nun had eyes only for Rashid and Komli. So what if Rashid Sahib had explained to the woman that she could not read or write, did the woman have to treat her like a mute wall in the background, she wondered pensively.

Although Komli was far from disgruntled, she, too, was happy to get out of the stifling office. She was too enamored by her metamorphosed self, to be saddened by rejection. Out of the blue she had a roof over her head, a soft, warm bed, clothes without holes or smells, and no hungry stomach! What more could she want? And if this was still rags, what the hell was rich, she wondered. The only thing she disliked about her new self was the restriction shoes and socks imposed. She missed feeling the ground under her feet.

Rashid offered to take them shopping, but Roshni assured him that they would be able to fend for themselves. In fact, she decided to speak up for a change. She was tired of the silence she had maintained for the last few days. Besides, the man looked harried and restless.

"Sahib, all I've wanted all my life is a room and enough food. Not only did we survive without it, but Ma, Komli, and I managed sometimes to laugh together in spite of everything. You've given me an apartment that has more, much more, than everything we need; you've stashed me with so many bundles of notes, it's scary. I know how many thugs there are on streets. We'll survive Patna, Sahib, I'm sure. There seem to be less thugs here than Calcutta," she added, surveying her surroundings a little skeptically. She suddenly felt calm and confident. After all, she now had the might of both money and a full stomach.

Rashid was relieved because he himself had little idea about basic necessities for running a house. As far as he was concerned, water came in glasses, food came on tables or thaals (huge metal platters around which Bohras sit for meals), depending on where he was dining, and clothes came from tailors who visited him at his convenience to measure him and to deliver the different apparel he required for the multitudinous roles he played in his day to day life. The closest he had come to the true source of nature was when he had tried to squeeze out milk from the teats of a cow.

Rashid bade them farewell. Roshni's serenity, together with her few humble words, had somehow lightened the burden in his heart. The journey back in the air-conditioned compartment was more pleasant than he had envisaged. Rashid couldn't help but appreciate the peace and sanity of traveling first class. Strangely enough, he found himself envying the simple lifestyle the two girls would have. He wondered what his life would be like if all he had to worry about was food, clothing and shelter. No wigs in court and fetas (turban) at mosques; no different rules of etiquette and dressing for home, for court, for mosque, for club; no rules for dining, for praying, for dressing. Was he really just one human being, he wondered suddenly as he marveled at his ability to be husband, father and master at home, treasurer of the Bohra community in Calcutta, judge at court, polished and westernized member of the Calcutta club and, as though that were not enough, he had also landed the job of being guardian angel of two helpless beggars! The two beggars had asked nothing of life but life itself, with a simplicity and humility for which Rashid suddenly had the highest regard. One sentence of his Catholic schooling suddenly made sense to him: *Blessed are the meek for theirs is the kingdom of heaven.* Dear Allah, bless the little child and her sister, he prayed, as the train whistled its way back to Calcutta.

Roshni and Komli felt more carefree after Rashid left. With full hearts and stomachs, they walked back to their apartment. Komli couldn't wait to get back, just to open and close her chest of drawers, just to feel the cold air from the refrigerator and, best of all, to sleep on a mattress again. Roshni, on the other hand, entered with some sense of trepidation, not knowing how she would handle the many locks and keys to life within walls.

Abdul was the living embodiment of old spirits that had looked after the house. It took him little time to realize that his Sahib was plagued by a sickness of the soul. He was convinced that it had something to do with that wretched beggar. The recent strange happenings had coincided with her arrival. Never before had this house been stripped of all servants. Both Sahib and Memsahib seemed to have little appetite for food. Sahib had never before taken two trips to Patna in such quick succession. But what was most unbearable for Abdul was the fact that his Sahib behaved more like his own shadow than a man with flesh and blood, a shadow that could survive on air alone.

Like a marriage of long years, Abdul didn't have to talk to his Sahib to detect what frame of mind he was in. He knew Sahib's moods had as many shades as the rainbow. And who could blame him for his many moods? After all, he had to deal with his modern wife, his pampered daughter, his sick mother, and his extended family. Then there were all his servants, the permanent ones and the transient ones who flitted in and out of the house. Saturdays were devoted to community matters and, word had it, he was the best judge in Calcutta. Abdul had no idea what his Sahib had to deal with in courts, but judging from the masses of papers Sahib poured himself into, sometimes until the wee hours of the morning, Abdul often thanked Allah for not being able to read and write. He had no complaints about his life, except perhaps that he didn't get enough of his wife during his youth. But that was how it was in his family, and that was that! His full name was Abdullah, meaning slave of Allah. He was content being slave of Allah and servant of an angel.

Abdul's role in his Sahib's life had changed from the *parent* who loves and reprimands to the *parent* who quietly retires to enjoy the fruits of his labor. He had held Sahib within an hour after his birth, for in those days women gave birth at home. He remembered fondly how as Chotasahib (little sir), Rashid often arose early in the morning when the dew was still wet on the grass, just to see the milk man bring in the cow. Alas, those days were long gone; milk came in plastic containers now! It was alright then for Chotasahib to beg that he be allowed to carry the bucket of milk up to the kitchen, and for Abdul to graciously consent. Abdul had known all along that in a matter of years his Chotasahib would become his master, when it would not be for him to question why or what his master did, much less spank him.

Even during his wedding Rashid had not forgotten his devoted servant. He had asked that Abdul be accorded the rare privilege of walking beside him while he rode on his horse. He had made such a romantic, mysterious groom. Abdul could still picture him, all dressed in white with gold tassels hanging over his face, striding a horse that knew to move slowly to the tune played by the band that marched in front of them. Abdul had watched Rashid turn from child to caring man. In many ways, Abdul understood his Sahib as well as he understood himself. The one difference between the two was that Sahib gave orders with quiet dignity, and Abdul delivered with quiet grace. It afforded Abdul much pleasure in his old age just to quietly smoothen out the little wrinkles in Sahib's life, so Sahib could deal with the bigger ones. Lovingly, Abdul ironed Sahib's clothes, dusted and polished his study, and, above all, made sure he ate right. Ever since he was a little boy, he had been told that health was wealth.

Abdul decided that if Sahib's fairy tale life was turning sour, he would simply have to assume the role of protective parent and get to the bottom of the mess. It didn't take a school education to figure out that there must be some connection between the fact that his Sahib's peace of mind and the three wretched beggars had vanished into thin air at the same time!

"Sahib," he ventured one evening when Zenub Memsahib was out, "I know it is not my place to say certain things, but I am going to open my mouth and say that I know you are terribly troubled. I felt something evil creep into our household the day Memsahib allowed that Hindu beggar in our garden. You are like a son to me; I know you better than my own wife and children. And when you hardly touch your meals, it bothers me greatly. You know, I can tell by the way you eat whether you are happy or worried. Lately it seems that you have been stricken by a sickness that is eating away at you. Look how quiet you are even now. You have not said a word!"

"You have left me speechless, Abdul!" Rashid said gently. The illiterate servant had seen through his soul and it simply felt good to see such a display of love and warmth when he had been cold and alone and unable to turn to anyone.

"So I'm right, Sahib. Something is bothering you! I'll be honest with you. I went out into the streets to accost the woman herself, but it seems that she and her family have disappeared. I hope I never see them again, although I do want to get to the bottom of it. I raised you like my own son, Sahib, please tell me what it is that is troubling you."

"That is exactly what's troubling me, Abdul, that Memsahib tried to help the beggars in a way unacceptable not just to you, but to me as well. That is why I've been in a state of turmoil. In time I will be alright. I don't think you have to worry about her coming here again, ever. I've sorted everything out. Trust me, Abdul." Although Abdul felt some sense of relief, he knew his master wasn't telling him everything. "Tell me, Abdul," Rashid continued, "Why do you think that a harmless Hindu, and a beggar at that, would hurt us? You must try and rid yourself of old-fashioned notions. It's one thing to believe only Muslims go to Heaven, but another to believe that a Hindu entering our house is an evil omen!"

"My father always told us that, Sahib. I'm concerned . . ."

"Believe me, Abdul, nothing's going to happen to me because an innocent Hindu stepped inside our garden. He looked up and smiled at his faithful servant. He had never said thank you to Abdul. The word did not exist in Abdul's vocabulary. So Rashid said simply, "It's good to have you around, Abdul. You just keep doing the things you do for me and I promise you I will get back to being my old self. How about getting me one of your good old cold lassees (yogurt drink)?"

"Are you trying to get rid of me, and have me return to the kitchen, Sahib?"

Rashid laughed, for the first time in many days. "Old is gold you know, Abdul. I would be a fool to get rid of you." He paused for a few seconds before adding, "Here's a little secret, Abdul. In trying to help that woman, Memsahib was about to sell some of our family jewelry. I was naturally quite upset and put a stop to it. But you know something? If she had sold it, I could have replaced it. You, Abdul, are an irreplaceable gem. Now, will you go get me some lassee?"

Abdul, in turn, wanted to say thank you, but did not know how to. So he prepared the perfect lassee for Sahib, while his heart sang a wordless, tuneless song of joy. More than fifty years of loyal service, and today he was paid the highest compliment of all—he was a priceless gem! At least his wise Sahib appreciated the old, even though most things old were fast being buried under modern garbage. All the sacrifices he had made in his life had been worth this moment, Abdul thought with a new shine in his eyes.

Rana went crazy for a few days. With hindsight, he realized that that chichree of a woman was really quite a treasure. He wanted her. He searched high and low for her, but to no avail. No vendors, no rickshaw-wallahs, no other beggars knew what had happened to her. He could only guess that their Ma had died and the two had decided to walk away. But surely one could not walk and vanish that quickly! After a few days the fox decided that Roshni had turned quite sour anyway and that he should concentrate on the other fish in the sea. After all, Calcutta had more women on the streets than he could handle in a few life times.

Rana decided to try even harder to get his visa for the Middle East. Too bad his was not a profession for which the Middle East expressed a need. There were no beggars in the Middle East, he had been told. The jobs advertised in the newspapers were for doctors, engineers, teachers, nurses and, at the bottom of the ladder, there were advertisements for manual laborers. Rana had no professional expertise to offer, and at first he refused to stoop down to the level of a manual laborer when he had not done a stroke of work in his life! But when he saw the gold and hard cash some of his colleagues of equal skill had amassed, his eyes began to twitch with envy.

"Life is hard in the Middle East," his friends had warned him. The rich Arabs treat us like dirt because we have no qualifications. We have to live like animals, twenty to a room. But we never starve. And if you are willing to work your butt off, and not get into trouble, you can return to India in a few years and live like a lord." The last four words appealed to Rana greatly. He had always wanted to live like a lord—have alcohol, opium, women, cigarettes, wake up late, gamble until the wee hours of the morning, whiz around in a Mercedes, and never worry about money. To some extent, he did live like a lord. But if he could take a short cut and fly to the Middle East to amass his fortune, acquire his Mercedes, and retire to languish in bed all day, why it might be worth some labor, he decided one day. It wasn't as if his hands had been hacked off.

In India, the mountains of applications from manual laborers wanting to go to the Middle East piled so high and deep that it turned into a thriving ground for bribery and corruption, the kind of ground on which Rana always performed best. Before long he, too, disappeared from Calcutta, having taken all the necessary short-cuts to acquire a passport, visa, work permit and airline ticket to fly him to Jeddah, the thriving commercial metropolis of Saudi Arabia.

Rana survived the initial hiccups of having an Arab customs officer hurl out the contents of his baggage for inspection. "What did you do that for?!" Rana asked angrily.

"Take off those sunglasses!" the officer ordered, shocked that this insignificant laborer was not quite as humble as the others who came in droves. Rana laid down his sunglasses on the counter and stared down at his well polished, black, leather shoes. "You have something to hide? Look at me!" the officer demanded angrily. Seething inside, Rana stared into the officer's eyes.

"Can I leave?" Rana asked impatiently, wishing the officer would stop scrutinizing his eyes.

"I do the questioning! Have any alcohol?"

"No. We're not allowed to bring any, I was told."

"Don't ever forget that," the officer barked astutely. "Next!" he shouted, looking over Rana's shoulders. He waved his baton at Rana's ruffled clothes to indicate to Rana that he could pack up and go through.

Bastard! Rana cursed under his breath as he stooped down to shove his clothes into his bag.

Next morning Rana met his Saudi boss, a man of means but little education. "Give me your passport," he demanded. After making sure all Rana's papers were in order, he added, "Tomorrow you start work. Be here at five."

"In the morning?!"

"We start early. The roads get very hot. You get an afternoon break. Then you work again from four to eight in the evening. Any questions?"

"No," Rana replied demurely. He was thinking of his friend's advice—*Do not argue with an Arab. And remember, your boss has your passport. You are at his mercy. He can keep you under his clutches as long as he wishes.*

"Take him to the main square on Friday," the Arab ordered one of Rana's colleagues. "He needs to understand how we deal with crime in our country."

At the main square the following Friday, Rana witnessed the public beheading of a young man who had committed murder. It seemed to be over quickly and quietly. Rana shuddered. The things he had done to children had made them howl in agony. He felt fearful and helpless, emotions that were totally unfamiliar to him.

Accompanied by thousands of other manual laborers, Rana quietly slapped cement on bricks, and spread tar on roads. The Arabs in Saudi Arabia came closer each day to their dream of catching up with the modern world, and Rana to his dream of whizzing around in a Mercedes.

Roshni kept to herself as much as possible. A simple lie, that she had been widowed early and therefore left Calcutta to start life afresh held many inquisitive questions abey. So long as one did not hurt others or flaunt money around, one did not get noticed that much in India Roshni soon realized. If she had a choice, she would be perfectly content to become a mere shadow that accompanied her sister wherever she went. Her life's singularly selfless ambition was to make sure her sister would be everything beggars were not— healthy, educated, respectable, and content.

Her neighbors simply accepted her as widowed Roshni with a young daughter. A decent, likeable twosome. The daughter must be like her deceased father, the neighbors decided, for unlike quiet, placid Roshni, Komli seemed to be a bit of a firebrand. What she lacked in one limb, she certainly seemed to make up with the other three; she rarely sat still for a moment. If the neighborhood children met on the street to play cricket or soccer or any other game, Komli was always there. Her handicap was never an obstacle. As far as she was concerned, spiders had eight limbs, man had four and she had three; one more than a bird, and if the latter could chirp and soar, why so could she!

Tara, Roshni's immediate neighbor, held back the first couple of times the smell of burned food wafted through her doors. The third time she went storming out. Youngsters these days never seemed to know anything, she had long decided. As far as Tara was concerned, life was an endless cycle of listening and dictating—when you're young you listen; when you grow up you get to be boss. You die, you get reincarnated, and the cycle starts all over again. It was now her time to dictate, to blow around colorful advice, even though it was rarely appreciated.

"Roshni!" she shouted with sugar-coated sweetness as she banged loudly on her neighbor's door, "Are you alright in there?"

"How are you, Tara Bahen?" (sister, mark of respect), Roshni enquired politely as she opened the door, wishing she did not have to refer to this woman as sister. Alas, it was a mark of respect, and Tara made sure all youngsters accorded her the deference elders had once demanded of her.

"This is the third time I've smelled food burning in your house. My daughter-in-law, Devi, did not know how to cook either until I taught her. Tell me, did you ever cook before your husband died? You can tell me, it's nothing to be ashamed of. Many wives from rich households never cook. The fact that Roshni appeared to come from a wealthy background made it easier for Tara to treat her with some civility.

"Not much," Roshni replied simply, relieved that this woman had found a good excuse for her ignorance.

"Let me see what's burning," she stated as she made a bee-line for the kitchen. "Hai, Bhagvaan!" Tara exclaimed, placing her right hand on her forehead. The cooker was caked with food that had overflowed many times over, it seemed, and it was obvious no one had taught her how to polish pots and pans to a shine. Why, Roshni's pots were the color of charcoal! Tara refused to let Devi put any kind of food into a pot until her daughter-in-law had scrubbed it to its original spotless, sparkle! "I can't stand too long on my rickety legs any more," Tara continued. "Let me call Devi. She will be glad to show you how to cook and clean. She's a little slow, but she'll be good for you." She was about to walk away when she decided to comment on the floral print on Roshni's sari.

"You know, Roshni, all good Hindu widows wear nothing but plain white saris. Next time Devi goes grocery shopping I'll tell her to take you with her. Maybe you can buy some. I do understand that life is not easy on your own, but at least try not to antagonize our Bhagvaan. He likes to see widows in plain, white," Tara added with the air of someone who was accorded the privilege of chatting with Bhagvaan all the time! *You people with full stomachs have nothing better to do, it seems, than prescribe colors for life's little events—red for brides, and white for widows, indeed,* Roshni wanted to retort, but chose to remain quiet.

Tara lived for her pride and joy, Mohan, her thirty year old son who was married to Devi. Tara disliked the name Devi because it meant angel! As far as she was concerned, Devi was the wily woman who did everything to estrange son from mother. Tara made sure Devi slaved for both mother-in-law and husband. The more affection Mohan showed for his wife, the harder Tara made her work. It didn't take Devi long to realize that in order to keep her sanity, she must become a passive listener. So Devi cooked and cleaned and sewed and followed her mother-in-law's every command. Devi, too, disliked her mother-in-law's name. It meant star—a star without any luster, Devi often thought as she jabbed her needle in and out of the cloth she was embroidering, wishing sometimes that it was her mother-in-law she could jab instead to avenge herself of the countless stabs Tara inflicted upon her day in and day out.

Devi was good for Roshni, and Roshni was heaven-sent for Devi. Before long, Roshni became a vessel into which Devi poured her every-day woes. Devi not only respected Roshni's quiet ways, but also began to look upon Roshni as a silent haven into which she could retreat when she wished to escape from her ever-droning mother-in-law with her countless stings.

Devi also knew from experience that sorrowful memories make silent, but steadfast companions with whom one can battle life's ongoing ups and downs. So if stoic, serene Roshni wished to savor her sad past in secret, Devi decided she certainly would not intrude. She knew how much she squirmed with disgust because it was impossible to keep any secrets from her mother-in-law. She had a nagging suspicion that Tara probably kept track of the times she and her husband made love. The walls of her bedroom were not quite soundproof, she knew. And the witch made no bones about being unpleasant every time Devi got her period. While many Hindu women hated going into seclusion during their menstrual cycle, Devi welcomed those days of peace and freedom from her tyrant of a mother-in-law. In fact, she prayed devotedly to the gods to keep her from conceiving until Tara was reincarnated into something else. *Thank God for reincarnation, at least you don't have to wish death upon your mother-in-law,* Devi's inner voice had quipped the first time she had made the wish.

Sometimes, however, Devi did summon up the courage to ask Roshni the odd question. Most intriguing to her was the fact that Roshni did not have a jamadaar (sweeper) come and clean her floors and bathroom. Why, even lower middle-class Indians could afford the pittance to pay the untouchables to whom it seemed India had relegated the wretched task of cleaning other peoples' toilets. No respectable woman defiled her hands with that job! Even Devi was spared that.

"If he is untouchable, why would I allow him to touch the floors of my haven?" Roshni asked quietly.

"You're strange, Roshni, but you're the best thing that's ever happened to me since marriage," Devi said with affection. She resolved that day to refrain from questioning Roshni unless it was absolutely necessary. And so Devi never did ask about minor things like why her new neighbors didn't have their ears pierced when all Indian women she knew wore ear-rings ever since they could remember. Wearing jewelry was a mark of standing and, judging from what Roshni could afford for her daughter, she must have been married into a family of some standing.

Unlike her daughter-in-law, Tara made no bones about voicing her suspicions about the two, seemingly rootless creatures. "If you ask me, that woman is hiding something behind her one-word replies," she muttered from time to time. "As saintly as she appears, there's an unexplainable smell of the gutters around her."

Neither Tara nor Devi found out that three mornings a week Roshni walked a few miles to a neighborhood her own neighbors knew nothing about and cleaned toilets for five families there. As far as she was concerned, Rashid's money was for Komli. To work as a sweeper didn't require an education and it paid for her food and the few white saris she needed. Although at first she resented Tara telling her what she ought to wear, Roshni soon realized that the less she defied people like Tara, the less she saw or heard from them. Also, people were less likely to notice a widow in white as opposed to an attractive, young lady in pretty saris. So she took Tara's advice and opted for the colorless garb of widowhood, which, as far as Roshni was concerned, was a blessing in disguise. It did not take unlearned Roshni long to realize that in order to live peacefully in the civilized world, she must show some desire to want to ape fellow-man. The more free-spirited Komli simply could not understand why her sister had to listen to bossy strangers like Tara. If Komli could have had her way, she would have preferred to be more belligerent in the hope that Tara would leave them alone.

Fortunately for Komli, she had Father Michael to take her mind away from the unpleasant neighbor. Father Michael was quite taken up by Komli's thirst for knowledge. He knew from day one that she would be a candidate for the Montessori school. Komli had worked hard at Sunday school. Like a sponge, she had happily absorbed Father Michael's engaging stories from the Bible, memorized the prayers, and downed each glass of free milk like it was the last glass of milk left on earth. It was not long before Komli received the triple honor of being baptized, attending the Montessori school, and learning how to read and write.

"Komli," Roshni said gently to her sister the day after she had been baptized, "You don't have to believe everything Father Michael says. You can take it in with one ear and let it out through the other. Listen to him quietly just so you can go to school. Ma raised us as Hindus. Just because he baptized you does not mean you have to forget our own holy trinity—Brahma is our creator, Vishnu is our preserver, and Shiva is our destroyer. You can think of all of them as our holy ghosts if you like. Just don't forget them."

Although Komli had nodded her head to appease her sister, what Komli did in reality was to retain every word that came her way. She had little time, and even less inclination, to sift the chaff from the grain. In her heart of hearts, what she truly adored was the word itself, regardless of whether it was prose or poetry, written or oral, religious or sacrilegious. And to show her gratitude to Bhagvaan, who was manifested in so many different forms, she asked Roshni one day if they could have Saraswati (goddess of learning) in the corner they had reserved for Ganesh. Komli had decided her favorite gods would be Ganesh and Saraswati. Roshni was delighted to oblige. Komli thanked both gods each morning before she left home.

In time, late evenings became the most precious times for Roshni and Komli. By that time each day Komli had been fed, done some school work, and had finished playing outside with the neighborhood children. The next couple of hours belonged to Roshni and Komli working together within the walls of a small paradise behind tightly locked doors. Whatever Komli learned in school, she repeated with fervor to her sister.

Learning was fun, especially at the Montessori school where Mrs. Fletcher often illustrated her stories with experiments.

"Do you know, Roshni," Komli stated one evening, "everything on earth is made of only three states of matter—solid, liquid and gas. Even you and I are made from only those three things. And those three things keep changing, depending on how cold or hot it gets. Mrs. Fletcher showed us how water freezes into ice and boils into vapor. How wax melts over heat and how that melted wax turns into a solid lump again when it is thrown into cold water. It was like magic! There are some very hard things that rarely change. Like iron. She burned it and burned it and it just stayed the same as if it could not feel a thing. I love school!"

"I'm so happy for you, Komli."

"You'll never guess where paper comes from, Roshni. Try!"

"Liquid turning into solid sheets?"

"Trees. Paper is made from trees, Roshni. Mrs. Fletcher gets kind of sad every time she sees us waste paper because she says we are wasting trees and since trees give us oxygen, we should do everything to protect trees."

"And what do we do with this oxygen, pray tell?"

"We breathe it and give the trees carbon dioxide. It's that magic giving and taking that keeps us all alive!"

"Oh Yeah! I'm pretty sure there wasn't a single tree on the streets where we begged. How come we're still alive?"

"It's like praying to Bhagvaan. Do you see him?" Komli asked precociously. "Mrs. Fletcher says you can't see all the magic."

"Sounds like the tree has worked a special magic on your Mrs. Fletcher, just as it had on our dear Ma. Remember all the wonderful stories she told us?"

"Yes, and I love them both. Trees are special. Without them we would have no paper, or stories, or food, or medicine."

"I'll remember that. Thank you for telling me," Roshni said indulgently as she looked into her sister's lucid eyes.

"I don't know what I enjoy more—school, or coming home and learning everything again with you."

In time, the two sisters treated themselves to a set of moveable alphabets. Watching them, one would assume that the two were playing with precious gems. "The vowels are blue, Roshni, they are the pearls. The red alphabets are the consonants. They are the other gems. String the pearls between the other gems and, wow, you create more magic! Let's take out two gems, h and t. Now give me the pearls—a, e i o u and sometimes y. Look what I've made! 'hat' and 'het' and 'hit' and 'hot' and 'hut' and 'hyt'. Sometimes, long after most children were fast asleep, the two jewelers lay awake, gleefully stringing words, some that would make no sense to the outside world. But they cared little for the world outside. For them, nothing was more precious than the novelty of learning together on full stomachs. Slowly but surely, the two tortoises were not only catching up with the civilized world, they were turning into content, healthy human beings who craved little.

Komli made friends quickly. If children tended to feel sorry for her at first, that sentiment was quickly replaced by admiration and fondness for one who was so immersed in the love of making new discoveries each day and in the joy of having children for constant companions that she had no time for self-pity.

Komli had won over her teacher during the first week of school when her teacher had narrated the Big Bang story of creation entitled, *God Who Has No Hands*. Komli had been so mesmerized by the story that Mrs. Fletcher noticed how far away Komli seemed that day, long after all the children had settled down to work.

"Komli, you seem to be far away. Can I help you?"

"Oh! I was thinking about the story you just told us. If a God without hands can create our world and have every thing follow His divine order, I think I'm going to be alright with one hand," she had said with refreshing confidence.

With a hug that had almost smothered Komli, Mrs. Fletcher had whispered, "You're going to be more than alright, Komli. If you put your mind to it, I bet you can do anything you wish! Here's something I want you to remember as long as you live: dreaming is not just for bedtime. You must never stop dreaming. It's good for the soul. And you must never stop working hard. It's even better for the soul."

"What's soul, Mrs. Fletcher?"

"It's the invisible person inside you that no one can ever, ever touch or take away. Some people call it Aatma. The harder you work, the happier your Aatma will be."

"Then I can dream about playing the piano some day?"

"Yes!" Mrs. Fletcher had responded, while she resolved to keep a special eye on this handicapped student who seemed to have all the essentials for success—a good head, a clean heart, an abundance of hope, and a dash of humility.

The next time the children played the piano, Mrs. Fletcher simply asked her students if they would like to volunteer to be Komli's left hand. There was hardly a child who had not raised a hand. Many were the songs that Komli learned to play, and many were the lessons that Komli mastered, with the help of other children.

It seemed that Mother Christina had done Komli a great favor by not accepting her in her traditional school. Komli simply thrived in the Montessori environment where she worked at her own pace, where children worked with children of different ages, where they taught each other as well, under the guidance of a warm, loving teacher. Most important of all, Komli was learning to think for herself. Her repertoire of stories of Creation increased by the day. Like candy, Komli learned to savor all the different stories, content in the knowledge that whoever it was who was looking after her, a God with no hands, Jesus with two hands or Durga with ten hands, was a very kind God, indeed. And her sister, too, was loving and kind, in that she never forced Komli to believe or disbelieve anything. The two knew instinctively never to barge into the inner sanctity of each other's souls. They were more like chalk and cheese, than salt and water that can be dissolved together to become a single entity.

Unlike Mother Christina's students who sat in front of a desk and listened passively to the 40-minute periods of prescribed knowledge teachers carefully clipped and pruned before presenting, Komli was soon able to walk around freely and virtually explore any of the different areas in a classroom environment that Mrs. Fletcher carefully prepared each morning before the children walked into class. There were special areas for history, geography, biology, botany, grammar, language, spelling, geometry, math, reading, and art. Komli could delve into any subject of her choice. As long as she worked within the parameters of the few rules of her class—respect one another, respect the materials in the classroom and try to choose from at least three or four subjects each day—she was left alone to explore her new world and to form her own conclusions. And if on the odd occasion it so happened that little Komli felt like studying nothing but ancient Egypt all day, she was allowed to do so, provided she was respectful of her classmates and her environment.

From a young age, therefore, Komli learned to delve into the subjects that interested her, and to form her own opinions. All Roshni asked of her little sister was to pretend she was her mother. It was not long before the lie felt like the truth, a beautiful truth, tainted though it was with a smidgen of lie. Like sand crabs disappearing into the wet sand, the memories of hunger pangs and itchy, lice-infested hair were silently swallowed by finer granules on the ever-changing seashore of life.

There was only one occasion when Roshni refused to indulge her sister. It was the day Komli came home from school with a stray kitten.

"Please can we keep her at home, Roshni?"

"No, Komli. Animals don't belong in homes."

"Why not? Some of my friends in school have pets."

"Not us, Komli. The money you receive is just about enough," she lied, "to live here, to go to school, and to eat well. And I am just about getting the hang of what it takes to look after home and human beings. We simply cannot look after a cat."

"Please, Roshni, I beg you."

Roshni knelt down on her knees, placed her hands on her sister's shoulders and looked up at her solemnly, "You can ask me again and again, the answer will still be no. There is one thing, though, Komli, that I never, never, never, never want you to say ever again in your life and that is, 'I beg you'. You are turning into a beautiful, educated, young lady. One day, when you grow up, you can have a cat, if you wish. But never, Komli, never, do I ever want you to beg for anything, do you understand?"

"Alright," Komli said with a pout, unable to understand why her sister had no empathy for stray cats when they themselves were street creatures once!

Roshni also had a way of confusing Komli from time to time about things the latter had learned in school. There was the one day, for instance, when Komli came home babbling as usual, "Do you know, Roshni, we have something in common with the cows and dogs and cats and rats that we slept with on the streets. We're all mammals!"

"Mam-mals," Roshni repeated slowly.

"You should see the pictures of mammals in books, Roshni. I wonder if there's such a thing as rich dogs and cats, and poor dogs and cats, because those mammals in books look rich, like we do now, with clean skin and combed hair and all that. I miss my dog and cat friends sometimes. I wonder if they miss me."

Roshni swallowed the lump that had risen in her throat. It surprised her that Komli missed any aspect of her miserable past. "So are you going to explain why we are all mammals, cats and dogs and cows and us? We lived with spiders and ants and cockroaches, too. Are they all mam-mals, too?"

"You know something, I asked Seeta that question myself."

"You told her we lived on the streets?" Roshni asked in dismay.

"No, Roshni! That's our precious secret, I know. I asked them why spiders and ants aren't mammals, and she just started laughing. She knows everything, Seeta. I love working with her."

"So what did she say about spiders and ants?"

"Cats and dogs have babies from their own stomachs, spiders and ants don't."

"So how come there were hundreds of spiders and ants around, if they don't have babies?"

"They do have babies!" Komli shrieked, "Remember Divine Order? It's like a master plan. Mammals have babies from their stomachs and spiders and ants lay eggs. Their babies come out of eggs."

"Eggs?"

"Not the eggs we eat. Little eggs."

"How come we never saw babies come out of eggs?"

"I don't know, Roshni."

"And all these things come from this creator with no hands?"

"Yes. If you believe the story of God Who Has No Hands."

"Have you forgotten our Brahma who created the universe, our Vishnu and Shiva and Ganesh and Saraswati?

"No, Roshni. You know I pray to Ganesh and Saraswati every morning before I leave."

"I know you do. But do you still love them?"

"I will never, never forget what they have done for me. Of course, I love them."

"Remember the other day you said we human beings have not been around that long. And you also brought me pictures of dinosaurs that you said died long, long before us. When I asked you how we know so much about them, if they died before we came, you started on this fossils business being like old books or something. Don't believe everything you learn, Komli," Roshni advised with a smile, "If you can see it, it's one thing; if you can't, it's another."

I can't see Brahma either, Komli wanted to say, but asked instead, "You mean what they tell me and what I read is not always true?"

"I don't know, Komli. Some of it sounds unbelievable sometimes. Like the stuff you told me about the hungry cat-pillar. I don't think Bhagvaan or Allah or Jesus or anybody's God could come up with that sort of stuff!"

"What sort of stuff?"

"That cat-pillars come from a egg, and the . . ."

"An egg! And it's cat-ur-pillar!" Komli corrected with a laugh. These times with her sister could be confusing, but they were always so much fun.

"Ya, ya, it comes out of *an* egg. Then it gobbles up leaves. Then, when it's full, it starts spinning some silk around it, like it can go shopping for needle and thread! Then it goes and hangs itself, like committing suicide, I guess, because it can't see a darn thing from that cocoon. And then, one fine day it just pops out of its coffin. And as though that were not enough of a fantastic tale, they tell you it starts flying around like birds, but it's not a bird. How can you believe such tales, Komli?! You don't have to believe Jesus walked on water just because Father Michael gives you free milk."

"Maybe it's free because it's water turned to milk! How come you believe all the tales Ma told us about Raam and Sita and Hanuman?" Komli asked.

"Ma never said I had to believe her stories. She said all people create stories. It's for fun, to while away the time on earth. If you ask me, all Gods are the same. Just like Father Michael and you and me, we're all the same. We make Gods in different colors, just like Gods make us in different colors.

"You know what, Roshni," Komli said slowly, "I think when Ma died she spun silk around us so we could have this beautiful place. Do you think Ma hung herself for us?"

"Let's go eat, Komli. My brain needs a rest from all this mumble jumble." She wanted to add, *no dearest Komli, it is because of me that you have been transformed into something else. You may never soar to the heavens, but at least you will never grovel in the filth either. Some day I will tell you. I hope you will forgive me.*

"Do we have to eat now, Roshni?"

"Yes! You cannot survive on reading and writing."

"I wish we could eat words. Wouldn't it be wonderful if we could just read and read and read our concoctions and have our stomachs fill up with words . . ."

"Would that be liquid, solid or gas, pray tell?"

"At least it wouldn't smell like the gas after we eat lentils," Komli said with a laugh. "I can't remember ever farting on the streets. Can you?"

"I refuse to have you side-track me any more. We're eating right now, although sometimes I wish those early men had never discovered fire. I wouldn't have to cook, and Tara Bahen wouldn't have to barge in to tell me I'm going to burn down the neighborhood."

In this way, sometimes in earnest and sometimes in jest, both sisters ate voraciously off the leaves of any and every book that came their way. Knowing nothing of the pressures of exams, since Montessori education did not believe in grades and exams, reading and learning turned into one exciting, wonderful adventure. Neither sister really saw the metamorphosis that was taking place within—the prostitute had turned into a unique nun who was so content in her cloister, she cared little about the hereafter. She prayed to Bhagvaan but also revered every book she could lay her hands on. Content to pray to her Gods at home, she rarely felt the need to visit the temple. Fear of bumping into Rana restrained her from going outside unless she absolutely had to. She started making an exception when she discovered a small library. Once a week she whiled away a few hours there before returning home, happily hugging two new books that she was allowed to check out at one time, for free!

As for Komli, she was turning into a butterfly that would not be content to flutter in only one garden. Her zest for learning and living only came to a screeching halt when her body insisted that it needed some sleep. The two sisters often read well past midnight, in heavenly silence. Sometimes they hardly exchanged a word, happy in the knowledge that the other was as content to be curled up in bed with a book. And since Komli never had any problems getting up in the morning, Roshni never did know that most school-going children went to bed long before Komli ever did.

"I can hardly wait to give Mustapha his birthday present," Tusneem said to her mother as they carefully wrapped his high-tech, digital, wrist-watch in expensive hand-made paper. It was her cousin Mustapha's twelfth birthday.

"None of the kids are scared of aunt Sakina during birthdays, are they?" Zenub asked.

"No; she makes birthdays so much fun! I know exactly where I'm going to park myself when she starts throwing out the candy. She throws more out at the corners than in the middle."

"Really! I thought you were after the money, not the candy."

"Both, actually. The toffees aunt Sakina has are the best! Where does she get them from?"

"I think she buys the imported ones just to give you children a thrill." Birthdays were always family affairs with grandparents, and aunts, and uncles, and more cousins than one could count on two hands.

Just after sunset, which marks the dawning of a new day for Muslims, Aunt Sakina propped a pillow in the middle of the room, laid a silk scarf on it and, with one of her sparkling, broad smiles, asked her son to sit on the pillow. The much-awaited ceremony had begun—with a topi (cap) on his head, Mustapha sat down on the pillow. His mother brought in a huge silver tray which she placed at his feet. On the tray was a green coconut surrounded by dozens and dozens of the children's favorite candies, and lots of coins, in all the different denominations. Starting with the eldest member of the family, each adult took it in turn to swirl the coconut seven times, counter-clockwise, around Mustapha's head. Each one tipped Mustapha's forehead with the coconut, and said mubarak (congratulations), before placing the coconut in the tray, so the next person could perform the ceremony. It was always fun when some of the youngsters jokingly threatened to hit the birthday person hard with the coconut. When everyone had had a turn, aunt Sakina held up the tray in the air, knowing that it was a signal for everyone to start shoving and pushing and jostling one another for a good spot behind the birthday boy. Sakina waited patiently for the commotion to die down. She knew it would be a few minutes before calm would be restored. She didn't really care how long it took the family to calm down; she enjoyed watching adults behaving like kids, and she enjoyed teasing them even more. When she finally saw adults and children crouched quietly, like cats ready to pounce, she cradled the tray in her left arm. With her right hand, she grabbed a handful of candy, and coins, and threw them over Mustapha's head. Again and again and again, she threw handfuls of candies and coins in different directions until there was nothing left on the tray but the coconut. As far back as Tusneem could remember, grabbing candies and coins was the best part of the birthday.

The coconut was then whisked away by a servant who split it open and brought back the coconut water in a glass. Mustapha took the coconut water around for everyone to take a sip. In the interim, everyone sifted through their loot. Counting the coins was fun. But it was even more exciting to unwrap the candies to see who had the umpteen IOU slips that Sakina had taken much pleasure in placing inside the candies the night before.

As Tusneem grew older, she started going to the birthday parties some of her school friends invited her to. The cakes, the candles, and the goody bags were lots of fun, too. In time, she ended up having two birthday celebrations—one with school friends, with cake and candles; and the other with cousins, coconut, coins and candies. She enjoyed them both, but if she were ever forced to choose one out of the two, she knew she would opt for the rowdy but fun-filled family gatherings.

With all the family obligations and school work, Tusneem had little time to sit and stare. Her 15-hour day started at 6 in the morning. After a hearty breakfast, she was driven to aunt Sakina's where, at 7.00 a.m. sharp Mullasahib arrived to giver her and her four male cousins religious lessons in Islam. At 8.15 a.m., the five cousins were driven to school, straight from the arms of Allah to the arms of Jesus, so to speak, because the school they attended was run by Roman Catholic missionaries. After a rigorous seven hours in school, there was always basketball, or soccer, or track practice, depending on the time of year. On Mondays, she also had ballet lessons and on Wednesdays she had piano lessons. One good thing about Wednesdays was that she had piano lessons at home, which meant that she got home a little earlier than usual, had time to relax and have a snack before her piano teacher arrived. There was always a couple of hours worth of homework to do, both for the nuns and for Mullasahib and sometimes, even on weekdays, there were functions to attend at the mosque, either social or religious. Although Tusneem's parents tried to avoid taking their daughter to social functions during weekdays, there were often times when they knew they were socially obliged to take Tusneem.

Sunday was Tusneem's favorite day of the week. That was the day all the aunts and uncles and children gathered at her grandparent's home, or went for a family picnic. Regardless of the venue, that was the day for the family to get together and play. Other than breaking up for namaaz (prayers), and lunch, even the parents played card games all day. The highlight of Sunday evening was getting ready to go to the movies. If there happened to be no appropriate movies for the younger children, they just got to go home early to get rested and be prepared for another hectic week ahead. From an early age, Tusneem had learned that no matter how busy one is, one must say the morning, afternoon, and evening namaaz. Indeed, for her parents and her entire family, life's busy schedule revolved around namaaz. Allah must never be forgotten, no matter what, she was often reminded.

Like Komli, Tusneem also curled up in bed each night with a book, for she, too, loved to read. But it was not long before Tusneem's eyes would close shut and all her senses happily succumb to the sweet oblivion of sleep. She slept the sound sleep of well-loved, hard-working, satisfied children who have not a care or need in the world.

"What's the matter, Komli? You look pensive today. Did someone upset you?" Roshni asked Komli one afternoon when she returned from school, unusually quiet.

"Did you see Mohan today?" Komli asked.

"Yes. Why?"

"Did he have anything on his wrist?"

"Yes, a string his sister gave him. It's Raakhi Bundhun today." Somewhat like Valentine's Day, Raakhi Bundhun was the day when all Hindus celebrated the special bond that exists between brother and sister. The sister ties a Raakhi around her brother's wrist as a symbol of her everlasting love for kith and kin. It was a day when brothers silently reinforced to their sisters that they would always be there for them. And for this bundhun, this tie, the brother always had a gift for her sister. However large or small the gift, Raakhi Bundhun was a day all Hindus looked forward to.

"Did Devi get a present from her brother?"

"Yes. She got a beautiful pair of gold earrings. Are you sad because you don't have a brother?" Roshni asked intuitively.

"Sort of. All the Hindu boys in class came with raakhi tied round their wrists. The girls were surprised that I didn't have a cousin or someone I could call my brother. Are we going to live like this forever, Roshni?"

"What do you mean?"

"In fear? Will we never make any friends? I don't understand why we have to live like thieves in hiding," Komli said precociously.

"You've always seemed so happy, Komli," Roshni exclaimed nervously. "I never thought of us that way. We don't have to live in hiding if it makes you unhappy."

"I'm not unhappy, Roshni. I just wondered today if we would ever have celebrations like other people."

"You know Komli, love is all around us. Even the cats and dogs on the streets showed it to their kind. Remember? Human beings have just devised all kinds of ceremonies to show it."

"And I hear those ceremonies are so much fun. I just feel we should be doing things other than reading all the time."

"What celebrations do you miss, Komli?" Roshni asked with a lump in her throat. There hadn't been much to celebrate on the streets as far as she could recall.

"Remember Holi?" Komli asked after a slight pause.

Roshni nodded with a broad smile. Yes, she could recall vividly how much her little sister used to enjoy Holi—the festival of spring. To commemorate the colorful bounty of spring, Hindu families and friends spent the day going from house to house and street to street with a free-for-all-license to spray and smear friend and stranger alike with colorful concoctions of paint. The squeamish and non-Hindus simply stayed at home that day, refusing to answer the doorbell. "You were pretty bold, you know. I used to laugh at the way you used to delve into other peoples' buckets and smear their own paint on them!"

"Remember the boy I played hopscotch with?"

"Nuttoo?"

"I used to help him mix paints. You know his family used to mix mud and grime and grease and sometimes even a little gasoline into their concoctions, so it would be hard to remove! They used to spend days amassing different colors. I used to dream that one day I would be able to have my own syringe and watch human rainbows squeal and scream and scram away from the fury of my syringe."

"You wait till Holi comes around, Komli, I'm going to smear you until you . . . ."

"I used to love getting smeared. That was one day no one could tell the rich from the poor. We even laughed with one another! Will you buy me a syringe, Roshni?"

"And every color under the sun. But Holi is a few months away. What would you like to do in the meantime so we can change from bookworms to . . ."

"Social butterflies?"

"How do you dream up such words, Komli? I'm serious. Tell me what you want. I'll see if I can make it come true."

"Can I have a birthday party? I'd like to invite some of my school friends," Komli asked looking intently into Roshni's eyes to see how she reacted.

Roshni felt uncomfortable at the thought of having other people over. No one other than Tara and Devi visited them. Rashid and Zenub had visited on a couple of occasions, just to make sure the sisters were doing alright. Komli had been in school on both occasions. Roshni had politely managed to put a stop to that by assuring them that their money order was coming in regularly and that they were doing alright, if for no other reason than to have Tara stop harassing her about associating with Muslims.

"Your past is none of my business," Tara had said hypocritically, "but I am telling you, Roshni, good Hindus never have anything to do with those hateful Muslims who think nothing of butchering us and our country. I would not touch my food if so much as the shadow of a Muslim fell on my plate!" Roshni had wished she had the courage to fight back obnoxious Tara. Rashid and Zenub were angels as far as she was concerned. She could not imagine them ever raising their voices at her the way Tara did.

And what is a birthday party, may I ask?" Roshni asked casually, hoping Komli had not sensed her discomfort.

"It's a celebration of the day you were born. The children in class invite their friends over. All the friends bring presents and play games and then go home."

It was Father Michael who had decided, or rather fabricated, a date of birth for Komli, after having explained to Roshni that one has to have that piece of information in order to go to school. The logic had escaped Roshni, but as long as her little sister could go to school, it mattered little what the priest wanted or what date he chose. The priest had mentioned nothing about birthday parties. "Sounds like lots of fun, but you've never been to a birthday party. How do you know what happens at birthday parties?" Roshni asked.

The children talk about it and I've seen pictures. I've been invited many times, but I've never brought the invitations home because I'm not sure if we have money to buy presents. Besides, we never go anywhere except to the library, so I didn't think you'd let me."

"You have money to buy presents, Komli." Roshni stated emphatically. "Next time, ask me instead of figuring out things yourself in that hot little head of yours!" She was piqued, more at herself than at her sister because deep down inside her heart she knew that she shouldn't be treating her sister like a prisoner. The other problem was that Roshni was content to live vicariously; if Tara was any indication of the real world, she would much rather opt for her present lifestyle. It occurred to her suddenly that her younger sister obviously needed more than just the pleasures she herself derived from staying at home and learning from her little sister; that she must indulge Komli's desires to associate with the people in her new world. She renewed the vows she had made a long time ago— to live only for her little sister. "I don't see why we can't have a birthday party. You'll have to guide me, though," Roshni declared, trying to look enthused.

"Do you know how to make a cake?"

"No, but I can ask Devi. What is a cake?"

"It's something round on which you light candles. Everybody gets to eat the cake after they sing Happy Birthday to me and I've blown out the candles."

"Do you think Devi will know what I'm talking about?"

"Probably. But it doesn't have to be a cake, Roshni. Just make anything sweet and we'll stick nine candles on it. We can buy the candles."

"Why nine candles?"

"Didn't Father Michael say I'll turn nine on the first of April?"

"Yes."

"One candle for each year stupido! What's so hard about that?

"Nothing! This stupido sister of yours learns from you every day, thank goodness. I'll tell you what, if you tell me exactly what needs to be done, you can have your friends over."

"Thank you, Roshni!" Komli said, springing up to hug her sister.

The birthday party turned out to be Komli's first lesson on human nature. At school, the six girls she had invited were wonderful to her, but at the party they were quite hateful. Komli could tell they were surprised that she had no dolls, no tea sets, no computerized toys, and not even a television! They did not have the sophistication of adults to snigger behind her back. To make matters worse, Komli's cake tasted awful and there was no 'Happy Birthday' inscribed in cool icing. As for her mother, the girls thought she behaved more like a maidservant. And the straw that broke the camel's back came at the time of departure—there were no party favors for the girls to take home. Komli had clean forgotten about them.

Komli was saddened, confused, and angered by the behavior of her school friends. Their shiny, black leather shoes were just a reflection of their meanness, she thought. But not a single drop of self-pity trickled down her cheeks. Never again, she determined, would she allow rich girls to enter her haven. The lesson empowered her with the courage to be herself and to accept that she was that 'rag' that would not always fit into the shoes of the wealthy. Wealthy children obviously lived in lots of compartments filled with different expectations. She would work with them only in school, she resolved. Insofar as socializing and playing was concerned, she would stick to the humbler and more fun-loving neighborhood children with whom she played on the streets. They were much more fun, she realized.

"I'm sorry you didn't have a good time, Komli. Next year I'm sure I'll do better," Roshni said humbly, hoping that by taking all the blame, Komli would feel less miserable.

"I'm never going to have another birthday party! All they did was go snooping around for things they have in their own homes. If I went to their house, I would be thrilled to find things I never had. Then it would be more fun to play with them. And they thought all our wonderful board games were boring! I should have invited the neighborhood children, but they don't have birthday parties it seems."

Roshni knew instinctively that she must turn this negative experience into a positive one for her fast-maturing sister. "I'm so glad you had this party, Komli. Look at all the wonderful things that happened. You now appreciate the neighborhood children, even though they don't go to schools as good as yours. Next year, just invite two or three girls . . ."

"Never. I'm never going to invite girls from that school. I can't believe how important it was for them to know what you gave me." She mimicked them viciously, 'I got a Barbie swimming pool!', 'I got a computer.' 'I got . . .'

"Hey, hey, hey, Komli," Roshni interrupted, deciding that she must put a stop to her sister's scathing sarcasm. "Are you jealous because you don't . . . ."

"No, I'm not jealous! They're stupid!"

"You should feel sorry for them if they're stupid. What's the anger for?"

"I don't know, she said, burying her head into Roshni's lap. "I dreamed about this party for weeks, but it didn't turn out that great. I'm different, aren't I? You know, when the girls asked me why I walk to school, I told them the doctor said I had to walk to strengthen my other three limbs. I bet now they'll feel sorry for me 'cause we don't have a car," she said mimicking them again.

"Do you feel poor, Komli, because you don't have a car?"

No. I just feel different, I guess."

"Let me tell you something. If you can stop feeling sorry for yourself and be proud of everything we have, I promise you, no one can hurt you."

"You know something, Roshni, I feel like screaming and telling them that I'm not ashamed of our wonderful home. How do you think they would react if I told them we were beggars once?" she asked, feeling a perverse streak run down her spine.

"The first thing you have to do Komli is to get rid of your anger. Ma always said, anger churns only in the stomach that is churning it, so get rid of it as fast as you can. Think of it this way; if you have too much food in your stomach you never have room for dessert. And if you allow anger to fill you up, you never have room for laughter. Your teacher tells me you are one of the cleverest girls in your class, and that all the children love you."

"Strange way of showing it, wasn't it!" Komli retorted, although she seemed to have calmed down a little.

"Listen to me, Komli. I may not know a lot like you do, but this much I do know—a good memory is the most precious thing you can give someone. Meanness makes a sad memory. In some people sad memories become monsters that gobble up the happy memories. Others take such good care of their happy memories that they turn into soldiers who kill all the sad memories. You always come home and tell me great things that happen each day. We did not have the time today. Tell me, what is the best thing that happened in school today?"

"Oh, I clean forgot! This is a good one, Roshni. You know why I had nine candles on the cake?"

"Yes, stupido, because you turned nine today. You already told me."

"But do you know why I turned nine today?"

"Cause you were born nine years ago!"

"So what's nine years?"

"January to December running around and around in circles."

"Well here's what Mrs. Fletcher did. It was the best explanation she ever gave. Everyone sat around in a circle. Then she placed a huge yellow picture of a sun in the middle. Around this sun she placed twelve strips of paper with the names of each month on them. Then she asked me to stand behind April. After that I had to walk slowly and go around the sun. When I came back to April, she asked me to place a candle on a beautiful cake she had baked for me. Then she lit it and said, "You went around the sun one time, just like the earth revolves around the sun. So you are one year old. Every time you come back to the same spot, you are one year older. She asked me to go around the sun again. Each time I placed a candle on the cake. I did it nine times. Then they all sang to me, after which I got to cut the cake. It was delicious. So that's why I'm nine, because the earth and I have revolved around the sun nine times since I was born! Get it?"

"Yes. How come old people never get giddy?" Roshni asked flippantly while the two sisters smacked together the palms of their hands, as they often did when they realized they had mastered a lesson.

"Without the sun we would have nothing, Roshni. No life at all."

"No wonder Ma had so many stories about our Sun god, Surya!" Roshni exclaimed.

"Are you going to open the presents the girls gave you?"

"Not yet," Komli said. She was not ready to think about them. Roshni got up suddenly. She brought back a little package, wrapped beautifully in silver paper.

"Happy Birthday, Komli!" she said, beaming with anticipation. She knew Komli would love her present.

"A watch! Oh, I've always wanted a watch. Thank you, thank you, Roshni. And thank you for everything you did for me today. Help me put on the watch until I can figure out a way to do it with this stump of mine," she said matter-of-factly.

"That Montessori school has made you very independent, little missy. You now make your own lunch and dress all by yourself. I'm so glad you'll have to come to me every time you need to remove or put on the watch."

"Don't count on it! I can do more things with my mouth than most people!"

"I know you can, Komli. I'm so proud of you. Just don't mouth off angry words. You can never take back words."

"Yes, wise one, I'll remember that!"

Roshni went to her bedroom, lifted her mattress and came back with one more package, a smaller one, wrapped in comic paper that she often saved to re-read.

"Another present?! Wow! What is it?"

"You can't open this one until you take a guess."

"Can't be a necklace," she said feeling it gently, "it's too flat. Tickets to Disney World?" she asked cockily.

"What's Disney World?"

"Don't know! Yasmin and Shirin said it's the most wonderful place in the world! Some day I'll take you there."

"Good! Then I don't have to buy the tickets. Come on, take a guess!"

"Birthday card with money?"

"Money? I'll never give you money. You have a guardian angel who spoils you with money."

"Am I ever going to meet this guardian angel?"

"Some day, probably. Take another guess."

"Train tickets for a holiday in a houseboat?"

"Close."

"Tickets for somewhere, huh?"

"Maybe."

"Here or away"

"Here. I can't afford away."

"Cinema?"

"Begins with the same letter, and the same sound."

"I knew I shouldn't have taught you how to read and write!"

"The only word I can think of is 'cycle' and even Bhagvaan couldn't wrap a cycle in a package this small, unless cycles also come out of eggs! Give up. I'm going to open it," she suddenly announced and ripped the newspaper.

"They're circus tickets. Devi told me about it," Roshni explained. She says circuses are a lot of fun for everyone. We're going next week, Fevrury eighth!"

"How many times must I tell you, it's Feb-roo-ary. And how can next week be February when it's already April?"

"Just kidding. It's fun to get you frustrated. The dates are on the tickets. Next week should be April eighth, right?"

"Right. You're getting good with the calendar! There'll never be another you, Roshni. I love you. I can't talk to anyone else like I can talk to you."

"Will you always remember that, Komli, that no matter what happens, you can always come and talk to me?"

"Oops! I clean forgot, Roshni, because I was so busy feeling sad!" Komli squealed as she leapt up. She ran to her dresser and returned with a package for her sister. "Since you and I don't know our birth dates, I decided that you, too, should celebrate your birthday on April first. That's a real prank we can play on each other! Happy Birthday, sister." She handed Roshni her present and explained with a giggle, "It's something to stop you from behaving like those nuns."

"What do you mean?"

"Open it!"

"What a beautiful book," Roshni said softly, trying to digest the fact that this was the first time in her life that she had received a gift.

"It's a diary, Roshni. Mrs. Fletcher says a diary can be anybody you want it to be—your friend, your mother, your aatma. You can tell it anything you want to. See this lock and key? You can also lock it up so no one can see what you've written. Ganesh and all our gods can't always remember what you say to them. There are too many people praying to them. Just make sure you put down the date before you start writing in it."

Roshni laughed and cried as she gave her sister a tight hug. "So how will this diary stop me from behaving like a nun?"

"Nuns keep their thoughts tightly locked up inside their minds, like they're different from everyone else. You need to start talking more, Roshni. I've noticed how Devi and Tara Bahen do all the talking when they come over. If you don't start writing down your feelings, you may burst! The only reason nuns don't burst is because they wear those tight things around their boobs!"

"Where do you pick up all these strange ideas, Komli?"

"Some come from seeds, and some come from eggs, and some come from out of the blue, blue sky," Komli said, waving her right hand dramatically in the air.

The two had a hearty laugh, before Komli added, "Roshni, I think the happy memories you gave me today have already gobbled up the sad ones."

Roshni's first entry in her diary was a question:

Ma, can reincarnashun let you come back as a diaree? Beleev and let beleev I always say to Komli. I beleev you have come back to me as this diaree. Komli made up a good story today. She decided that I was born today but 25 years ago. Please send me a sine to show me that you forgive me for what I did to her. I should be suffering for my sin but Ma I am so so happy. Komli goes to school and she teeches me new things evry day. All I ever lerned on the streets was to add coins that got taken away. In school Komli has to multuply and share. She is better at counting than I am. Sometimes I praktis with rice and lentils. Yes Ma we have rice and lentils to spare now. In your storys there were no dates. Komli and me are trying to understand calendars. One day I asked her to find out the birth date of her two teachers Father Michul and Miss. Flecher. Father Michul has no children. Sometimes it is hard to understand all the things I am lerning. Anyway, Komli told me it is rood to ask people how old they are. Today she explaynd to me that age has to do with the earth rivolving around the sun. So if the earth has gone round the sun 55or 67 times since Father Michul was born, why is it rude to ask him that? Lerning is fun. Asking questions can be tricky.

*Not counting you and Komli I love reading the most. One day I
want to teach beggars to read. I hate jamadaarni work. I want to get
another job. I just don't know how to.*

*It is so much fun talking to you and praktising writing at the
same time and—Komli better never see this part—no Komli to chek
my mistakes. She is always korrekting me. But I love her so much and
you. Ill write tomoro.*

As time marched on, the pure white pages of Roshni's diary were crammed with notes
because Roshni had begun to firmly believe that her mother had miraculously been
transformed into a silent receptacle for all her outpourings.

It was around the middle of October when Tara and Devi started to feverishly clean
their apartment. Mohan helped out with the painting of the walls in each room after he
returned from work.

"What's going on?" Roshni asked Devi one afternoon. "Are you going to have a baby?"

"No, Roshni! You know Divaali (New Year/Festival of Lights) is around the corner. I
haven't had the courage to ask you before, but what did you do in your husband's
house? Every one I know, ever since I was a little girl, cleans their house before Divaali.
It's my favorite festival. Even Tara Ma is human that day!"

"Devi," Roshni started softly, "I think the time has come for me to tell you something."
Roshni had realized ever since Raakhi Bundhun and Komli's disastrous birthday party
that she needed Devi's guidance in order to have some semblance of normality in the
sterile cell in which she was raising her sister. There was no way she wanted a broken-
hearted Komli wondering ever again why they did not partake in Hindu celebrations.
Besides, although she knew little about celebrations, the one thing she had loved about
Divaali was the way all of Calcutta was magnificently lit up with hundreds of oil lamps
glowing from window sills and parapets. It was the one night when it seemed that all the
stars of heaven had descended on the roof tops of Calcutta. It was a sight that had never
failed to ignite a light of hope in her soul.

Devi waited patiently, knowing instinctively that Roshni needed time to brace herself
for whatever it was she needed to confide. Roshni continued, "Devi, Komli is not my
daughter. She is my sister. I have never been married, and until we came here, Komli and
I were beggars on the streets of Calcutta. We have no family."

"Hai Bhagvaan!" was all Devi could utter, as all the missing pieces of the puzzle that
was Roshni locked into place.

"You've turned me into a decent cook, Devi, for which I will always be grateful. I can
live here happily for the rest of my life without asking for anything more. But Komli is
growing up so fast. The other day she came home all sad because she had no one to tie a
raakhi around."

"Oh no! Mohan would happily adopt her as a sister," Devi exclaimed.

"I cannot bear the thought of my little sister being sad again because we did nothing for Divaali. Can you help me? Can you prepare me with everything I need to know, so my sister does not feel like a lonely prisoner inside these walls."

"Of course I can, Roshni. But please don't ever tell Tara Ma what you have just told me. She comes from the high and mighty Brahmin caste. She might just decide we should have nothing to do with you."

"Someone I met once told me that the caste system and untouchability has been abolished."

"It has been, and yet it hasn't, Roshni. By law it does not exist. But we cannot etch in and etch out laws in people's hearts and minds. Many people like my mother-in-law still consider themselves to be of the highest class . . ."

"What about you, Devi? Will you still come see me now that you know where I come from?"

"Do you have any idea where I come from when I visit you?" Devi asked emotionally.

"What do you mean? You come from next door, from the highest Brahmin caste . . ."

"Yes. And from hell, into this peaceful, heavenly nest that you have built. So often I want to come running to you, to get away from some of the things my mother-in-law says and makes me do. But you say so little that I'm never sure if I should." The two women exchanged quiet smiles as the doors to their hearts creaked open a littler wider, leaving a warm glow in their eyes. The very same walls that Komli viewed as a prison had turned into a haven for the two older women who were persecuted by a society that victimized innocent, unschooled, selfless women.

In her diary that night, Roshni wrote:

Ma,

Devi helped me start kleening today so I can get redy for Divaali. We got rid of so many cobwebs! Komli and me are invited to her house. Im so happy that Komli can be like other children and pay her respekts to her elders. And maybe get presents. I havnt yet told Komli. She has no respekt for Tara. I like our white walls, but I told Komli she could paynt our bedroom in any color she wanted. When she comes back from skool tomoro, we are going shopping. Devi tells me I have to buy at least one new utensil, lots of oil lamps, fire-crakers, and all kinds of food stuff to make sweets. Komli is so excited! And oh, I have to get a stachew of Laxmi (Goddess of wealth). I dont feel the need to pray to her but Devi says that I must have her in our home for Divaali.

Visiting people did not turn out to be such a bad thing after all Roshni had to admit to her little sister after celebrating Divaali at their neighbor's house.

Tara Bahen turned out to be a charming hostess and a splendid story-teller. Dozens of earthen oil lamps had been placed all around the house and even on the veranda, but they had yet to be lit. Once all the guests arrived, Tara took them to her Puja room and solemnly offered prayers to Laxmi and Ganesh. Then she narrated the story of Divaali:

> *Once upon a time there was a king who lived happily with his beautiful, spoilt wife. Early one Divaali morning, the queen got an extremely expensive diamond necklace. Unfortunately, the queen laid the necklace by the banks of the river in which she always bathed each morning. A crow happened to come by just then. He spotted the necklace and took it away, thinking he could eat it. When the king heard of the loss, he ordered his drummers to announce that he would give a huge reward of money to anyone who could find the necklace before the onset of Divaali celebrations that night.*
>
> *While flying away with the necklace dangling from his beak, the hungry crow spotted a dead rat at the doorstep of a poor, old woman's drab hut. He traded the tasteless diamond necklace for the dead rat. The poor woman had been out, looking for wood. She had also heard the drummers. When she found the necklace at her doorstep, she marched straight to the king and returned the necklace. When the king offered her a huge sum of money, to his surprise she refused it. She had something else in mind. "I want no one to light any lamps in their homes tonight," she demanded. What a strange request, the king thought. He had no choice but to agree to her request. No one dared to light any lamps that night, even though it was Divaali. That Divaali night, the only place that was brightly lit with oil lamps was the poor woman's hut.*
>
> *Our goddess of wealth, Laxmi, was angry. She loved light, and she specially loved to visit the homes of her devotees on Divaali. When she saw the lights in the poor woman's hut, she went knocking on her door, "Please, please let me in. I cannot bear the dark!" Inside the poor woman's house was her life-long companion, Poverty. He was used to living in darkness all his life. "Please, please let me out," he wailed, "I cannot bear the light!"*
>
> *"I will let you out, Poverty," the old woman said, "if you promise never to return again." And to Laxmi, the poor woman said, "I will let you in if you promise never to leave me again." When both agreed, the old woman opened the door. In came Laxmi and out went Poverty and the old woman lived happily ever after.*

After the story, Tara got up and began to light each oil lamp, one at a time, knowing in her heart of hearts that, like her, each guest would experience a spiritual awakening of some kind.

Between the fireworks and celebrations that followed, Komli and Roshni slipped away for a while to do puja and light their own lamps. It was then that Komli asked her sister to close her eyes for a minute. She led her into their bedroom which was in darkness.

"That's for you," Komli said excitedly, "You can open your eyes now."

"A bedside lamp! How wonderful!"

"Now you can read at night instead of tossing and turning." Komli said matter-of-factly.

"And I can write in my diary when you are fast asleep."

"You seem to write forever sometimes. Can I read your diary?"

"One of these days I am going to get you one. Diaries are like gods. They don't come to us in human form and so it's easier to tell them whatever we want to."

"So why can't I read your diary? I thought there were no secrets between us."

"This diary came with a lock, remember? You'll understand when you get older."

"You should have been named Roshni (light) and I should have been named Komli (bud)," Roshni said as she laughed and hugged her sister. It's been a day of so many illuminations! I'm so happy"

CⳆ ☙

CHAPTER 3

PRIME

"Roshni!" Komli yelled from the bathroom one morning, "Come look at my underwear. I think I've got my period!"

"Oh my goodness! How do you know it's your period?" Roshni asked as she approached the door."

"Come, look!"

Roshni confirmed that it was, asking, "Do the girls in school talk about it?"

"Yes. They say once you get your period, you have to always watch out for when you don't get it. That's when you get pregnant."

"Well, miss know-it-all, you can go tell your educated friends that you don't get pregnant when you don't get your period. You get pregnant when you have sex with a man. It's because you're pregnant that you don't get your period. That's how it works."

"Now who would have thought that my hermit of a sister would know anything about men or sex?!" Komli retorted with some humor.

"You can lose your innocence from too much reading, you know. I know more than you think I know," Roshni said matter-of-factly. "You have to start using sanitary towels now."

"I know. I've seen you take them to the bathroom."

"Well, I've run out of them. Can you wait here while I run to the store for some?"

"I don't think I have too much of a choice, do I? Don't be long, Roshni."

Roshni indulged in the luxury of taking a cab. She thanked Bhagvaan that her sister could afford sanitary towels, instead of the brown rags that she had once used, month after month. Rags that her mother must have washed and kept somewhere because she always produced those same old rags every time she got her period. They seemed browner each time, but the blood had always disappeared. Did anyone ever canonize such selfless mothers, she wondered.

Two days later Roshni found herself knocking on her neighbor's doors. Devi was out, unfortunately, so it was to Tara that she posed her question, "Komli is having severe cramps from her period, is there any thing I can do to help her?"

"When did she get her period?" Tara asked immediately.

"Two days ago."

"But I saw her playing outside yesterday! Why hasn't the girl been secluded to one room while she is under the curse of the menstrual cycle?" Tara admonished.

"I never was. Why is it a curse?" Roshni asked defiantly. For a change, she showed some signs of irritation. All her dear mother had said was that the period was the body's way of rejecting unfertilized eggs. Both mother and daughter had considered the period a heaven-sent blessing because Rana had refused to touch her during those uncomfortable but precious few days of the month. Why, thought Roshni, it could turn into a blessing even now, should Tara decide to have nothing to do with her neighbors.

"You must come from a very modern family, Roshni. I don't know many people who so openly flaunt our age-old Hindu customs. I know I cannot force you to do anything but, believe me, this child of yours will not be happy if she grows up wild, without customs or beliefs."

"She does have beliefs! We . . ."

"By now she should be fasting every Tuesday so she can get a good husband. You should be training Komli in the delicate art of weaving her way into a man's heart. She should be learning to cook and clean and sew. It is us women who have to play the twice blessed role in life to please and to procreate. The road to a man's heart is a long and arduous one. After a grand wedding, life for a woman turns into endless weeding. It takes years to pluck out the thorns of lust and hunger and anger and greed, until one fine day you finally see the flower that has blossomed inside the heart of your man." Tara had never actually let anyone know if her husband's heart had ever blossomed. That was her secret. "There is no time to sit and stare, except when the red river flows each month. If you sit idle, the snakes come slithering in to hiss out their venom and rattle their cranky tails at you and, believe me, there are countless snakes lurking in every husband's household!" Roshni shuddered in silence as she thought to herself how well Tara seemed to know about these snakes, but never saw herself as the hissing snake in her wretched daughter-in-law's life. Roshni swore she would never subject her sister to the life of servitude sweet Devi was subjected to.

When tactless Tara stung Roshni by suggesting that Komli would need a large dowry to entice a man to marry a girl with two handicaps—being both mud-apple skinned and one-handed, Roshni almost thanked Bhagvaan for her sister's stump. A man would have to love Komli, she decided, before she would throw her out in the jungle of life that Tara and Devi accepted with the same resignation with which she had accepted prostitution.

Over the years, the birth of a grand-daughter had sharpened Tara's stings. She resented the 'curse' that was Amrita, because she so wanted her home to be blessed with a first-born grandson. These women now-a-days were so spoiled, Tara thought, compared to what she had to go through when she had returned home to her in-laws with a first-born baby girl. To make matters worse, these young women nowadays thought nothing of laughing outright at advice they considered old-fashioned.

Although Tara was unable to assert herself with her neighbor, she was obsessive about perpetuating the circles of servitude among the females she was destined to dominate: First, there had been Tara's younger sister-in-law on whom she had had the pleasure of practicing; then came Devi, her daughter-in-law, and now, Amrita, her grand-daughter. Yes, she was determined that the women under her would accept servitude and sorrow with the stony stoicism she herself had cultivated to combat the seniors in her life, seniors who had treated her far more harshly than modern-day youngsters could tolerate, Tara thought with some self-pride.

"Look at our Devi. She fasts every Wednesday for her husband's health and welfare. But I suppose having Komli go without food for a few hours has not so much as entered your head!"

"No, to be honest with you, it has not!" Roshni said quietly."

"Between your modern ways and that other fancy school she goes to, she knows little about our religion. She will grow up with a mumble jumble of nothing, like a beggar who lives on other people's left-overs! No wonder our priests say the world has entered the fourth, horrible Kali Yuga (age of degenerate virtues). Everywhere I see people mocking religion and customs and traditions and listening to no one but themselves; people who abandon their religion and morals and families and think nothing of one's caste or creed or honor. This age was predicted thousands of years ago in our Hindu epics. Do you even know something about them?" Tara asked sarcastically.

Although Roshni had learned long ago not to argue with Tara, this time she stood her ground. "We do pray to the same gods that you pray to, Tara Bahen. I'm sorry. I will not treat my child like an untouchable girl just because she has her period. I cannot see the sense in it. I will suffer the consequences, whatever they might be." She looked straight into Tara's eyes as she resolved firmly that she would never allow Tara to impose restrictions on her beloved sister.

There was something about Roshni that made it hard to argue with her. First of all, Roshni rarely argued. But when she did, she did it so quietly and with such conviction that Tara knew instinctively to back off. She would have to get Roshni some other way, she determined as she returned to her apartment.

"What is this Kali Yuga?" that your mother-in-law was yakking about?" curious Komli asked Devi when the opportunity presented itself.

"Oh, just ignore her. She's always narrating tales from the Ramayana and the Mahabharata. I'm not as knowledgeable as she is, but she believes this particular phase on earth is composed of four cycles. We're in the fourth stage of chaos and crisis, known as Kali Yuga."

"And what are the other three stages?"

"I think the first one is innocence, then comes confusion, followed by an age of prime and glory, after which comes the age of vice and chaos. According to her, after this the world will be consumed by fire. There will be total devastation."

Komli had little patience for Tara's high-handedness. "You can tell your mother-in-law that I think I'm going through the second yuga of confusion myself, thanks to her!

And you can also tell her, the knowledgeable Hindu that she is, that there is no such thing as total devastation. After death comes reincarnation!"

"She'll kill me if I talk like you do, Komli." Devi replied with a diffident giggle. Although she hated her mother-in-law's ways, she definitely had more respect for what her elders told her than Komli seemed to have.

"And ask her how come I have to fast on Tuesdays for a good husband. Do men ever fast for a good wife? Or is it not necessary to fast for the welfare of a slave?" After Devi left, Komli exploded again, "I hate that old woman! She thinks she knows everything. Bet you she's never been to school in her life!"

"Hey, hey, hey, remember you cannot laugh on a stomach filled with anger," Roshni said, trying to calm down her sister. "You know, Ma didn't go to school either but, like Tara, she too had lots of stories to tell. I learned lots of good things from Ma. Her stories often kept me going, in fact. I've been thinking a lot lately of the Wish Fulfilling Tree."

"What's that?" Komli asked.

"Ma used to tell a story about this old, gnarled tree that stood outside a village. All the children of the village knew that if they stood under it and wished for something, their wish would be granted. So, of course, they would go under it and ask for all sorts of things such as candy and toys and money. What they did not know was that every time the tree granted a wish, it also gave them the exact opposite of what they asked for."

"What's the opposite of candy?" Komli asked immediately.

"Shhh! I've barely started the story. Let me finish," Roshni responded, pressing her index finger to her lips. "So when the children got candy, they also got stomach aches. When they got toys, they also got boredom, and when they got money, it came with lots of worries. One day, a boy with only one leg came to the village. Naturally all the children told him about the Wish Fulfilling Tree. Of course, the boy was tempted to ask for his other leg. But first he decided to watch for a while. He was so fascinated and moved by the two opposites that everyone received that he completely forgot to make his wish. He became one of the few people on earth who was content because he had wished for nothing."

"Maybe he was the only one," Komli retorted. "It's impossible to wish for nothing!"

"I know."

"What if one wishes for death?" Komli asked, tongue in cheek.

"Then one gets its opposite—life or reincarnation!"

"Did Ma read from books?"

"No. She couldn't read or write. She just had lots of wonderful stories to tell, about Ram and Sita and the Pandava brothers."

"But I bet she didn't make them sound like all doom and gloom, like old Tara does!"

"No she didn't," Roshni replied as she reminisced about her loving mother.

"So why have you been thinking about this Wish Fulfilling Tree lately?"

Roshni started laughing. Think about it, Komli. I wished you wouldn't starve; you got food. Now you have food; Tara thinks I should starve you every Tuesday at least, so you can get a good husband! Ma used to say that the tree was our world, giving us what we want."

"And what would be the opposite of a good husband? A bad husband or a good wife," Komli asked in jest.

"You're getting too smart too quickly, Komli. Sometimes I wish . . . ."

"I wouldn't wish, if I were you, Roshni. Never know what else you might get!" Komli snapped. "But you know something, Roshni, I wish you tons and tons of love. So what if you get the opposite? At least you would get to experience the good and the bad. I'm not so sure I want to live life sans desire?"

"What desire?"

"Sans desire. Means without. I was quoting mighty Shakespeare. In school, when you get your period, they begin torturing you with Shakespeare. And at home you get introduced to philosophy, it seems!"

"You didn't like the story?"

"I loved it!"

"I'm not used to you being sarcastic!" Roshni said with a pout.

"I mean it. I really liked it. It's just that it sounded like one of Father Michael's million parables."

"Then maybe some day you'll tell them to your children."

"I'll never remember them! I'll read to them from books."

"You don't have to remember them exactly the way you hear them. Remember what Ma used to say—the leaves rustle with a million unwritten stories. If people hadn't told them before man invented writing, who knows, some of our best stories may never have come down to us."

"Know what else I like—that you and I are such opposites! Would that have anything to do with the Wish Fulfilling Tree?"

"You're impossible! I have a present for you now that you're all grown up."

"Birth control pills?"

"Hai Bhagvaan, how can you talk like that! You're too young to even think like that. I'm not so sure about this school of yours. Maybe . . ."

"I'm just teasing, Roshni. Love means you can tease and say silly things. Can I have my present?"

"It's the diary I promised you. Remember?"

"Aah! So now I get to write silly things in my diary so my sister won't get shocked."

"You won't shut me out, will you?"

"Not as long as I can tease you."

Roshni's diary entry that night read as follows :

Ma,

Today I told Komli about the Wish Fulfilling Tree. I dont know if she got it. But then I am not sure that I get it myself. Sometimes I think

I do, and then it eskapes me. Take the period for example. If your
bleeding your not with child, but if your with child you dont bleed.
You always bled for us, didnt you, Ma?
I hope you think it is okay that I refuse to have Komli fast on
Tuesdays for a good husband. If you ask me, she has fasted enuf to last
her nine life times of husbands! I pray every day though that she gets
a good husband who will make her happy. Please send me a sign
when a good man comes around.

As soon as Tusneem got her period, the family started preparing for the joyous occasion of Mishaq (holy communion)—the most important event in the life of a young Bohra.

"Once you've taken Mishaq, Tusneem," Rashid explained gently, "it's like Allah starting a separate account for you for all your good and bad deeds. Up to now, you were in a joint account with us, but after Mishaq you are accountable for everything you do. Your sins will be on your own head, not ours." Having no guilt to speak of, that did not bother Tusneem. The fact that she would have to sit in front of a Bhaisahib (priest) who would perform the rites of Mishaq in front of the entire family, several priests, and honored guests terrified her.

"Mustapha says Bhaisahib will grill me with all kinds of questions. Do I really have to memorize everything I've learned so far?"

"You say your prayers all the time. You know them all by heart, don't you?"

"But will I be asked to recite something in front of everyone?" Tusneem persisted.

"Sometimes Bhaisahib asks a question or two but I know you'll be fine, Tusneem. Have you ever failed an exam? You'll come out with flying colors, as usual. Do you remember the Aameen celebration we had for you on your seventh birthday?"

"Vaguely. I remember getting lots of presents . . ."

"Because on your seventh birthday you had finished reading all 30 chapters of the Koran. That's quite a feat!"

"And am I the only one with such an accomplishment?"

"No. Many Muslim children do it. But it takes discipline and perseverance and since you have those qualities, you have nothing to worry about."

"Pappa, merely reading is different from being questioned or asked to recite something in front of all the guests! If I fail, will I have to face the humiliation of having to go through Mishaq again?"

"You're not going to fail, Tusneem. I have all the faith in you. But you have to have faith in yourself, too. If you feel shaky, spend a little more time memorizing whatever you need to. Ask Mullasahib. You still have time, you know," Rashid said gently, but firmly. He knew well how much hard work it took to be where he was in life, and he wanted his daughter to have the same high standards!

"This is going to be far more nerve-racking than any other exam I've taken in school, Pappa!"

"Here's a little secret for my grown-up daughter; nerve-racking exams are good preparation for all the nerve-racking that comes when you're grownup and away from your parents."

"How come your nerves are never racked?"

"They are, sometimes," Rashid said stoically, hoping that his daughter would never have to suffer his kind of anguish.

"Give me one example."

"I'll give you one if you promise to go study."

"Promise."

"I worried like crazy for nine whole months before you were born."

"So that's why I have no sisters and brothers! You couldn't handle it!"

"I could handle a dozen you," Rashid said laughing, "but I guess Allah poured so much good into you, He decided He wouldn't indulge us any more. Now go study before your head swells up too much."

As his daughter walked out, Rashid couldn't help but think nostalgically about the three wonderfully special occasions when they had honored their precious daughter—when she had been named, when she was shorn of all her hair, and when they had celebrated Aameen. After those celebrations Zenub and he had retired to their bedroom like innocent Adam and Eve—happy, content, and guilt-free. But within a handful of weeks after Aameen, after that fateful afternoon when Zenub had meddled with two beggars, it was in the haven of their bedroom, when the two were locked out from worldly distractions, that the burden of guilt lay heaviest on their shoulders. Zenub had apologized to her husband at every opportunity that presented itself. She had tried everything she could think of to convince him that he was not guilty, that he should not go around looking like someone who had committed a murder. After a few months she had given up, realizing that her husband, the judge, could not stop judging. With elbows resting on his desk and forehead bent down on two tightly clasped hands, Rashid prayed fervently—please Allah, spare Tusneem the consequences of the sins of her parents. She is innocent and pure and I love her more than anything else in the world.

Little did Rashid know that Zenub sent up the same prayer night after night and every time her conscience played havoc with her soul—please Allah, spare my husband and my Tusneem the consequences of my sins. They are innocent and pure and I love them more than anything else in the world.

As luck would have it, Tusneem got a few extra weeks' reprieve from Mishaq, courtesy of aunt Sakina who announced one day that there was talk about Bawasahib coming to Calcutta.

"Zenub, we must try and get Bawasahib to perform Tusneem's Mishaq. Wouldn't that be wonderful!" Although it was rare that Bawasahib performed Mishaq for one person alone, the Khans enjoyed special privileges. Add Sakina's determination to that and the family had a perfect recipe for success.

It was not long before Zenub handed Moonshee, the tidings-bearer of the community, a handful of scrolls filled with the names of practically every Bohra family in Calcutta.

After lengthy deliberations with Sakina and the elders of the family, Zenub and Rashid had meticulously checked off the appropriate grids in the scrolls that indicated exactly how many men, women, and children from each family were invited. It was Moonshee's duty to go from household to household and make sure someone from every household made a note of the date, time, occasion, and number of people invited by initialing beside his or her family name. Since no specific names were mentioned, it was taken for granted that each family would be able to comply with the invitation simply by sending representatives; if a father was unable to attend, his son, or son-in-law could always fill in.

Regardless of how embarrassed Tusneem felt on the morning of Mishaq, Zenub insisted on going into the bathroom with her to make sure her daughter knew how to get namazi (purify the body through ablution). After Mishaq, Tusneem would have to perform ablution each time she bathed. The only time she would be exempt was when she got her period. One did not purify one's body, much less pray or step inside the mosque when one got one's period, she was informed. So, on a day as auspicious as Mishaq, Zenub knew she had to ensure that every inch of Tusneem's body was purified.

"You must shave your pubic hair every forty days. They must be no longer than grains of rice," Zenub said matter-of-factly. Tusneem nodded her head, hoping that the less she said, the quicker this ordeal would be over. She could think of nothing more mortifying than standing stark naked in front of her mother, especially after having all those embarrassing pubic hairs sprout from nowhere!

When Tusneem stepped out of the bathroom, she looked like an angel dressed in dazzling white, cotton orna ghagra. The night before, Zenub herself had lovingly purified and hung out her daughter's special clothes on a clothesline which, too, she had purified herself. Mishaq was too auspicious an occasion to entrust the task of purifying Tusneem's clothes to servants. Zenub had placed a pair of namazi wooden clogs outside the bathroom, and it was on these clogs that Tusneem emerged from the bathroom. When her feet were bone dry, she slipped into white socks which, too, Zenub had purified. There was not a spot of anything that Tusneem wore or touched that was not namazi. Zenub made sure that none of Tusneem's younger cousins, who might have wet, sticky, fingers, came anywhere near Tusneem until the Mishaq ceremony was over. And until Bawasahib arrived, Tusneem herself made sure she hung around like a white bed-sheet dangling from a clothesline that was beyond the grasp of anything napaak (impure). The only creatures within close range were the butterflies that fluttered in her stomach.

Bawasahib was also dressed in dazzling white clothes. He smiled graciously as he passed by each member of the family. Rashid had the honor of placing both his hands under Bawasahib's hand as he guided him slowly to the seat of honor—a beautiful white namazi masalla (prayer rug) that had an ornate hand-embroidered gold border on all four sides. Trembling inside, Tusneem walked out and sat down quietly on another, less ornate masalla about four feet in front of Bawasahib. One end of a namazi, white cord was handed to her. Bawasahib held the other end of the chord and solemnly performed the rites of Mishaq, asking Tusneem to swear from time to time that she would abide by the laws of Islam. She managed to answer all the questions that Bawasahib asked her. He smiled a gentle smile and blessed her when she went up to do salaam. She was done! She had passed with flying colors! Zenub cried with joy while the guests congratulated Tusneem and her family.

Zenub had taken out her best china for the occasion. In a beautiful Belgian crystal glass she served Bawasahib a sweet sherbet, of which he took but a sip. Tusneem handed the glass to Sakina who made sure she put it aside in a safe place. All the immediate members of their family would later take a sip from the same glass that had been graced by the lips of Bawasahib. But first they had to serve Bawasahib the hearty brunch that Zenub and Sakina had gone to great lengths to prepare personally. Together with Rashid and a few elderly members of the family, it was their great privilege to serve Bawasahib. The servants stayed in the kitchen for a change while their master and mistress served Bawasahib.

It was only after all the guests had left that the family relaxed to enjoy a quick brunch themselves. However, they did not have all day to relax. The entire Bohra community would have representatives at the lavish dinner the Khans would be hosting that night at the community hall.

It had taken Zenub, Sakina, and a couple of other ladies at least three months to design and to hand-embroider dozens of little pink rosebuds on the orna ghagra Tusneem wore that night. To add a little sparkle to her clothes, her orna was strewn with subtle little shimmering mother-of-pearl sequins. The two-yard border of the orna that Tusneem would drape over her head had matching, miniature rose-buds embroidered back to back. Tusneem's jewelry, one among many sets she would one day take with her to her husband, matched her clothes. Sakina, Zenub, and their mother had deliberated for about an hour as to who should wear what jewelry; together they had decided that Tusneem should wear the delicate diamond and ruby set rather than the heavier one which would be more appropriate for a wedding.

That night, together with her mother and some of her aunts, Tusneem stood at the entrance to the hall as each guest came in, did salaam, handed a gift to Zenub, usually in the form of an envelope with some money in it, before they went inside the hall to find a place to sit down. Tusneem's grandmother sat in a corner on a special couch that had been brought in for her. Although she rarely went out because diabetes had taken its toll on her, this was too important an occasion for her to stay at home. She sat on the couch and beamed happily at all the guests who came up to her to pay their respects.

The men and women were segregated by a huge, hand-carved wooden partition. Tusneem couldn't help but enjoy the many little eyes she saw from time to time, trying to peek in from the men's side to take a look at the blushing new blossom in whose honor the dinner was being held. She couldn't help but enjoy the dozens of women who couldn't take their eyes off her beautiful clothes.

It was customary among Bohras to personally serve the food to their guests, no matter how large the number. Together with their extended family and with the help of some close friends, the thousand guests were served a seven course dinner, which always started with a dessert. After dinner, platters of paan (betel nut leaf, to aid digestion) were taken around to all the guests. When the guests started to leave, Zenub and Tusneem went back and stood at the door again, this time with beautifully hand-carved crystal bottles containing rose attar (perfume). Hostess and guest smiled at each other as they did salaam again. Graciously, Zenub and Tusneem dipped into their bottles of attar and gently smeared the palm of each guest's hand with a dab—a fragrant gesture of gratitude for attending.

It was well past midnight before Tusneem returned home. Having been treated like an angel all morning, and a princess all night, it was an exhausted but exhilarated Tusneem who finally fell asleep that night, tucking away yet another splendid memory of the rites and passages along the pathway to heaven.

"Want a piece of my bread?"

Rana nodded, showing no signs of energy.

"What you in here for?"

"Alcohol," Rana whispered as he wolfed down the bread. He had lost count of the days he had been in the prison. The stubble around his jaws suggested at least three.

"They going to deport you?"

"I don't know."

"You have any friends or relatives?"

"A friend, Kaloo."

"Does your friend know you're here?"

"Yes."

"You have no one else?"

"No."

"Your friend knows they don't feed you in prison here?"

"I don't know."

"Relatives and friends are supposed to bring you food."

"How long will I be here?"

"Hard to tell."

"Are you from China?"

"Korea."

"What did you do?"

"Car accident. Killed an Arab. He was jay-walking but, man, you injure those bastards and you're done!"

"What will they do to you?"

"I have friends. They're trying to get me out."

"Those other three men who are sleeping, what did they do?"

"That bald one on the left was caught shoplifting. The guy beside him murdered his fellow-worker. His days are numbered. That one staring into space refuses to talk."

Two more days passed by without Rana having anyone visit him. Sleep was the only way out of Rana's misery. The hungrier and weaker he got, the more he slept.

"Here, have all this bread and beans," the Korean said to Rana on the sixth day. "I'm getting out of here tomorrow."

"Can you help me?"

"What work did you do?"

"Road construction."

"How much money do you have?"

"About three thousand dollars."

"How long have you been in this country?"

"About six years."

"You have family back home?"

"No."

"Absolutely no one?"

"No one."

"Then you're lying, you bastard! By this time you should have at least ten. If you want to get out of here, I'll do it for ten thousand."

"I swear I don't have that much money."

"Seven?"

"Maybe."

"If I get you out of here and find that you have more, I'll bring you back in here, you understand?"

"How will I go back home without any money?"

"You need money and a passport to get back home, remember."

"My boss has my . . ."

"Passport," the Korean finished smoothly. I will forge papers for you. You will be able to work under me."

"I just want to return to India."

"Then wait here for your friend to come and free you."

Tara's idea of backing off her neighbor's lifestyle was to get someone else on Roshni's back.

"Devi, come sit by me. I need you to do something," she commanded one afternoon. I've had many suspicions about that neighbor of ours. I'm convinced she comes from some lowly, untouchable class, although she pretends to be a respectable widow. No matter how many servants they have, people from rich families know something about keeping house. If it wasn't for me, this woman would have killed us all with the fires that could have started in her kitchen. She's out every morning from eleven to two. I've noticed her sari's always a little muddy at the bottom. I don't believe she goes to the library every day as she says. To read as much would be a sin in itself! I am convinced she is into something worse. I don't have the legs to follow her. She seems to like you. Find out what she's up to, Devi. Maybe she'll talk to you. If not, you could even follow her. I'll let you have the morning off. We need to get rid of her or at least keep away from her at all cost if she's into anything unclean or sinful.

Devi trembled with fear. She knew her mother-in-law was capable of doing anything. Her rickety old legs may not support her too well, but her eyes and ears worked better than most. She could not allow Tara to get rid of the only woman who brought some light into her life. She could not bring herself to spy on her friend although she, too, knew in her heart of hearts that Roshni was working somewhere. But Roshni never mentioned it and Devi loved and respected Roshni too much to probe into those areas that Roshni was not yet ready to talk about. Devi decided to take Komli into confidence. In some ways, Komli was the more mature of the three, and certainly the most knowledgeable.

"What are you doing home so early, Komli?" Roshni asked when she returned home from work to find Komli sitting on her chair, pretending to read.

"I did not go to school today. I felt sick on the way so I decided to turn around and come home. I guess you've been at the library?"

"Yes, I have two new books I checked out. But tell me first, where do you feel sick?"

"In my heart."

"In your heart?" Roshni asked fearfully.

"I feel sick that I share every thing I learn and do with you, as we promised. It seems to me that you have not been keeping your end of the promise."

"What do you mean?"

"Here's what I mean, Roshni," Komli said angrily. "I felt sick to my stomach watching you come out from one building and move to another with bucket and mop in hand. Why, Roshni?" Komli shouted. "Why are you doing menial work when you can afford to send me to a good school and give me everything I ask for? Why do you choose to live like a nun when you can go out there and make some man so happy? You can raise some children without having a witch like Tara to torment the hell out of you. Don't you ever feel like being a normal woman with normal desires?"

"I do feel like a normal woman, Komli. I have you. I love you. I will do anything for you. I think that's how most mothers feel."

"I can understand that perhaps you are content to live your life vicariously. But I simply cannot understand why you are secretly doing the work of a jamadaarni when you simply don't need to work."

"How did you find out?!"

"I hate to admit it, but I have to thank Tara for getting suspicious about your comings and goings . . . ."

"She knows?!"

"No. She wanted Devi to follow you. Devi was petrified, so she confided in me."

"So you followed me and skipped school?!"

"Yes," Komli said without losing her composure, "and unless you explain to me why you work, and promise that you will stop working as a jamadaarni, I refuse to go to school. In fact, I want to know everything, Roshni, everything. I've been waiting for the right moment. I want to know why we suddenly acquired a roof over our heads and who this guardian angel is who sends us money every month. I am no longer a child, Roshni. In a couple of years I will be going to college. But I promise you, I will not step inside another institution of learning unless you treat me like an equal and tell me some truths."

Komli stared so hard at her sister that Roshni felt she was being stripped of any integrity she had. Quietly she asked, "Komli, do you remember with whom you slept every night when we lived on the streets?"

"Huddled close to Ma."

"Was I ever around?"

"I can't remember. Why?"

Using the best euphemisms she could, Roshni said simply, "I was made to huddle close to men, different men." She paused for a moment to swallow the pain and then continued coldly, "For the favors I rendered, those horrible men paid another beast of a man who was like our boss. He gave me an allowance which helped us to survive."

"You mean he forced you into . . . ." The word 'prostitution' hovered in the air but Komli refused to utter it. Her sister was a saint. No one in the world could change that. Both sisters realized that to hug one another then would be even more painful. Komli quickly decided it would be easier to ask more questions. "How come one fine day we just came to live here, Roshni? That man who brought us here on the train, was he the man who forced you?"

"No, Komli, no! That man is a true saint. He is the one who saved us from the other brute. Will you just believe for now that what brought us here is the most painful and sinful thing I ever did. But I did it thinking it was the only way I could save Ma. The only way I could prevent you from falling into the same trap that I was in, because, believe me, you were getting too close in line to taking my place. I managed to save you, I think, but I could not save Ma." The tears coursed down Roshni's face. Komli fetched her a glass of water while she recalled that it was around the time that Ma died that she had slept in someone's bed and something painful had been done to her between her legs. She decided to ask no more questions for the moment. She had never seen her sister in tears.

Roshni continued humbly, "I thought that being a jamadaarni was a few rungs above being a prostitute. The money order we receive each month is for you. I cannot bring myself to touch it or bring myself to talk about it right now."

"Roshni, in my eyes you are nothing but a wonderful loving woman whose only crime is that she never goes out to have fun and tries to hide things from me. I know that when you are ready, you will tell me everything. All I want from you right now is a promise that you will never again work as a jamadaarni. Do you know something? If we needed to, I would gladly leave school and go sweep myself. I have nothing against sweeping. I just refuse to let you go clean other peoples' shit while I sit back and enjoy school and have you cater to my every need! I mean it; unless you promise me, I refuse to go to school."

"You know something, you are my little savior, in more ways than you realize. I am so utterly sick of the work I do. But I just don't know how to go about getting another job," Roshni added simply. "Do you think I could work as an ayah for some little children?"

"Why do you have to work?"

"Komli, I cannot sit here all day and do nothing. As much as I love to read, I cannot do it all day. It would drive me crazy."

"There are a million men out there who would do anything to marry you, I bet!"

"I've had my fill of men, Komli. Thinking of them sickens me even now. Work helps me take my mind off them. Will you help me find another job?"

"Maybe. I'm surprised you haven't found one in the newspaper you read from end to end."

"I've been tempted to apply but have never had the courage to go out and make telephone calls or send out applications. I don't know how to go about it, Komli."

"Does it have to be tomorrow? Can you wait a month or two or even a couple of years until I finish high school? Things are getting tough. You could help me . . ."

"You know I can't help you with that crazy algebra and stuff! But guess what, I'd love to take a break from that stinking job."

"Thank goodness! You could always work on your spelling you know!" Komli exclaimed as she sprang up to give her sister a tight hug.

"Work on spelling instead of toilets?! More torture! Torture! Torture! But I'll take it, Komli, thank you, thank you, thank you!" Roshni laughed as she returned Komli's hug.

By the time the stench, the unyielding rusty iron bars and the filthy floors of his prison cell helped Rana realize that freedom and food for his aching belly were worth every penny he had amassed, he found that there was absolutely no one around him that he could bribe. Was he left there to die, he wondered. He wished death would come upon him sooner than later. But even death chose to ignore him. He passed out, he prayed, he hallucinated, he slithered around a little, and then, one fine day, the door creaked open to bring in a ray of hope.

"You have one minute to decide," the Korean whispered, holding up a blank passport. Give me your savings and I will take your photo and put it on this passport. You work for me. Yes or no?"

"I can leave now?"

"Now."

"Yes," Rana hissed.

In the underground jungle of hunting and gathering, yet another prey had been trapped. It turned out that the hunter and the prey were equally crafty. Both understood the limits of an escaped prisoner with no money and forged passport that Rana had yet to see.

I'll bide my time and get even with you, you son of a bitch, Rana said to himself once his body had regained its physical strength. He knew he would have to save and slave for a few years at least before he could pounce. Of this, he was sure: that if he was prepared to be patient, an opportunity would sooner or later present itself. The world was full of opportunities. Some grabbed and some grovelled. It was his turn to grovel.

"Found it!" Komli exclaimed one afternoon as she was browsing through the *Help Wanted* column in the newspaper. "Look, Roshni, this English family in Patna needs a nanny to look after their children. Want to apply?"

"I've never been to school, Komli. I can't work in some British Sahib's house! They need people like you. You have all the confidence. I don't!"

"If you want, I'll apply for the job, and you go to school, Roshni. I could handle that."

"Never! Besides, you'll be graduating from high school in a few weeks."

"Then listen to me, Roshni. I bet most people who will apply for this job will barely be able to read and write. Can you see educated Indians working as a maid servant? Although, I know one who thought nothing about working as a jamadarni once!" Komli added with respect for her humble, selfless sister. "You'll be perfect for the job! You can read and write and have no airy-fairy notions about what you can and cannot do." She could not imagine anyone more loving than her sister, anyone more graceful, more dignified and more honest.

"It is you who has airy fairy notions about what I can and cannot do," Roshni said lovingly.

"You're damn right I do," Komli responded with a grin. "I'm the plain, practical one. I know you can accomplish anything you want to if you put your mind to it."

"I don't want to go to work for some white lord when I don't even know how to deal with our own lords and ladies."

"Let's take one thing at a time," Komli said with the patience of a mother. "First, we will just apply for the job and see if you can get an interview."

"An innerview?! I don't want some outsider to have an inner view!"

"It's inter-view, Roshni. You view him and he views you," Komli said with a smile.

"I don't want to be inter-viewed, Komli!"

"You can't live like a hermit all your life, Roshni! Even the nuns see more of the world than you do!" Seeing how nervous Roshni looked, Komli softened her approach. "Roshni, if only you could see yourself through my eyes. I can't think of anyone better I would trust my children with. Please Roshni, for my sake, will you just try for the job at least. You may not even get an interview. And if you do, no one will bite you!"

"How do you know all these things? You're so grown-up some times!"

"Someone has to be! And here's something else to think about. Soon I'll be going to college. I know you're dreading my going back to Calcutta. Would you like to sit here, twiddling your thumbs and worrying about me, or would you rather be happily occupied with a job?"

"I'd like you to go to college in Patna, and for me to be working here somewhere."
"Roshni, it's not going to happen that way. I'm going to Calcutta College. It's supposed to have the best Education program. I want to teach, remember?"
"What happened to the little sister who always listened to me?"
"What happened to the big sister who wanted only the best for me?"
"You win, as always!"

"What will I do without you" Devi sobbed when she first heard that Roshni was moving in with the Johnsons for a couple of years.
"I get time off one day a week. I'll be back to visit you and check on our place."
"That's not the same as having you around night and day, whenever I need you."
"You won't even miss me. You now have little Amrita and another one on the way." She patted lovingly on Devi's stomach. "This one's going to be a son, I can tell."
If it wasn't for you, Roshni, I don't know how I would have survived Tara Ma!"
"You can survive anything, Devi. I am the one who will be forever indebted to you. You taught me more about life than you'll ever realize. You are like one of those skinny roots that look fragile but cannot be easily broken." While the two went through the emotions of crying and embracing one another, Roshni's thoughts whizzed around in circles. Life itself seemed to run around in circles, she thought. Beginnings and endings with so many different names such as departures and arrivals; cleaning and cooking; reading and reflecting; waking and sleeping, yearning and yielding—they were all circles, endless circles, that had no definite beginning or end; circles that were never lacking in someone, somewhere running the course. Women run too many courses now-a-days, and that is the curse of modern society, Tara had told Devi not so long ago when Devi had wondered if she should get a part time job so she could afford some of the things she would have liked for her little one.

All through her miserable pregnancy Devi had prayed fervently for a son. She was convinced that it was for the sins that she had committed that her prayers had not been answered. The cruel treatment Tara meted out to her served only as fuel to ignite the fire of hatred that raged in her heart. Alas, the fire did not rage enough to squelch the deep-seated Hindu belief that one's destiny is not something one fights. Her mother-in-law was her destiny. She could not fight her. She would simply allow rage to simmer within her; it would never boil over. If the insides of her stomach burned with anger, so be it, Devi thought. At least she now had a precious daughter who soothed and cooled down whatever remained of the scorched lining of her stomach. Besides, Roshni herself had brought Devi so much relief. While Tara seemed to thrive in the dark, leaving no room for the exchange of human emotions, Roshni and Devi had thrived on the friendship that had evolved over the years.

Living in her dark world, it was unbeknown to Tara that over the years Devi and Roshni and Komli had flourished in a secret paradise of learning from one another. If Tara was right, and if reading and writing were supposed to be the sole prerogative of men, then these three women had sinned secretly, and with great pleasure. Although, academically speaking, the youngest appeared to be the oldest, in spiritual terms the three were equals—females feasting together on the forbidden fruit!

"What will I do without being able to come over when I need a break, Roshni?"

"I'll tell you what; I need someone to check on the apartment from time to time. So you get the keys of course. Come over with little Amrita whenever you want to. Tell Tara you're going over to dust my place. That way she won't go with you!"

Devi bade Roshni a sorrowful farewell. Tara, on the other hand, was secretly delighted to be rid of a woman who brought so much sunshine into the life of her daughter-in-law.

The Johnson household fell in love with Roshni. She was diffident, but wise, literate but unassuming, dignified, gentle and oh so humble. In time, six year old William and four year old Tessa, too, fell in love with Roshni. Although she was but a nanny in the eyes of the Johnsons and a mere ayah in the eyes of the hierarchy of native help the Johnsons enjoyed, as far as Roshni was concerned, she was literally transported to a life beyond her imagining: she accompanied the children in a chauffeur-driven car that she swore was longer than the little room she and her sister slept in. She was convinced that the garden in which she sometimes played hide and seek with her wards had to be better than the Paradise Father Michael had promised Komli. In the garden, Roshni often removed her slippers to feel the cool green velvet under her feet. She loved looking at the flower beds of vibrant pansies, marigolds, and petunias interspersed with rectangular emerald green bushes. The garden was clipped, pruned, and diligently maintained to perfection by an old gardener whose sole passion, it seemed, was to tend it lovingly. He had learned long ago that nothing on earth was as peaceful and joyous as nurturing a garden hemmed in from the outside world by majestic Magnolia trees. No one knew that one of the main reasons why he had such a great affinity to the flowers and trees was because they attracted gorgeous butterflies that flitted in and out of the garden in a manner similar to the way in which he tended to his flowers—in stone silence. If the birds twittered and the bees buzzed around him, it was in a language other than man's, and that he did not mind at all. Neither did he mind the fact that he never did get to see the nocturnal, social butterflies who flitted in and out of his master's garden with stems of champagne and wine, gathering gossip and depositing it with reckless abandon.

Roshni often took the time to stop and stoop and smell the flowers in the garden that was so lovingly cultivated by the old gardener. Often, she stayed down for a few seconds longer than necessary, to thank Bhagvaan, and to ask Him what she had done to deserve this Paradise.

At first she had been scared of the clothes washer and dryer, but after a while she realized that they were somewhat like her little sister, Komli—they rumbled and rattled and removed all the dirt. What came out always smelled good.

As for the kitchen—Roshni couldn't help but wonder if the Johnsons ever appreciated the power and beauty of human hands. She was somewhat subjective, she realized, because her sister often claimed she could achieve so much more if only she had two hands. And here was a family with gadgets that did everything man could do with two hands—open a can, squeeze out juice, chop and grind, bake bread, make coffee, suck up dust, and as for sewing and embroidering, why madam had a special room in which to house those honored gadgets that spat out the most exquisite designs. Even the sunbeams seemed to dance and linger in there, as though they enjoyed watching her create brilliantly colored, magical patterns merely by pushing buttons.

Once the fear and fascination of machines and gadgets had worn off, Roshni settled down to the more important task of concentrating on William and Tessa who simply grew to love her, and she them. This nanny did not know the meaning of raising her voice. Little did the children know that her urge to scream had been smothered years and years ago when she had realized that one less man could mean two more hungry stomachs. Besides, Komli had unwittingly passed on a great deal about what makes happy children by telling her how Mrs. Fletcher dealt with children. Many a times when Roshni could have said 'no' or 'don't do that', she found herself using a positive approach that won the hearts of her two wards. In the eyes of the entire Johnson family, Roshni was a gentle blessing from heaven itself.

Dear Devi,

How are you and everyone at home? I miss you a lot but I am very happy with this English family. It took me a long time to get used to them and their grand house. You would love them if you saw them. I wish I could bring them over, but madam would probably have a fit if I asked her. Actually, she would not have a fit. She is the most polite woman I have come across in my life. Do you know madam never orders me to do anything. She always asks me! Of course I don't have a choice, I know. But it feels nice. Wonder how Tara Bahen would react if she had to live with madam for a few weeks. I think both of them would have a heart attack, although I'm not sure which one would have it first!

You know, I think of your little Amrita every time I visit their ball room (not for cricket or football. They use it for dancing). I feel so tempted to take my scissors and cut off a yard from their shiny brocade curtains that hang from floor to ceeling. It would make such a beautiful dress for Amrita and, believe me, nobody would notice the little snip in the yards and yards of material gathered together. I think there are at least ten such curtains in the beautiful round room. This room is so huge that you can't see the necklace madam is wearing if you stand at the other end of the room! Of course the children and I never go in when madam has guests. Sometimes she asks me to polish something in there because she knows I don't like to sit around doing nothing.

And guess what? Some of the Indian servants are jealous of me because I get to sit and eat at the table with William and Tessa. Actually I feel very uncomfortable but they force me to. Madam keeps saying sorry to me because she thinks her children are so rude, but I just love them because they are so honest. They try to teach me how to eat with a fork and spoon and knife. Beats me why they eat with them. A fork is just like a hand with four fingers and you can think of the spoon as the thumb. Problem is you can't bend the fork and spoon like fingers. I think our way of eating is much easier. And food also tastes better when you eat with your own hands, believe me. But it's fun learning new ways, especially when your teachers are two darling children! When I go to their kitchen I eat with my hands, although I have to suffer the taunts of the servants who think I am miss high and mighty who should be eating with fork and spoon!

Life can be very confusing sometimes. There I was in my little room, thinking I was a good neighbor and an angel of a sister. Now I know people who call me miss high and mighty! And there is a gardener who thinks I am a pest, I am sure. He doesn't actually say so. It's just the way he walks away every time he sees me. I think he thinks the way to happiness is to pretend to be deaf and dumb. If it wasn't for the loving way he looks after flowers and runs away when he sees me, I would swear he was blind as well! Then there are the darling children who think I am so much fun. And there is Komli who thinks I am too serious and never have any fun. As for Tara thinking I am bold and brazen and all that, the Johnsons think I need to be more bossy with their children! And you think I am so clever, while these people treat me as border-line literate!! As for the head cook (yes they have three cooks), he thinks I am a rose with thorns because I don't like the way he eyes me, and I tell him so!

Makes me wonder who I really am!

Komli is ajusting well to college. Although I was scared at first to send her back to Calcutta, I realize now that Komli has turned into an extremely brave and intelligent young woman. She will be able to look after herself, I know. Will write again soon. You can write to me at the address on the top of this letter. Look after yourself. Give a hug to Amrita. I miss you a lot. Hope you get this letter. I am mailing it to your husband's office, as you suggested.

Love, Roshni.

When Tusneem and Komli first attended class together at Calcutta College, Komli looked like an earthy brown moth camouflaged behind the decaying, old, wooden desk in front of her. Tusneem looked like a splendid butterfly whose resplendent colors changed from day to day. Although Komli had not realized it herself because she paid little attention to what people wore, some of the more envious girls had noticed that Tusneem could go for a whole month without wearing the same clothes twice.

Tusneem rarely questioned her professors. She had long learned from Mullasahib and from her family that it was less hassle to simply accept and do what she was told. The one common lesson all the adults in her life had imparted to Tusneem was that discipline was the key to success. Like a perfectly brought up child, she did everything in accordance with the rules laid down by her family, her community, and her college professors. There was a time and a place for everything in Tusneem's life. She dressed right, she prayed right, she behaved right, and she did all her papers right, too. She was simply a 'straight A' human being. If she had any faults, it was perhaps the fact that she was a little too meek.

Komli, on the other hand, was neither a 'straight A' student, nor meek. If Komli did not wear the watch on her hand, Tusneem would have sworn the girl knew nothing about time. She breezed into class at the nick of time, hair carelessly bundled into a knot that looked like it was sliding down by the minute! It never seemed that she took the time to iron or to color coordinate anything she wore, dress, sari, or sulwarkurta. The irony was that while Komli had all the time in the world to go for pedicures and manicures and the removal of unwanted bodily hair, it was Tusneem who managed to squeeze in appointments for all the cures her society demanded. As for Komli's slippers, they had two qualities that suggested they were purchased with the intention of being a part and parcel of her for life—they were two sizes too big, and they were a neutral brown, so she could wear them with everything.

The only time Komli took off those slippers was when she ran track. It was at the first tryout for track that the girls got to know each other better. In the hundred yard dash, Komli beat Tusneem by a fraction of a second.

"Would you like some of my water?" Komli asked Tusneem, when she noticed that Tusneem was the only girl huffing and puffing without a drink of water beside her.

"No, thank you. I'm fasting."

"You're kidding me! How can you fast and run track at the same time?"

"It's not that hard. I've been fasting on and off ever since I can remember."

"For a good husband?"

"No!" Tusneem exclaimed with a laugh. "It's the month of Ramadan. All Muslims fast during the month of Ramadan."

"You can't possibly go without food for a whole month!"

"We just don't eat from sunrise to sunset. When I go home today, there'll be quite a feast waiting for me!"

"And you can't even have a drink of water while you fast?"

"Nope! Although that's not the hard part; the hard part is getting up at four in the morning, to pray and eat . . ."

"You mean you stock up on food in the middle of the night?"

"I wish it was as easy as that. The stocking up on food is not what we focus on. I have to go through ablution, then pray, then eat, then stay awake to say another prayer before I can finally go to sleep for a blessed hour. Then it's time to get ready for college! We're up every night for over two hours. That's the hardest part."

"Wow! I don't know if I could get up in the middle of the night to pray!"

"So do you fast for a good husband?" Tusneem asked with a slight frown?

"Some do. Not me!"

"Have you ever fasted in your life?"

"If I did, I can barely remember!" Komli replied, a little too casually. "I have an old-fashioned neighbor in Patna. Her favorite pass-time is to meddle in our lives. According to her, I should be fasting every Tuesday to get myself a good husband. The logic totally escapes me. Right now I'm just glad to have escaped from her clutches!"

"What about your parents?" Tusneem asked, "don't they have any say in the matter?"

"I was orphaned when I was young. I live with my sister. This is the first time we've been separated." There was something sweet and simple about Tusneem; Komli did not feel the need to lie to her about Roshni being her mother.

"You're lucky!"

"Why, because I was orphaned?"

"No! I'm sorry. I meant to say you're lucky you get to stay in a hostel. My parents refuse to let me stay on my own until I get married."

"How come a good Muslim like you gets to run track in these slinky shorts?!"

"We're a crazy mixture of strict and liberated. Doesn't bother anyone in my immediate family, although we used to have an old servant who mumbled angrily under his breath every time he saw me in western garb!"

"I've noticed your driver comes to get you every day at lunch time. Why do you rush home for barely thirty minutes? Besides, you're not supposed to have lunch if you're fasting!"

"My cousins and I have gone home for lunch-break since we were kids. We go home to pray. We have to pray within certain prescribed times, depending on the rising and the setting of the sun."

"Why can't you pray right here in college? Just look up to the sky and pray! From what I've gathered, Bhagvaan, or Allah or God or whoever it is that monopolizes heaven, plays I spy with my little eye all the time."

Tusneem giggled as she, too, warmed up to Komli. "Don't you have any rules and regulations for praying? Or do you not pray at all?"

"As long as I started each morning with a prayer, my sister left me alone. Actually, I say thank you to Him-up-there more often than that. I just look up and thank Him whenever I feel like it," Komli said with a smile.

"That sounds so easy! I have to go through ablution, put on special clothes, lay out my masalla, make sure it faces west . . ."

"Why west?"

"Because holy Mecca is to our west."

"So if you were living in America, you would face southeast?"

"Yes. And see that stray dog there? If he so much as touches me, I have to bathe to purify myself before I can pray."

"So all animals are untouchable?"

"Kind of."

Feeling sorry for Tusneem, Komli suddenly took the rest of her water and poured it over Tusneem's head. "I hope that cools you down a little. Besides, you won't have to go home and perform ablution now!"

"Oh, I wish you hadn't done that, Komli!" Tusneem exclaimed in dismay.

"Why? It's good old water."

"Exactly! It's not namazi water. Namazi water is purified water. You know how everything has to be sterilized when a baby drinks milk out of a bottle?"

"No. But carry on."

"Everything we use for ablution has to be purified with a prayer."

"Meaning that the bottle that contains the water has to be purified first?"

"Yes. Even the clothes I wear are purified."

"And what if a bird innocently poops on your clothes?"

"You're making fun of me, aren't you?" Tusneem asked, a little piqued.

"I'm sorry. I should know better than to be facetious. So, in order to touch the namazi clothes your hands must be purified, right?"

"Yes."

"And now that I've poured unpurified water on you . . . ."

"I will have to go home, bathe, purify myself, and change into namazi clothes."

"I'm sorry, Tusneem. I was just trying to cool you down."

"I know. When we fast, it's a fast for all our senses. I can't see a movie, or watch television, or listen to the radio, or smell food, leave aside cool down with water poured over me!"

"So what do you do if you have to go to the bathroom in college?"

"I try not to. But if I absolutely have to, I have to perform ablution and wear clean underwear before I can pray."

"Wow!" Komli exclaimed in fascination. "You've been brought up so strictly. What rules do you have for praying itself?

"Many. They're not easy to explain. It's just a side of me that I've never discussed with a non-Muslim. Maybe someday you can come over and see for yourself. Do you know, we had an old-fashioned servant like your neighbor. He's retired now. When he was head servant in our house, I could not even have Hindu friends over."

"That's how Tara is. She won't allow Muslims into her house. She's probably afraid she'll be reincarnated into a pig if she defiles herself with Muslims!"

"We Muslims don't believe in reincarnation, only in heaven and hell. Which means that if you're right, I'll be reincarnated into some creepy, crawly creature, and if I'm right, you'll burn in the fires of hell!"

"If you ask me, Tusneem, heaven and hell and reincarnation all happen while we're living here on earth."

"Meaning?"

"By the look of things, you are probably living in heaven already. And to be honest with you, I think I have already been reincarnated once in my life. We were very poor once. And then, for whatever good deeds we performed, my sister and I were reincarnated into what I consider healthy, happy people. Money is a means to material things. Wealth is a state of mind. My sister and I are as content as can be. Are you, Tusneem?"

"I've never thought about it. I'm too busy thinking of all the things I have to do or cannot do. Did you ever have religious lessons, Komli? You sound pretty grown up and all-knowing."

"No. Unless I can count Father Michael's Bible history lessons. Is that what you mean?"

"No. You said you were Hindu. Did you ever have lessons in Hinduism?"

"Only by way of wonderful stories that Ma used to tell us. Maybe I sound confident and all-knowing because I'm not as polished as you are. Aren't the less educated usually the ones who are more cocky?" she asked with a humble, but cheeky smile. "If you got to know me better, you would probably say that my beliefs are a hodge-podge of things I picked up here and there."

I think I'm going to like you, Tusneem said to herself before she remarked, "You must have had a trouble-free childhood."

"You seem far away. What are you thinking?" Komli asked, without bothering to answer Tusneem's question.

"Oh, I was just thinking of Mullasahib, our religious instructor. He was so different from the nuns in school and from our professors in college."

"Whom do you prefer?"

"You know what, I've grown up to prefer the one I feared and hated the most, our dear old Mullasahib! He was this roly-poly, fat guy with beady eyes as black as thunder. He had a humongous brown mole on the side of his chin, like a third eye that seemed to warn us not to mess with him because he would erupt with anger! And he often did, if we skipped lines in the Koran. His voice seemed to come from 20,000 leagues under the sea. That's pretty scary for a child!"

"How many sisters and brothers do you have?"

"None. Believe it or not, first thing in the morning I was driven to my aunt's house where we cousins had religious lessons together. Then we were packed in a car and driven to school."

"I went through something similar every time I went to Sunday school, except I went home to Ganesh and Saraswati."

"I know something about your gods. Isn't Saraswati the goddess of education?"

"Yes. I do pray to her every morning, by the way."

"I am always fascinated by all the gods I see during the Puja festival. What I can never figure out is why you immerse all the gods in water at the end of the festival."

"I'm not sure. Maybe it has something to do with going back to water from where all life emerged, although sometimes I prefer Father Michael's story about humans evolving from a spec of dust. He forgot to mention, though, that as the spec of dust gathers momentum, it turns into quite a forceful whirlwind that huffs and puffs and blows away things, before it whimpers down into a harmless spec of dust again. Awesome, if you ask me."

"Sounds like what Mother Xaveria taught me in school. She didn't mention the huffing and puffing either."

"No, those that huff and puff rarely mention such words!" Komli said with another cocky smile.

"You might be the exception, Komli," Tusneem said calmly.

"Ooooh! That stings!" Komli admitted. "Guess I'll have to watch what I say."

"I like you the way you are. You can always blame it on your teachers!"

"Thank you! Guess we'll never get rid of the influence of our Catholic fathers and mothers, will we?"

"I guess not. You know something, I have never told this to anyone, but my image of hundred-year-old, bearded Allah floating among white clouds is always mixed up with 30-year-old Jesus walking on water!" Tusneem said, enjoying the opportunity to admit to this warm, feisty girl that her image of mighty Allah had been watered down by the nuns. "Want to hear a jump rope rhyme we made up about our daily Islamic and Bible lessons? It went, Aleeph, bey, tey, sey, jeem, hey, khay, juhunnum (hell) if you don't pray five times a day. 1, 2, 3, 4, 5, 6, 7, all good Catholics go to heaven."

"We were possessed by two spirits, I guess, one for the missionaries and one for home. One less than the holy trinity!"

"Did you blaspheme like that in school?" Tusneem asked laughing.

"Do I look that stupid? Tell me more about your Mullasahib. Why did you dislike him when you were young?"

"He was everything the nuns weren't. And we thought the nuns were Gods! The nuns taught us never to slurp our soup or our tea and that's exactly what Mullasahib did each morning, slurp his tea as loud as he could. And he never seemed to know how to have fried eggs without making a terrible mess. Still, we could hardly wait for the servant to arrive with his breakfast because in those fifteen minutes while he wolfed down his heavily buttered toasts and eggs, we could skip lines galore!"

"Your Mullasahib sounds like a glutton!"

"Perhaps. But now I realize that he probably wolfed down his food because he never got enough at home. He was poor. It has taken me all these years to realize that Mullasahib was probably closer to the poor and meek who enter the kingdom of heaven than those rich and righteous nuns."

"I know someone who never had enough to eat. She pecks like a bird, but with the grace of a queen. Her younger sister often pigs out though, I have to confess."

"Well," Tusneem continued, too lost in her thoughts to pay serious attention to Komli's asides, "I prefer Mullasahib because I understand him better than I ever will our indifferent professors or those mysterious nuns in school. Did you have nuns in school?"

"No. But I saw them often in church on Sundays. Couldn't see their boobs, their hair, their anything except hands and face. They could have been men in hiding! No wonder they're called penguins. Who can tell a penguin's sex?!

"I'll say this much for our Mullasahib, at least he was genuinely interested in making sure that we did everything right to obtain a ticket to heaven. You know, I think he had just one set of clothes. He came every morning in this navy blue saaya (knee length jacket), a limp white izaar (pants) and an ageless, black topi with a barely visible gold rim. In this uniform he arrived each morning at 7 o'clock sharp!"

"Between Ramadan and your Mullasahib and praying, did you ever get enough sleep?"

"Sometimes! You should have heard Mullasahib bellow at those cousins of mine who were still in bed! Sometimes he even threatened to wake them up with a glass of cold water callously hurled at the face. My cousin, Mustapha, had the pleasure on a couple of occasions. And for the next hour a reign of terror prevailed. He sat on the carpet, with his back cushioned comfortably by a pillow propped against the wall. Between him and us cousins were more pillows on which we propped our Korans, Ammas and Saifaas (religious books). Like Allah, it seemed he could hear all of us at once, so simultaneously we recited the different verses, swaying backwards and forwards. Like busy bees we droned on and on, quite mechanically, for our senses hadn't quite awakened yet. Why are you laughing?"

"I can just picture you! Carry on."

"Mullasahib was wide awake, of course. He probably got up way before sunrise to say the morning prayers. Perhaps he could hear us all at once, or maybe that was just a trick to keep us on the alert. When he was served his breakfast, I sometimes dared to nudge one of my cousins to watch me skip from line one to line fifteen. It was such a thrill not to get caught. I never did. Poor Mustapha, he got the worst of Mullasahib's thundering rage!"

"What's Mustapha like, meek as a mouse, or rebellious?"

"A little bit of both, but in a quiet way. Can I share my favorite memory with you?

"Hope it's a little better than what I've heard so far!"

"It is. This happened when I was about eight, I think. As I said, in our eyes, Mullasahib was some kind of a wizard who had the amazing ability to gobble down his breakfast and still keep his two ears attuned to the different Arabic lines five sleepy kids were reciting simultaneously! Well, one day Mustapha suddenly stopped reciting. Mullasahib's breakfast must have been especially good that day because he didn't notice anything immediately. I did. Carefully, without turning my head, I cast Mustapha a sideward glance. Slowly, slyly, I allowed my eyes to wander to where his were transfixed—at this soft ball of human flesh with thousands of little black hairs sticking out. Unfortunately, I too, stopped reciting then. The droning must have dropped quite a few decibels. Mullasahib pounced on us suddenly. What are you two staring at, he bellowed. Mustapha jumped out of his skin and started mumbling something, anything, from the Koran. Unbeknown to us, Mustapha's younger brother had picked up on the goings on and simply blurted out, you have a hole in your izaar, Mullasahib! There was no time to murder the little devil then. Mullasahib was too busy raving and ranting about how wicked and shameless we were and how Allah would punish us for our sin and how many extra pages we'd have to recite to atone ourselves."

"So that's why you prefer Mullasahib; you saw more human flesh on him than on the nuns, huh?" Komli said with a hearty laugh. "You just don't look like the type who would eye men's balls from the age of eight!"

"Stop being so crude, Komli!"

"How can you have any sympathy for someone who hollered at you and scared you?! Didn't you ever protest or complain to your parents?"

"We didn't know the meaning of protesting. And who ever complains about their teachers? They're supposed to be infallible, especially nuns and Mullasahibs! But now, when I look back on Mullasahib, I see him as this poor man trying to support wife and six children in some dark hole of a room, on the pittance he must have received giving a handful of religious lessons to rich kids who had no clue about poverty and sacrifices. Let's change the subject. Tell me something about yourself."

"I have a saint of a sister who lavishes all her love on me."

"What about your cousins and uncles and aunts?"

"I don't have any," Komli said coolly, although a twinge of sadness nabbed at her.

"Wow! I can't imagine a life without cousins. I've lost count of how many I have!"

"I have something you don't have, I bet."

"What's that?"

"I have a guardian angel who looks after me. I've never met him, though."

So what does he do to make him your guardian angel?"

"Sends me money for my education." Sensing that Tusneem was beginning to feel sorry for her, she added perversely, "And I have what you would call a hole for a hostel room. Does that bother you?"

"No, Komli! I've already told you that I wish I could live in your hole. I'm dying to be independent and live by myself. I hate being picked up by my driver, while most people walk or bus it to college. I hate being the rich freak that everyone envies, or dislikes for all I know."

"Then I must be the freak that likes you," Komli declared with a smile. What's your major?"

"I haven't yet decided. What's yours?"

"Education. I'm going to make sure little children aren't fed foreign crap!"

"Our crap is alright, you mean?" Tusneem asked with a laugh.

"Does your own shit ever smell?"

In time, Tusneem grew to marvel at the ease with which Komli dealt with her handicap, rarely complained, questioned her professors without fear, made quick decisions, and found humor in most things. Komli, on the other hand, grew to appreciate the grace and goodness with which Tusneem always conducted herself. While Komli gained confidence in herself and her ability to deal with the outside world, she grew to love sweet, gracious Tusneem who seemed to have everything but confidence in herself. Tusneem had little time in her busy schedule to make decisions, it seemed. She had to pray to the dictates of the rising and setting sun, she had to eat what was served, wear the right clothes for the right occasion, and attend religious and communal functions regardless of the demands of college affairs. For Komli, Tusneem's saving grace was that she seemed so unlike those rich, cruel girls who had come to her birthday party all those years ago, when she had resolved never again to socialize with the wealthy.

"You know, Komli," Tusneem stated out of the blue one day, "even though you pretend to be so open-minded, I have a suspicion you're not allowed to socialize with Muslims."

Komli shrieked with laughter. "What if I said yes, would you stop having anything to do with me?"

"No! It's just that I wanted you so much to come to my birthday party. You always make excuses, every time I invite you."

"Maybe I do hate Muslims after all!" Komli said in jest.

"Why do Hindus and Muslims dislike each other so much?"

"I was just joking!"

"I know that. But that doesn't take away from the fact that Hindus and Muslims don't really trust one another."

"If you ask me, it's because they know so little about each other. But I think it also goes way back in history, from the time of the Moguls probably."

"We learned mostly about British history in our school."

"Bet the nuns never mentioned anything about their high-handed forefathers partitioning our country into India and Pakistan, did they? Imperious old Brits! I mean Brats! Clip a little territory here and there, give it another name and then leave the circumcised country to deal with its problems! How did we get onto this subject?"

"Your little joke about hating Muslims!"

"I don't think I hate anyone, Tusneem. As a matter of fact, you're the closest I've ever come to loving anyone other than my sister and Devi."

"Then why do you always find excuses to decline my invitations to come home with me. I think you'll like my family. They are far from bigoted, narrow-minded people. In fact, Pappa always tells me that if we educated people communicated more and understood one another, we would have less problems in the world."

"Here's the catch though. Educated people get rich and, from what I've read, the richer they get the more problems they have; they socialize only with their kind, and have little or no time at all to think about others, forget about truly communicating!"

"I wish you wouldn't sound so all-knowing all the time. Listen, I'm staying at my aunt's right now because my parents have gone away for Haj. Next week we're celebrating Bakri Eid. It's the day we sacrifice a goat. You're always questioning me about my customs and traditions. I think you'll find this occasion extremely interesting and lots of fun. Will you spend Bakri Eid with me, Komli, please?"

Something about the sacrifice appealed to Komli in a strange way. She succumbed and accepted the invitation.

Early Friday morning, an excited Tusneem whisked Komli to the back yard in her aunt Sakina's house, from where they would get the best view of the ceremony.

"This is where the goat will be sacrificed. After it's over, the ladies get busy preparing for the feast. I tell you, Komli, it's the best bar-b-q'd meat in the world!"

"What are we supposed to do?"

"Just enjoy. We usually play a cricket match while the women marinate the meat and get the food ready. Relax, Komli, no one's going to hurt you. I wish my parents were here. I know they would love you." Just then there was quite a commotion at the gate. "Here comes the goat, Komli, watch!" Tusneem said with bated breath.

Komli tried not to wince as she saw two butchers struggling with a bleating goat that they were tugging by its horns. Judging from the pathetic sounds it made and the way it seemed to be resisting with all its might, it seemed that the goat knew instinctively that it's time had come. However, being a creature that knew nothing about accepting fate with a resigned air, it bleated and wailed and fought the two butchers with all the might it could muster. To no avail.

The rest of the family came out and gathered around the goat. It took six human hands to force the goat to lie prostrate on the ground. Tusneem's uncle Kasim read out a prayer, after which he took a knife and slit the goat's throat, making sure he went back and forth as prescribed by Islamic laws. Komli had never seen anything quite so gory. "What is the reason for this sacrifice?" she whispered. Everyone else seemed to accept the ceremony so matter-of-factly that Komli felt it would be improper to ask such a question out loud. She did not realize that her question was drowned in the agonized bleating of an animal pleading to be relieved of its pain.

"Remember our Bible history lesson about Abraham sacrificing a lamb instead of his son, Isaac? This ceremony stems from the same belief."

"I thought you were Muslim."

"I am. But we believe in all the prophets of the Old Testament. Muslims and Christians fell apart when Jesus came along. We believe Jesus is a prophet, not the son of god."

"And is this the bar-b-q'd meat we'll be eating later?" Komli asked, regretting that Tusneem knew she wasn't a vegetarian.

"Some of it will be distributed to other people in the community."

"Will the beggars on the street get some?"

"No. This meat can only be distributed among Bohras. Remember what I told you Mamma sometimes tells me about us Bohras being the cream that settles on top of a pan of milk?"

"How can I forget being told I'm totally non-fat!" Komli retorted sarcastically. The two girls enjoyed joking and jabbing at each other from time to time, knowing that neither harbored communal, caste or religious prejudices.

"Well, I'm afraid this meat only goes to the people in our community."

"Yeah!" Komli retorted, "butcher the innocent, non-denominational creature, and then elevate it to something sacrosanct that only you Bohras can eat!" Komli shuddered, but was unable to take her eyes off the goat whose suffering was quickly brought to an end by the butcher who proceeded to efficiently disembowel the creature with the dexterity of a master who knows his tools. Once the goat stopped writhing in pain, and the bleating whimpered down to a deathly silence, Komli herself calmed down a little. For the first time in her life, she was witnessing an anatomy lesson come to life—the gullet and stomach and large and small intestines, the liver, the kidney, the heart, and head were deftly cut and placed in different heaps on drab, gray concrete that suddenly came alive with pools of thick, red blood embracing each lifeless heap of body parts. Repugnance was soon replaced by a sense of fascination she always felt when she learned or understood something better. This was a live lesson. Unlike the illustrations in her books, which were pretty, but soul-less, stench-less, and blood-less, this was the real stinking stuff, she reflected quietly—muted spare parts that but a few seconds ago was a magical whole that could walk and communicate; now waiting to be collected, cooked and consumed by the chosen! She had read about Hindu sacrifices and about the sacrifices of ancient cultures. What kind of gods were they, she asked herself, who created magical creatures such as these and then asked that they be brutally disseminated. For what? A ticket to heaven? The goriness of the moment leant a morbidity to her reflections. How would her own life end, she wondered; at the hands of fellow-man or at the hands of nature's unrelenting cycles?

"Alhumdolillah!" someone said out loud, looking at Komli who had sneezed just then.

"What's he saying to me?" Komli asked, embarrassed that perhaps her loud sneeze had caused some kind of a disturbance.

"You know how some people say 'God bless you' after you sneeze . . ."

"To keep the soul from being carried off, according to Father Michael."

"Well, we say 'Alhumdolillah'. I think it means Allah be praised."

Allah be praised, indeed, Komli thought to herself with the first hint of a smile. If You hadn't blessed us with orifices, how would we sneeze and fart and burp and babble and explode with a million ingenious ideas about right and wrong?!

"You didn't enjoy the sacrifice very much, did you, Komli?"

"You said I would find the occasion interesting. I did. Although I can't say that I enjoyed it. There were no cars during Abraham's time, were there?" she asked suddenly.

"You ask the darndest questions. What the hell are you thinking now?"

"God should have asked man to sacrifice cars instead of innocent little goats. After all, cars are also made up of parts that enable them to function. At least there would be no pools of blood around each dismantled part! More importantly, cars are so expensive, it would really test man's faith in God, wouldn't it?"

"I just hope none of my relatives heard you!"

"If they did, just tell them I am an unschooled heathen!" Komli whispered gleefully.

Tusneem just shook her head. Although she had become used to her friend's jokes and strange way of thinking, she wasn't always sure when Komli was joking and when she was serious.

Komli was relieved to be escorted out of the backyard and into a garden where she was silently welcomed by the fragrances of an herbivorous world of colorful flowers and majestic trees swaying gracefully in the breeze, oblivious of the stench of meat and blood from which a nauseated Komli had emerged intact.

It was in this garden that Mustapha first saw the strange, one-handed creature with coarse, black, untamed curls cascading down her shoulders. The cousins were playing their traditional game of cricket. It took two hands to bat, but one to bowl. With ease of confidence and a winning smile, Komli asked to be bowler and runner while someone else batted for her. Komli had learned very soon after she started school that people were too embarrassed about her handicap to ask her to join in any games they felt she could not play. Her passion to participate in any and everything left her with no choice but to take the initiative and to prove that with a little help she could overcome her handicap. Komli turned out to be a good bowler. Everyone stared at her with sympathy and curiosity, while she seemed to radiate her individuality without a trace of self-consciousness. The poet in Mustapha viewed her as a forget-me-not that showed no signs of feeling out of place or forgotten, unlike some of his better-endowed female cousins who thought it was an art to look fragile, forlorn, and forgotten. Interestingly enough, this creature seemed to add a spark to Tusneem who, as far as Mustapha was concerned, had never before played cricket with the enthusiasm she showed in the presence of this friend of hers.

Later that afternoon, it was Komli who approached Mustapha and asked if she could help him fly the kite he was trying to get off the ground.

"Sure," he responded with a smile, "These strings have been sharpened by glass, so be careful you don't cut your fingers on them. The aim is to get our kite as close as possible to the other kites and see if we can cut them down. On the other hand, if you see a kite that's about to cut ours down, you must quickly yank ours out of the way."

"Cut throat kite-flying, huh?" Komli asked with a smile as she yanked his kite and watched it jostle and soar under a clear, blue sky. "How come you weren't around for the slaughtering of the goat?" Komli asked casually.

"I used to love watching it as a child. I could hardly wait for the day. Keep an eye on our kite!"

Alas! Komli was too new at kite flying to be able to handle the strings with agility. Before long their kite came wafting down, having been cut by the strings of another. "I'm sorry," Komli said simply.

"You don't have to apologize; it's just a game. Sooner or later most of them come down as well. Want to try another one?"

"Maybe later," she answered politely, and headed back to find Tusneem.

It had been a day of so many wonders for Komli. Never before had she witnessed an animal being sacrificed. What a nice euphemism for butchered, she thought. Never before had she participated in a family gathering of countless uncles and aunts and cousins having so much fun together. Although each one seemed different, it was not hard to see what strong family ties bound these people together.

As loud and boisterous as they had been playing games and fighting for each point, when they congregated for the afternoon prayer preceding lunch, Komli could not help but wish she could participate with them. Tusneem's maternal grandfather, Motapappasan, led the prayers. The men lined up in three rows behind him. The women lined up behind the men. Each one had his or her own special prayer rug on which to pray. Komli watched from a distance, respectfully this time. They did not pray in one position. They stood, they knelt, they sat, they went down on their knees, their foreheads touched the floor from time to time. Each action was repeated again and again. No one looked beyond the rug on which one was praying. Yet each action was perfectly synchronized by the lead word, Allaho Akbar (Allah is great), Motapappasan said out loud from time to time. Even their hands kept changing position. Wow, Komli thought as she watched from the doorway, Allah must love this family.

"Your prayers are like exercising in slow motion. It was wonderful to watch," Komli remarked, feeling a strange sense of peace.

"Even our lips move all the time. We're not supposed to keep them pursed together. I just wish I understood what I was saying. We pray in Arabic, you know."

"Why?"

"It's the language of the holy Koran."

"I thought prayer was about communicating, asking, or thanking."

"I guess that's why my favorite part of namaaz is doa. That's when we go down on our foreheads and ask Allah for whatever we want in a language of our choice. The rest, as Mamma always says, is like taking medicine—it does us good, even though we do not understand why."

"Well, think of it this way," Komli said cheerfully, "it's a wonderful way of getting your body in shape for both this world and the hereafter."

"If you think this is good exercise, you should watch us on the night we have to keep awake and pray until sun-rise!"

"Pray all night?!"

"Yes!"

"How often do you have to do that?"

"Once a year. It's enough, believe me!"

"Bet your people never suffer from joint aches!"

"You can ask Motapappasan, my grandfather. He also gets up at one every morning to say some special prayer. Then he wakes up again before sunrise!"

Komli could only shake her head in awe before she said, "By the way, I noticed one of your cousins kept going to the bathroom while you prayed. It seemed he caused a lot of sniggering among your cousins. What was that all about?"

"That was our devout Esmail, the one who told Mullasahib he had a hole in his izaar! He's so intent about doing everything exactly right that he keeps breaking wind."

"As in farting?"

"Yes. Now this is going to blow your mind away, but since you asked, I'm going to tell you. Before we pray we have to do vuzu, which is a short ablution, with prayer of course, of our hands and face and neck and feet."

"So that explains why everyone made a beeline for the bathroom. I couldn't quite understand that, I must admit!"

"Well, vuzu is broken, so to speak, if you break wind. So, if you fart in the middle of a prayer, you have to go and do vuzu again and start that prayer all over again. Esmail simply cannot complete his prayers without doing vuzu at least two or three times. His older brothers have told him they'll give him a hundred rupees if he can finish a prayer without going to the bathroom! He's just got some kind of phobia, poor guy. But he's a darling. We all love him!"

"And if I dare to ask you why you have to do vuzu again if you fart, you're going to tell me you have to simply swallow the pill because it does you good?"

"I'm afraid so. Actually one of my cousins, Mustapha, did summon up the courage to ask Mullasahib once. The rest of us started sniggering since we were young and immature, so Mullasahib got annoyed with us, and I'm afraid to this day we've never found out."

"Can't your parents tell you? I want to know the reason."

"Why?!"

"There's got to be a logical explanation for it. I can't see how anyone can dream up something like that without some valid reason! You know one of the first things I learned in school was that everything in our world is made of three states of matter—liquid, solid, and gas. That's about the only thing that comes to mind. See if you can find out from your parents. I'm curious."

"We end up going around in circles when we ask too many questions. Our parents tell us that they cannot reveal everything to us unless we go for advanced religious lessons. And, of course, most of us youngsters don't feel like going for more religious lessons than we have to because there's never enough time to fit in everything as it is. So then we end up being told that since we can't be bothered to make the extra time to find out the reasons, we have to simply listen to the elders. And to be perfectly honest, I'd rather go to a movie than go for advanced religious lessons!"

"Thank goodness you're human!" Komli said with a warm smile. I often wondered what an angel like you found in a heathen like me!"

"Wanna know?"

"Go ahead."

"The ability to fart freely."

"Yeah! It's amazing how much one can fart on a full stomach!" Komli said, wishing that her sister was with her to enjoy her play on words.

"You're quite spiritual yourself, Komli, and you damn well know it."

"Thank you," Komli said as the two girls looked intently at each other. Worlds apart though they were in many ways, they acknowledged at that moment that they had become inseparable soulmates.

"It's time to change the subject. Let's go eat."

And how graciously they feasted, Komli would reflect again and again. Everybody sat on the carpet, around six huge thaals that were placed on brass rings that served as legs. About ten people sat around each thaal. Before everyone sat down to eat, two young girls had come around with elegant pitchers of water sitting on a container. They went around individually to each person, starting with the elders in the family.

"Just put out your hand and wash it, Komli. The container under the pitcher will hold the water as it is poured over your hand."

"Is my hand being purified?" Komli whispered.

"No, you twit! It's simple hygiene! You wash your hands before you eat, don't you? It's customary for the host to come to you with a pitcher of water so you can wash your hands."

Motapappasan sat at a thaal with some of his grandchildren. Komli learned later that the 'san' was added to 'Motapappa' because he had lived in Japan for several years. 'San' was a mark of respect in Japan, and it had stuck to him, even after he had returned to India. Quite a mouthful, Komli thought, but decided Motapappasan had a nice ring to it. And he had such an enigmatic personality. Had he become an oriental sage, she wondered. He had smiled at her when she was introduced to him, but had said nothing. In fact, she had not heard him speak a single word. Yet, he seemed to be aware of all the goings on, perhaps even inside the hearts of all his children and grandchildren. It seemed that he had been around for so long, that he did not need to communicate verbally with anyone. Old is gold is what he epitomized.

The most fascinating thing about Motapappasan was the way he silently conducted himself at the thaal. A young girl, no older than eight or nine, stretched out her right hand, palm turned upwards. In the palms of her hand, she held out a beautiful miniature crystal bowl containing salt. Motapappasan placed his index finger into the salt and tasted it. All his grandchildren followed suit. We never start a meal without first tasting salt and giving praise to Allah, Tusneem explained later. Neither did anyone delve into any of the different courses that the servants kept bringing, before Motapappasan tasted it first. As for the delicious, freshly baked rotlees that the servants brought in every fifteen minutes, Motapappasan simply placed the platter of rotlees under the thaal. He handed out rotlees to each grand-child as and when he or she needed one. No one asked him for one, though. No one had told them not to ask. Over the years, the children had simply picked up what constituted good thaal etiquette. The children seemed so sure that Motapappasan always watched out for them. How wonderful it must be to have a grandfather like him, Komli thought. She wished she could have him alone for a few hours each weekend, just for companionship, and perhaps to unravel some of the mysteries of life. She wished all children could experience the comforting silence of Motapappasan. She felt sure that if she had him for a grandfather, or just for companionship, she would probably never feel insecure. They had not exchanged a single word, and yet he had touched her deeply.

Komli parted company that evening with a newfound appreciation for Tusneem. She realized that it was not monetary wealth that had worked its magic on Tusneem; it was the grace and nobility that ran in the veins of her family for no one knew how many generations. For a few brief moments, Komli was also struck afresh by a newfound sense of her own poverty—without grandparents, aunts, uncles or cousins, she felt as though she had been raised in a desert where her only oasis was a sister. Fortunately, she had little time for self-pity since she had a couple of papers to write.

But first Komli decided to write a quick letter to her sister.

Dear Roshni,

I really enjoyed your last letter from the Johnsons. I love college. Not having Tara knocking on my door is an added bonus! I have to be careful though. I've made friends with a sweet Muslim girl called Tusneem and sometimes I find myself jabbing at her like Tara used to jab at us! I take that back. I don't think I could ever be as mean as Tara. She invited me over to her aunt's house to celebrate Bakri Eid. Was a gut-wrenching eye opener that I'll describe personally when I see you next. Here's a question for you to ponder in the meantime—some don't eat pig; some don't eat cow; some only eat fish on Fridays, some don't eat on Tuesdays, some don't eat on Wednesdays, some eat Kosher, some eat halaal, some don't eat after dark, all in order to get their ticket for heaven! Irony is, kingdom of heaven is reserved for the poor and the meek. When the hell do the poor and the meek have a choice of food or any idea what day of the week it is?!! I'd love to go around the world to see if the rest of mankind is as crazy as we are in India.

Have to confess, the meat was the best I've ever had. It was cooked on special stones that get naturally treated in the scorching heat of the desert of Saudi Arabia.

By the way, I think I came across a person like the cripple in the Wish Fulfilling Tree, except he wasn't a little boy and he wasn't a cripple. He was Tusneem's grandfather. He seemed so content. I wish I could chat with him to find out how he got to that stage. I've already got the opposite of my wish—he didn't say a word!

Write soon. With all my love,

Komli.

It was during a World History class that Mustapha became more interested in Komli. The professor had started his lecture by pronouncing that the driving force behind all historical events was man's fundamental need for food, clothing, shelter, and spirituality. Komli had argued with him, quite convincingly at first, that food was the only fundamental need of man; that Calcutta's homeless would survive without clothes; that if the homeless wandered around with some semblance of clothing it was only because the conscience of the rich could not stomach stark truths about starved skeletons; that it was easier for the rich to part with a few pennies and unwanted clothing so they could carry on with the more important matters of adorning their bank accounts and their castles and cathedrals.

"We're discussing history, not the poor," the professor had remarked at one stage.

"They don't often go together, do they?" Komli had asked, a shade too sarcastically.

"Actually they do. You need to catch up on your reading. Many revolutions have been ignited by the poor." He had stared at her for a second, to gauge her soul it seemed, before adding, "They are also poor who are starved of other fundamental needs besides food!

Komli had backed off. The professor had been right.

Mustapha began to look forward to history classes. His cousin's strange friend had some strange notions, but at least they added a spark to history lectures. Sometimes, she raised questions that he himself had wondered about but had chosen to figure out by himself.

Tusneem was delighted when Mustapha asked one day if she would mind if he joined her when she was with Komli. Everyone in the family loved gentle Mustapha, even though he was not the easiest person to understand. He was an amiable young man of few words. For companionship, he preferred the silence of a book to the chatter of people. About the only person whose prattle Mustapha tolerated, and even enjoyed from time to time, was that of his loving mother, Sakina. If it wasn't for her, there was a good possibility that he would have steered clear of customs and social obligations and climbed the lonesome path of a hermit camping out on the Himalayan ranges.

In time, Mustapha was simply bowled over by Komli. In his eyes, she was the tomboy under whom lurked a woman who was sensitive to all creatures great and small, regardless of caste or class. He began to enjoy her prattle a little more than his mother's. Like his mother, it seemed that she, too, had the courage to say what she thought. The difference was that Komli rarely passed judgment and, better still, never expected anything from anyone. And what Mustapha found most refreshing was Komli's bottomless appetite for learning.

The two found themselves whiling away hours by the banks of the river Hooghly. While Komli did not have to hide her secret rendezvous from anyone, Mustapha was fortunate that he had Tusneem for alibi. It was Tusneem who first started thinking how wonderful it would be if Komli could become a cousin-in-law. Times were changing, slowly but surely; she had heard of a few Bohras who had married outside the community.

"Komli," Mustapha asked one day, "what do you see in that spoiled cousin of mine? You two are so different!"

"Opposites attract, they say. And, by the way, she's not as spoiled as you think. We talk to each other for hours sometimes."

"About what? All she thinks of is clothes and makeup, doesn't she?"

"That's all you men think women are capable of thinking about. We make all kinds of serious plans about how one day we'll knead men's bodies, same way as we're trained to knead dough. We'll pat you and smack you and roll you, and after you're flattened and fried, we'll toss you on the plate of marriage and devour you!" Pleased with her analogy, she bared her teeth at Mustapha who felt the ripples of some truth course through his being. His mother could certainly knead his father any which way she pleased. Ironically, as though he needed to be kneaded, it was at this point that he popped the question he wanted to ask, but dreaded, knowing what battle lay in store for him.

"Will you marry me, Komli? Mustapha asked while they sat under the shade of the sprawling Banyan tree that had witnessed thousands of young lovers meeting secretly under its protective canopy.

"What are you saying, Mustapha?! I had a glimpse of your family at Bakri Eid, and I learn things from Tusneem all the time. You come from a family of noble, wonderful people. I may not agree with everything they do or believe in, but you should know better what marrying a Hindu would do to your family!"

"But you have to say yes first, before I can ask them, Komli. Will you marry me?"

"You ask your parents first. I'm not even going to think about it yet."

"Why not?"

"I would never hurt my family, especially since I have no one but my sister. If the love she showers me with is any reflection of what your parents give you, how can you hurt them, Mustapha?"

"And how do you think your sister will react?"

"My sister has so much faith in me, Mustapha, that even if I brought a rogue into the house and assured her that he was a gem, she would welcome him with open arms. I'm afraid when I visit your house, I'll be looked down upon as an unclean Hindu, won't I?" Sensing his discomfort at the stark truth she had nailed, she squeezed his hand gently and commanded, with a twinge of sadness, "Smile! Your parents are paying for you to go to college to get a real education. We should at least be able to laugh at their ways, even if we don't always understand them. I'll be able to handle your parents if by some miracle they do want to talk to me. I'm not expecting anything from them. It's when you expect something that you have to worry."

"So you're already saying that you don't expect anything, which means that you're not really considering my proposal."

"You're right, Mustapha, I'm not. Trouble with you is that you think too much. I'll start thinking seriously after you've spoken to your parents. Want to know why I think Him-up-there chose women to bear children?"

"Why?" Mustapha asked quietly, knowing her well enough by now to expect some shade of truth in her jokes.

"Because we're more mature and we can handle pain better than you men can," she said smugly. "Want to know why He created man before woman?"

"Not really, but I'm sure you'll tell me anyway!"

"Because you have to prepare the garden for us. Work and work and work. In fact, now I really understand what you were trying to tell me the other day about Voltaire and working in the garden. I think Him-up-there wants you to go out to work so we can deal with the more important task of raising children!"

"Komli, why are you joking when I am dead serious? I love you. I want to marry you."

"Joking just relieves the tension, Mustapha. You know that I love you dearly. I couldn't think of a better man to spend the rest of my life with. But now that I can have you all to myself, I'm scared you'll be taken away. I had nothing to fear when you had nothing to give me. Do you understand?"

Mustapha suddenly saw the vulnerable side to Komli. It gave him the courage to take her in his arms and reassure her. "I will not let any human being take you away from me, I promise."

Komli held Mustapha tightly, wondering if she was ready for a world outside of her sister and college.

"What are you thinking, Komli? You're too quiet."

"You know so little about me, Mustapha . . ."

"I've always wanted to know more about the Durga Puja festival. Want to take me to the pandals (tents) and tell me more about your beliefs, and your gods?"

"Durga Puja is my favorite time of the year! Ten wonderful days of drums and songs!" Komli exclaimed, eyes lighting up. "You really want to go?"

"My mother won't exactly be thrilled. I'll be honest with you, most Muslims find the ten days quite a nuisance! Every lane, every alleyway has music blaring all day. And since there are pandals of gods and goddesses in every street and alleyway it is almost impossible even for those who want to have nothing to do with them to avoid seeing them. And since we've never really bothered to understand your beliefs, we end up ridiculing your gods with ten hands, elephant-head, and red tongue sticking out . . ."

"What do you say about them?"

"How can one criticize clay gods? It's their creators whom we criticize as idol worshippers!"

"Idols they may be, but if you could hear some of the wonderful stories Ma used to tell me you would love our gods and goddesses."

"I don't know about that! All I know is that I love you and I want to understand you better."

"Let's head towards some of that blaring music. Let's see what the gods reveal about me." Komli said with a grin.

"That's one of the reasons why I love you so much, Komli. You can laugh even as I am insulting your religion!"

"You weren't insulting my Gods; you were just airing your ignorance. I don't think you'll say nasty things about them once you understand their wonderful significance. If you do, then watch out! I have quite a temper, you know."

"I can hear the conch shells," Mustapha said as they approached one of the pandals. "It's such a mysterious, haunting sound, like it's coming from some far away place."

"There you go, you already dig it and you don't even know it! Ma used to say that embedded in the music of the conch shell is the music and mystery of the cosmos, given to us by Bhagvaan himself. She also used to say that music is one way we can reach our Gods. Agree?"

"Hmm . . . I thought that applied to human beings."

"Don't you sing in your mosques?"

"Sometimes. We call them Marasiahs."

"Marasiahs, bhajans, hymns—different names, same sentiments. See that goddess in the shimmering sari and beautiful jewelry? That's goddess Durga."

"Why is she riding on a tiger?"

Durga has the power to subdue the proud, angry tiger's ego and do you see the different weapons in her different hands? That's to fight evils like hate and anger and greed and jealousy and envy and pride and passion. Durga is supposed to answer all our prayers."

"So what do you ask of her?"

"I usually pray to Saraswati, and to Ganesh, the goddess of learning, and the remover of obstacles. Look, there's Kali Ma! My heart always skips a beat when I see her ferocious black face and that fiery red tongue sticking out!"

"Why does she look so angry? And why does she have a garland of skulls around her?" Mustapha whispered.

"Kali Ma is actually Durga when she's angry. The garland of skulls is to reminds us that sooner or later we all die."

"Why is she so black and scary?"

"The black's our future. No one knows what it will bring. But we must pray at all times so our future is brighter than our present. Want to try?"

Mustapha was glad Komli seemed distracted and distant suddenly. He could not bring himself to pray to Kali Ma.

"Komli had suddenly been transported to her childhood days when she used to love listening to Ma's stories of love and abduction, of valor and courage and sacrifice, of right and wrong; stories that had transported her to far away green pastures. They had been stories that had nourished her soul and put her to sleep. And they had been times for Ma to rest a little, knowing that during those sacred times of oblivion, hunger pangs would not assail her little daughter. There was another reason why Komli ached for her mother—she would have liked to take her permission to marry Mustapha.

"Why are the gods drowned in the river Hooghly at the end of Durga Puja?"

"From mud to water, from one life force to another, I guess. I'm not sure. I used to long to get on those trucks when I was a child, but Ma never let me," Komli replied, a shade quieter.

"Could you blame her? With all those frenzied people jostling and dancing, you would have been crushed to death!"

"It's getting late, Mustapha. I need to get back to my dorm to study."

"Are you hungry?"

"A little. But I really must get back."

"I had no idea it was so late! I need to get home, too. My parents are sure to ask me where I've been. You're lucky you have no one to answer to."

"So do you understand me a little better, now that you've had a glimpse of my gods?" Komli asked, wondering suddenly if people like Mustapha could ever relate to her many hunger pangs.

It was unbeknown to Tara, although she sensed it occasionally, that Devi had successfully battled through the many obstacles of an arranged marriage and penetrated her husband's heart. Having done so, she was now able to manipulate her man. And so, every Wednesday, Devi waited with more enthusiasm than usual, for her husband to come home. More often than not, he came home on Wednesdays with a letter for her from Roshni. A secret that was well hidden from Tara since she firmly believed that reading and writing was only for men.

Devi always allowed her husband to use the letters as his weapon; on Wednesdays, Devi never refused to make love to him. In turn, he rarely let her have Roshni's letter until she had satisfied his animal needs. This was just as well, because it was when the entire household was fast asleep, Tara, her husband, and her two children, that Devi indulged in the precious letters that brought back Roshni to her in the quiet of the night. With great anticipation, she quietly ripped the envelope, like a seamstress carefully ripping a hemline. Devi could never be absolutely certain how long or when Tara eavesdropped on them.

It was unbeknown to Devi that Tara rarely eavesdropped on them now that their household had been blessed with a son.

Oh what a joyous occasion that had been for Mohan and Tara. Devi, too, was overjoyed with her new-born son, although it saddened her to see the glaring difference between the way her two children had been received. After twenty hours of agonizing labor, Devi had been thrilled beyond measure when the doctor had laid Amrita in her arms. She was too exhausted at the time to notice that her husband's reaction had been somewhat tempered. It was only after she saw her husband leap with joy and cradle their newborn son in his arms, as though the babe was Lord Krishna himself, that Devi felt a twinge of anger. It was one thing that her old-fashioned mother-in-law had old-fashioned ideas about girls being a liability; but for her relatively modern husband to treat their children like one was gold and the other plain aluminum was a hard cross to bear during those sensitive times when a mother needs to be calm and relaxed for her mammary glands to flow.

And to compound matters, as soon as she had returned home from the hospital, the Hijras had come knocking on their door, asking for a huge sum of money since the household had now been blessed with a son, named Shakti. Hijras were born eunuchs who made a living by going from household to household during auspicious occasions. She had seen them many a times on the streets—a proud group of skinny human beings dressed in saris, but with manly faces and flat chests, singing and strumming at their instruments without any hint of shame or embarrassment that they were neither men nor women. Out of superstition and fear, it became customary to placate the Hijras and to obtain their blessings rather than incur their wrath. The Hijras had actually inspected her son. Mohan had explained to Devi that had her son been born a eunuch, the Hijras would have taken him away. But since he was born whole and healthy, the Hijras were content to receive a sum of money in exchange for their priceless blessings.

Hai Bhagvaan, help me to understand human beings, was Devi's quiet response to all the money that she saw being given away to the Hijras at a time when they had so many other expenses to think about. And as though Bhagvaan had answered her prayer, indirectly, Roshni visited her soon after she had given birth. Like a bottomless vessel that has the capacity to receive an ocean-full of tidings, Roshni listened and laughed and was able to make Devi laugh, too.

"Do you think your mother-in-law plays with Shakti's marbles?" Roshni asked facetiously when she heard how Tara doted on him.

"Roshni! How could you! I can see Komli saying something like that, not you!"

"Poor Komli, she has the guts to speak her mind and people think she's wild. And you and me, we're quiet, and docile, we ask little, and people like Tara Bahen treat us like flowers without fragrance, and sons like roses without thorns!"

"Those male roses carry the family name, and their special perfume, don't forget," Devi said sniffing the air with a rare burst of sinful expressions.

"Now you sound like Komli!" Roshni responded as she doubled up with laughter. "She visited me recently, and when I showed her the fabric softner the Johnsons use to make their clothes smell beautiful, she just shrugged her shoulders and said 'who needs artificial scents when each one of us has our own scent.'

"How is Komli? Is she happy?"

"Oh yes! That girl loves life, although I sense some anger under some of her jokes. Oh I must share this with you, before I forget. Komli insisted on reading an essay to me by this famous English writer called Jonathan Swift. She said every rich Indian should read it."

"We're not rich."

"I know. But it's so shocking and kind of funny that someone could even think such thoughts that I have to tell you about it. Everyone in college has to read it, she told me."

"Go ahead, shock me some more."

"It's called a *Modest Proposal*. The writer was angry because he saw that people allowed their children to starve on the streets so he proposed in his essay that poor people should cook their children and sell them."

"Really!"

"That way children wouldn't suffer for years and years, only a few minutes in the cooker, and that way poor people, who have more children any way, would make money, money, money, selling them!"

"Ugh! You pay for her to study that?"

"It's supposed to be deep. Profound was the word Komli used. She was quite taken up by it. She asked me to try and imagine what would happen if our beggars were allowed to start making money off their children."

"Everybody would be making babies at night; no one would go around robbing homes and no one would starve! World's problem solved, right?" Devi asked sarcastically.

"Swift also said that the children's meat would taste better than other animals' meats."

"Is this Swift guy a writer or a cannibal?"

"Who knows. I was as shocked as you are, Devi. Komli said it's supposed to make rich people re-read, and think, so they help the poor, although she added with the same breath that the trouble is the only thing rich people read is their currency notes!"

"You know what, I'm glad I'm not that rich that I have to read such stuff, and I'm glad I'm not that poor I have to cook my children. I wonder if male babies would taste better than female babies."

"Don't even go there, Devi. I might say something so crude that you won't want to have anything to do with me!"

"That will never, ever happen, you know that. Want some advice?"

"Don't tell me I need to have children . . ."

"That would be wonderful, but I know how you feel about men! What I was going to say, though, was that perhaps you should look for marriage proposals for Komli."

"It's been through my mind. I'm waiting for her to finish college."

"Do you think she sees boys?"

"The only one she's mentioned casually is a guy called Mustapha. I think she likes him because he writes poetry. I know she doesn't tell me everything."

Tara knocked on the door just then, to say that Shakti was hungry.

"I'll be there in a minute, Ma. Let me say bye to Roshni."

"She really has mellowed hasn't she!"

"I'm mellowing, too, just from being able to talk to you. Come back soon, Roshni, I miss you."

Mustapha had grown up to be very much like his father, Kasim, who was extremely quiet, although Mustapha never found out whether his father was quiet from birth or had opted for silence after marrying his mother. It seemed that Sakina shut her mouth only when sleep immobilized her. Mustapha and his younger brothers had long learned to tune out of her endless barrage of do's and don'ts, knowing that under her huge frame lurked a warm, well-meaning mother who loved to laugh and joke with her husband and four sons. Few people saw the mischievous smile that transformed her overbearing personality to that of a harmless child. Sons and husband often laughed at mother, for they knew a good heart ignited the fire that always seemed to rage within her. All the men in her family understood that she could handle most matters with an earthy practicality that other women lacked. Having grown up in a family that usually ate together, prayed together, picnicked together and had many a laugh and argument together, Mustapha knew that an opportunity to talk about Komli would present itself sooner or later.

It was at a peaceful, Sunday picnic when his younger brothers were playing ball, and Sakina was crocheting that Mustapha broached the subject, indirectly at first.

"There's a Bohra guy in college who's going out with a Hindu girl. They seem to be serious about each other. What are their chances of getting married?" Mustapha asked as casually as he could.

"What's his name?" Sakina snapped immediately, ignoring Mustapha's question. If she knew his parents, and she knew most parents, she would help them avert the calamity, she thought quickly.

"I don't know him. Someone else told me about him."

"Find out and let me know."

"So what would happen if they decided to get married?"

"You find out about him before matters get out of hand, Mustapha. I'll help his family."

"Mamma, you've yet to answer my question, what would happen if . . . ."

"Mustapha, there's no point in discussing something I've never dealt with. I don't know any Bohras who've married Hindus. Christians, yes, but Hindus, never! By the way, since we are on the subject of marriage, how do you feel about marrying Tusneem? Marrying first cousins is considered to be a very good alliance. I know Zenub and Rashid would be delighted, but one never knows with you youngsters any more!"

"Then how come you and Pappa aren't first cousins?" Mustapha asked with all the calm he could muster. He wasn't really interested in the answer. He was just searching for a way to stop his mother's speeding engine. If not, he knew she would just blast her loud horn and carry on, expecting everyone to move out of her way.

"Pappa's father and my father were the first two Sheikhs (coveted title Bawasahib bestows on devout Bohras) in Calcutta. We didn't even see each other until we were married, but we never questioned our parents' decision."

"Pappa, did she really marry you without saying a single word?" Mustapha asked, hoping a joke would side-track the topic of conversation.

Kasim smiled to himself as he thought nostalgically of their first night. Strangely enough, he had been quite enamored by her forthrightness. That first night he was convinced that her jabbering was just a defense mechanism to ward off the consummation of their marriage. She was a mature eighteen and he a less mature twenty-one. He was in no hurry for the entrée himself. If the first course of their marriage was to be appetizing prattle, so be it, he had decided. It was only weeks later, when a spark had been kindled between husband and wife that they had finally consummated their marriage.

"You're just like your mother, Mustapha. You believe in miracles! She started jabbering the moment she set eyes on me! Our world will come to an end the day your mother refuses to say a single word!" Kasim was smiling. He was in no hurry to push his sensitive Mustapha into talk about marriage. He knew in his heart that there was a poet in Mustapha; that, like him, Mustapha also didn't quite agree with the ways of society and the world at large. But he knew that if he had learned to love Sakina and to quietly cope with the unnecessary spices that she needed in order to stew life to a tasty meal, that his mature Mustapha would also somehow find a way to cope with the women in his life.

"Yeah! We'd never have had children if I didn't do all the talking!" Sakina retorted as Kasim let out one of his rare, loud guffaws.

"Told you she believes in miracles!" Kasim said, looking at his somewhat embarrassed son.

"I think I'll go and play ball for a while," Mustapha said, attempting to walk away.

"Don't try to escape me, Mustapha. Tell me, what do you think about marrying Tusneem?"

"Mamma, that's impossible! I see Tusneem almost every day of my life. She's like a sister to me!"

"I would think that that would make it easier for you to fall in love with each other, rather than marry an absolute stranger. At least you won't have to go through what those idol-worshipping Hindus go through—marry a stranger just because of the dowry she brings!" Sakina argued.

"Hindus don't worship idols, Mamma! They just choose to make clay images of their gods, just as Christians do of Jesus and their prophets. And you're the one who says Jews, Christians and Muslims are like different tributaries branching out from one river."

"But not Hindus. We have nothing to do with their so-called Holy Ganga (river Ganges). That river will never join ours."

"You know nothing about Hindus, Mamma!" Mustapha said, raising his voice sharply. I've done some reading about their pantheon of gods. They have wonderful, human attributes."

"See, Kasim, does this prove to you at last that too much reading is bad for you? Our educated son seems to have fallen in love with idols. Mustapha, there is only one god, Allah, and he is not like us humans, thank heavens!"

Mustapha stared out at the grass, thinking lovingly of his impish Komli. The thought of Komli and his mother arguing over religion scared him. He could see his mother getting furious while Komli would probably walk away wisely, with that smile he had grown to love so much. Like his mother, Komli also used milk and cream as a metaphor for mankind. Homogenized milk, she had claimed, was digestible; it's when the cream is allowed to settle on the top that one can have indigestion.

Suddenly Mustapha got into a more belligerent mood. He decided to change tactics. "So what would you say, Mamma, if I came up to you and said I was in love with a Hindu girl?" he asked, a little too calmly.

"You wouldn't dare, Mustapha!"

"Supposing I did dare. Pretend, Mamma. How would you react?"

"For once in your life you would see me dumbstruck."

"Meaning you would quietly let me marry her?"

"No! I would quietly wring your neck!" Sakina replied in jest.

Mustapha decided suddenly that this was the moment of reckoning. If he was to be slaughtered, he might as well get it over with since he was already bleating.

"Mamma, I'm serious. That Bohra boy I mentioned earlier is actually me. There is a Hindu girl I've fallen in love with."

"You don't know what you're saying, Mustapha!" Sakina said fearfully, because it suddenly dawned on her that her son was dead serious. "As far as I'm concerned, you've just given us a very good reason to make marriage plans for you. We won't force you to marry Tusneem, but you need to think seriously about settling down with a Bohra girl. There are hundreds of girls in our community who would give an arm and a leg to marry you. Go call your brothers. Let's leave."

"That's one of the special things about this girl I love. She couldn't give me an arm to marry me even if she wanted to! Her beauty is in her soul and she cares little about the money we have! She already warned me that she stood no chance with our bigoted way of thinking!" Mustapha dared, unable to control his emotions.

Kasim's heart skipped a beat. He had noticed how intently his son had watched Komli play cricket that Bakri Eid. Later he had helped her fly a kite. Was that the girl, he wondered.

"Don't you ever dare use the word *bigoted* again, Mustapha. For years and years and years Pappa and I have been for sabak (religious lessons). Just because you're too busy delving into everything outside of Islam and don't bother to go for sabak, does not make us bigoted!"

"I used that word because you referred to Hindus in such a derogatory manner. I don't think any one has the right to ridicule another's gods."

"Gods! Monstrous clay Gods that they dump in the Hooghly each year for what reason they alone know!" Sakina screamed.

Exactly, Mamma. They alone know, and they have faith in their Gods, just as you alone know certain things about Islam and have faith in Allah. Water is a great purifying agent. Maybe their gods go for ablution. We go through ablution every time we pray, day in and day out."

"The subject is closed. Let's go home"

"Mamma, I am not renouncing Islam. I just don't believe that we are the only ones destined for heaven and that all Hindus are heathens. Will you at least meet Komli?"

"Komli? Isn't that the girl Tusneem brought over for Bakri Eid?" Are you telling me you like her?" Sakina asked in a tone of disbelief.

"No, Mamma, I don't like her; I love her. Will you please agree to meet her at least?"

"Why? You cannot marry her, Mustapha."

"Not even if she converts to Islam?"

"Kasim," Sakina implored, betraying the first signs of helplessness, "don't you have anything to say? Explain to your son that it's not just a question of Hindus and Muslims, but our reputation as well. Our fathers are Sheikhs. How will we face our community?"

"Let's go home, think about it calmly and discuss it again, shall we? Kasim said with more calm than he felt. There was a part of him that empathized with his son. However, he also knew that as a parent he was helpless; he could provide no outlet from the circle of family, communal and religious ties that had bound them together for generations. There were times when Kasim wondered about man-made laws, especially those made by the Bhaisahibs with whom he had to deal from time to time. Inner tranquility meant more to Kasim than he cared to talk about. Rather than get into senseless arguments with priests who, as far as Kasim was concerned, often took liberties as self-appointed agents of Allah, he was content to give a few hours of his time to community service, and then come back home to his family and to his books. Sakina never knew what he read, which was just as well, because he had delved into the holy books of many different faiths, only to discover, like his son, that in essence all religions simply expected its followers to be human, not super-human. He was convinced more than ever before, what a captive was this creature called man who had no control over his birth or his death. In the interim, however, the reigns were yanked quite tightly by parents and teachers and preachers. His inner tranquility had been shattered suddenly. The prospect of having to preside over a war between mother and son was the last thing he wanted, especially when he knew in his heart of hearts that his son made more sense than his wife. It was definitely the worst crisis in their lives.

Sakina had no patience for Kasim's silence. She had worked herself into such a frenzy that, within five minutes of reaching home, she announced, "I'm going to phone Zenub and Rashid. I cannot think clearly, and you won't talk. Maybe discussing this with my sister will help."

Rashid breathed a quiet sigh of relief when he heard about the crisis. He had known in his heart of hearts that it was just a question of time before Sakina would suggest that Mustapha and Tusneem get married. But he knew his Tusneem would never consent to marrying someone for whom she felt nothing but brotherly love. He was relieved that he would not have to live with the pressure of having to fight Sakina, had Mustapha consented to marry Tusneem. Still waters run deep, he thought; quiet Mustapha goes out and falls in love with a Hindu!

"So how did you react?" Rashid asked, politely addressing the question to both Kasim and Sakina, knowing full well that Sakina would do all the talking.

"How do you think we reacted?! A Hindu!! In our family?!!! How can we even think about it! We're just going to have to deal with Mustapha himself. Zenub, do you have any suggestions?"

"I can't think right now. This is quite shocking."

"You won't like this, Sakina," Rashid said quietly, "but my suggestion is that you do not openly oppose Mustapha. We . . . ."

"What do you mean do not oppose him? Let him marry that Hindu?!"

"No. I didn't say that. We need time, to think, to talk to him, and to hope that maybe it's just infatuation, and that he'll get over it in time. If you oppose children these days, they tug harder in the opposite direction. It's the price we have to pay for sending them to school. They feel liberated, and they can think for themselves. We have to let him think we're thinking too." Rashid paused for a few seconds, and then added, "Maybe there is a solution! Isn't Bawasahib coming to Calcutta next month?"

"I refuse to even mention something so degrading to Bawasahib. He holds our families in such high regard!"

Zenub agreed with her husband. "Think about it, Sakina. If you tell Mustapha you are prepared to let Bawasahib make the decision, he will believe that you as parents did not oppose him, and we get a whole month to hope he'll fall out of love. Where did he meet her?"

"In this house, when you were away for Haj. They go to the same college."

"I agree with Rashid," Kasim said to his wife. "Every important matter in our lives is taken to Bawasahib. We never undertake anything major without his blessing. Let's talk to Mustapha again when both of you have calmed down."

"Let's have some tea and play Rummy," Rashid suggested, hoping to alleviate the tension.

"How can you think of cards at such a time?!" Sakina asked.

"I never thought I'd hear you refuse Rummy!"

"Tea is the only thing I can handle right now," Sakina confessed, as she called out to the servant.

Mustapha seemed somewhat contained when he heard that his parents were at least prepared to place the matter in the hands of Bawasahib. He had been no older than five when his mother had explained to him lovingly that Bawa meant father and that Bawasahib was the father of all Bohras; that he was so fortunate that he had two fathers, one that lived with him and one that he could visit from time to time. Through many conversations he had overheard and through many examples set before his very eyes, Mustapha had realized over the years that his parents had such implicit faith in Bawasahib that no travel, no major business undertakings, engagements or marriages had taken place in his family without first seeking Bawasahib's permission or blessing, the two being synonymous. Even with a major medical condition that the doctors had said required an operation, it was Bawasahib's blessing that had ultimately convinced his mother that to be operated upon would be alright. *You must have faith in Bawasahib, we never question him* were words he had heard again and again over the years.

Having been educated in a convent with non-Bohras, and having been exposed to college students from all over India, little seeds of doubt about implicit faith had sprouted in Mustapha's mind. It was difficult for him to understand how grownups could leave all decisions in the hands of Bawasahib; how they could magically transform themselves to little children who could go nowhere, who could undertake no project without first asking Bawasahib.

The roots of Sakina's faith went back several generations. Her father and her father's father had served Bawasahib and the Bohra community all their lives. For the selfless services rendered, Bawasahib had bestowed the much coveted title of *Sheikh* upon both her father and grandfather. It was an honor that was extremely rare to come by those days, for it was bestowed on the elderly only after they had performed years of community service and had proven to be extremely devout Muslims as well. As a result, Sakina and her family had been treated like royalty ever since she could remember.

In the eyes of the younger generation, things had changed a lot in the last few decades. It was rumored that the title of Sheikh was now bestowed upon the wealthy because of the huge salaam it brought in. Sheikhs had sprouted everywhere, young and old. Mustapha had an uncle, his father's brother, whom he had loved dearly. He had died when he was seventy years old, and, as far as Mustapha could remember, he was a devout Muslim who had served his community all his life. "Pappa," Mustapha had asked one day soon after his uncle had died, "Is it true that uncle Shabbir never got the title of Sheikh because he had no money? That's what some folks say anyway."

"I don't know, Mustapha," his father had replied. To admit to Mustapha that perhaps some of Bawasahib's priests had become corrupt might be construed as pointing a finger at Bawasahib. Kasim could never do that. He had too high a regard for Bawasahib. Besides, he did not want to unnecessarily incur the wrath of his well-meaning wife. A non-committal, *I don't know*, seemed to be the easiest way out.

"I loved uncle Shabbir. He was so humble and devoted to our community. I watched him take the pennies he had made from the sale of old newspapers and put them lovingly in a jar. He said he was saving the money so he could have his turban polished for Bawasahib's next visit to Calcutta."

Kasim looked lovingly at his sensitive son who had brought back fond memories of his older brother. "You know, Mustapha, your uncle Shabbir always struggled for money. His saving grace was not just his humility, but also his wonderful sense of humor. Here's a secret. I, too, believe that he should have received the title of Sheikh."

Mustapha decided to take the question to his more outspoken mother.

"We never question Bawasahib. You should know better than to ask such questions, Mustapha!" had been his mother's response.

"I am not questioning Bawasahib, Mamma. I am questioning his priests. It is they who recommend who becomes a Sheikh and who doesn't. There are thousands of Bohras all over the world, Mamma. There's no way Bawasahib can keep track of who is worthy of the title and who isn't!"

"And since when have you been able to keep track of what goes on in Bawasahib's household?" Sakina had asked angrily. "Mustapha, we never ever question Bawasahib. How many times must I tell you that?"

"I am not pointing a finger at Bawasahib, Mamma. People are talking about corruption among his priests. It goes on all over the world, not just with us Bohras. Money is a means of control. That is what our priests are trying to do to us, control us."

"Mustapha, I don't want to hear talk like that, ever."

"Are you telling me, Mamma, that you are turning a deaf ear to corruption or that our community is immune from corruption?"

"I am telling you that I will never, ever question Bawasahib. Is that understood?"

Whereas most women demurely paid their respects to Bawasahib and retreated quietly after they were blessed, Sakina always found the courage to talk to Bawasahib. And Bawasahib always accorded her the privilege to chat and to use him as a sounding board for the most trivial matters. The father in Bawasahib understood that the child in Sakina had never grown up, insofar as her faith in him was concerned. He knew and understood that even though she dominated her community and family with a firm hand, in his presence she was but a child yearning for his blessings and guidance. Mustapha himself knew that Bawasahib devoted most of his time to his community and to prayers. He exuded nothing but learning and purity. Mustapha himself had a deep regard for Bawasahib's spirituality. But he was not so sure about the integrity of the people who surrounded Bawasahib. He had heard too many rumors about their high-handed ways with the humble and the meek.

Mustapha reacted with mixed feelings when he was told by his parents that they were willing to place the matter of his life's first and only love in the hands of Bawasahib. What would he do if Bawasahib refused to bless the marriage? He could argue with his parents until he turned blue; he could never do that in front of Bawasahib. Although he was not consciously aware of all his feelings for Bawasahib, love had slowly crept into his reverence and regard for their community's spiritual father.

During the breathing time Mustapha and his family had before Bawasahib's arrival, life for devout Bohras in Calcutta became extremely hectic. Elaborate preparations had to be made to host Bawasahib and his family who would be staying in Calcutta for three entire weeks. Homes were painted and patched and sparkled to a shine. Bawasahib would be able to bless the homes of many families during this long stay. It was rumored that the fortunate were not chosen by lottery, but by priests who had their ways of finding out who could afford what salaam. And since money was no obstacle for Sakina, she knew her house would be blessed by Bawasahib's presence. If it took her entire family a whole month to prepare for the occasion, it would be the happiest month of the year for sure.

Roshni's diary entry when she heard about Mustapha was brief :

Ma,

Of all the fish in the ocean, Komli goes and hooks a Muslim guy.
They want to get married. I haven't met him yet. Please guide me.

Komli seems to have clean forgotten that I am just her sister. She says that as long as I approve, she will marry Mustapha. She said she is so lucky that I am her mother, best friend, sister and priest all rolled into one. I don't have the wisdom to play all these roles. I just want her to be happy. Will she be happy marrying outside her religion? Please send me a sign.

"Oh Komli, I'm so excited," Tusneem squealed as she hugged Komli when they met in college.

"Pappa and Mamma came home from aunt Sakina's last evening and asked me all sorts of questions about you."

"And no doubt you told them the earth would shake under their feet when they behold my beauty, my brains, my boobs and my sexy buttocks!"

"No, I asked them which life they were referring to since you Hindus keep coming back from previous lives!"

"You didn't?!"

"You should have seen the look on Pappa's face. He tried to hide his smile but couldn't. He had me scared for a while though 'cause he said it was time for me to consider getting married to Mustapha. It was only when he had me almost reduced to tears that he admitted that he was kidding."

"Are you supposed to marry Mustapha? Why were you reduced to tears?" Komli asked nervously.

"You can be so dumb sometimes! My aunt Sakina was hoping Mustapha and I would marry each other. Marrying cousins is considered to be the best."

"Why didn't you tell me?!"

"Tell you what? There's nothing to tell. Mustapha and I do not love each other that way. I have a suspicion Pappa was just checking to make sure I wasn't in love with him myself!"

"So what did you tell them?"

"That I wish you had a brother so I, too, could have a love marriage with a wonderful Hindu!"

"You're a twit, Tusneem. Can you get serious for a second and tell me how they reacted, otherwise I'm going to class."

"Bye."

"Don't worry, my time will come when I'll tell you nothing!" Komli started stalking off to class when Tusneem shouted out, "Pappa said your chances of marrying him are pretty good."

"You mean I can bring Ganesh into your lives?"

"Nope! No animals. We consider all animals unclean, remember?"

"I think Ganesh is purer and happier than any human being I know," Komli retorted with a smile.

When they met again after the last class that afternoon, a somewhat disgruntled Komli complained to Tusneem, "The only day Roshni can come over to meet Mustapha is the following Monday. He tells me he can't meet her that day because that's one day in the year all Bohras have to go to the mosque. Are you telling me he can't take a couple of hours off to meet my sister?"

"I'm afraid so, Komli. Can your sister come another day?"

"I suppose so, depending on how flexible her employers are. I thought Mustapha was pretty easy going about religion. How come he *has* to go to the mosque that particular Monday?" He doesn't strike me as some religious fanatic!"

"He's not, Komli." You have to understand, the tenth of Mohorrem is the holiest of holiest days for us Bohras. We mourn the martyrdom of Maulana Husein, who was the grandson of prophet Mohammed himself. He died on the battlefields of Kerbala, fighting for the cause of Islam. Even less devout Muslims who don't attend all religious functions come to the mosque on the tenth of Mohorrem."

"So there's absolutely no way he can meet my sister that day?"

"No. That one day, he can't. I wish you could come with us to the mosque, just to get a glimpse of the tenth of Mohorrem. It would help you understand."

"Well, why can't I go with you?"

"You'll get mad, Komli, but only Muslims can go to the mosque. We'll go together next year, after you're married."

"I want to go this year, Tusneem. I want to see what I'm getting into. Will I be challenged, if I were to walk in?"

"If you don't wear the ridaa you will?"

"What's ridaa?"

"Something like what the nun's wear except ridaas don't have to be black and white."

"So all one can see is one's face and hands?"

"Yes."

"Perfect, Tusneem. Loan me one of your ridaas. You don't have to acknowledge me. I'll just come there on my own."

"I don't think so, Komli. It doesn't sound right."

"Stop being such a wimp, Tusneem. I'm going to marry your cousin."

"You know what? If I agree, you'll get to see Bawasahib," Tusneem said, as though she was trying to absolve her conscience.

"*The* Bawasahib?"

"There's only one Bawasahib, Komli! Yes, *the* Bawasahib from whom Mustapha has to obtain permission to marry you."

"All the more reason why I should go, Tusneem. Please say you'll loan me a ridaa. I promise not to embarrass you. I promise not to so much as say hello to you, please."

"You realize I could go to hell for this?"

"You'll never go to hell, even if you try. You're too good, just like my sister. So you're going to loan me a ridaa, yes?"

"Let me think about it. We still have a few days.

Dear Roshni,

If this letter sounds like I'm possessed, think of me being possessed by a good, pure spirit that invaded my being while I was playing I Spy on Mustapha and his people at their mosque.

I was a little piqued at Mustapha for saying that there was no way he could meet you today. I now understand why.

Today was the 10ᵗʰ of Mohorrem when Bohras mourn the martyrdom of the grandson of prophet Mohammed. The mosque was so crowded by eight in the morning that there was literally not an inch of space between people sitting beside each other, shoulder to shoulder, knee to knee, no exaggeration! The men sit on the ground floor and the women sit on a mezzanine floor with windows from which they can look down at all the men. I never saw one man look up to the women (pun not intended!). The exciting part about the morning was the arrival of Bawasahib. The entire community was in an uproar when he came in. I have to admit, Roshni, Bawasahib looked ethereal as he walked in, dressed in dazzling, white, gossamer-like clothes. If it wasn't for the wall of priests that protected Bawasahib, I am sure he would have got trampled on by his people. A thousand hands clamored that Bawasahib look at them, bless them with a glance at least. As soon as he was helped up on the raised platform he smiled at his people, including the women on the upper level. When he finally sat down, there was a hush; a wonderful sense of peace prevailed. It seemed that Bawasahib's presence itself had satisfied a spiritual hunger in their souls. When I finally spotted Mustapha, looking like a little dot sitting about twenty feet away from Bawasahib, I somehow understood the look of reverential awe he had on his face. There was something extremely sacrosanct about Bawasahib.

The adults listened intently to Bawasahib's sermon, but, judging from all the fidgeting among the children, it seemed that the younger ones were being lulled to sleep. Apparently, everyone fasts that day and has, therefore, been up from around four in the morning!

I bumped into Tusneem during the afternoon prayer break. She smelled like some mysterious incense. She did something beautiful to me then, more in jest I'm sure, but it really touched me deep down, Roshni. She took my right hand in hers, placed it on her forehead, brought it down to her lips and released it saying, Bowloo Chaaloo

Maaph. She said she had just asked me to forgive her if she had in any way hurt me for anything she had said or done to me. I had seen Dozens of Bohra women do that all morning. Tusneem explained that on this holiest of holiest days all Bohras make sure they have been forgiven by fellow Bohras. What a wonderfully humbling gesture—to ask fellow-man personally to forgive you and to forgive them their trespasses in turn. And do you know what, Roshni, I think they truly mean it. They seemed so imbued with the sanctity of the occasion that I think they find it in their hearts to forgive and be forgiven in turn. What could be healthier for one's soul than to get rid of the burden of harboring anger and guilt, and relieving others of any guilt they may have themselves? And as though that were not enough, Tusneem asked me to remember her in my prayers. Bohras ask their friends and family for two things on this holy day—forgiveness and remembrance in their prayers. I shall never forget it.

After the afternoon prayer, everyone seemed to be waiting impatiently for Bawasahib to return. What was really enthralling this time was the procession of specially chosen men that followed Bawasahib—men fervently singing a heart-rending marsiah (hymn) to the beat of which they did maatum (flagellate one's chest) with their right hand. Every single Bohra, man, woman, and child, joined in the maatum as Bawasahib walked in. There were no drums, no bells, no instruments; just the marsiah and a few thousand Bohras doing maatum in unison—thud, thud, thud! Some had tears coursing quietly down their cheeks, some wept, some children just looked around in bewilderment as to why the adults were crying so unashamedly, but one and all, including the little children, were doing maatum. The ocean of men somehow parted to allow Bawasahib to ascend his platform. When he stood on it and started doing maatum himself, the people went crazy. The mourning and the maatum got even louder. All my senses were inflamed. I was simply mesmerized.

After a few minutes, Bawasahib signaled to everyone to sit down. Everyone settled down to listen quietly to Bawasahib. Around four in the afternoon, things started to stir again. Bawasahib had started narrating how each member of Hussein's family was slain one by one on the battlefield of Kerbala. Each year they relive the tragedy that Hussein and his family faced. The last few seconds were unbelievable; so many things happened at the same time that it seemed like one big blur. Sobbing uncontrollably himself, Bawasahib had hardly finished uttering the last words about how Husein was finally slain at the neck, when hundreds of men around him leapt up with folded hands, clamoring to touch him, to catch his eyes, to ask him to remember them in his special prayer from the alcove to where he was carried on a sea of clamoring hands, it seemed. Everywhere I looked, men were doing maatum as hard as they could. Some in circular groups, some on their own. Some fainted, some actually bled around the chest, while some volunteers sprayed rose water on them to help them revive. Women everywhere were sobbing and shaking uncontrollably. Some women turned hysterical and did maatum as hard as the men downstairs while some stared at them aghast, knowing that women weren't supposed to beat themselves so hard there, where little babies are nursed.

Slowly but surely, every Bohra went down on his forehead—it was time for doa, the most important doa in the year I would assume, for surely you would think that Allah would answer everyone's prayers at this sanctified moment. I heard a thousand murmurs, wailing, wanting, beseeching. I felt like going down and praying myself. But I chose to watch instead. I could pretend to the world that I was a Bohra, but I could not pretend to their Allah, could I? It seemed wrong somehow. So I watched, feeling like the only impure person in the mosque. I am convinced that during that grief-stricken half hour of maatum and doa, all the different prayers of mankind were represented. Gone were the hunger pangs, gone was the fidgeting.

When people started to leave, they did not look exhausted at all. Rather, they looked like people who had been purified and cleansed; people who had unburdened themselves and were therefore returning home with lighter hearts. There was something euphoric that I will carry in my soul forever. I imagine the older one gets, the more one has to unburden, so the better one feels.

The tenth of Mohorrem is something to experience, Roshni. It is a holy, private day of mourning such as I have never seen in my life. I could tell, looking at all the faces, what a cathartic experience it had been for them. I saw Tusneem leave but chose to stay away. I didn't want to take away from whatever good feelings she was experiencing then.

At least I understand why Mustapha said he could not miss it to meet you. No good Bohra misses it. And I'm glad that my prospective husband is a good man, to say the least. I am sure you will love him. On the one hand, I love and understand him, but on the other, I am left with this niggling doubt as to whether I can ever fit into the house of these noble people. There must have been several thousand men, women, and children in the mosque that afternoon. And it was Mustapha's uncle upon whom was bestowed the honor of leading the prayers. The

*thought that a man from such a family wishes to marry me scares me,
Roshni. The beauty of Mustapha is that he is extremely knowledgeable
and tolerant of other religions. I'm just so confused, because I love
him even more after watching him today. He and his cousin Tusneem
seem such a wonderful blend of deen and duniya (religious and
worldly).*

*Has anything dramatic been happening at the Johnsons? I can't
wait to see you.*

With all my love,

Komli.

Mustapha's heart sank when Bawasahib asked Sakina and Kasim to send Mustapha to him on his own the morning after he had dined at their house. Mustapha had never had a private audience with Bawasahib. Normally, this would be something to brag about, but it was a tremulous Mustapha who knelt before Bawasahib the following morning. He cupped his left hand under his right, gently held Bawasahib's right hand in both his and proceeded to do salaam by gently lifting Bawasahib's hand to his right eye, then to his left, then to his forehead and finally to his lips. Letting go of Bawasahib's hands, and the money he was holding, he proceeded to kiss his right knee, and then his right foot. Like a meek lamb, still kneeling, he then looked up at Bawasahib with bated breath and trembling hands folded in front of his face. He looked at Bawasahib in agonized anticipation. His future happiness lay in what would transpire in the next few minutes, he thought to himself. Other than the stiff white turban Bawasahib wore on his head, everything about him seemed soft and pure. His snow white clothes simply radiated his inner purity.

"Your mother tells me you wish to marry a Hindu, Mustapha. What is her name?"

"Komli."

"Do you know what it means?"

"I think it means fresh bud."

Bawasahib nodded his head as he smiled down at Mustapha. It was the warm, reassuring smile of a gentle, educated, holy man. "So why do you wish to marry her?" he asked softly.

"I . . . . I . . ." Mustapha could not bring himself to utter the word 'love' in the presence of someone who radiated only the sacrosanct and the ethereal.

"I know something about love, Mustapha. I have a wife and seven children. I knew you would find it hard to talk to me in the presence of your parents. That is why I asked that you see me alone. Tell me, whom do you love more, your family or Komli?"

Komli, Mustapha wanted to say, but hesitated. Understanding the young man fully, Bawasahib said kindly, "It seems to me that you already love her more than your parents. That usually happens after marriage." A few beads of perspiration trickled down

Mustapha's armpits as he realized that Bawasahib was more understanding and knowledgeable about love than he had realized. Would Bawasahib guess that they had already made love to one another, Mustapha wondered with trepidation, as Bawasahib continued, "You do realize that your wonderful parents have devoted their lives to our religion and our community, don't you Mustapha?"

"Yes."

"That they would give their lives for what is right?"

"I think so."

"That if you do something to embarrass their standing in the community, it would hurt them terribly?"

"Yes."

"If you had a choice between hurting your parents or Komli, whom would you sacrifice?"

"Komli," Mustapha whispered fearfully, after a slight pause. He felt as though their heads were already on the guillotine. His parents were too noble; they had been too good to him; he could not marry Komli if it would bring them pain. Bawasahib had brought that home to him, better than any one else could have, he realized.

Bawasahib gave Mustapha one of his gentle smiles for which he was so loved in the community. "I was hoping to hear that, Mustapha. You come from one of the most noble families in our community. You know there was a time when my forefathers did not have the kind of wealth we have today. It was your grandfather and his father who helped my forefathers when we were in need. Don't do anything to hurt your parents. They can never be replaced." Mustapha nodded helplessly, as he felt the blood in his body turn into a watery substance that was barely able to support him on his wobbling knees. Little did Mustapha know that Bawasahib was used to seeing humanity by the hundreds, humbly struggling under crosses far heavier than Mustapha's. Little did Mustapha realize that Bawasahib understood his anguish because he had six sons of his own. Sons with whom he wished he could spend more time, but could not because of the pressing needs of his religion and his community. He gazed intently at Mustapha for a few more seconds before he continued, "Introduce Komli and her parents to your parents. If Komli will consent to converting to Islam, bring her to me and I will give you both my blessings to get married."

"You will?!"

"I will," Bawasahib said, smiling and nodding his head at the same time. He reached out for a handkerchief from the pile that lay on a table beside him. For every salaam, Bawasahib gave out a handkerchief which all Bohras treasured, since it was both blessed and handed to them personally by Bawasahib's very own hands. Mustapha knew this was a sign for him to depart. Suddenly, the blood gushed back to his legs. His lips had dried up with fear, but somehow he managed to stretch them a little to form what looked like a smile. As he wobbled up to his feet, he decided that when the time came he would request that Bawasahib himself bless their wedding, instead of one of the local priests. He knew that the salaam to Bawasahib would have to be very big for such a privilege. But Komli was worth it. And he would not get a handkerchief on that glorious day but, hopefully, a beautiful woolen shawl that Bawasahib himself would drape around his shoulders. On at least three occasions in the past, he had watched how graciously his grandfather and his father, too, had accepted shawls from Bawasahib for whatever great service they had rendered. He was too young to know the reasons. He only recalled how the eyes of his father and grandfather had shone with pride as they bowed their way out of Bawasahib's presence.

"Thank you!" Mustapha said as he retreated respectfully, bringing a twinkle to Bawasahib's eyes. 'Thank you' was not a word the older generation used in his presence. Times were changing. This new generation had a new vocabulary.

Rashid, Zenub, and Roshni felt the earth quake under their feet as they were introduced to one another. They tried not to sway as they felt tremors of shock course through their beings. Everyone managed to have tea without a drop being spilled; everyone managed to exchange a few civilities, before Sakina charged forward, "So, are you happy about Komli marrying our son?"

"Yes, indeed," Roshni replied quietly. She had already met Mustapha. She had fallen in love with his charming personality. She was greatly looking forward to meeting his parents. She had come in beaming, only to have dark clouds, in the form of his aunt and uncle, cast a terrible shadow over her happy disposition.

"Has Komli told you about our Bawasahib?"

"Yes."

"In our family, we don't do anything without our Bawasahib's blessings. Fortunately, Bawasahib has agreed to the marriage, but would like to meet Mustapha and Komli before the Mishaq ceremony."

"What is the mishaq ceremony?" Roshni asked.

"Oh, it's the ceremony that will initiate her into Islam. Every Bohra has to go through that."

"But Komli is not a Bohra."

"We know. But we cannot perform Nikaah (marital rites) unless Komli has gone through Mishaq."

"You mean she has to convert to Islam to marry Mustapha?" Roshni asked without any attempt to conceal her surprise.

"Didn't you explain this to Komli and her mother?" Sakina asked Mustapha.

"I did mention it to Komli," Mustapha stated with some anxiety.

"I forgot to mention it to my sister," Komli said with a smile. Over the years Roshni had learned everything Komli had picked up about Christianity and Islam. She never did mind what Komli learned, as long as she thanked her deity first thing each morning. If Komli chose to pray to Ganesh or to Shiva or Vishnu or Brahma, the creator himself, that was her choice. As far as she was concerned, they were all different rays of the same sun.

Roshni treated other religions as a part of education and Hinduism as her way of life. And if she did not like certain things that Tara claimed to be the way of Hindus, she simply thanked fate for not cursing her with a mother-in-law or a forced-old-law. When she had begged on the streets of Calcutta, her mother herself, and Rana, had taught her to invoke the names of Bhagvaan or Allah or Jesus, depending on who it was that was about to dole out the precious pennies. If invoking the names of the gods of different religions had helped sustain her on the streets, she saw no harm in allowing history to repeat itself if that's what it was going to take for Komli to be married. As long as Komli was happy and behaved like a decent human being, she simply had not felt the need to walk her on the straight and narrow path.

"Is it settled then that Komli will go through mishaq?" Sakina asked, mistaking the momentary pause for the affirmative.

"Why is it necessary? I mean, why can't they get married as Hindu and Muslim?" Roshni asked, just as a matter of curiosity.

"That's impossible!" Sakina exclaimed while all the other adults in the room also looked at Roshni in disbelief. It would have been one thing if she had said she would not have her daughter convert. But to actually suggest that a Hindu and Muslim could live together as Hindu and Muslim, why that was unheard of! "We do not know much about your religion," Sakina continued with unusual humility, "but we believe a Muslim must marry a Muslim or at least do what our religious leader tells us to do. In this case, he has agreed to this marriage if Komli accepts Islam."

Roshni felt a perverse streak slowly surface out of the depths of her being. She was with Rashid when she had heard Mother Christina say that silk and rags cannot blend together. Well, she decided, she would show these rich people that not all rags considered it an honor to be patched to a piece of silk. "So you mean they must both be of the same religion to get married?"

"Yes." Sakina replied.

"Would Mustapha consider becoming a Hindu?"

"A Hindu?!" Sakina asked, without trying to conceal the shudders that coursed through her being.

"You make it sound like a crime!" Roshni responded with quiet dignity.

"Mustapha, do you really think it would be a crime to convert to Hinduism?" Komli asked suddenly. She could read her sister's mind to some extent. Besides, she wanted to test Mustapha who seemed so tolerant or, at best, indifferent to religions."

"If it hurts my parents, it would be a crime, wouldn't it?" Mustapha asked, a little hesitantly.

"And would it not be a crime to hurt my family if I convert to Islam?"

"Yes. But I thought you were easygoing about religion, Komli. That it wouldn't be a problem for you to convert if you really love me."

"Then you must not really love me, Mustapha, if you can't convert for my sake. Is that right?"

"No that's not right, Komli," Mustapha shouted, forcing Kasim to intervene by suggesting that he calm down a little. Paradoxically, the heated arguments had rendered Komli stone cold. She felt stifled by the wealth, propriety, and religious laws to which she and her sister were totally unaccustomed.

Suddenly, Roshni did not care about hiding her past as she had all these years. Besides, Zenub and Rashid already knew about her. Without concealing her anger, she stated quietly, "I was fortunate enough to live on the streets for a few years. What the streets taught me about Allah, Bhagvaan and Jesus was different from what the books say. Tell me, do Bhagvaan, Allah and Jesus live on land, water and air? Am I to suppose that they don't often meet, and that when they do, they fight! Is that what thunder and lightning is about? I'm uneducated. I've never been to school. Maybe you can tell me!" Roshni asked with a sarcasm that totally surprised Komli.

"I don't think it's time for being facetious," Rashid said. "Let's try to . . .

But Komli had had enough herself. No one was going to tell off her sister. "That's the trouble with adults, you know. They teach us to read and write and learn about other countries and cultures, history, geography and biology and zoology, but when it comes to religion, they restrict us to just one. Don't think! Just accept! I refuse to stop thinking, and I refuse to just accept."

"Our children are not raised to talk back this way to adults," Sakina said icily.

"Of course not. I understand you're the cream that settles on top of the milk. Roshni and I are homogenized, totally non-fat milk. Let's leave, Roshni," Komli added suddenly, determined not to betray her emotions in front of anyone. She knew that the best way to make these educated people think was to leave with calm and dignity. A show of anger would only convince them that they were superior. Komli desperately wanted them to realize that she was not some poor, wilted flower that was ready and willing to be clipped and stuffed into the first vase that offered to sustain her.

"Komli, we have to find a solution," Mustapha implored, "otherwise . . . ."

"There is no solution, Mustapha. When adults cannot cooperate it saddens and confuses children, but at least I know now that they're not to blame—it's our gods who confuse our parents." And with those words of wisdom that endeared Komli to Kasim and to Rashid, Komli led her sister out, while Sakina gesticulated to Mustapha to stay back.

Rashid, too, desperately wished he could do something. Roshni and the little brown bear in his Goldilocks' bed had acquired the grace and poise of swans, he thought. Alas, some pride and anger also had come in the wake of the education and shelter he had so zealously ensured they received. All these years of trying to atone for his wife's sin had somehow resulted in their family hurting this girl once more. How could he tell them he admired them for their pride and poise? How could he tell them they looked so vulnerable that he wanted to embrace them; how could he tell them he would love to have dinner with them because it would be like having a refreshing talk with children, instead of all-knowing adults? He wanted to run out and do something. Instead, he sat and stared, hopelessly stuck in a traffic jam of emotions hooting and honking at him for getting into a jam from which there was no escape. Of Roshni, Rashid mused—twice you walked into my life, and each time you left me more human, more humbled, more compassionate, and more understanding. You who have not even been to school.

At the hostel that night, after Roshni had forced Komli to eat a simple meal of rice and lentil, Komli brought up the inevitable question.

"Roshni, Tusneem's father looked exactly like the man who came with us on the train, only a little bit older. Her mother, too, was an older version of the woman who took me to that bedroom where something painful was done between my legs. I could tell from the way they reacted to us that they were horrified. You told me once that you weren't ready to reveal certain things about our past. Is it because you can't handle it or because I won't be able to? Right now, I feel I can handle anything!" The two sisters looked straight into each other's eyes, soul, searching soul.

"Some secrets are like toys, Komli, they are fun to share. Some secrets become private treasures that you share with no one. And some turn into daggers that cause pain even if there is no one around to turn the dagger inside you. They are like our skin; we have to carry them with us. I wish so many times that at least they could be like snake skins so we could shed them if we needed to. The one I have not been able to share with you all these years is the last kind."

"I'm sure I will be able to deal with it. Try me, Roshni," Komli urged. Roshni knew her time had come. She revealed everything.

"So, Tusneem, my best friend, is the girl I saved from being circumcised," Komli reiterated in a flat tone that revealed little. How could she be angry with Tusneem? Besides, ironically, Tusneem had already asked her for forgiveness on the tenth of Mohorrem, that Bohra gesture that Komli had found so heart-warming.

"If I had known some of the things I know now, I would have done battle all those years ago. I know you would have found another solution, Komli. You're braver than I am," Roshni said humbly.

You're damn right I would have done battle, Komli wanted to scream.

"I could see no way out of the vicious circle we were in," Roshni added defensively.

"Did you ever try complaining to a passer-by about Rana? Wouldn't one in a million have done something?"

"It never occurred to me, Komli. Ma raised us to quietly accept our lot," Roshni replied as she passively accepted that her sister had every right to be angry with her. The tears coursed down her face as she said simply, "I hope some day you will forgive me."

"I do understand," Komli lied. It was difficult for her to understand how any human being could take so much abuse and oppression without putting up a fight. One thing she did know, though, her sister was an angel, too much of an angel perhaps. She went up to her and quietly laid her head between Roshni's bosom. "There is nothing to forgive, Roshni, and, by the way, you are very courageous, you know. I was so proud of the way you stood up tall in front of Mustapha's family today. I always believed nobility came with money and culture and education. You have an inborn nobility, Roshni. I am the one who needs to work on it!" Komli moved back and smiled at her sister. "And if it wasn't for what you did for me, Roshni, I'd never have the second kind of secret, the kind that becomes a private treasure, to be shared with no one."

Roshni looked at her intently before asking, "Have you and Mustapha made love?"

"A private memory to be shared with no one, remember?!" Komli repeated. Roshni let her question go, knowing from the glow in Komli's eyes that the answer was probably, yes.

Neither sister read in bed that night. With eyes closed, both indulged in their private memories.

Komli thought back on the afternoons when Mustapha had visited her in her hostel. At first they had both been content to wait for sex after marriage. Mustapha represented everything her childhood had lacked—father, uncle, brother, a warm, wonderful male figure to love. Everything he said and did was endearing. For him, too, she was a novelty—she was poor, forthright, with no one jiggling her around like a puppet. The sensitive poet in him had sensed that she had built a fortress around her vulnerability. Something told him that she had been wounded in more ways than one. Above all, he wanted to take care of his beautiful, brave Komli. And then, one evening, he had told her that marrying her depended on his audience with Bawasahib, and that he wasn't very hopeful of a positive outcome.

"Can we consummate our love?" he had asked in a whisper that was barely audible. "I would at least like to take away that memory with me. Good memories are the only baggage worth carrying," he had added simply. He had searched deeply into her eyes, hoping to find something that suggested that she understood him. Morals and desire did battle for a few seconds. Morals blurred to take a back seat while desire leapt forward.

Mustapha's parents had been preparing so feverishly for Bawasahib's arrival, that they had failed to notice that their son was often gone for long hours. Like Zenub, Komli, too, was relieved to realize that those orgasms that escaped her weren't because there was something inherently wrong with her. But at least it hadn't been impossible for her to enjoy sex. Mustapha had made her go wild, occasionally. Those were her secrets. Her private treasures.

"You've made me the happiest man in the world. No one will ever love you like I do," Mustapha used to say. "If you seek beauty, you'll find it, like I found you. I used to sit by the water and imagine a creature like you. I knew you were out there, somewhere. I wrote so many poems about you even before I had seen you. I put you out to the universe, as some say, and you came to me. Think beautiful, Komli, and it will come to you, I promise." She tried to think beautiful, she tried to think positive, but couldn't help wondering if he would ever come to her again, knowing that she certainly would not go to him until he offered, just offered, to convert for her sake, as she had been prepared to for his sake. It had not even occurred to Mustapha to offer to convert for her sake. Just offer, at least. The thought ran like a vein of iron through her being. Nothing, and no one could soften that blow.

Roshni lay in bed and wondered what it would be like to have a gentleman like Rashid for husband. He had looked at her with tenderness, it seemed. She had seen the warmth in his eyes. Was it admiration, or both? It was just as well that she had asked him all those years ago not to visit her, she thought suddenly. For reasons she could not figure out, a teeny tiny, fiery red spark of ember had come alight in the cold, gray, un-raked ashes of sentiments she harbored for men.

That night Tusneem hypothesized with her parents as to what would happen if some day she wanted to marry a Hindu.

That would be worse, Tusneem, because the boy would have to go through circumcision, Rashid wanted to say, but could not bring himself to discuss that subject. Instead, he had the presence of mind to quickly change it to, "You would have to live in a Hindu household. Would you be able to do that?"

"Is there someone? Zenub asked quickly, just to make sure.

"No. There's no one."

"Tusneem, you get a proposal a week from Bohra families who would love to have you as their daughter-in-law."

"Because I'm rich, right?"

"No, my darling. You should have more faith in yourself. You are so beautiful, inside and outside. It's time you take these proposals seriously and think about marriage."

"I will one of these days, Mamma, when I meet a boy who interests me."

When Rashid and Zenub retired that night, they decided to make arrangements to send Tusneem to England for a few months to stay with Rashid's brother. Something might click between their daughter and his brother's son. And if nothing came out of it, at least it would get her away from Komli for a while. Not that they thought she was a bad influence so much as they were terribly uncomfortable that the sacrificial lamb had reared its head as their daughter's best friend!

During moments of desperation, Mustapha had actually toyed with the idea of approaching Bawasahib again. It was Bawasahib who had been the most gentle and the most understanding, he thought. Was it possible that Bawasahib would allow him to marry her without Komli converting? But then Bawasahib's words came back to haunt him: *Don't do anything to hurt your parents.* In fact, he recalled, that even Komli had said she would never do anything to hurt her sister. He decided he was the one who must be strange and selfish for loving her above all else. He blamed himself and, more angrily, he blamed the many Gods for their monopolistic ways. Yes, as his dear, wise Komli had said, if it wasn't for the Gods of mankind he would be with his Komli now.

Take me back, you Gods, he muttered, one unbearably, lonesome evening when he could no longer cope with the pain of belonging to no one, and having no one to talk to either. Mullasahib, if you were right about Allah and Islam, then no doubt the worms will gnaw at my body for all the sins I have committed, and for the one I am about to commit now, Mustapha thought coldly. But surely worms gnawing at my body will not be near as horrible as this wretched parasite, loneliness, that will not leave me alone for a moment, gnawing at my mind and my soul and my heart. And if Komli is right and I will be reincarnated, send me back to her, Durga, Kali, Shiva, Ganesh or whichever of you Gods is in charge of that department, just send me back to her, he implored, as he dove into the depths of the river Hooghly, to be reincarnated into a human corpse floating on the headlines of every newspaper in Calcutta.

Kasim sought out Rashid before he sought out his wife so they could change 'suicide' to 'accidental drowning'. He seemed to recall that burial according to Islamic rites was denied to one who had taken one's own life. He very much doubted if his wife would survive the double blow of death and denial to bury their son according to Islamic rites.

Komli went to the river Hooghly where she and Mustapha had often whiled away quiet hours—talking, holding hands, indulging in the luxury of saying nothing for long intervals—and sobbed. The sensation was strange; she couldn't remember when she had last cried. She cupped her hand, reached into the water and washed away her tears, hoping that somehow, somewhere, sometime her tears would mingle with whatever tears Mustapha had shed. She had learned in school that water carves, creates, and deposits. So does sorrow, she thought—carve, create and deposit memories in the unique but sacred sanctity of one's soul.

Although at first it was hard for Komli to face Tusneem in college without feeling guilty about being the cause of Mustapha's death, both ladies discovered that the root of their friendship was based on love and understanding; a root that was too tenacious to snap under the recent storm they had weathered.

When Tusneem told Komli about the implications of suicide on burial rites, Komli couldn't help but think of the way Parsis disposed of their dead—the deceased were simply left in an open tower for nature's cleaning crew to come swooping down to devour, and to regurgitate the human body so it could be recycled into a state of matter mother earth could use, regardless of how or why it had perished.

"My parents want me to go visit an aunt and uncle in London for a while," Tusneem mentioned to Komli one afternoon.

"To separate us, right?"

"I think so. But you know, my parents are very understanding. They were a little taken aback when I told them that if they were sending me away to separate us, it would not break up our friendship. They denied it, a little too quickly, and claimed they just wanted me to take a break. And to tell you quite frankly, I'm looking forward to going to London." Suddenly she removed a broach she was wearing. With it she pricked her finger and then turned around to Komli and asked, "Can I prick yours? I used to see kids do it in school. We rub together the blood on our fingers and become sisters for life."

"Have to draw out blood, huh?" Komli asked with a smile as the two put up their index fingers and smeared their skins with each other's blood.

"So when I come back, you won't have disappeared on me, right?" Tusneem asked with tears in her eyes.

"You mean you're not going to write to me?"

"Of course I will!"

"Then how can I disappear on you?"

"You seem preoccupied about something. What is it?"

"How long will you be gone, Tusneem?" Komli asked.

"I should get a three month visa, but can extend it to six months if I want."

"I might be a mother when you come back," Komli said quietly.

"What?!"

"I'm expecting Mustapha's baby."

"Does Roshni know?"

"I was planning to tell her first since she was the only sister I had, until now that is. Do you know how fortunate you are, Tusneem, to have a large family? I get very lonesome these days. I'll miss you." Suddenly Komli put her hand on her face and started sobbing. For exactly what reasons Komli was crying even she did not know. She loved Roshni dearly but her world had expanded dramatically with college, Tusneem and Mustapha. The prospect of raising a child, the way Roshni had raised her, frightened her. She did not want to live like a saint or a slave. She had had a peek at the world; there was more to raising a child than binding it in a cocoon of learning. She wanted her child to have a father and a mother and brothers and sisters and aunts and uncles. She was angry with herself and with Mustapha; he had let go too quickly; and she, with her immaturity, arrogance, and her false pride, had not known how to yank the strings of love that had soared for but a few moments.

"Is there anything I can do to help you, Komli? It would mean a lot to me if I can somehow help you."

"Here's a promise, if I need help, I'll holler."

Tusneem wasn't satisfied that Komli understood what asking meant. She wrote to her parents that night. A letter she decided she would hand to them when she bade them farewell at the airport. It said :

Dearest Pappa and Mamma,

It's hard to tell you how much I appreciate what you've done for me. Actually if it wasn't for Komli, I would probably just take this vacation to London for granted, too, because throughout my life you have denied me nothing. But over the last few years in college, I learned to be thankful for a ton of things that Komli doesn't have.

You'll never know how much she helped me. Believe me, being rich and sheltered and chauffeur-driven is not a ticket to popularity among thinking students in college (the kind of group I yearned to belong to). Although Komli and I often argued or disagreed about things, at least she made me think. Here's an example : When I told her we Muslims cannot pray or go to the mosque when we get our period, she told me that Hindus, too, treat the period as something unclean. Then she stated simply that she thought the period should be revered, like water, because all it is is the remnants of unfertilized eggs. And without water there would be no egg and without egg there would be no life. We argued and laughed and learned from each other about many, many things.

She's a tough cookie, some said of her, and I believed it until recently. My heart broke when she sobbed uncontrollably before we parted. She didn't ask for any help. She just said I was so lucky that I had a large family.

She's expecting Mustapha's baby and I know she feels very alone and very lost.

I wrote down her address in our telephone book. Luckily they live in Patna. When you go there next on a business trip, Pappa, do you think you could take Mamma with you? It would be so wonderful if some members from the family involved in her tragedy could support her in whatever way she needs. I realize Mustapha's family would not be able to handle this. But I know in my heart of hearts that I am blessed with parents who will understand and offer whatever help Komli needs.

Komli helped me realize what a great sculptor is this thing called love. With joy and sorrow and understanding and anger and pride and prejudice and sacrifice and hope and despair (such powerful tools!) it hammers away relentlessly at flesh and bone and blood. And then, with laughter and tears it fires and polishes each human being to a shine one cannot always see, unlike the cold masterpieces sculpted by man. It is always love for something or someone that pushes us in strange directions, doesn't it? I always wanted a sister. Little did Komli and I know that love would one day chisel us into sisters. I love her dearly. No one can take that away from me. I am so glad I have you for understanding parents because I know that after you read this letter, you will never try and take her away from me.

But my reason for writing is not that you allow us to be sisters, but that you visit Komli and offer her whatever help she needs. She thinks she's tough. I think she's about as tough to crack as an eggshell.

Thank you for understanding. I love you very much. Thank you also for sending me to college instead of just marrying me off. I think I am better prepared now to handle life. I am able to see myself a little more clearly by looking into Komli's soul. I could think of no better person to use as a mirror into which I could gaze to see what I am truly about. Komli has left me with the courage to be honest, so here's a promise—I will always be honest with you because I know how much you love me. Understanding and love go hand in hand, don't they?

With all my love,

Tusneem.

At the prayer service for Mustapha, Sakina sobbed so much and so loud for her son that it shocked the entire community. This big, strong woman whose role in life had been to teach, to command, to reprimand, to take complete charge and to have no qualms about calling a spade a spade, was vulnerable after all. The humble women who had been scared of her, did not know how to go up and console her; did not know what to say to her when all she needed was for people to hug her tightly, to say that they understood her grief; that they understood her for not understanding why this should happen to her when she had done everything Bawasahib and the holy books prescribed. Why, why, why, she kept asking, without receiving any answers, only tears and torment following each other in frenzied circles.

And it was not until the following Bakri Eid that Sakina truly saw her Mustapha again. As the goat bleated and wailed, knowing it was about to be sacrificed, Sakina realized with horror that life truly enacted some of those religious lessons she lapped up with such fervor and enthusiasm. This was no theory, no kitaab (holy book), she thought as she ran up the stairs to sob privately in her bedroom. Suddenly she realized the great, great significance of Bakri Eid—it was the meaning of life, life that was one big, bleeding sacrifice at the altar of religion and laws and love and children and parents; nothing but a sacrifice, she thought, as she sobbed uncontrollably, unable to shut out the sounds of the bleating goat. She realized how deaf she had been in the past to the bleating of the goat.

As though to reflect the change in her personality, her hair had turned a soft, powdery ash-grey. Many people missed the fire that had raged in her. The only person who could sometimes ignite the embers to a warm glow was her husband. But even he had no choice but to accept that, like him, a part of his wife had been sacrificed at the altar of her love for her son.

"Komli, I understand how hard life is for you," Roshni began one evening when she was visiting Komli. "Devi knows a boy who she thinks will make you a good husband. Would you consider meeting him at least? He is educated and Devi tells me his parents won't ask for a very big dowry."

"Dowry?! I will never, never, never marry a man who wants money to marry me! People say women are hard to understand. I think men are far worse. For the favors of sex outside of marriage, they want to pay us. For marriage, for cooking and cleaning and slaving for them, for blessing their homes with little children, they want us to pay them?! Does it make sense to you?"

"No. It never has. I just so desperately want to see you happy again, Komli, that I thought perhaps you would bow to custom and meet this boy at least."

"To hell with custom and tradition! I'm sick of hearing about everyone's customs and traditions and concerns about honor and reputation," Komli lashed out. Roshni had never seen Komli so angry before. She understood that Komli needed to let it all out, so she decided to listen quietly while Komli continued, "Now I would understand if a stranger wanted money to marry me if I was carrying someone else's baby. Because without that shit of a piece of paper that constitutes marriage, an innocent child becomes a bastard, doesn't he? Now does that make sense?"

"No, Komli. Are you carrying Mustapha's baby?" Roshni asked in a whisper.

"Yes. And here's what I've decided, Roshni. I'm going back to Patna.

"I'm going with you."

"For once, you're going to listen to me, Roshni. I'm not a child any more. I want to be left alone for a while. I need to get in control of my feelings, my anger at Mustapha and the world and, most of all, myself. I got myself into this mess. Please, Roshni, allow me a little time to myself. I promise you, as soon as I need help, I will get in touch with you. You're happy at the Johnsons. Seeing you fret over me will make my burden still heavier. We grew up together. There is nothing you can do, that I can't do, other than being an angel, of course. And remember, I can always go to Devi if I need something. Now that she's expecting her third little one, I imagine she knows everything about pregnancy. Write and tell her I found my man, at no cost whatsoever. Ask her if there is a dowry one can pay for reincarnation!" she jabbed.

Roshni held her sister quietly in her arms, knowing words would be useless.

That night Roshni wrote to Devi, asking her to keep a special eye on her sister.

In her diary she simply added:

> *Ma, prostituting myself and begging for food was easier than seeing Komli suffer. I've never seen her so lost and angry before. I wonder what good all the learning and books has done her. I wanted so much for Komli to be happy. Leave aside the three Rs, even the six basic Rs— reading, writing, 'rithmetic, religion, rupees and a roof over our head, is not the answer to happiness. What is, Ma? I feel so helpless.*

ଓଞ

CHAPTER 4

REINCARNATION / INNOCENCE

As the plane took off for the skies, Komli's spirits soared. It had been a long, long while since she had felt good about anything. Thank you, thank you, thank you, dearest sister, she said to herself, hoping that some day she could do something equally wonderful for Roshni. In her hand luggage, she had packed the diary her sister had given her all those years ago. At first she had been too busy to take the time to write. She had felt like it during the last few months, but her thoughts had been too morose; she wanted her first entry to be a happy one. The moment was at hand; she fished out her diary, turned it over fondly as she thought of her sister, and began to write :

Aatma (soul),

What a good omen! A stewardess came up to me and said, 'Madam, Mr. and Mrs. Johnson have requested that you join them in first class. There's plenty of room up there. Would you like to join them?' They're crazy, these Brits! Would I like to, indeed! They could have slapped me in the butt, kicked me into first class, and I would have happily said a dozen thank yous! I think some of their politeness has rubbed off on Roshni. Everything in first class is spotless and sparkling. No, I'm not drunk! The champagne was bitter! The caviar, supposed to be fit for kings, tasted like fish eggs without any spice. I'm smiling and saying 'yes please' to everything the stewardess offers. She smiles back, but I can tell exactly what she's thinking—greedy bitch! I'm going to try everything—in the air and in the ground. What's the use of traveling if one can't do in Rome as the Romans do? It seems that Bhagvaan enjoys yanking us up and down like a yo-yo. Yanked up Mustapha, yanked me down with pregnancy and then, on another one of His million whims, just yanks up my premature baby. Did He think I wouldn't have been able to cope? So here I am, up in the air, while Roshni gets to baby sit Devi's newborn baby. Never can tell how He'll yank His strings. He's yanked me to first class, and I'm enjoying every minute of it! Can't wait to land! I feel like the pussycat who's going to London, to London to visit the queen!

It is now 8 in the evening. I miss Roshni already. The Johnsons keep dropping by to chat. They make sure the stewardess cuts any food I can't cut with my stump. I've been tempted to just pick it up with one hand and eat it, but I know that would mortify the genteel Johnsons. Besides, I don't particularly want to be yanked out of first class! People travel by planes to go to other destinations. I think people should travel by planes just to see what comes popping out magically from the plane itsel! Ask and you shall receive must be the motto of this airline! I have less space in front of my seat than I had on my desk at home, but this space contains a telephone, a television, a magazine, a newspaper, a bag for throwing up (can't imagine, though, why any one would want to vomit in here), socks to keep my feet warm, pads to rest my eyes (or to keep them from popping out), toothpaste, toothbrush, a sewing kit, and a perfume, if you please. I also have my own special light, my own special fan, my own special music (nine different channels), and my own special button, to call my butler, I guess! And as if all this is not enough, the stewardess keeps coming around to ask me if there is anything I need—a juice, some fruit, some crackers, a candy . . . No wonder the Brits ruled the world. I can hardly wait to see what their country's like.

The Johnsons tell me we'll be landing soon and I have to fill out some forms to be able to see the land of our ex-masters!

Religiously, every morning, Roshni cupped a few drops of coconut oil in the palms of her hand. With it, she gently massaged Deepak's arms and legs and chest and back, mechanically moving back and forth, back and forth, until both masseur and child were transported into another world; Deepak into the blessed world of sleep, and Roshni, into the sanctuary of silence which, she had begun to realize, was a luxury few people enjoyed. She took longer than most women to massage Deepak. It was during these tranquil moments that she, in turn, massaged the rough and smooth edges of her memories and freshly kindled desires. She needed to massage her soul so she could have the strength to carry on. It was she who had quietly borne the mental suffering of a miscarriage, while Komli had writhed and shrieked out the bloody, clotted remnants of her short-lived but tragic affair with Mustapha. It was she who had borne the anguish of not knowing if Komli would survive; it was she who had tearfully thanked the doctors when they had finally come out to proclaim that Komli would live, although it was doubtful if she would survive another pregnancy.

It was Roshni who had quickly realized that she had to do something lest her sister's soul wilted as prematurely as her unborn child. The Johnsons were retiring; they were returning to England. It was Roshni who had summoned up the courage to ask the Johnsons if they would sponsor Komli so she could obtain a visa for England. It was she who had finally lit a spark in Komli and convinced her to go away. "You know, Komli, I'm tired of hearing that riches and rags and religions don't mix. We barely spend a fourth of the allowance Rashid sends you. If he can send his daughter abroad, so can I!" And with that little jab, she had somehow fired her sister to swing west for a few months. "Find out if their gods are prejudiced like the gods of Hindus and Muslims; go see if they have our crazy caste system; find out if their neighbors come barging into other people's lives and what their attitude is towards the period and beggars and husbands and untouchables. Go seek some new truths, Komli. Go find out why the British ruled the world. Write me long letters about everything you see and do."

Secure in the knowledge that Komli had the Johnsons to help her out, Roshni had bade farewell to her sister, hoping that she herself would be able to survive life without Komli and the Johnson children on whom she had selflessly lavished her nurturing instincts.

When Devi hinted that she could use the help of a baby-sitter, Roshni readily offered to look after Deepak. Each morning, while Devi tended to her ailing mother-in-law and to the other members of her family, not one of whom could do without her, Roshni massaged the newborn. It must be nice to feel so needed, Roshni thought. How she would have loved this baby to be her nephew instead of her neighbor's child. Roshni hated to think of her dignified, serene Gods yanking people up and down like yo-yos, although she did wonder sometimes if Komli was right, especially now that her very own heart was suddenly being yanked around uncontrollably.

First there had been that tender look from Rashid on that fateful afternoon when they had met again after so many years. She would have forgotten about him, had he not visited her again with his wife. She had understood that the visit was only to offer her pregnant sister any help she needed. She had said they were fine. And then, to compound matters, Rashid had come again one day, by himself this time. This time her heart had somersaulted uncontrollably. He had said he was on one of his business trips. He wanted to make sure Komli was alright. She had assured him once again that Komli was fine. He had stayed a few minutes longer than necessary; it seemed he wanted to say something, but could not find the words. Roshni had offered him a chair to sit down. He had smiled a little smile, but had declined. She could pretend to all the world that she was just being civil to a kind man. She knew better. In her heart of hearts, she knew she was disappointed that once he found out that Komli had left for England, he would never come again. For the first time in her life, she had come across a man who fitted her idea of being an insaan (human). But, like everything else fate had churned out for her, he belonged to somebody else.

She continued to massage Deepak and, with it, some of the cruel memories that had re-surfaced now that she was alone. She could not have been more than three feet tall, she recalled, when the brute who belonged to her Ma, whom she referred to as Abba (father), had first yanked up her dress and started petting her body at night. She had been too scared to call out to her mother in case the brute beat her up just as he used to beat up her mother. Although mother screamed sometimes, most times she remained quiet. Even when he came home tottering with a bottle under one arm and a woman in the other, Ma took it quietly. Was it because she was scared of being beaten, that Ma maintained a stony silence, or had Ma suffered quietly in order to maintain some semblance of sanity for the sake of her daughter, Roshni wondered with hindsight.

Ma had taken it all until that one night she had found her animal of a husband on top of her beloved child. All Roshni remembered was a sound like thunder and a scream that had pierced her ears—someone had hit her father on his head with a frying pan. He had rolled over, to reveal her mother standing above her. There had not been a single tear on Ma's face. Mothers must somehow muster all the strength they need at times of crises. She had grabbed Roshni and walked out; mother and child, with nothing in their hands but each other's hands. Ma had walked and walked until Roshni had begged her to stop. Roshni never stopped begging from that night on. Mother's stomach had grown big at some stage. Komli had arrived. She was too little to understand that woman needs man to procreate. Roshni had just been happy to have her first and only doll; a playmate she had grown to love because she was often abandoned on the streets, to look after the infant, while mother went about looking for food, or so she said.

Rana had perpetuated the cycle of abuse. Zenub had saved her. And now the very woman's husband was turning into a tormenter of sorts. Although a part of her was resigned to the fact that she was destined never to have anything she could call her own, she could not stop her heart from skipping a beat when Rashid dropped by; she could not stop her heart from hoping that he would come again, from wondering what it would be like to have a man like him for keeps.

"I've really got to know my mother-in-law in the last few months, Roshni," Devi said one afternoon. "She actually cried the other day, and asked me to forgive her for treating me so badly."

"You sure you heard right?"

"I think the hardened part of her heart has already died. She actually told me that she hated me because I had such an easy life with her son, compared to what she had to suffer when she first entered her husband's household."

"She treated you like a slave!"

"She was not only slave to her mother and father-in-law and her husband, of course, but also to the three older daughters-in-law and their husbands as well. It seemed like all of them took every opportunity to make her life miserable!"

"Makes me wonder what is better, being single, or spending the rest of one's life with hateful in-laws!"

"She said she could have borne it all better had they not taken away her first-born girl who simply disappeared a few days after she was born. She thinks they killed her. Even her husband said nothing."

"Oh no," Roshni cried in horror, "I've read about it, but I never thought I would ever know someone to whom it had really happened!"

"She kept saying how lucky I was that times have changed and girls are not put to death any more. What a shame, no, Roshni, to have to live life like a stone that's chiseled by hatred. Mohan and I try to give her all the loving we can. I think she appreciates it, especially my sweet Amrita of all people! She hardly asks for anything anymore because I think, at long last, she's content. I think she's finally got rid of all the bee stings."

"Getting stung herself, or stinging you?"

"Both. We are so lucky we can talk to each other, Roshni. If only Tara Ma had talked to me earlier, I could have given her some sympathy and love."

"And you would have been happier, too."

"At least I had Mohan and now I have my little ones to keep me going. I can't imagine what I would turn into if my little Amrita was taken away from me and killed, Roshni."

"You are an angel, Devi. You've forgiven her everything, haven't you? How's Mohan dealing with Tara Bahen's illness?"

"I know it bothers him, but you know how men are."

"I do?" Roshni quipped.

"Sorry. He goes to work, brings in money, gets fed, makes love, sleeps and goes back to the same old cycle, while we women can get on with the more important task of raising children, instead of cooking them!"

"You've never forgotten that story, have you?" Roshni asked with a laugh.

"Strangely enough, Tara Ma's helped me realize what an important role we cooking, cleaning women play at home. Little Amrita clings on to her with big, shiny eyes and laps up all the wonderful things she tells her. You would be surprised how gently she tells Amrita about the stages of life."

"Those stages that Komli got mad about?"

"I remember that! This has nothing to do with the world. It's Amrita's individual cycle. The first stage of her life will be lots of fun if she works hard because that's the time she is a student, regardless of whether she learns in school, under a tree, or on her grandma's lap. Then comes the second stage which she says is the hardest for both men and women because you become a householder. Want to guess the third stage? Very few people reach it."

"Having babies?"

"I said very few people reach it. Besides, that's part of householder"

"Being thankful?"

"Detaching oneself from all worldly desires. Tara Ma thinks we're heading in the opposite direction. At least that's what she said when Mohan bought a computer because he needs it for work."

"Has she reached the third stage?"

"I guess. She wants nothing worldly."

"So is that what life's all about, going from learning, to suffering to renouncing everything?"

"Renouncing everything is different from renouncing worldly things. When you renounce everything, you become a Sanyasi. You live with nature. You survive on whatever man or nature gives you, and you meditate."

"Sounds like Komli and I were Sanyasi's first," Roshni said facetiously, as the two laughed together.

"Will you have dinner with us tonight? You might find that you actually enjoy listening to Tara Ma."

"I would love that." The ways of Bhagvaan may be unfathomable, Roshni thought as she saw Devi to the door, but it seemed He always sent little droplets of joy to keep one from shriveling up completely.

Tusneem was at the airport to meet Komli. Her friend looked extremely radiant, Komli thought. She introduced her to a tall, handsome, young man who had the air of a confident, westernized Indian.

"This is Abbas," she said, touching him possessively on the arm. The Johnsons watched politely as the two girls jabbered endlessly. They had been in India long enough to understand that some Indians simply failed to realize that airports were not meant for socializing.

"I think Komli's friends are waiting for her," Abbas intervened politely. He, in turn, had been in England long enough to understand that the British had yet to realize that the tongue was a muscle that could be utilized for talking.

"Are you sure we can't take you home with us for a little while?" Tusneem asked.

"No. I'm spending a week with the Johnsons. After that I'll be at your mercy. I'll phone you as soon as I can." Komli replied. The two parted company happily, knowing that it would not be long before they would catch up with the goings on in each other's lives. Komli watched Tusneem walk away, hands interlocked with Abbas's hands. Sending Tusneem to England had been a good decision, it seemed. Komli couldn't wait to find out, and wondered why Tusneem had not been more informative in her letters.

"I'm sorry I kept you waiting, Mr. Johnson."

"Don't worry, Komli, we have to wait in line anyway, for a taxi." And with those lines, Komli became the spectator who watched the dramatic metamorphosis of her sister's ex-master and mistress: it was Mr. Johnson who politely held open the door of the taxi, shut it gently after she had stepped in with all the dignity she could muster. Gone was the Indian chauffeur who had saluted the Johnsons, who had held open the doors for them, who had shut it gently and then walked around quietly to drive them where they commanded, like a robot that had been programmed by his foreign masters.

In the week Komli spent with them, the Johnsons were miraculously transformed into humble, hardworking commoners. It was Mr. Johnson who scurried around their beautiful cottage, making sure everything was alright. The man used his hands so dexterously. Komli wondered from where Roshni had acquired the notion that the man only knew how to put on his reading glasses and flip the pages of the newspaper, and maneuver knives and forks at the table. Other than that, Roshni had claimed, the man was totally helpless.

A few days after her arrival Komli wrote her first long letter from England:

My dearest Roshni,

The Johnsons are wonderful, wonderful people. I couldn't be happier. I know I get in their way sometimes, but they couldn't be nicer and more thoughtful. I have one strict order to follow—not to say sorry again. Mrs. Johnson said she is tired of hearing me apologize all the time. I can't help it! Living in this house is like living on another planet. I can't even take a shower without asking them how the gadgets in the bathroom work! And by the way, these people are far from helpless. They work like a co-operative—collectively they're cooks, cleaners, carpenters, chauffeurs, gardeners, you name it! About the only thing they don't have a handle on is cooking. I can't wait to go to Tusneem's and pig out on some spicy anything. Didn't you ever tell the Johnson cook number 1 or 2 or whatever they had in India to at least throw some garlic and ginger into their food? If it wasn't for the fact that they wear clothes, and eat with knife and fork, I would swear they were just one generation removed from cave men! Boil the potato, heat the meat, and eat the treat they know not how to treat. Sounds idiotic? Their food inspired me!

Do you know what really baffles me? If these people have so much regard for manual labor, why the hell don't they eat food with their two hands? The snooty Indians, who look down on manual labor, should be the ones eating with knife and fork, don't you think? But I'm so glad we're creatures of contradictions, otherwise life would be dull. The fork is a good instrument for jabbing. Little do the gracious Johnsons know that every time I jab at their tasteless meat and potato, which they cut up for me so graciously, I thoroughly enjoy the opportunity of having a good stab at the tasteless food. Sorry, Roshni. I know you love and respect the Johnsons. But we promised to be honest with each other. I also know what you're thinking—that I've become oh so ungrateful, considering there was a time when I happily devoured anything that came my way. Well, I'm off the streets and I've been introduced to knives and forks and sometimes my mind itself feels like a fork that wants to jab, jab, jab! At least I jabber it out of my system. Obviously, I haven't forgotten what you said about vacuuming my stomach of all anger, so I can laugh more! Want to know why I'm like a potato? Mrs. J told me that if you don't prick holes in potatoes before placing them in the microwave they explode because of all the steam that builds up inside. *It's a good thing she hasn't served me anything spicy, I'd probably wolf it down with my bare fingers and lick the plate to a shine. That would squirm the hell out of them and, as wicked as I sound, I really don't want to do that to the Js. I actually like them. It's their food that's driving me crazy. And oh, I clean forgot to tell you, they haven't even heard of black pepper. Their idea of black pepper is this tasteless gray stuff that's neither salt nor pepper!*

Here's more positive stuff about the Js. They live in a beautiful, small cottage in the outskirts of London. It's real small compared to the mansion they had in Patna. The size of it makes them more human somehow—more like family instead of master and mistress. When I first saw their cottage I thought it was over-run by neglect. I learned later that it's quite an art to get ivy leaves to creep and crawl around walls like that. Imagine a cottage covered with green lace on the outside and you'll get the picture. As for their garden, Mr. and Mrs. J tend to it with so much love and care that it helps me to understand better what lies inside their souls. Walking barefoot in their garden felt like being Eve (before she turned wicked). I've no idea how many different kinds of flowers they have. I've learned the names of some. I'm usually too embarrassed to ask. It's like asking an Indian about ginger and garlic. I've got it! Gardening is the spice of their lives! Each flower bed is a work of art—little flowers in front of taller flowers, interspersed with little green bushes here and there. It's hard to do justice to their beautiful garden. Maybe they take Voltaire literally. Mustapha told me once that Voltaire said everyone should work in their garden. Mustapha was deep, more deep than I realized. So are the Johnsons I think. I hope they invite you some day. You will go crazy about the English countryside. The little that I've seen so far is one exquisite garden!

You know Roshni, they say the British treat their homes like castles. Well, guess what, they treat their commodes like thrones. Mrs. J. polishes it to a shine with her own two hands and then proudly moves on to her next job, head held high. I wish our dear sweepers in India could see her, just so they would walk with head held high even though some of our arrogant rich still have the gall to treat them as untouchables!

Let's see, I've been to Buckingham Palace and the Tower of London so far. Everybody goes to see the changing of the guards at Buckingham Palace. They say that that's the only thing that changes at Buckingham Palace! The palace was gray and drab. The guards looked glorious in red, black and white. I have a suspicion they feel about as lifeless as the palace—they're not allowed to flinch a single muscle on their face and, while marching, they're not allowed to flex a single joint.

The Tower of London was definitely more exciting. People used to get imprisoned in there (though they say some people also get imprisoned at B. Palace). Got to see the Kohinoor the Brits took away from us. Don't ask me why it's imprisoned in the T. of L. I thought jewels were meant to be worn.

Life can be oh so confusing but oh so interesting, and I'm oh so happy, Roshni, thanks to you! I am coming to terms with losing Mustapha and his baby. I often feel calm and content, so please, please don't worry about me. In fact, I hope you're coping well without having the J's children to look after. I'll be happy when I hear you've started doing something for yourself!

I must go now and see what help Mrs. J needs in the kitchen. I can't wait to see Tusneem! Say hi to everyone and write long letters, like me.

With love,

Komli.

Abbas had grown up in Karachi, Pakistan. He had come to England to study and, like many hard-working Asians, he had become a successful chartered accountant. Like some men with double standards, he had enjoyed his share of western women, knowing that for keeps he would marry a virgin from back home. Back home where he knew he would be received like a prince; where parents would clamor to claim him for a son-in-law; parents who knew or cared little about male virginity, so long as he was foreign-educated, which translated of course to material security for their daughter.

Abbas's dream woman was destined to be shipped to him instead. As soon as he set eyes on Tusneem, he knew she was the girl of his dreams—beautiful, poised, educated, and the daughter of a well-established uncle from India. She fit the bill perfectly and, as luck would have it, they even liked each other.

Komli was more than delighted when she heard that for the engagement ceremony she was going to be Tusneem's only female friend and representative from India.

"How come your parents aren't flying over for the engagement ceremony?" Komli asked in surprise.

Pappa phoned the other day. Mamma's not keeping well. He said it's nothing to worry about, but rather than make two trips, for the engagement ceremony and then again for the wedding, Pappa and Mamma are going to come here in three months, for the wedding."

"Wow! That's fast!"

"I have a sneaking suspicion that things are being rushed a little because Mamma is more sick than they're letting on. I also wish things were better for you, Komli."

"They are, believe me. I will always love Mustapha, but I am no longer angry with the world! Where are we going today, Tusneem? There's too much to see in this country. Do you think your uncle will mind if you and I go somewhere on our own. Could you bear it yourself, come to think of it?"

"Bear what?"

"Being parted from Abbas."

"I think I'll survive. What do you have in mind?"

"The land of Chaucer and Shakespeare and Oliver Twist, Scotland and Wales and Ireland," Komli said with a broad smile. "Mr. Johnson is looking into the possibility of finding me a temporary job so I will have a little more money to spend. And I'd like to blow it with you, before you get married, to see any and everything we can."

Mr. Johnson not only helped Komli find a temporary clerical job at a bank where he had some connections, he also helped to find her a simple bed-sit she could afford on her weekly salary. Tusneem joined Komli whenever her prospective in-laws let her. Every once in a while, Tusneem was even allowed to go away for an entire weekend with Komli. The English pound was expensive. Both Komli and Tusneem knew that they did not have the kind of money they had in India. Making sure they had enough pennies was always a part and parcel of everything they did. However, within the space of a few weeks, they had made whirlwind trips to the Lake District and Devon and Cornwall and Oxford and Cambridge, with concerts and theater thrown in from time to time.

Reading maps was not an everyday part of life in India. The rich were chauffeured around and the poor rarely had money to go anywhere. Tusneem and Komli rarely referred to tourist maps. They found it much easier to ask passers by for directions. One Saturday afternoon, after they had walked around Canterbury and savored some of the streets and taverns mentioned in the pilgrims' tales, the two realized they needed to find a bed and breakfast for the night.

"Excuse me please. Do you know if there is a bed and breakfast nearby?" Komli asked a passerby.

"I'm sorry, I don't. I believe the priest in the cathedral is a kindly man. Ask him. He might even let you stay there."

"Did you hear that, Tusneem? Let's go find the priest. Let's tell him we've lost our party and don't know where to stay."

"Why?"

"Maybe he'll feel sorry for us and let us stay for free!"

"You can stay in the back room of the cathedral if you like," the priest replied with a twinkle in his eye. If you can survive the hard benches, that is. That's all I have I'm afraid."

The two thanked him profusely and curled up on two solid, wooden benches. Much to their embarrassment, he came along an hour later with a bowl of soup and a loaf of bread. Warmed to the very cockles of their heart and hungry stomachs, the two fell asleep, as best they could on narrow, wooden benches that creaked and groaned every time they tossed and turned.

Tusneem was up as soon as the first sunbeam hit the apology of a single, one square foot window-pane that graced the otherwise dingy little room. "God, my back is so sore!

Get up, Komli. I know I should never have listened to you!" she said as she tried to stand up straight the following morning."

"Ooooh! I'm sore, too. Was it worth saving the money we did?"

"No! You know, I think Pappa was right," Tusneem said in jest, "you have a strong influence over me. I would never have dreamed of conning a good old priest!"

"If you ask me, he conned us!" Komli retorted with a laugh. "You know what, I bet he knew all the time that we were lying to him about being lost. He knew darn well what treats our bodies were in for! If you ask me, it was his clever way of teaching us a lesson without using harsh words."

"Yeah!" Tusneem agreed, "I'll never forget how hard a free-b can be!"

"Stop looking so disgruntled. I'd rather learn a lesson laughing than crying. We're both in one piece.

"Let's go thank the priest and get out of here."

"Come back again," the priest said as he waved goodbye and chuckled to himself. Life was full of tales, he knew; he enjoyed some of the tall tales the most.

Although Tusneem ended up laughing about the episode, Komli did some serious thinking that day. Perhaps she should not always be the leader and the initiator of things, she resolved. It was not right on her part to make genteel Tusneem uncomfortable. She wanted to be Tusneem's friend, not her temptress!

That evening Komli decided to test her. She ordered wine for herself and offered it to Tusneem. "Come on, you're in England now. Take a sip."

"No! What are you doing, Komli?! You know Muslims don't drink!"

"I understand that drinking's a sin if you allow alcohol to fuzz up the brain Allah's given you. A sip of this wine is not going to do that! Come on, try it."

"Komli, stop it. Let's live and let live, please."

"Are you sure you won't just take one sip?"

"I'm sure."

"Phew! I feel so much better," Komli said squeezing Tusneem's hand.

"Why? Because for once I refused to listen to you?"

"Yes! It was only this morning that you said that there was some truth in what your father thought—that I was a bad influence on you. I took it quite seriously, you know. I had already decided that I would knock the glass out of your hands had you decided to try the wine. I want to be your friend, Tusneem, not someone who leads you astray. And, by the way, I'm sorry I forced you to sleep at the cathedral last night."

"I'm sure it will be one of those memories we'll enjoy sharing with our families. Don't worry about it. Other than knock the glass out of my hand, what would you have done, or thought, had I said okay to the wine?"

"I would have let you live and let live by keeping a little distance, impose less on your time, let you come up with suggestions as to what we do when we meet . . . ."

"And you never would have told me why, would you?"

"Probably not."

"And I would have assumed you'd made new friends! Please don't ever do that. I'm extremely happy with Abbas and his family, but no one can replace you, Komli. I can talk to you about anything. I have no secrets from you. Remember our blood bond in college?" Tusneem asked with a smile.

"I remember."

"Then you must always be open with me, promise?"

"Promise," Komli said, knowing full well she could never tell Tusneem that she had once been made to sacrifice a little more than a mere drop of blood for her.

Aatma,

> *I'm so happy for Tusneem. Her engagement ceremony was quite romantic! I could tell, though, that Tusneem missed not having her parents with her. And I'm a little ashamed that I envied her for all the people who shower her with love. I can't even imagine what it would be like to have uncles and aunts and cousins loving me so much. And as though she doesn't have enough family from her parents' side, she now has countless more from her in-laws.*

> *It also happened to be Abbas's birthday today. Although Tusneem was unable to tell me why his relatives had to swirl a coconut around his head, I was impressed with the fact that they had gone to great lengths to find green coconuts in non-tropical London. Traditions, family, money, love . . . I feel quite beggarly, but better now that I've got it out of my system. Roshni knew I would need you for soul-dusting, didn't she? I wonder what she writes in her diary.*

> *Tomorrow we're going to the theater to see the longest running play in London, The Mouse Trap. It's a murder mystery, although I first assumed that it was about women and marriage. Judging from the way young English girls talk back to their bosses in office, I doubt if marriage turns English women into meek little mice scurrying around to cook and clean for their husbands. I wish somebody at the bank would invite me to their home so I can see for myself. Wonder what kind of a wife Tusneem will make. Would I have made Mustapha a good wife? I would so have loved to cook and clean and raise his children. You know what, although I'll never admit it to Devi or her mother-in-law, being trapped in the house like a mouse with plenty of little mice scurrying around wouldn't have bothered me one bit!*

> *Writing to you sure does dust my soul. I feel so much better*

Rashid stood at Roshni's door one morning and said simply, "May I come in? I need to talk to you." Roshni wondered if she was imagining it, but he had the air of a beggar at her threshold.

Without saying a word, Roshni pointed to the two chairs in her sitting room. Rashid was struck afresh by the stark simplicity of Roshni's surroundings. As usual, she was dressed in a simple, white sari. There was nothing between her and the equally stark, white backdrop behind her. If it wasn't for her earthy brown face, her charcoal eyes, her black hair that she had knotted simply at the nape of her neck, and her ten slender, ringless fingers dangling down gracefully by her sides, she would have blurred into the white wall behind her. He knew he provided her with more than enough money for basics. Surely she could afford to adorn her home with some luxuries. But there were none. All he could see were two chairs, two tables with books on them, and a naked light bulb dangling from a wire. If a light bulb is meant to give light, why adorn it with shades, it seemed to suggest. In one corner there was an over-stacked bookcase that one could tell was in constant use.

For a fleeting moment, Rashid reflected upon the fortune he had paid for the Czechoslovakian chandelier that never failed to stun his guests as they walked into their ornate pink and gold sitting room. Every few months, Abdul's son spent an entire day cleaning the crystals on the chandelier. But of late, glitter had lost its sparkle. This pristine room before him contained everything he needed—a chair and books and the companionship of a woman with whom he yearned to discuss the books she read, knowing that he had probably read most of them himself. Unlike his beautiful library, with wall to wall mahogany shelves containing expensive, leather-bound books that gathered little dust, thanks to his servants, Roshni's inexpensive paper-back books looked like they had seen a lot of loving use. In his eyes, she epitomized peace and contentment. Ironically, she was very much a part of the reason why peace and contentment had eluded him for so many years.

Roshni said nothing. She would speak when she was spoken to, as she had done for most of her life. At long last Rashid looked up at her and said, "Zenub is dying. She has asked if she could see Komli, to ask her for forgiveness."

"But she was well when she visited last time. Of what is she dying?" Roshni asked with genuine concern. The mother in Zenub had long struck a chord in Roshni's heart. Even on the rare occasions when she had visited with her husband, it was Zenub with whom she had felt more at ease. Also, she knew that Zenub was a fallible human being and therefore more approachable than her husband, the judge, who had probably never wronged anyone in his life, nor been wronged by anyone either. In her opinion, such human beings were the most untouchable.

"According to the doctor, she has breast cancer."

"You sound as if you don't agree with the doctor," Roshni remarked, wondering why he had hesitated for a split second.

"I thought there might be other complications, but the doctors have found none. She does not have long to live. Do you think Komli will agree to go see her?"

"Komli had a miscarriage. I sent her away for a few months. She needed a holiday."

"I'm sorry to hear that. Is she alright?"

"Yes."

"Will she be returning any time soon?"

"Not for a few months. She's in England. I worked for an English gentleman who offered to sponsor her."

"Does Tusneem know she's in England?"

"Does that alarm you?" Roshni asked calmly.

"On the contrary, I hope they're in touch. Although Tusneem is very happy in England, I know she gets lonesome from time to time. Besides, she loves Komli."

"I am happy for them."

"Will you come and see Zenub?" Rashid asked humbly.

She wanted to say, yes, just to be able to see him. But she stood still and said stoically, "It is for Komli to forgive Zenub, not me."

Rashid looked as if he had been slapped in the face. "I need to get going. Is there anything you or Komli need?"

"No. Thank you." Roshni's heart went out to Rashid as she walked him to the door. The rich man looked so lost. It was obvious men needed their women. She felt she had to say something to make this sad man feel better. "Will you convey a message to Zenub?" Roshni asked suddenly.

"Yes. I hope it will help her."

"Tell her we wish her peace. Komli would not have had an education if it wasn't for her. She would not be where she is right now, if it was not for your wife. Tell her Komli is having the time of her life in London. She writes to me often, saying how wonderfully life is treating her. Tell Zenub we're never hungry, Komli's happy and I love reading and learning. None of that would have happened without her." Roshni's good nature got the better of her; she looked into his eyes and gave him a radiant, warm smile to indicate that she meant every word of it.

Rashid responded with the faintest glimmer of a smile, as if to indicate that some of the fog had lifted. Out of the blue, perhaps because of the smile she had granted him, he asked, "May I ask you, Roshni, why do you wear the clothes of a widow when you've never been married?"

"It's the easiest way to avoid questions from inquisitive neighbors. I'm happy this way."

He nodded his head to indicate that he understood. Since there was little more he could say or do, he said goodbye, wishing suddenly that he could sit down and eat a simple meal with her. No servants, no chauffeurs, no niceties. He forced himself to snap out of his day dreams. He had to go to the hospital, and then to the airport to fetch his daughter. These were hard times, doing the things that his wife did so well. He felt lonely and guilty that, while his wife was dying, he was indulging in strange thoughts about being with a woman he barely knew.

In her diary that night Roshni confessed:

Ma, I dread the times when Rashid walks into my life because it makes my heart beat so fast. And yet, as soon as I close the door on him, I wonder when he will be back again. Is it a sin to dream about stroking his hair and comforting him and telling him to stop tormenting himself because he is not to blame for his wife's actions? For the first time in my life, I'm glad Komli is not here. She has sharp eyes. I am sure if she saw me when Rashid was around, she would know that I do not think like nuns any more. She always teased me for behaving like one. When men were forced on me, I thought at least I was pure in my heart. Now I live like a nun, and think impure things. Tara Bahen seemed so horrendous once. Now she's changed into a smiling, loving person. Komli's lesson about the three states of matter changing again and again depending on how hot and cold it gets makes more and more sense.

"All the plans are made for your wedding, Tusneem, but it seems like I will not be there," Zenub said tremulously. Zenub had ignored early signs of a lump in her breast. She had thought the shooting pains would go away, that they were heartaches being manifested in another part of her body; they were the result of seeing her husband and her nephew and her sister suffer so much, she had convinced herself. When the pain became unbearable and she finally did see a doctor, she was told it was too late. When she had taken a turn for the worse, and was hospitalized, she had asked for Tusneem and Komli. She had to see the two girls. She wanted to leave this world peacefully. So it was Tusneem who flew to India to see her mother.

"Tusneem, there is something I must tell you before I die. I hope you will forgive me."

"Just rest, Mamma. There is nothing to forgive," Tusneem replied, assuming that her mother was asking for the customary forgiveness that all Bohras asked of each other regardless of age or seniority. To forgive and to feel forgiven is a part of spiritual cleansing no amount of ablution can do for you, her father had told her several years ago when she had asked him why saintly people like Motapappasan needed to ask his grandchildren for forgiveness. Sometimes, unintentionally, even the best of people commit sins, he had added.

Zenub carried on, "You know Bohra girls get circumcised at seven, don't you?"

"No. I thought only boys get circumcised. Did I?"

"You would remember if you did. That's why I need to tell you something, so I can die peacefully. I did not want you to be circumcised so I offered to help a beggar with all the money she needed to live comfortably if she would allow me to have her little sister circumcised instead of you."

"Did Pappa agree to this?" Tusneem asked, knowing that her father was too great a judge to acquiesce to something so heinous.

"No. No one was supposed to know. It was supposed to be my secret crime. Pappa came home unexpectedly and found out. He was horrified. Neither of us have ever truly recovered from it. Love for you blinded me, Tusneem. That's all I can say."

"Are all Bohra girls circumcised at seven?"

"So I am told."

"Why did you not want me circumcised if other Bohra girls are, Mamma?"

"I learnt that it curbs sexual pleasure. You will soon find out that sex is a beautiful part of marriage. I did not want to take that away from you." She wanted to explain that her sex life had not been the best, but that was not something for mothers and daughters to share. Tusneem wondered herself with some sense of discomfort what sex had been like for her parents. They seemed so happy together.

"Pappa and you are so broad-minded. Why did you simply not defy society, and refuse to have me circumcised?" Tusneem asked.

"That's what I should have done. Times were different then. I had to think of your grandmother, and the honor of our family at large. I'm sorry, Tusneem. I just had to tell you before I die. You will be a mother some day. I hope you will understand then what it is to love one's child; what a lioness will do to save her cub. Maybe you will forgive me then. I'm sorry I did not have the courage to defy society and . . ."

"Mamma, I don't have to have children to understand. Besides, you did not force the beggar to have her daughter circumcised, did you? Did you not save two women from the streets?"

"I don't know, Tusneem. When I was young I thought I knew exactly who needed what. Now that I'm about to face Allah, I can't help but ask myself, who am I to know who really needs to be saved in this world?" Zenub's voice was fading away.

"Stop talking so much, Mamma. You need to rest . . . ."

"I need to tell you one more thing, my child. The two women are Roshni and your friend, Komli."

Tusneem was unable to utter a single sound.

"I had Komli circumcised, Tusneem; the girl you have grown to love so much. Can you forgive me?" Zenub implored.

Tusneem stroked her mother's hand, unable to say anything. She realized that, ironically, Komli was not only her soul-mate who could help her talk this one through, but also the only person she could not dare approach. Would she ever be able to face her again, she wondered. She realized her mother was waiting to be forgiven. "Mamma," Tusneem said slowly, knowing she had to choose her words carefully to help soothe her, "I've been thinking, if I was faced with the same dilemma, I would . . ." she wanted to say, *run away*, but said instead, "do the same, and be comforted in the knowledge that I saved human beings from a life on the streets. I love you, Mamma. You're an angel. All mothers are angels." The tears rolled down Tusneem's face as she squeezed her mother's hand and added, "I forgive you, Mamma."

"Please ask Komli to forgive me. I love you, Tusneem."

"Does Komli know, Mamma?" Tusneem asked quickly, realizing that her mother was breathing her last. There was no reply. Tusneem decided Komli could not possibly know. If she did, she would never have anything to do with her. Besides, it was only the other day when Komli had worried about being Tusneem's temptress when in actual fact she had been her savior! Crying quietly, she closed her mother's eyes. As she kissed her on each eye-lid, Tusneem whispered, "Help me, Mamma, to summon up the courage to carry out your last wishes and ask Komli for forgiveness."

"Just be thankful she was not in pain very long," Rashid said to his grieving daughter. They looked into each others eyes, at which point it occurred to Tusneem that perhaps her parents had suffered ever since that fateful day Komli had been circumcised. "Did she suffer a lot, Pappa?" Tusneem asked suddenly.

Father smiled gently at daughter, as he remarked philosophically, "With all my book knowledge, I used to think that I had all the answers. But it seems that our Judge up there prefers to scatter the important answers in the air somewhere—we think we've captured the answers, but have we, Tusneem?"

You sound like Komli, Tusneem wanted to say, but decided that neither she nor her father were ready for that name to be brought up just yet.

Rashid thought back on the time when they had power outages in Calcutta. Zenub used to love watching the candles flicker and soar and drip away until they finally turned into insignificant mounds of wax. After he had shoveled mounds of earth over the white sheet that covered his wife's body, he thought of her also as a flame that had soared and flickered and faltered and soared again, until her flame, too, had been extinguished, leaving behind nothing but an insignificant mound of earth. It was all the same, he decided—in the end there was nothing but a mound of earth, or dust, or ashes, or wax.

He thought back on the one funeral he had attended in America when he was studying there. The casket of the deceased had been so beautiful. He had thought then that it was such a civilized way of bidding farewell to one's loved one. But now, as traumatic as it had been for him to go down six feet into the dug out earth and lay his wife to rest, he was glad he had had one final opportunity to hold her body under the pure, white sheet they had brought back from Haj. It was customary among Muslims to bring back a shroud from the holy city of Mecca. They had put away the white sheets, without thinking for a moment that they would need one so quickly. There had been something so inexplicably satisfying about laying his wife to rest himself; about making sure the tip of her delicate nose faced Mecca, and touched the earth as well. Mecca and Mother Earth—such powerful equalizers, Rashid thought philosophically; during Haj, it was impossible to distinguish between the rich and the poor because everyone was draped in simple, white cloth; everyone was but a pilgrim in the eyes of Allah; and perhaps one is also but a pilgrim in the eyes of Mother Earth, where one comes to rest sooner or later, shorn of all appellations. He felt assured suddenly that his wife was at peace and in good hands. Rashid, too, felt at peace when he finally came up again to be embraced by his male relatives. Only men were allowed to go to the cemetery for burial rites. Women were only allowed to come and pray and pay their respects after the burial rites were over.

The closest Tusneem came to realizing that her mother had finally left her was when she saw her father return home amidst loud mourning. It was not his tear-stained face that she would remember for the rest of her life; rather, it was his dirt-stained, white izaar that had conveyed to her with an unquestionable finality that her father had laid her mother to rest, that Mother Earth reigns supreme; that it is she who finally restores peace upon man.

"Death can be an awakening, Tusneem," Rashid continued. "With your mother's passing away, I have also laid to rest the unpleasant things we shared. I can now focus on the wonderful things she did for us. You know, in some ways I'm thankful that she passed away before I did."

"Why?"

"I would hate to think, had I preceded her, that my dear widowed wife would have to sit for Iddut (four-month and 10-day period of seclusion when, other than blood relatives, the widow is allowed no male visitor).

"Men don't have to sit for Iddut, do they?"

"No."

"Why do widows have to sit for Iddut?"

"I'm not sure. The roots and reasons for customs often get lost in time. Ten people will give you ten different answers. You think everyone knows why Santa Claus comes down the chimney or why the Easter bunny brings a basket?

"But those are fun things, Pappa."

"It's the same with customs that are no fun. All I know is that although your mother fought some customs and traditions in the name of love, in the name of love itself she would have sat for Iddut for my sake. Iddut is a very hard time for women. I saw my mother go through it. She was always so terrified that a male servant, or some stranger, would see her and that she would have to start Iddut all over again."

"You mean if a man saw her during the last week of her Iddut, she would have to sit again for another four months and ten days?!"

"Yes."

"How come we never fight senseless traditions and customs, Pappa?"

"Some do, Tusneem. Those that don't, cling on to faith to keep them going. I'm not sure at this point in my life that fighting customs is the answer to happiness. It is not the fighting that brings joy and sorrow. It is love. All I know right now is that I'm glad Zenub has been spared further pain. You and I are so fortunate; you had a wonderful, devoted mother, and I had everything a man could want from a wife. Strangely enough, her grace and nobility came from the customs and traditions of her forefathers. Don't ever forget that, Tusneem."

During the time that Tusneem was away in India, Komli managed to keep herself busy with her first job, in a foreign country at that. Although in her letters to her sister Komli claimed that she was very happy in England, she left out the instances that saddened her. Other than Scott, who was American, and with whom she had lunch from time to time, no one at the bank seemed to know anything about the world outside England. After the initial fascination over a handicapped foreigner was over, Komli found that there was nobody with whom she could hold a conversation during lunch time. Much to her disappointment, nobody seemed interested in socializing with her after work or during the weekends. It was during those few weeks when she decided to stay away from the Johnsons and Tusneem's prospective in-laws, that Komli first understood the meaning of being truly alone in the world. She dealt with it quite well most of the time. It gave her a strange sense of freedom.

She enjoyed her little room. It was large enough for a sofa to be turned into a bed. There was a sink in one corner, a cupboard in another and a television between the two. That was it. Perfect for her books and her few clothes. When she felt like hearing another human voice, she turned on the television. When she felt like communicating, she wrote long letters to her sister. Most of the time she enjoyed being with just her thoughts, her actions and her memories; it afforded her the opportunity to drift and to think about how she had evolved from a beggar who was always hungry into a young lady who was still hungry; the only difference was that she wasn't quite sure how to go about satisfying this new emptiness. Fortunately, she had the good sense to treat herself like a tourist at all times. There was too much to explore instead of sitting around feeling sorry for herself.

When she heard the news about Zenub, however, being alone did bother her a lot. She wrote to Roshni that night :

My dear Roshni,

How are you? I am sure by the time this letter reaches you, you will have come to know that Tusneem's mother finally passed away. Abbas phoned me this morning to tell me. It feels so strange to have my best friend's mother pass away, and no one here that I can talk to. So I'm sorry if I sound a little depressed. I need to talk to someone! It won't be too long now before I return to India. Boy, am I excited. As much as I have enjoyed the few months here in England, I think I am ready to come back, finish my teacher's training and think seriously about teaching little children. I think I am going to enjoy that very much.

It seems like it was just a few days ago that you told me to go find out what the other side of the world is like. You've gathered from my letters how much I've loved it here. England is very beautiful, Roshni.

I was supposed to go to the theater with this American guy at the bank. His name is Scott. I'm always looking up to him, because he's about a foot taller than me and because he knows a lot. He's like a walking encyclopedia, with about as much expression on his face! Although I must admit that he smiles a lot when we have lunch together. I think I confuse him because I am the best speller at the bank, I finish all my work efficiently, unlike the cheeky teenagers at the bank; I seem to know a lot compared to them, but very little compared to Scott.

When I heard this morning from Abbas that Tusneem's mother passed away, I told Scott I couldn't go to the theater. Theater tickets are expensive, but I think he understood, although he did not say much. He's the only guy at work who seems to know that in India we don't have to go jumping over lions and tigers to cross streets! It's amazing how little the Brits I work with seem to know about the country their forefathers once ruled! I would love to enlighten them, but they don't seem to know how to make conversation, not with me at least. The only time I really hear them talk non stop is on the television!

I remember you wanted me to go find out about their castes and creeds and Gods and all that. Well, there's no caste system in England so there's not much to find out. They have their rich and poor, but you can never tell if one is rich or poor, unless they open their mouths, I am told. And since they rarely open their mouths, I absolutely cannot tell the rich from the poor. Everyone carries a black brolly (umbrella), wears navy blue or gray coat and matching gloves. In Oxford street where the world assembles to shop and on the underground during rush hour, everyone is extremely touchable; the rest of the time I get the distinct impression that the Brits would like me to treat them as untouchable Gods. I am at long last in love with our Goddess, Kali, for sticking out her tongue. At least she shows some emotion!

You wondered if British people have neighbors barge in like Tara. Other than a boat, I don't think the British even understand the word 'barge'. Their homes and their hearts are exactly alike; you pass them by, day in and day out, maybe for months, but you never get to step inside. At least Tara's comings and goings were like the sunrise and the sunset, of which we got regular glimpses. Within a few weeks of our arrival in Patna, didn't we know about the lives and comings and goings of all our neighbors? Hadn't we talked to them all several times? And I know, had you not been so scared of our past, we would have been eating and socializing with them in no time. Well, in all the months I have been here, and Tusneem who's been here even longer, neither she nor I even know what our neighbors look like. It seems everybody has different times to go to work, which is the only time they open their doors, and different times to return, which is when they must quickly lock their doors shut behind them. And since I come and go at times that don't coincide with my neighbors', I have no idea what they look like. I might be working with one at the bank for all I know!

Yes, the Brits make me angry sometimes. Other than the Johnsons, these Brits open no doors and let out nothing. Nothing! Not even gas! If there's any stench, it's in the minds of the people, mine included, I know. Funny thing of course is that when we opened our doors in Patna we resented Tara barging in! But perhaps we wouldn't have minded so much had she bared her soul a little.

I thought fate had dealt me an unnecessarily large number of deaths—Ma's and Mustapha's and my baby's and, now, Tusneem's mother's. But I tell you, Roshni, the Brits beat me, hands down! There are all kinds of dead people walking among them. Some people actually pay to go walking down lanes and alleyways rumored to have ghosts! I see ghosts all the time, and I've yet to pay a penny. I do believe some go to Spain to look less deathly. To be honest with you, I am at a total loss as to how the Brits ever ruled the world. Maybe silence is more powerful than I realize.

I am so glad I have had this opportunity to understand the true meaning of loneliness. While you and Tusneem and Mustapha were around, I was never ever alone. Other than the Johnsons, I cannot say that I have been able to befriend a single Brit. It seems they are all dipped in some cold crust that rarely cracks to bare the warmth inside. They're human, so I'm assuming there's some warmth lurking in there somewhere. Maybe I would see things differently if I was born and brought up here. Maybe these are just tourist impressions. Too bad I get to take them home with me!

Do I sound like a lonely, miserable wretch? Actually I'm not that alone. Fortunately, or unfortunately, I have a constant companion these days. I've decided to call him Fixit. I guess he's been around forever. I just never paid much attention to him while I was so busy satisfying my hunger pangs for food and knowledge, and love. Now that I am alone, this little, invisible voice surfaces all the time, and since I have no one to talk to, I pay a little more attention to him. Most times he disagrees with me. He's forever telling me what to do and what to say and trying to fix my life for me. For example, when I'm eating with a fork, he keeps telling me to be gutsy and eat with my hands since I dislike the fork so much. I don't want people to think I'm a dog, I tell him. Well, they think you're some lowly creature anyway, so why try to prove to them that you're civilized! Fixit thinks I need some passion in life, other than jabbing people. He thinks I should return to Calcutta and help the needy.

I can't wait for Tusneem to return. I hope she won't postpone her wedding plans for too long. I want to be here for her wedding and I know she won't take no for an answer. As happy as she is in London, I think she misses her relatives in India. And I miss you terribly. I can't wait to return. Write soon,

With all my love,

Komli.

P.S. Surprise, surprise—I actually spoke to a neighbor tonight. Turned out to be a milkman's wife. I would have thought all milkmen's wives *are illiterate. At least that's the way it is in India, isn't it? Well, when I was being all smart and cynical with her about our crazy world, she told me ever so sweetly, 'there's a lot of good going on in this world, love; trouble is only the bad gets reported.' Which means, Roshni, that had I stayed away from reading, I would have remained as sweet and innocent as the milkman's wife. How come reading hasn't affected you at all? Is it because you run shy of the human race?*

Tusneem returned to England after a forty-day mourning period. Another auspicious date was set for her wedding. But it was not Abbas, or her wedding, that was uppermost in Tusneem's mind when she returned. Tusneem could not bear to live without knowing how Komli would react to what she had learned from her mother.

As soon as the two were able to have some time alone, Tusneem broached the subject, indirectly.

"Komli," she started cagily, "I heard a bizarre story when I was in India. I want you to tell me what you think. Has anybody ever told you that we Bohra women get circumcised at seven?"

"No," Komli lied as her heart started to beat a little faster. She knew immediately that Zenub had told Tusneem everything and that the time had come for drama and emotions; something she would much rather have avoided. In many ways, she looked upon Tusneem as her innocent, younger sister. She saw no point in making her feel guilty. She realized that to ask a simple 'were you?' would be the natural question to follow. But she could not bring herself to pretend she knew nothing. So she waited for Tusneem to continue.

"Aren't you going to ask me if I was circumcised?"

"I thought you were going to tell me a story," Komli responded.

"Well, a wealthy lady in our community did not want her daughter to go through circumcision, so she found an imposter, paid her a great sum of money which the woman desperately needed for her family. What do you think about it?"

"What's 'it'? The rich woman, or the poor woman, or the story?" Komli asked coldly.

"Whose is the greater crime, Komli?"

Komli had no doubt in her mind that the rich woman had committed the greater crime. But what if Tusneem was playing games with her, what if she knew that the rich woman was, in fact, her deceased mother. She could not be that cruel to her friend. "It's hard to tell, Tusneem. I come from a far poorer background than yours. I've heard lots of horrific things that go on among poor people. Things that rich children from rich families are rarely aware of."

Tusneem began to feel frustrated. She was expecting a more dramatic, belligerent reaction. "How would you feel if you were that imposter?" she asked suddenly, sensing that perhaps Komli knew something. She could also sense the tension in the atmosphere. In many ways, the two were like a long-married couple who could gauge each other's moods, predict questions and answers from the slightest of gestures, or even from a stony silence.

"I would feel pretty mad at first that I was sacrificed for money. On the other hand, I would find out how desperately she needed the money, because I can't see a mother sacrificing her child just for money, can you?"

"If I were to tell you that I am that saved lamb, and that my mother is the woman who bribed and bought a beggar, what would you think of us?"

"Can I think about it?" Komli asked calmly. She was deliberately under-reacting because she needed time to figure out if Tusneem knew that she was the imposter. She still wasn't ready for an emotional drama, especially since Tusneem was still mourning the death of her mother. She added quietly, "You know something Tusneem, it's hard to react to ifs. One reacts one way to a story and another way to something that really happens to one. So why don't you tell me the truth, as we always do, and then ask me questions. Let's leave out the ifs." Tusneem felt a little intimidated by Komli's tone of voice. She sounded as if she was losing patience.

"It's true. My mother did save me," Tusneem said. She could not hold back any longer. If Komli was losing patience, she may as well get it over with and face the worst. She covered her face and simply sobbed. Komli felt the tears welling up inside her, but managed to look calm.

"Do you know what happened to the girl who was circumcised," Komli asked as calmly as she could.

So Komli didn't know, Tusneem thought. She would have to tell her. Or was Komli playing games, too? Surely she remembered being circumcised. Maybe she did not, maybe she was put to sleep. Mamma was no longer around to ask questions. She looked at Komli, tears still streaming down her face. Yes, Komli, I know the girl. I don't know what happened to her inside her soul. On the outside, she's educated, headstrong, knows exactly what she wants, and her friends simply love her."

"Do you?"

"More than I love you," Tusneem said calmly, suddenly feeling an upsurge of strength that only love can unleash. Like a water cycle, the tears evaporated on Tusneem's cheeks, but came down again on Komli's. Rare tears, as rare as the rain that falls on a glistening, brown desert.

"You know something, Tusneem," Komli replied, crying and laughing at the same time, "Roshni thinks the world of me, too. She thinks I'm that gem with the best sparkle of all. But let me tell you something, if I'm that gem that sparkles, it's because your parents quietly nurtured me; they protected me from mightier waves that sweep over the streets of Calcutta, waves that come in the guise of men who would have crumbled me to dirt under their feet. These Brits can work a million wonders, even rule the world, but I doubt if they can change the hand of destiny. You and I were meant to polish each other. That's why we're still together. I would not change our friendship for anything, Tusneem. And you know, you're right, you really don't know how I feel inside. You can never put yourself in my shoes. But let me tell you, I see myself better sometimes through you. I feel very, very lucky because I have you for a friend. No one can take that away from me."

"Then do you forgive me, Komli?"

"No. You haven't done anything that needs forgiveness. Besides, remember the tenth of Mohorrem when I sneaked into your mosque? You asked me for forgiveness then!"

"But you did not say then that you forgave me. The last thing Mamma asked was that you forgive her. Do you?"

"If I didn't have Roshni, I would wish I had a mother like yours. Of course I forgive her! Can you and I even begin to understand the burden your mother was prepared to shoulder in the name of love? Ma and Roshni took quite a beating, too, in the name of love.

"Thank you, Komli!" Tusneem hugged her friend with all the strength she could muster.

"These are the times when I wish I had two hands, so I could give you a hug that feels as good as yours."

"How long have you known, Komli?"

"Since that ill-fated day when Roshni and I talked to Mustapha's parents."

"And in spite of that, you were worried that you might turn into my temptress?!" Tusneem asked in disbelief.

"Everything changes in time," Komli said with a shrug of her shoulders. "So what are the wedding plans now?"

"We won't do anything for three months."

"Tusneem, I need to get back to India," Komli exclaimed in dismay.

"Not until I'm married, you're not. Besides, there's a ton we still have to see together."

'Komli," Tusneem explained a few days before her wedding, we have a pre-nuptial Kaathaa ceremony when four different aunts have to pound things like cardamom and turmeric and other spices with pestle and mortar."

"Why?"

"I don't know. Pappa told me the other day that reasons get lost in time. So will you please just listen to what I have to say, so I can get married!"

"I'll try," Komli said with a smile, "Carry on. I won't interrupt."

"My father's sister is here and my father's brother's wife is here. Aunt Mariam, one of my mother's sisters is coming tomorrow. The fourth aunt has to be Mamma's brother's wife. Will you play proxy and be that aunt?"

"What an honor! Are you sure your family won't mind?"

"No, Komli, I've already asked."

"What do I have to do?"

"Just pound the ingredients with the pestle. You cannot look up though until we tell you."

"Why can't I look up?"

"You'll find out tomorrow. Can you wait till then?"

"Do I have a choice?" Komli asked, looking puzzled.

"No."

"Alright," Komli responded with a dramatic pout. What else does tomorrow's ceremony entail?"

"Once the pounding is over, you might get a gift from me, after which we get to eat of course. The end of all celebrations is food, thank goodness!"

"And what do I do with the pounded ingredients?"

"They get put in a clay pot which is then immersed in a natural flowing body of water, like a river. And if you dare ask me why, you might find yourself floating on the river Thames yourself!"

And it was while Komli was pounding the ingredients in her mortar, looking down and demure, as she had been told to, that she realized that everyone else had stopped pounding, but her.

"You can look up now, Komli, at the aunt sitting opposite you." Tusneem said, hardly able to contain her excitement.

"You look like my sister, Rosh . . ."

"It is," Tusneem shrieked. All else was drowned in the laughter, tears and chaos that ensued.

Rashid went up to his daughter and said quietly, "Your mother would be proud of you. You couldn't have done anything more wonderful for your friend, although for a moment I was worried the two sisters would have heart attacks! I would not even have dreamt of such a once-in-a-life-time surprise. They will thrive on the memory forever."

"Thank you for bringing her, Pappa," Tusneem said, squeezing her father's hand. "Just to see the look on their faces was worth every penny."

Indeed, Roshni had not put up too much of a fight when Rashid had knocked on her door one afternoon to ask if she would accompany him to England. He reiterated what his daughter had said to him over the telephone, that if all those years ago Roshni could make Komli play proxy for Tusneem, Tusneem now wanted Roshni to play proxy for an aunt.

Roshni was being offered a trip to see her sister. The *nun* was not superhuman. Besides, she often felt unbearably lonely herself.

It had never occurred to Roshni to offer Rashid anything for his kindness during his visits. This time she felt she should ask him at least. All she could think of was a simple glass of water. He accepted it graciously. If water was meant to purge and purify, for once he actually felt it doing so as the water coursed down his parched being. Give a man an inch, it is said, and he becomes a ruler. He put his hands on her shoulders and said, "You treat yourself like an untouchable, you dress like a widow and my daughter says that you live like a nun. I refuse to take you to England as any one of the three. I will come back tomorrow morning at ten to take you shopping."

"Yes, Sahib," Roshni had replied saucily, showing a spark of humor that she saved only for Komli and Devi.

"You'll never understand how much that glass of water meant to me. But tomorrow, make sure you have two cups of tea ready," he had commanded with a smile and walked out.

What a double-edged sword is this thing called memory, Rashid thought to himself as he flew back to India. The foundation stones on which one lives, securely or insecurely, depends so much on memories, he reflected. Good, sound memories had probably played a major role in his many achievements in life. And then, like a bolt of lightning, one bad deed, one sordid memory had slowly but surely caused major upheavals in his life.

With each passing minute, Rashid felt he was being pulled further and further away from the physical reality that was his daughter, his deceased wife, his extended family in India and his devoted Abdul who had long retired. He was returning to nothing but a house full of memories. He glanced at Roshni, sleeping peacefully beside him. She had looked so beautiful at his daughter's wedding. He had made sure he did not stare at her for too long, lest his eyes reflect that the animal in him had surfaced suddenly, after being dormant for several, long years. The animal in him had slowly died after that fateful afternoon when his wife had bared her soul to him, in more ways than one. They had made love over the years because that's what husbands and wives are supposed to do, but the spark had slowly been extinguished; sex had turned into a perfunctory act each performed for the sake of keeping up pretenses. In time even that had become unnecessary. Like traffic lights that automatically turn red, yellow and green, Rashid and Zenub had allowed social and religious obligations to control the comings and goings and turning points of their lives.

Rashid was delighted that for his daughter, too, life's ever-changing traffic lights had steered her in the right direction. Although he wished that his wife could have been present for Tusneem's wedding, and that his daughter could have experienced the grandeur and glory of weddings in Surat, instead of the relatively less glamorous wedding in London, he was glad that she was happily settled now, in the secure house of his own brother's family.

He wanted no part of his mansion any more; only the memories. Yes, they had mostly been wonderful memories.

But now he wanted to run a red light—to summon up the courage to ask a Hindu if he could visit her on a regular basis. Was he ready to allow others to judge him, for a change? More importantly, did the saintly woman beside him harbor any passions? Or had the dark memories of her past truly broken her to the point where she desired nothing for herself? Too bad there was no gauge for painful memories, he thought. Only the knowledge that memories crash in to live with one regardless of whether they're wanted or not.

When Roshni stirred, she found herself staring into the palms of her hands. Although the swirls of brick-red, celebratory henna had already started to discolor, she was happy in the knowledge that it would take decades for the memories of her whirlwind stay in London to fade away. Subconsciously, she was grateful that happier memories were usurping unhappier ones. She had laughed so much at Madam Tausaud's, she had peed in her underwear, all because her ever-babbling sister had mistaken a wax statue for a real guard.

"What are you smiling about?" Rashid asked, jolting her back to the present.

"My sister at Madam Tausaud's."

"Any other fond memories?"

"Every minute was unforgettable."

"Was the wedding hard on Komli?"

"I don't think so. I think my sister was too immersed in Tusneem's happiness, although it's never easy to tell what one's thinking deep down inside," Roshni replied, subtly sliding her right hand down to her lap. Rashid's elbow was too close to hers. She couldn't make up her mind whether she wanted the plane ride to go on forever or whether she wanted to shut herself up in her room in Patna. No, he mustn't read her mind; so she continued to talk. "About the only thing Komli found hard to digest was that you and Abbas took the oaths of marriage, while Tusneem had to sit and watch."

"At the end the priest did get Tusneem's consent, you saw that, didn't you?"

"What happens if the girl doesn't have a father?" Roshni ventured, thinking how close Komli had come to marrying his nephew.

"One finds a proxy. It happens from time to time, especially nowadays with everyone whizzing around the world!"

"You had no shortage of relations, even in England," Roshni marveled. "It was very heart-warming to see all the different aunts and uncles play significant roles in the wedding."

"Why was it heart-warming? It can be nerve-racking, trying to please everyone!"

"Really! I just got a sense of how secure Tusneem was with so many well-meaning relations around her. Speaking of security, I hope you'll take this in the right spirit, but after the Nikaah ceremony, Komli asked me if deep down all men were insecure because they always want to play leading roles in everything! Even in our Hindu weddings, the bride walks demurely behind the groom."

"I'll have to think about it," Rashid said with a laugh, wondering if this simple woman would ever realize how un-superior he felt in her presence; how much he yearned to spend time with her as her simple equal.

"Is there anything you truly need?" Roshni asked suddenly, making Rashid jump out of his skin so to speak.

"I'm not sure what you mean," Rashid replied, a shade breathless.

"Komli said I should give you something to say thank you for all you have done for us, but we couldn't come up with a single thing that might be meaningful for you."

"You and your sister are very wise. Things don't mean anything to me any more." Their eyes met. There was no need for words. Roshni understood clearly how lost he was without his wife.

"Your wife was a very sweet lady. Tusneem's just like her."

"Thank you."

"Lately I feel like I'm the luckiest woman in the world. If I can't thank you, whom should I thank? Your Allah? My Bhagvaan? The Jesus that got Komli into school?"

"Wouldn't hurt to thank them all, would it?"

The wedding, the excitement, the rounds of sightseeing with Roshni had come too quickly to an end. When Komli's life resumed to normal, she felt lonelier than ever. Her sister was back in Patna, Tusneem was honeymooning, and she was in limbo land, it seemed; working to pay off her credit cards before she could return to India. Life was neither good nor bad; it was just cold and tasteless. During one of her lunch-breaks, she found herself walking aimlessly inside Green park, wishing desperately that she had someone to talk to. She watched the passersby instead. Some were with their children, some were with their lovers, some were exercising, while the majority seemed to be rushing to their respective destinations. She decided to go sit by an old lady who was feeding the pigeons. Maybe she could strike up a conversation with her. But the birds flew away as soon as she approached. Feeling guilty, Komli crossed the street to find out what the long line was about outside Albert Hall. She found out that people were waiting patiently to get tickets for a concert. All was quiet and serious. She decided suddenly that she would just stand and smile and wave and say hello and see what happened. The first passer-by sensed she was trying to draw his attention. Being civilized and polite, he just nodded his head and continued to walk. The second one accelerated his pace as he passed her by, as if to suggest that the streets of London were, after all, full of strange, loony bins! And on they came, and away they went. Hardly anyone took the time to smile back. One, half-demented tramp did make a saucy suggestion, "I would stand at Soho if I were you. That's the place to catch 'em love."

"So . . . what?" Komli asked innocently, not knowing that Soho was one of London's red-light districts.

"So screw you!" he retorted and shuffled away, thinking the world was full of tramps like himself. Some just dressed better than others.

Within a few seconds another waif passed by and said, "You have a beautiful smile. What's a good girl like you doing that for?"

"Doing what?"

"You know what! You look like no hussy!"

"I'm not!"

"I know, but the rest of the world probably thinks you are. So stop smiling, sweetheart. I'm glad I saw that smile, though. Don't see too many these days, do you?" he added and walked away. This smiling business was for the dogs, Komli decided, although she wondered if any creature other than man was blessed with such elasticity around the mouth.

"What the hell are you doing, waving to strangers?" the next passer-by asked. It was Scott.

"I felt like a smile and a chat for lunch. I got a couple of smiles at least!"

"Would you like a sandwich with it?"

"Sounds good!"

"Are you really that desperately lonely, or are you just crazy?"

"Probably the first. Because if I was crazy, I wouldn't know that I was, would I?"

"Then how come every time I've asked you out lately you've said you're busy? Have you been lying?"

"No. I have been busy with a friend's wedding and, to top it, my sister visited as well. Everyone's back to whatever is meaningful in their lives, and I guess it just hit me today that I am just drifting in a country where no one has time for a WOG."

"As in Worthy Oriental Gentleman?"

"But it sounds derogatory, doesn't it?"

"Don't worry about it. As far as I'm concerned, you're a worthy oriental woman, which converts to WOW!"

"I like that!" Komli said, thankful for the laugh.

He watched Komli closely as she unwrapped her sandwich with one hand. "What happened to your hand?" he asked gently.

"It's not a story for lunch time," she said. She could have lied and said she was born like that, but she felt he was an honest man who deserved the truth.

"I've seen worse at war. I could handle it."

"You've fought in a war?"

"You make it sound like I've performed at the Kennedy Center!"

"What war?"

"Does it make a difference? A war is a war. Between my grandfather, father, uncles, and cousins, we've fought in two world wars, in Vietnam, in Korea, and in the Middle East. Since war is not a fairy tale, those who survive do not live happily ever after. My grandfather drinks away his memories; my father gets so lost while he's digging his yard, I wonder what it is he's digging for; my uncle runs around in his wheelchair and smiles a lot, but few people on two legs seem to notice him down there. My cousin is married and divorced and nobody knows what's made him more miserable, the war or marriage. And here I am, drifting, hoping to cast off my memories somewhere."

"That's not always easy to do, is it?"

"Nope!"

"So are you going to tell me what war you fought in?"

"Those who don't fight in wars give wars names and dates—all the better to remember them by! While those who fight in them simply want to forget it all." War's the same old hell, that just gets transported to different grounds, with different names, on different dates. That's the most I've ever talked about it. You should be flattered! So now will you tell me about your hand?"

"I will, another time."

"I don't know if there will be another time. I'm moving on in a few weeks."

"Where to?"

"Tripoli."

"Tripoli?"

"It's on the north coast of Africa, where Colonel Gaddafi rules."

"I've heard about him. He's supposed to be crazy. You're brave. Want to know why I'm down in the dumps today?"

"Tell me as we walk back."

"Did you use toilet paper on the battle field?"

Scott looked at her quizzically, "I thought you were going to talk about yourself."

"I am. I just wanted to make sure you could handle what happened in the office this morning."

"Don't tell me you were caught stealing toilet paper from the bank?"

"No!" Komli exclaimed, giggling. "But thank you for making me laugh. I need it! Until I came to England, I never used toilet paper. We clean ourselves with our hands and a pitcher of water. I'm so used to the water that I feel unclean, just wiping myself with toilet paper. So, what I've been doing at the bank is to take some toilet paper from the toilet, wet it in the sink, take it back to the toilet and wipe myself with the wet toilet paper instead of dry toilet paper. Well, a couple of days ago I forgot to take in the wet toilet paper before I went to the toilet. So I reversed the process. After I finished, I went out to the sink with my pants down. Just as I was wiping myself with wet toilet paper, Mrs. Smith walked in."

"You're kidding me!" Scott shrieked, making a few heads turn around. What did she say?!"

"She was so shocked, she just spluttered, oh excuse me, as though she had committed the crime, not me, and scampered out. In India I would have got a raucous *what the hell are you doing?* or something. These people and their stony silence is something else. All I was doing is cleaning myself, with the help of a little water! Tell me Scott, how did man clean himself before paper was invented?"

"I wasn't born then, honey, thank goodness."

"Do you know where paper comes from?"

"Trees, I believe. Everybody knows that. You make it sound like some great mystery," Scott replied as he gave her another questioning look.

"If everybody knows that, how come people think little about using the poor tree's metamorphosed trunk to wipe their asses?"

"So they don't itch, I would think!" Scott replied facetiously.

Komli ignored him as she carried on, "Just think, Scott, trunks, trillions of trunks, transformed into tons of toilet paper while bewildered birds and beasts helplessly screech and flap their wings, wondering what they did to deserve the rape and pillage of their habitat. But man is so full of shit . . . ."

"I know! Otherwise he wouldn't need toilet paper . . ."

"Man is so obsessed with himself that I'm sure he never thinks of the birds and beasts while he's cleaning his rear end!"

"Did you say that to Mrs. Smith?" Scott asked laughing hard.

"Hell, no! Every time I saw her, her face looked as red as a baboon's ass."

"God! You have quite a tongue on you!"

"Better than hurling insults by saying nothing! Anyway, Mrs. Smith called me in today. I guess she had the weekend to recover. She said that the bank would not be able to renew my temporary work permit. So this week's my last week at work."

"I'm sorry, Komli. I can't say that I'll miss you, I'm leaving the bank myself. There are a ton of jobs out there. You'll get another one."

"I'm here on a tourist visa. The only reason I got this job is because of an English family my sister knew in India. There's no way I'm going to ask them to pull more strings for me."

"So what do you propose to do?"

"I'm in a bit of a fix because I've run up quite a credit card that I need to pay off before I leave."

"We're almost at the bank. Give me your phone number. I might come up with something."

Three days later Scott asked her to meet him after work. "It's a nice day, would you like to go to Green Park for a while, before we go and sit inside somewhere?"

"Yes, I'd much prefer that myself," Komli said, since it was a nice, unusually warm June evening.

"Tell me, what brought you to England on your own? I thought single, Indian women . . . ."

"Stay at home and cook and clean and sew their lives away?"

"Something like that. What brings you here, on your own?"

"I'm in what some might call an extremely fortunate situation in that I have no parents to tell me what to do, and an older sister who thinks I am the sun around which she must revolve."

"And are you trying to run away from her?"

"On the contrary, she suggested I leave India for a while, to recover from some things that should never have happened. Tell me, Scott, if a Catholic and a Protestant couple want to get married in America, how would their parents react?"

"As long as they're not both of the same sex, most parents would heave a sigh of relief and bless them, I would imagine."

"God, it never occurred to me that there could be worse scenarios! I'm Hindu. I wanted to marry a Muslim. We couldn't. He ended up taking his life and I ended up losing our baby."

"I'm sorry . . ."

"So here I am, trying to find out if the rest of the world's Gods and religions and customs and cultures are as crazy as some of ours in India. At least that's what my sister asked me to do when she urged me to get away for a while."

Scott decided then that he would do all he could to persuade her to work with him in Tripoli. Not only was she hard working, something about her honest, unselfconscious ways appealed to him. "So what have you found out so far?" he asked.

Even though Scott was not English, he was white. Komli decided not to tell him what she thought of the British. Besides, he had accused her of having quite a tongue! So she pointed to a flower and remarked casually, "I wonder what it would be like to be a flower, rooted to one spot. Never go out of your way to talk to anyone, never get pricked by another's thorns, just sway with the breeze, listen to the music of the bees and the butterflies, soak up the sun and the rain, make some food for who knows what magical creature on planet earth, let out one's fragrance when one matures and then silently fade away, leaving behind a few seeds to carry on one's work. Sounds like heaven, doesn't it?"

"Boring after a while I would imagine."

"Well, if you believed in reincarnation, you wouldn't have to be a flower all your life."

"So what else would you like to be?"

"I think human being's the most interesting, but I could handle being the wind for one life. That would be fun."

"You realize that's the exact opposite of flower. You would be rootless, without fragrance and blow your life away."

"That's what you might do! I would whisper in people's ears . . . ."

"To stop using toilet paper!" Scott retorted with a laugh.

"I would pick up the fragrances of flowers and waft them in and out of homes with open doors. I would never sit still, that's for sure. I would travel over seas and mountains. Imagine being able to stand right on top of Niagara falls one day, and Mount Everest the next, and breeze in and out of rain forests on the way! What would you choose, Scott, if you had a choice?"

"Anything that's deaf, so I wouldn't have to listen to man."

"Seriously, is there anything you'd want to become?"

Scott thought for a moment, wondering how to amuse this creature who sought the silence of flowers but could not stop talking. "My first choice would be God Almighty, since I'm not sure there is one. My second choice would be dog."

"Master and slave. Opposites, too, like flower and wind. What would you do as master?"

"Have wine, women and cigarettes for the rest of my life."

"And that would make you happy?"

"Very happy."

"What would you change?"

"Nothing. If I'm happy why would I care? That might be one of the answers you are seeking. God's happy; He doesn't give a shit what happens down here. You can tell your sister I solved one mystery for you."

"Actually, you haven't. My God likes wine, doesn't womanize, doesn't smoke and He cares about what goes on down here."

"And what wine does He drink?" Scott asked with a smile, "Maybe He and I have the same tastes!"

Komli started laughing herself. "Father Michael is the reason why I sometimes picture god in flowing white robes, sipping red wine from golden goblets."

"If you're Hindu, why did you have to listen to this Father Michael, who I assume was a Catholic priest?"

"I was orphaned early, remember? Father Michael helped me get admitted to a good school, on the condition that I listened to his stories."

"Did he try and convert you?" Scott asked with the slightest hint of anger.

"Hell, no! It was I who milked him. We got free milk after each session. My sister asked me to listen to his sermons quietly with one ear and take it out of the other. Some of it got stuck in between though," she said giving him a broad smile.

"You must have a lot of weeding to do!"

"Maybe, but I can't be bothered. It gets especially wild when I chat with my best friend, Tusneem. She's Muslim. The three of us should have coffee some time. We'd make quite an unholy trinity, I'm sure."

Scott did not let Komli know that he already knew a fair amount about the religions of the world; about prophets, priests, rabbis, messengers, monks and disciples, either in exile, in hiding, or in the making. He had seen enough in his travels to arrive at the conclusion that wherever they roamed, or wherever they hid, in the interim man had to make do with images, concrete or otherwise. Right now he was more interested in the amusing images living in the inner recesses of Komli's mind. He had never consciously tried to rid himself of the Father, the Son and the Holy Ghost on which he had been raised. It just so happened that memories of stench and blood and death and the agonizing moans of wounded soldiers had usurped that corner of his mind. As far as he was concerned, wars and religions were alike—glory only came after death and, in both cases, there were lots of little people following their commander in the fear that if they disobeyed all hell would be let loose.

"How would you like to work as my secretary in Tripoli?" Scott asked suddenly. He had decided he would definitely like her to work with him.

"With that mad man, Gaddafi?"

"He's not the only mad man in our world, as I am sure you already know. So that shouldn't bother you too much. The pay is excellent, about four times what you make here," Scott threw in, knowing that she needed the money.

"Are you telling me you can get me a job there?" Komli asked. The prospect of being able to pay off her credit cards quickly so she could return to India sounded very enticing suddenly.

"I'm climbing up the social ladder, so to speak. I'm going to be the data base manager for Libya's oil company. And, guess what, I get to have some say as to who I want for my secretary. If you're interested, get hold of today's newspaper and apply for the job. Two Libyan gentlemen are coming down here to interview secretaries. You can be one of the candidates."

"What makes you think I can be an efficient secretary?"

"I've seen you work at the bank. You may not be Miss Efficiency, but judging from what I've seen here, you'll make a better secretary than some of the girls I've worked with." Seeing that she wasn't sure, he added, "What have you to lose simply by applying? You don't have to make up your mind today, you know. Come for the interview, meet the Libyans, see how you feel about them. Believe me, not everyone feels comfortable with the Libyans. I have a strong feeling though that you won't have any problems."

"What about this stump of a hand of mine? Mr. Johnson pulled strings for me, that's why I got the job at the bank."

"All I can say to the Libyans is that I've seen you function better with one hand than I've seen some function with two. By the way, I wish you wouldn't call it a stump."

"Why not?"

"'Cause ice-cream has no bones."

"'Cause what?!"

"'Cause it makes you special."

"Beauty lies in the eyes of the beholder, huh?"

"I guess. By the way, I can think of a very good reason why you'll definitely prefer Tripoli to England."

"Why?"

"They have bidets beside the toilets in all their bathrooms."

"And what pray tell is a bidet?"

"It's something like a toilet with a water fountain. So you go to the toilet and then sit yourself down on the bidet to wash yourself! No one will fire you for using water instead of toilet paper!" Scott said with a smile.

"I wasn't fired for that reason, but you can make fun of me if you want to. I don't mind that."

"I'm not. I probably have more respect for water than you have. I've been in situations where I've been without baths for weeks at a time. Believe me, it makes one appreciate water. Are you hungry? Would you like to go have a bite somewhere?"

"Sounds wonderful. I'm starving."

"What do you fancy eating?"

"Anything that's not English."

"My, my, you really do need to get out of this country, don't you?"

Aatma,

> *Tusneem thinks I'm crazy to even think about going to Libya since it's ruled by Gaddafi who's supposed to be some crazy fanatic. But Scott tells me that there are so many crazy people in the world, that if he decided to stay away from them, he would have to stay at home all the time! He quipped about not being sure if he himself was safe to be around! I like him. He's funny and very down to earth. He's fought in some war, but refuses to tell me which one. If you ask me, he lives in the trenches most of the time. Maybe that's why he's so nice and down to earth!*

> *If I accept the job, I'll be working for Scott in the Computer department of Libyan Oil Company. He told the Libyans he would like me to work as his secretary, which made it a lot easier for me to land the job, I suppose. I looked so prim and proper for the interview,*

Roshni would have been proud of me! I looked like a serious school teacher with hair in a simple knot on the nape of my neck. Fixit advised me to make sure the two Libyans who interviewed me see my stump as soon as I walk in, to indicate that I was not afraid of being one-handed. Well, the guys didn't so much as mention my hand, like it didn't exist! All they mentioned was that Tripoli wasn't like London and there was very little to do outside of work. They wondered if I would be able to handle being alone. Maybe those lonely days in London were fate's way of preparing me for Tripoli. I assured them that I love my own company as long as I have plenty to read. Scott had advised me, under no circumstances, to air my opinions and to answer their questions as briefly as possible. He said Middle-Eastern men don't expect women to think and that since I had some strange ideas anyway about trees and toilet paper, I should say as little as possible. So I smiled a lot, said as little as possible, and landed the job!

I know Roshni will be upset with me, but I'm sure she'll understand once I explain my credit card situation. Besides, she was the one who insisted I go and find out what the rest of the world is like. Do you think I should pass up such an opportunity? This job is so perfectly timed. It pays about four times what I make in London. To top it, I get one month's vacation and twice a year I get something called R &R, which means that the company I work for will actually pay me to go away somewhere to Rest and Recuperate! I leave for Tripoli in about a month after I accept the job. Scott's already there. Scott's advice to me before he left was to travel light. The less baggage you bring, he said, the longer you'll tarry in the hearts and homes of foreigners. Maybe that's why I couldn't stomach the Brits; I carried too much baggage from India! From now on, wherever I go, I'm traveling light.

It was Fixit who had finally convinced Komli to jump at the opportunity to go to Libya. Use it as a stepping stone to see Africa, he had said. You got little warmth from cold, old England; see what the hot desert has to offer. Besides, it's not as if you're leaving behind a husband and children or being irresponsible in any way. If something should happen to you, it won't be such a great tragedy for anyone! Only Fixit would dare say such a thing, Komli thought wryly. But she knew he was right.

On the eve of her departure for Tripoli, Komli laid back in bed and looked lovingly at the scroll that graced the otherwise bare walls of her bed-sit. *DESIDERATA*, it said in bold red. By now she had memorized the first sentence of the scroll, *Go placidly amid the noise and haste and remember what peace there may be in silence.* She stared at it and smiled to herself. It was definitely the best gift she had received from an Englishman. She would never forget that Sunday stroll in Green Park, much less the tramp through whom she had first become acquainted with the famous words of Desiderata. The tramp had propped up a stand on the sidewalk outside Green Park. He was a tattered and torn, wizened and withered piece of humanity with a bald head sprouting soft, patchy tufts of white hair. His gums were swollen and spongy. A dental prong would have confirmed a serious case of gingivitis. His few teeth looked more like miniature remnants of a burnt, wooden fence that had been hammered in willy nilly. The cigarette dangling out of his mouth would have long been stubbed out by one more genteel—it was no more than a centimeter long! Komli tried to draw his attention but it seemed he was gazing into another world. So she started reading some of the old parchment scrolls he had stuck here and there at random. This was no Harrods. Scrolls were propped up on a couple of easels. Some dangled on the iron rail of the park, some were scattered on what looked like an old suitcase. She wondered if it contained his worldly possessions. When Komli came across *Desiderata,* she was simply enthralled by its truth and simplicity. She asked the tramp if she could buy it.

"This is an old scroll. Give me five pounds and your address and I will mail a new one to you." Yeah, right, Komli thought to herself cynically, you probably can't even read and write. You'll pocket my money and I'll never see the scroll.

She had started walking away when she heard him recite a line from the scroll, *Exercise caution in your business affairs for the world is full of trickery. But let this not blind you to what virtue there is. With all its sham, drudgery and broken dreams, it is still a beautiful world. Strive to be happy.* Then he had added, "You must believe in Desiderata. Come here, love. Give me your address. You don't have to pay me now. I'll send you the scroll and you can pay me afterwards." Komli had given him her address, sure of two things—she would never get the scroll, and he was too old to come and rape her.

Two weeks later the scroll had arrived in the mail, but without the tramp's address! Komli was left breathless. That old man was no tramp! And although she never saw him again, as far as she was concerned, he was metamorphosed into a shining star in her sky of memories. She wondered if there was a religion somewhere that believed Him-up-there was a homeless tramp. After all, nobody really knew God's address.

She decided, no matter how light she had to travel, Desiderata would go with her wherever she went. It was the last thing she took off the wall Monday morning, when Tusneem arrived to take her to the airport.

C♋80

CHAPTER 5

CONFUSION

It was a dull, dismal, chilly morning when Komli said goodbye to Tusneem. The farewell party Tusneem had held for Komli the night before had already put quite a damper to her departure. Neither Tusneem's in-laws nor the few friends she had invited had anything but negative things to say about Gaddafi. If there had been anything positive, it was their admiration for Komli for venturing out into unsafe territories.

"You're so gutsy! I would not dream of going to the Middle East on my own."

"I'm going to Tripoli. That's North Africa."

"Gaddafi's as close to an Arab as you are to India. He's a mad man. He's supported lunatics like Idi Amin!"

"And terrorists everywhere."

"Russia's backed him with weapons that are dangerous in the hands of a mad man."

"He's bombed embassies . . . ."

"Leave her alone," Tusneem had asked, although in her heart of hearts she knew there was some truth in what her friends were saying. She herself had tried to talk Komli out of going, but to no avail. She had offered to pay off her credit cards, or at least to loan her the money.

"You only live once, Tusneem. Besides, most people treat me kindly because of my stump. Just remember that, every time you start worrying about me."

"If we don't hear from you in a couple of days, we'll know you were machine-gunned at the airport itself!" some smart alec had quipped before bidding Komli farewell.

Keep smiling, Fixit had advised; *this is supposed to be a party. These people have no business crushing your spirit! If you really want to experience life, you can't afford to be a wimp!*

Without betraying any emotions at all, Komli found her seat on the plane. She felt worse than a wimp. This time, nothing about the airplane fascinated her. She sat back and thought gruesome thoughts about her life. Wretched beggar in need of money to pay off her credit cards, maimed hand, circumcised, single, miscarriage, rootless, and now off to get machine-gunned at the airport itself, by the sounds of everything she had heard the night before! No one in the world really needed her, so if she got machine-gunned, she got machine gunned, she said to herself bravely. Feeling sorry for her, Fixit brought up the positive side of her life—*at least you're attempting to see the world; you have a loving sister, a caring friend, warm memories of Mustapha, you've traveled a little, and you're gutsy, not that bad, if you ask me.* Komli could hardly wait to land. If she survived the airport, maybe she would crawl out of the morbid state of mind into which she had slumped.

Holding her breath, Komli stepped out of the plane. She was expecting a dirty, dusty airport with shabbily clad, hot-tempered Arabs pointing machine guns at her. To her relief, there was not a gun in sight. Instead, the airport was spotless, sanitized, and extremely quiet; so unlike the zoo that had been Heathrow airport but a few hours ago. Unable to find a single sign in English, she followed the other passengers. Wow, she thought to herself after a few minutes, all the signs are in one language alone, Arabic. She had assumed all airports had signs in at least two or three languages. She had taken it for granted that all the world bowed down to English, the queen of languages; that everywhere people felt that they must know English in order to be considered educated. Here was a dictator who invited experts from all over the world to modernize his country and to draw out its oil, but when they arrived at the airport he had no qualms about telling them, without a single spoken word, that Libyans didn't feel the need to conform to western standards; that if foreigners couldn't read Arabic, tough! It was the first time Komli had seen something silently suggesting that there were people in the world who didn't give a damn if English speaking people didn't understand! How about trying to learn our language for a change, the Arabic signs seemed to suggest. She was impressed.

It looks like this race does not lick the white man's ass, Fixit observed bluntly.

The immigration officer was smartly dressed in crisply ironed khaki trousers and shirt; a far cry from the dirty, disheveled, illiterate Arab she was expecting. He looked at her stoically and then proceeded to examine her passport and work permit. *Look dignified and serious*, Fixit advised. *You're Indian, in your early twenties, and not married. You're probably suspect!* The immigration officer asked her a few, courteous questions in pidgin English and let her go.

The customs officer was equally stoic, until he noticed a scroll in her hand.

"Show me," he demanded, pointing to the scroll. Komli handed it to him with a smile, quite certain that he, too, would fall in love with *Desiderata*. He cast a cursory glance at the scroll before asking, "It's your religion? No religious documents allowed." He chucked the scroll in the trash can.

"Please, sir," Komli pleaded, "it's a beautiful saying. It's very precious to me."

"Why?" the customs officer demanded.

Don't tell him a tramp gave it to you! He won't understand, Fixit quickly advised; *succor up to his sympathy, tell him your teacher gave it to you when you lost your hand.*

"My teacher gave it to me when I lost my hand in a car accident," Komli replied, looking genuinely stricken.

"Ah! Keep it," he said, as he fished out the scroll from the trash can and handed it to her. You have any other books, magazines?"

"A few. They're in my bag."

"No magazines!" he said, "Show me." Happily, Komli handed him the magazines she had picked up at the airport. They were replaceable. He nodded to her to leave, chucking the magazines in the trash can.

"Thank you," she said, heaving a sigh of relief. She hadn't been gunned down, physically or otherwise. Her spirits lifted as she walked out to the arrival lounge to meet Scott. A sea of strange faces greeted her. Most of the men waiting outside did look unkempt and unemployed. The handful of women she spotted were in purdah (veil). She felt as though she was being stripped naked by the galaxy of eyes that seemed to be piercing through her very being as she stood still, with suitcase in hand, eyes searching for a familiar white face. I don't even know where my place of work is; I don't speak the language and this certainly does not seem to be a place for a single, stranded woman, Komli thought, while she wondered what she should do. *Don't look anyone in the eyes, they'll think you're waiting desperately to be picked up*, Fixit advised cheekily. Komli did not appreciate his joke, and was thankful she could ignore him. Her eyes continued to search for Scott, but alas, there were no six-footed white men around; he would be easy to spot in a crowd of strange looking men with curly, black hair and light brown skin.

Suddenly there was a tap on her shoulder. "Miss Komli Seth?" a man in a spotless white robe asked her.

"Yes!" Komli replied, spinning around and, at the same time, curbing her desire to leap up and embrace him—somebody in the world knew her, was all she could think of. 'Miss Komli Seth'. What a magical sound! He beckoned to her matter-of-factly to follow him, without introducing himself or offering to assist her with her suitcase. I guess this is my first glimpse of the uncivilized Libyan, Komli thought quietly, although she was relieved that at least she had been met.

"Where's Scott?"

"Who?"

"I mean Mr. Duncan, from Libyan Oil Company. He was supposed to meet me."

"Oh, I have a note for you," he said casually, handing her a folded piece of paper.

The note was from a Mr. Saleh, saying that Scott sent his apologies. He would see her in a day or two and that, in the meantime, she would be received by a few ladies who would be waiting for her in the office building. There was no time to allow either fear or anger to surface; the Arab had started walking off. Komli had little choice but to struggle behind him with her heavy suitcase that contained more books than clothing. Fortunately, it wasn't too long before they came to a shining, pale blue limousine, waiting for her, chauffeur and all! Maybe this Arab is the chairman or someone who handles important people, Komli thought naively.

Yes, he's definitely something that does not handle baggage, Fixit said sarcastically.

The chauffeur took her luggage and placed it in the boot. No one was introduced, no names were exchanged, and since both men climbed into the front, Komli assumed that she was expected to slide quietly into the back of this plush, leather-upholstered piece of luxury.

What if they take me somewhere and rape me, Komli asked herself, as she hesitated at the door. Fixit encouraged her to take the risk, *your choice is to stand and be stared at by strangers, or trust these guys. Your luggage is already in the boot, by the way.* Komli decided to trust the two strangers. She slid into the back seat. The two men began jabbering in Arabic, oblivious of the baggage behind them. Komli longed to ask questions, but Fixit convinced her to be quiet. *In these people's eyes you are mere chattel, to be relegated to the back seat. You must play the role of a docile Indian, and a woman at that, as is expected among Arabs.*

So Komli gazed out into the desert, into the billion specs of sand that passed her by. Father Michael's words came back to haunt her, 'Dust thou art, and to dust thou shall returneth'. She wondered if the sand dunes they whizzed past had once upon a time been people. Was the little sand dune England? The slightly bigger one Spain? And was the real big one India? Maybe they were mounds of dead Jews, Christians, and Muslims.

Strange, what goes through your mind when there are no human beings to talk to, Fixit mused.

Komli was surprised to see healthy, hailed-from-Switzerland type cows grazing on beautiful patches of lush, green grass. Scott had told her that Libyans had the money to import anything they wanted—water for grass, grass for cows, cows for beef, beef for people, people for drilling oil, oil for wealth, wealth for power, power for control. He had also warned that Gaddafi had the power to keep out what he did not want and that she must be careful what she said to people. He had made her promise to be forthright to no one but himself. Well, she had no choice right now but to keep quiet. Komli shut her eyes for a while and invoked the name of Vishnu. Preserve me, mighty Vishnu, she implored, I'm not ready to be turned into a spec of dust. I've had glimpses of the east and the west. Please let me survive what lies in between. And with that prayer out of her way, she wondered with some trepidation what plans the two men had for her. When the car came to a smooth halt in front of a tall, multi-storied building that said Libyan Oil Company in bold, black letters, Komli heaved a sigh of relief—the men were not out to get her; so much for skepticism!

Brenda, who had been in Tripoli for just about a month, was waiting for her in a lavishly adorned foyer. Exotic, tropical plants in huge, colorful pots welcomed Komli. The spotlessly-buffed, marble floor had ripples of earthy blues, greens and copper meandering in free form. Three, plush, sage-green sofas around a table strewn with magazines suggested anything but uncivilized. Brenda also turned out to be warm and friendly. Like Komli, she loved to talk. Just the dose Komli needed for her parched, dwindling spirits and her new-found sense of security.

Wow, Komli thought, I could be in a sophisticated office building in Singapore, for all I know!

"Don't you have any more luggage?" Brenda asked.

"No, just this suitcase."

"Then let me show you your apartment. The first five floors of this building are offices. The three floors above it are residential, for expats."

"What's expats?"

"Short for expatriates; all the non-Libyans who live in this building are expatriates. We'll have dinner together, so you can meet some of the other expats. Sheila and Jane were supposed to be here to welcome you, but they're up cooking dinner. You'll meet them tonight."

"Do you know anything about Scott Duncan? He's only been here a few weeks. He was supposed to meet me at the airport."

"Yes. We were expecting him at a party last night, but he didn't show up. We've tried his apartment, but there's no reply. Hopefully, he'll show up tonight. Do you know him well?"

"We worked at the same bank in London. He's the one who told me about this job."

"He'll be around, don't worry. There are essentially two kinds of expats here—the kind that keep to themselves and the kind that stick together and socialize because there's not much else to do here. If you like socializing, you won't have a dull moment, believe me. There are tons of nice people around." If Brenda was an example, then she would survive, Komli thought, as she was shown into her apartment.

"I believe your roommate is arriving in a few weeks," Brenda added as she turned the keys to Komli's apartment. You'll have the apartment all to yourself until then. Choose the bedroom you want. You share everything else with your roommate. I'm going to leave you to unpack and settle down. Whenever you're ready, just come down to apartment number 602, one floor below. If you need anything, just let me know."

Komli went straight to the kitchen. It was at least twice the size of the Johnson's kitchen. Casually she inspected the contents of the drawers and kitchen cabinets. It was well equipped with all the gadgets she had seen at the Johnson's. The rest of the apartment consisted of a dining room, utility room, two huge bedrooms with attached bathrooms and a huge sitting room with pale blue sofas that looked terribly lonesome.

You could start socializing, Fixit suggested, as Komli rattled through the spacious apartment with him; *you can have big parties in this room, that's for sure! Let's check out the bidet Scott was talking about. I wonder if, like him, that, too, is non-existent!* Komli inspected both bedrooms and decided to choose the one with the better view. There sure was a pretty peach colored bidet by the toilet. Scott wasn't lying after all. Hopefully, he would show up for dinner, she thought.

Komli found some thumb tacks in the kitchen drawer. She nailed *Desiderata* to her bedroom wall. Having nothing else to do, she unpacked the linen which she had been advised to bring, made her bed and propped herself up on the pillows. She could read the scroll clearly from where she was. She read it twice through. *I think we're going to have lots of time to memorize it,* Fixit assured her. *Why don't we go down and meet some people instead?*

Most of Brenda's friends were white. However, unlike England, where Komli always felt that WOGS were unwanted, Brenda's friends warmly welcomed her. They were from many different parts of the world, she found out later, although Brenda and all the other female secretaries were hired from England.

Most of the guests seemed to be sipping red or white wine, which confused Komli because she had been told very categorically at the interview that alcohol was strictly forbidden in Libya.

Ask them where it comes from, Fixit urged. *But K*omli wasn't interested in finding out. One of her ears was attuned to the doorbell. Every time it rang, she looked up, hoping to see Scott.

Around eight in the evening, a straight-faced, unshaven Scott stood at the door, patiently waiting for the sarcastic remarks to abate before he shrugged his shoulders coolly and remarked, "No, I wasn't dead drunk and I didn't oversleep either. Wish I had, though! I strolled down to the souq (market place) yesterday and got picked up by the police!" He couldn't see Komli quietly standing in a corner. Was the continuous twirling of his moustache an indication that he was a little nervous, she wondered.

Why? What for? what happened? different voices asked simultaneously.

"Don't know. This police just tapped me on the shoulder and started talking in Arabic. Then I was escorted to the police station where they asked me questions I could barely understand, about where I worked and what I did. It took them over 36 hours to look at my papers, make telephone calls, who knows what else, before they decided to release me, just like that!"

"But on what grounds did they take you in to begin with?"

"Libyan, I guess! I haven't the faintest idea!"

"Bet they thought you were an East European spy; you look like one!" Geoff retorted, giving him a glad-to-see-you-back thump on the shoulders. "I warned you about safety in numbers, didn't I?"

"The bastards allowed me to make one telephone call. By the way, does anyone know if a Komli Seth arrived this morning? I phoned Mr. Saleh and asked him to make sure he sends her a note."

"Are you referring to that shy, young lady there?"

Scott apologized to her for not being able to meet her at the airport, but was relieved that she had arrived safely.

"Hey, Geoff," he called out a few minutes later, "you've been here long enough. Why don't you give Komli the do's and don'ts talk. Don't want her making the mistake I made yesterday!"

Geoff had been in Tripoli several years. He played the dual role of brother to all and devil's advocate, too, depending on the needs of the expatriate. He sat himself down beside

Komli and advised her, "Never go anywhere without your Identity Card which you'll get on Sunday in the office. Weekends here are Friday and Saturday, since Friday is the holy day. You heard what happened to Scott. Don't go out on your own. There are no theaters or cinemas or places to go to other than the beach. Expats simply stick together. The Libyans don't trust us; they think we're all promiscuous devils, and that's a blessing in disguise, believe me. You don't want to trust them either. There's a lot of gossip. You'll soon learn to sift out the truth from the exaggerations, although sometimes the truth seems like exaggeration and exaggeration like truth! There's a story a day, like the one we just heard from the horse's mouth! If you toe the line, you'll have fun, I promise."

"Is alcohol allowed among expatriates?"

"Expats, you mean?"

"I like the sound of 'expatriates', I rarely abbreviate words."

"Good! You can help me out in scrabble. Abbreviations are not allowed."

"What else do I need to know."

"Ah, yes, never, never say anything in public against Gaddafi or the Libyans. Remember, they are always right; that's the golden rule here.

"She asked you a question about alcohol. You may as well tell her what we stash under our beds."

"The forbidden wine is delicious, Komli!" Geoff said, dramatically kissing the tips of all five fingers on his right hand and thrusting them out in the air. When I see expats buying gallons of grape juice, tons of sugar and little packets of yeast, I make sure I get to know them. That's where the next batch of wine will be sooner or later. Sooner or later depends upon how desperate one gets about consuming it! A lot of expats have a little cottage industry that keeps them busy during weekends; they brew and bottle batches of bubbling wine. All the better to drown their sorrows with!" He's pretty entertaining, Komli thought, as she laughed at the clown. 'Frail' was the word that came to Komli's mind as she studied Geoff. He was short and skinny. She wondered if he sported the salt-and-pepper goatee beard to make him look a little more respectable.

Hope you made a note of the fact that they drink to drown their sorrows, Fixit whispered.

"You mean people stash wine under their beds?!" Komli asked in disbelief.

"Yup! Helps you sleep better! And if someone warns you about a police raid, you have to stay up all night and guzzle the wine down! You can never risk being caught with it red-handed, and I think it's an even greater crime to flush it down the toilet!"

"You're scaring her, Geoff. Stop it!" Scott commanded, although he couldn't help laughing at the harmless comedian.

"There's one more thing you need to know because you'll find out sooner or later. There's a big black money racket going on."

"What's that?"

"You get paid a fat salary in pound sterling. You send it to your bank in England of course. But you need some dinars for living expenses here. You write a pound check to me for your living expenses. I give you more dinars than the official rate here because the local people want your pound check. British money, you know. Everybody wants the Queen's money! I am told the Libyans have tons of pounds stashed away in Swiss banks!"

"I don't think I get it."

"They say that back home all the time—if you don't get it, you don't get it! Don't worry, Komli," Scott added, "you just toe the line and ignore the bit about the wine and money laundering."

"Laundering?" Komli asked.

"Just ignore it, Komli, I'm hungry. Let's go see what food there is. Geoff's a good guy, although a little crazy. He's been here too long."

"I heard that!" Geoff retorted. "I've been here long enough to tell you that what you two do in private is your business. In public, keep a low profile and you'll find it's quite nice here, really, especially the increments! I'm a living example. I've been here seven years! Let's drink to that!"

Later that evening, Scott offered to take Komli back to her room. "May I see what your apartment's like? Or is that a no-no?"

"No, it's not a no-no," Komli said confidently. "I wasn't so much as touched by two, strange Arabs who picked me up at the airport. To top it, I've been warmly welcomed, you haven't turned out to be some con man, and the apartment is fit for a queen as far as I am concerned. It's equipped with more goodies than I've ever owned in my life. I feel totally invulnerable now!"

"Is there anything you need immediately?" Scott asked as he glanced around the apartment to make sure everything was alright.

"I could do with some tea and milk for the morning. Other than that, I'll be alright until tomorrow. Where do I have to go to buy basic food supplies?"

"I believe Brenda has arranged for Melissa to take you shopping tomorrow. Talk to her. I hear it's quite an experience for those who don't eat out of cans!"

"Is that all you eat?"

"Fast foods and restaurants make good alternatives. I see you already have something on the wall," Scott remarked when he saw *Desiderata* on her bedroom wall.

"That goes with me wherever I go."

After Scott glanced over the lines he remarked, "From the sound of things, it looks like you'll have to forget that line about speaking your truth quietly and clearly. I think what Geoff was hinting at is that you don't speak much at all, just listen."

"That would be a nice change from England. I love listening to people. By the way, I tried the bidet. What a nice invention!"

"I'm glad you like it," Scott replied. "Others also think of saving trees, it seems."

"I wish I'd never mentioned that toilet paper incident to you," Komli said with a laugh.

"Be thankful for your views, Komli. At least you won't panic like the rest of us when there's a toilet paper shortage in this country!"

"What do you mean?"

"You'll see, when you go shopping tomorrow. Goodnight."

A tired Komli went to bed that night, happy in the knowledge that she had not been let down by Scott.

Around noon the next morning, Melissa knocked on Komli's door. Komli noticed that Melissa was not as sun-tanned as some of the other expatriates. With her short-cropped, un-styled hair, and plain, cotton pinafore she looked more like a dedicated school teacher than some of the more attractive single women she had met the night before. As Komli would find out later, Melissa's body and mind did not adapt well to change of climate or culture.

"Have you made your list of what you need?" Melissa asked, getting to business straight away.

"No. I just need basic things like salt and pepper and bread and milk and rice and . . . ."

"Stop, stop! Melissa exclaimed, "This is Tripoli. There's no supermarket by our office. And the one downtown is not worth trekking to with most of its shelves empty! Let's deal with salt first. It's easier to get oil here than water, and diamonds than salt!"

"What do you mean?"

"Let's go. I'll explain as we walk to the local stores." Komli noticed that the streets were clean, but quiet. Melissa continued, "For some strange reason, salt is very hard to find in Tripoli. Sometimes you can buy it under the counter, if the storekeeper is in a good mood. So we end up treating the darn stuff like some rare gem! Don't worry, I'll give you some. Most of us bring back salt when we go on vacation. You can return it to me when you get your supply.

Melissa had been right. More than half the shelves in each and every store they went to were empty. They looked as sorry as some of its older, more wizened owners who seemed to have little choice but to resign themselves to their hapless fate—demand was high but supply was often non-existent. Fortunately, no one starved. And no one dared to complain to Gaddafi. Komli managed to get bread and oil. Butter and eggs happened to be out of stock.

"Tomorrow, Inshallah," (Allah willing), the kind, old men said to the ladies, in the hope that they would return when their shelves were better stocked. Fixit reminded her that this was a desert; that it was understandable why vegetables were hard to find. Komli was surprised to find Melissa happily helping herself to a sorry, shriveled assortment of tomatoes and green peppers. Worse still, she saw Melissa grab an ugly cauliflower that looked like it was suffering from a severe case of chickenpox.

"Times are lean," Melissa explained with an earthy practicality. "When there's not much you can get, you just grab what you see. Come on, don't look so put off, you won't get any better elsewhere. It may be completely different in a couple of weeks. One never can tell. But if you don't buy what's available now, you might not last until the season of plenty!" Melissa had a dry, caustic sense of humor. Added to it was the ability to mimic people to perfection and to bring much needed laughter to expatriate gatherings.

Pick those two, half rotten tomatoes, Fixit urged, *you'll get one whole edible tomato after you salvage it.* Komli found some potatoes, canned cheese, and soups, but no fresh milk.

"Get yourself a can of Nido," Melissa advised, "it's not so bad once you get used to powered milk." Father Michael and London had spoilt Komli. She loved fresh milk. Seeing her disappointed look, Melissa added, "Fresh milk is so erratic here, we've given up looking for it. Shortages come and go. You'll get used to it. There's a party each weekend, and no one starves, believe me. You just have to get used to buying up in bulk whenever you see something you like. There's not much to spend our salary on anyway, so everyone can afford to hoard!"

"Stock up on what?" Komli asked sarcastically. Even onions were hard to find. How does one cook without onions she was about to ask, when Fixit reminded her calmly that it would be futile to ask a Brit about onions, knowing that their diet was limited to broiled meats and boiled vegetables. As for basic Indian spices, even the shopkeepers hadn't the faintest idea what she was talking about, although Melissa said she knew an Indian guy who might be able to help Komli.

"How do these poor storekeepers make a living?" Komli asked in frustration.

"Gaddafi makes sure no one starves, so I guess no one cares. I hear all these privately owned stores are going to be turned into cooperatives. Can't get any worse, can they?" Melissa pointed to the cans of tuna and mackerel. "Grab a few," she suggested, "don't know what the butcher will have. We'll go there next." Komli was sure she detected a glint in Melissa's eyes, as though she was getting some kind of perverse pleasure out of this.

"How long have you been here, Melissa?"

"Five years."

"Has it always been like this?"

"It's getting worse. But since we get better at the game, it doesn't seem so bad. Just remember, you get two R and Rs a year, which everyone needs, I assure you! You get another 30 days' vacation, and a fat pay check each month. If I can hang on for a few more years, I won't have to worry about a mortgage or working when I get back to England. Isn't that something to keep you going, eh?"

Komli had no idea what Melissa was talking about so she remained quiet until they came to the butcher's. "Oh, good, he's open," Melissa remarked. "None of these shopkeepers adhere to any kind of nine to five hours. If they have goods to sell, they're open, if not they go for camel rides or take their four wives and nineteen children to the beach in their Toyota—husband and camel in front, the rest at the back!" Komli managed a polite, half-hearted giggle as Melissa shrieked with laughter.

It was obvious the meat had just arrived at the butcher's. There were a few sheep's heads hanging on hooks, with blood dripping into little red puddles on the floor! Even Melissa was a little taken aback by that, but she decided to hang around herself until the butcher decided to come out. No, one couldn't afford to be squeamish, it seemed, when fresh meat was available.

"He's just got a fresh supply of meat," Melissa said enthusiastically. "I've been dying to have roast lamb. Maybe I'll treat you this weekend!" She reeled off her order— a few kilos of this, a few kilos of that and half a dozen chickens. The butcher just brought out a carcass from the back room and hacked off what he pleased. It was hard to tell what animal it once was.

Looks like camel to me, Fixit said matter-of-factly. Komli lost all interest in meat suddenly. *Perfect grounds for dieting considering you put on some weight in London!"*

"Aren't you going to order anything?" Melissa asked as the butcher bagged her order in sheets of unread newspaper.

"I'll wait," Komli managed stoically.

"Get some chicken at least," Melissa urged, pointing to dead fowl hanging from smaller hooks. The order of display was reversed Komli noticed. Chickens hung with all but their heads nicked off, while lambs' heads dangled with all but their bodies.

"Will he clean the chicken for me?"

"No," Melissa said, taking much pleasure in saying so. "We've tried money, smiles, even chatting him up, nothing seems to work. He will not clean them for you."

"I've just decided I prefer being vegetarian."

"You'll get used to it. You think I cleaned chicken in England?! That's why it's best if you buy a whole lot together. Clean them, get it over with, freeze them and then you don't have to worry for a few weeks! It's not as if we're pressed for time you know."

"I'll buy some another time. I'll pass for today."

"Pass out, you mean, by the look on your face," Melissa said with a chuckle. "Wait till you see the butchers out in the desert," she added enigmatically.

"Dare I ask why?"

"No. It would spoil the fun."

"Thank you! I can hardly wait! Can we call it a day?" Komli asked suddenly, feeling quite exhausted. The prospect of fending for herself in that huge apartment with no music, no television or radio to drown out the over-powering silence didn't help her disgruntled state of mind. If only she could talk to Roshni or Tusneem, she thought, instead of being lumped with irritating, old Fixit.

"Hey, cheer up, before long you'll be having people over for dinner just like the rest of us."

"What would I feed them? Canned soup with a loaf of bread? Or do the loaves and fish multiply in the desert?"

"There's hope for you! You're already joking. After my first shopping spree, I almost took the next plane back to England. There's only one rule to follow when you have guests—you don't plan a menu and then go shopping; you go shopping and then plan your menu around your haul. The creative come up with some wonderful concoctions! Come, let's go to my apartment. I'll give you some salt, eggs, and butter. That should keep you going for a while."

Just as they were nearing the office building, Komli heard the Azaan (Muslim call to prayer). It brought back fond memories of predominantly Muslim areas in Calcutta where she had sometimes heard the Azaan. But never before had she heard the Azaan being recited simultaneously from all four corners of a city. Never before had she heard such a loud, beautiful, universal call to prayer. Even though she was Hindu, a dormant religious chord struck in her somewhere. It was while she was reveling in the sounds of the Azaan that she heard Melissa rudely interrupt with obvious irritation, "There they go again, wailing like lunatics. Never fails to wake me up at an ungodly hour in the morning!"

"It's the Muslim call to prayer," Komli explained politely, but in a tone firmly suggesting that it ought to be respected.

"More like a bawl to prayer," Melissa retorted. She was so wrapped up yodeling what she thought was a perfect rendering of the Azaan, that she failed to notice that Komli was far from amused. Even though Komli had often questioned Tusneem about praying in a language she did not understand, and for abiding by customs and traditions about which she had no clue, Komli found that she had little patience for the likes of Melissa who, she was to discover, ridiculed anything alien without first trying to understand at least.

"Here, keep this chicken for yourself," Melissa said impulsively as if to make up for annoying Komli's sense of respect for prayers. "You might need it. I'll give you the eggs and butter as soon as we get to my apartment. Believe me, I know how you feel. I went through it myself when I first got here."

On her first day at work, Komli found out that she was not assigned to work privately for Scott but to the Accounting Department in general. It did not take her long to realize that all senior Libyans and white men had white secretaries. White secretaries were, in fact, quite a status symbol! So she had been relegated to work for no one in particular. Scott found that he could not do anything about it either. The Libyans had changed their mind and that was that. Poor, confused Libyans, Komli thought with anger and some sympathy—ostracizes white people socially but dreams that a white angel will work under him when he reaches the top rung of the ladder. Even the Libyans treated the Indians as inferior WOGS, Komli thought with a dash of self-pity.

At least color prejudice is not the sole prerogative of the white race, Fixit remarked wisely. It was a hard blow to digest, but digest it she did, with the help of Fixit who was thoroughly enjoying the opportunity of having her undivided attention in that football field of an apartment.

Immediately after work one evening, Komli made a bee-line for the refrigerator. She tore off the newspaper package that Melissa had given her and started brutally attacking the chicken in an attempt to rip off its skin. *Calm down*, Fixit said sympathetically, *in time I'm sure you'll be able to rip off the Libyans' pre-conceived notions about you, skin-tight as they seem to appear!* But Komli tugged at the chicken's legs and hacked at its joints, while she fought her inner battles about man and his blind prejudices. So what must she have to be truly accepted by her fellow man, she asked herself—same color skin hail from the same country, same religion, same caste, same class, same family, same sex, same thoughts, same what else? *You'll find you can narrow it down and narrow it down until all there's left is yourself,* Fixit said smugly. *And you can thank Melissa for the chicken; looks like it came in quite handy after all!* The brutally dismantled chicken looked so ghastly, Komli threw it all out. She heated a can of soup, had it with a slice of plain bread and decided to go to bed.

The last couple of lines of *Desiderata* stared back at her to comfort her. '*With all its sham, drudgery and broken dreams, it is still a beautiful world. Be careful. Strive to be happy.*' She was glad only her pillow felt the tear trickle down her cheeks. She thought of the tramp who had introduced her to Desiderata. She, too, had harbored preconceived notions about him. She did not know whether it was that thought, the tramp, or Desiderata that calmed her down. She slept well. In fact, it was quite a calm, composed lady who walked in to work the following morning.

After Komli recovered from the initial shock that the Libyans had taken her inferiority for granted, she found that they could actually be very naïve but kind and considerate. She especially liked the way most Libyans greeted her with an *Us-salaam-o-alaikum*. It means peace be upon you, one of them had explained. *Wa-a-lai-kum-salaam*, she had learned to say back—meaning, and peace be upon you, too. The Libyans in her department were far from the fighting lunatics she had been warned about. If anything, they were always kind to her; they never seemed to forget that she was handicapped. Also, most of the Libyans felt more at home with her than they did with the white expatriates. They enjoyed chatting with her. They had no qualms about asking her things like, "How come you're not married yet? Or, "Surely you were married once and are divorced now, hmmm?" It seemed that they were used to female divorcees and spinsters seeking refuge in the desert.

In time, Komli realized that the average, middle-class Libyan was a very likeable blend of innocence and arrogance. She couldn't help doubling up with laughter when one day she decided to tell them that she knew something about Islam because she had made a good Muslim friend in India. "Oh, they are not true Muslims in India," one of them had retorted arrogantly, "the only true Muslims live here, in the desert."

Between the Libyans and Bohras and Father Michaels, Allah and Jesus are doling out quite a few tickets for heaven, Fixit observed with a chuckle. Komli thanked Bhagvaan for thinking of reincarnation. At least she would not have to fight for a place among the cream of mankind in jam-packed heaven.

Tripoli wasn't a bad place at all in which to be reincarnated, Komli discovered. Within a couple of months, she had been transformed into quite an experienced expatriate. She had lost count of the dinners and lunches to which she was invited. At work she enjoyed the little tidbits of information she gleaned from the Libyans and after work there was always something to do.

On Mondays, she went to Arabic classes with a few expatriates.

Tuesdays, she played tennis. She and Scott usually played together as doubles partners. Nobody minded that Scott served for Komli.

On Wednesdays, she usually kept to herself, to write letters, read a book, or simply to enjoy her own company. Newspapers in English always arrived two days late and were often censored. Sometimes they did not arrive at all. But Komli enjoyed reading them occasionally, to keep vaguely in touch with the outside world. As Fixit had casually remarked once, *since news is always about people one never knows or meets, what difference does it make whether you read it today or tomorrow?* Any hot, news-making item always drifted in on the grapevine from those who had the luxury of a radio.

She looked forward to Thursdays, not because it was the last day of the work week, but because on Thursday nights she played scrabble. She was good at scrabble, but more than that, she loved laughing with the expatriates, especially with the British and Americans who, she found out to her utter amazement, often failed to understand one another's English! She herself had been the cause of much laughter one evening when she had innocently put down the word 'hump'.

"Dirty, four letter words are not allowed, Komli!" some American had shrieked.

"But this is not a dirty four-letter word! It's hump. Like hump on a cow."

"Is that what you do in India?" Geoff had screamed while everyone roared with laughter.

"Do what?"

"Hump on a cow!"

"The cows in India have humps . . . ."

"I bet! You have a ton of them loitering around, don't you?!"

"Komli," Scott had said softly, "in America 'hump' is slang for fuck!"

"And in England 'on the job' is slang for 'hump' so you better watch what words you use, girl!"

"I didn't know!" Komli exclaimed, a little embarrassed, but nobody heard her. Scrabble was always a time for drinking, eating, and merriment.

As for weekends, Komli was convinced that was when heaven came down to earth. There was always a group of expatriates who went to the beach, either at Sabrata, or Leptis. Komli had no idea that the Italians had once occupied Libya, much less that colossal, milky-white marble statues and intricately carved marble columns had been abandoned to languish lazily in the sun and the sand. Scott had been with her that first time when she had been so utterly shocked to see the stunning ruins. Each ruined semblance of city or temple or noble statesman that had once stood upright seemed to have its own story that was lapped up and corroded by frivolous, frothy, white waves that came and caressed it flirtatiously from time to time.

"Wow," Komli had remarked with envy, "imagine spending your life on this gorgeous coast."

"The Romans knew how to live, that's for sure," Scott had remarked, while Komli sat cross-legged on the beach and happily lapped up historical tidbits that fell her way.

Dear Roshni,

Hello there! Hope you received my brief letter saying all's well. I'm really anxious to hear from you, although I've heard that one cannot always rely on the mail here! Please get a telephone line. If that's difficult, get in touch with Rashid. I know he can pull strings. I don't have a telephone in my apartment, but I'm allowed to make calls from the office.

Here are some impressions about good old Tripoli. So many interesting, strange things have happened in the few weeks I've been here that it's going to be impossible to tell you everything. The expatriate gang I go around with is at the beach. That's where we spend most Saturdays—picnicking on the shores of the Mediterranean. Spoke to Tusneem the other day. Pregnancy's treating her well, it seems.

You know how cold, and damp and miserable it can be in London? Well, Tripoli is just the opposite. It seems that the sun just knows exactly how much heat to radiate. It's never cold and I've yet to find it unbearably hot. The skies are always a beautiful, clear blue, and as for the Mediterranean sea, wish you could spend some time here, Roshni, to see it for yourself. It's simply breathtaking! I've never seen so many colors in the water. Compared to our brown Hooghly, the sea here is a jewel, with patches of aquamarine, and powder blue, and royal blue, and frothing white surf all basking together contentedly under a gentle sun that never seems to want to stop shining on this gem of a city. And the few clouds you see in the sky always look like they've had an over-dose of bleach. How can you expect the breeze in a paradise like this to be anything but gentle and mellow?

I didn't tell you because I knew you would worry, but when I first came here I was pretty depressed. People in London had scared me so much, I was almost convinced I wouldn't make it beyond the airport. As you can tell, I am far from dead! The workload is so low, it's boring! Other than that, life here seems to be one long holiday with parties thrown in over weekends. I chose to stay in today because I needed a break from partying and being with people (yes, that's how much we expatriates socialize). When the Libyans in London warned me that there was nothing to do in Tripoli, I assured them that I was perfectly content with just books for companions. Believe it or not, I don't get time to read! No, the truth is, I haven't made much of an effort. Too busy meeting people!

The Libyans and the foreigners rarely socialize with one another. The Libyans think all foreign men are greedy sinners out to squeeze every penny they can get for their expertise, and that all single, foreign women are promiscuous, sex maniacs who go around the world bed hopping! The foreigners think all Libyans are dumb, crazy, and uncivilized. Neither extreme is true of course but, betwixt the two opinions, and Gaddafi's strict orders to stay away from foreign devils, there's no ground left for socializing or attempting to understand one other. Neither the Libyans nor the expatriates have any idea how the other half truly lives.

Being neither Libyan nor white, sometimes I find myself getting a little irritated with all the negativity. I'm beginning to realize what the Brits must have been like when they ruled India—bitch, bitch, bitch about uncouth natives must have been an entertaining pastime for them. It is often the case here with the group I go out with. I think the only difference between the expatriates in Tripoli and the Brits in India is that while in India the Brits left behind a humongous railroad, and this language I speak, and the laws by which we still abide, the foreigners in Tripoli are out for just one thing—money, money, money (self included, I'm ashamed to admit).

Most people think Gaddafi is crazy. I think the man is a visionary whose Utopian dream is crazy. He wants to unite all Arabs under the cause of Islam and to set his people free: free from foreign rule, and free from desires and ambitions, by giving each one as much as necessary, no more, no less. It seems that no one dares to ask Gaddafi the million dollar question—how can he tell what is necessary and what is not necessary for another human being? So, this fanatical fervor to revolutionize his country, and an undying hatred for all white imperialists, seems to spur him on. And what does the crazy dreamer do when he discovers he has the potential to realize his dream if he can just drill out the precious oil with which his sands is blessed? He goes and imports foreign expertise, from every country imaginable. Expertise of the devil himself! So what does he do for his people whom he must protect from the corrupt devil? He sets up schools and military that churn out an arrogant people in whose head it is drilled that they are the chosen, and that Gaddafi is their infallible leader (chosen or otherwise) and that all foreigners, especially westerners, are untouchable devils. So much for Gandhi abolishing untouchability. It runs rampant in the minds of people everywhere, Roshni. The good thing is that it helps me realize that people like Tara are not as evil as I once thought.

If a Libyan disagrees with Gaddafi, he doesn't tell anyone—because anyone could be Gaddafi's I-spy-with-my-little-eye something beginning with a T for Traitor! And we foreigners are so scared we'll get bumped out of the country and lose our fat pay checks, we don't dare push Libyans around. We treat them with mock deference and pretend they're always right. If a foreigner gets uptight about not having any rights, he's quickly reminded that Gaddafi's interested in his expertise, not his rights. The only right he has is to leave and that, too, only when Libyan officials grant him the exit permit to leave! But, like quicksand, money sucks us all in, and sucks out all respect! In the eyes of the Libyans, we are alien prostitutes out to pick up every penny we can lay our hands on, having abandoned our country, our people, our culture, some of us our religion, all for the sake of money, money, money!!!

The great irony, Roshni, is that money and power have blinded Gaddafi. These pure sands, so close to the source of three great religions, has been turned into hardened concrete to house machinery and modern marvels. In his euphoria, poor Gaddafi is blinded to the fact that destruction of innocence comes in the wake of wealth. His people, many of whom were once content to live the life of simple nomads, are now confused with an onslaught of unimaginable amenities for which they crave. Gaddafi, who so feverishly wants to set his people free from western imperialism and capitalism, imports more and more westerners, and more and more materials, which, alas, unwittingly but relentlessly tempt his people. Worse still, he imports more and more weapons with which to defend his once fearless Bedouins. So, if the devil himself is here, to toil in the soil, and rip off its oil, with it, Gaddafi is also ripping off any glimmer of hope he has of realizing his Utopia. To put it in a nutshell, the once-innocent Libyan seems to be caught up in the western disease of perpetually wanting more!

Scott drove me far out into the desert one night when I saw an unforgettable sight: simple Bedouins warming their hands by a roaring fire, and sipping gahwa (coffee). They were sitting on the sand itself, with a star-studded sky for roof. Stars that seemed content to sparkle in huge clusters in the untouched desert, but run shy under the glaring eye of blazing city lights. It was hard to tell if the Bedouins were quietly conversing or simply contemplating the stars. Their camels were untethered, but made no effort to run away from their masters. It seemed that beast and Bedouin knew they were linked to each other and to the sand by who knows what stars in the sky above. I was dying to go up to them. But Scott refused to let me out of the car. He had not only taken the risk of driving out miles into the desert, and late at night, too (could be mistaken for a spy), Scott wasn't so sure that the Bedouins would appreciate our intrusion. 'They're unschooled and pure. We do not have a right to defile them,' Scott said. It blew my mind away. Imagine anyone saying that of our unschooled people!

I'll never forget the sight Roshni, as long as I live. The closest I ever came to it was when I was awakened by vicious mosquitoes on the streets of Calcutta. I used to get mad at the mosquitoes. Now I am thankful that at least their jab awakened me to gaze at the stars while the rest of the city was asleep.

I'm confused, but happily learning, and my fingers are cramping so I'm going to take a break and have a cup of tea.

Komli not only needed to rest her aching fingers, she felt the need suddenly to indulge in the memory of that unforgettable night when Scott had driven her through the Libyan desert. There had not been another soul or car in sight. She had felt like she was on another planet with a human being who, in reality, was turning out to be quite different from other human beings she had met in Tripoli or anywhere else for that matter. Unlike other expatriates, he rarely discussed money and mortgages and the stock market; he didn't seem to be interested in sex and, with the twirl of his moustache, he seemed to have the wonderful ability to smile away what seemed like a big crisis to other expatriates.

"Thank you for taking the risk and bringing me out here. I wouldn't have missed it for the world," Komli had said to him as he turned around to drive back.

"Thank you for coming with me," he had responded quietly, "I'll never forget it." He had looked deep into her eyes and smiled. His eyes had crinkled together, like tributaries of mirth, branching out from two hazel-green pools. Her heart had missed it's first beat since she had known Mustapha. His had, too, after quite a few years. It had been too beautiful a moment to be shattered with any more words. Silently they had driven back, savoring soft classical music, the stars that twinkled over an otherwise pitch black desert, and the heavenly silence of meaningful companionship between two human beings whose souls had been momentarily united.

Komli's thoughts went further back, to the afternoon when they had picnicked at an enchanting oasis with one, lone, mellow palm tree, bent with age, swaying gracefully over a ribbon of a stream that ran beside it in perfect peace and harmony. The palm tree had looked like it was patiently waiting for someone to come and relieve it of the heavy burden of ripe, golden-brown dates it was graciously dangling, but barely able to support on its skinny, old trunk.

Just when they had finished their lunch of roast chicken and freshly baked bread, a group of Libyan children had stopped about twenty feet away and started chucking stones at them. The braver expatriates had tried to shoo them away; the more timid ones had started loading their cars, cursing under their breath at such barbaric behavior. When everyone had finally climbed into their cars, a few local women had joined the children and had started trilling as they set fire to the spot where the expatriates had picnicked.

It had been a gruesome sight. Komli remembered how in India women trilled to ward off evil. Were the Libyan women trying to purify their defiled land, Komli wondered. She chose not to tell anyone, knowing that it would enrage her group even further, and justifiably so. She recalled some of the confused questions and answers :

"Were they scared we were going to rob them of those dates?"

"What dates?"

"The dates on the palm tree! Their only means of survival, probably!"

"And loaded with nutrition . . ."

"Shut up, Scott. These people are maniacs. Let's get out of here!" Geoff had interrupted.

Komli had quietly agreed with Geoff. She had noticed the little children's eyes; they had gleamed with hatred while they had hurled stones, as hard as they could. There was no giggling, no childlike mischievous expression to indicate that they were enjoying their little prank. It seemed they had been thinking harsh thoughts while casting stones.

When things had calmed down a little, Komli had turned to Scott. "Aren't you angry at what those Libyans did to us?"

"If I were your son's teacher, and brainwashed him into thinking all foreigners were bad just because some of them had ruled over his forefathers, would you feel sad or angry?"

"Both I think. I wouldn't let my son go near you."

"Well, the sad thing is that these children don't have a choice of teachers. They're probably being fed with facts like dates are nutritious and everything else is poisonous, for all I know. It's too bad their mad ruler is having such a negative effect on innocent children," Scott had said with a sensitivity that had not gone unnoticed by Komli. "But then again, it's not as if we never cast stones ourselves," Scott had said with a shrug of his shoulders.

Maybe he's referring to your remarks about the Brits, Fixit pointed out. The more Komli thought of Scott, the fonder she was growing of him.

Komli's eyes strayed to *Desiderata*—Listen to others, even the dull and ignorant; they too have their story. She wished suddenly that Scott was around. She felt like a chat.

After finishing her tea, Komli continued with her letter :

> *Before I say bye, Roshni, I guess I should assure you that I am not doing any bed hopping. Don't intend to either! I think sometimes the white man thinks like the Libyans—that all single women here are promiscuous. Went out for lunch with a Dutch guy who told me brazenly that he was vasectomized. Said he even had a tie that said so! Meaning, dear, innocent sister, that I could go bed hopping with him and never worry about having a baby because he has his tubes in his big pipe tied up (and his sense of decency, too, if you ask me!). And these white people have the gall to think the poor Libyans are crazy! Scott brings*

sanity and calm to the mini storms in my life by telling me that there are many sex-starved men in the desert, but that I should take things with a pinch of salt. (which by the way is usually available only in pinches). I actually bought a small packet of salt for, let's see what it converts to—about 400 rupees. No, I'm not exaggerating. I know what you're thinking—how the hell does one ever throw something so expensive on food! As far as I know, the only race that has mastered the art of eating food without salt, is the Brits. So everyone else pays a fortune to get it, if they can. Maybe that's part of the Libyan plan! We foreigners certainly don't know why salt is so hard to find. We grab it and hoard it when we can. That goes for other items as well. It's not uncommon to be working in office when some white seer comes around prophesying that the butter ship is due soon. To market, to market rush all the fat pigs, who come home again, home again, jiggety jig, with mountains of butter to freeze and to whip. I hate to tell you Roshni, I've done so myself! Fixit often wonders how I ever survived on the streets!

I'll write another long letter soon. Reply fast and say hi to Devi and family. With all my love,

Komli

"May I come in?" Rashid asked, as Roshni stood at the door, trying to figure out the reason for his visit.

"Yes. Please sit down. Is everything alright?"

"As far as I know. I received a call from Tusneem recently. Komli asked her to find out if you had been in touch with me, so I could help you get a telephone line. I am here on business, so I decided to drop by."

"Oh."

"I would love to help you in any way I can, Roshni, you know that don't you?"

"Yes."

"Then why didn't you get in touch with me? It seems like your sister wants to be able to talk to you from time to time. Am I such a monster that even for her sake you would not get in touch with me?"

"I didn't want to bother you. You've done so much for us already. I asked my neighbor's husband if he could help me get a line."

"So it's all taken care of?" Rashid asked, trying to conceal his disappointment.

"He said it would take at least a year."

"That's not bad. Sometimes it takes longer. Fortunately, or unfortunately, sometimes you can get things done faster, depending on who you know. If you like, I can get you a line in a week."

"You can?!"

"Yes," he said, without mentioning that in reality he was weary of pulling countless strings for countless people. He wished bureaucrats, and Bhaisahibs and people at large would treat all people equally, but life had proved otherwise. He often wondered if he would have all the friends and contacts he had, if he were just a common merchant of some sort.

"I see you've gone back to wearing the white sari."

"It would cause too much stir in the neighborhood, if I were to suddenly change colors." They smiled at each other, knowing that the pun was unintended.

"Do you miss your sister?" Rashid asked for want of something to say.

"Terribly, just like you must miss Tusneem. And your wife," Roshni added after a second's pause. "I realized when Komli fell in love with your nephew that I had lost a part of her to someone else, even though she was still in India then. And now, even though she is away, I know I will never lose that part of her that is mine. It is comforting." How simply and quietly you speak your truth, Rashid thought to himself as Roshni continued, "I'm glad I got to know Tusneem better in London. Komli is lucky. She has a good friend."

He stared at her for a long while, unable to say anything.

"Did I say something to offend you?" Roshni asked.

"No! No! You don't know what a burden you've lifted from my shoulders. I wish Zenub was here to hear you."

"What burden?"

"The burden of taking advantage of Komli all those years ago."

"But that was my choice. Can you not see with your own eyes how much you have done for Komli and for me, or do the words of your written laws blind you?"

"So you do forgive us our sin?"

"You have to forgive yourself, Rashid. I do not understand, or wish to understand, all the written laws in your books. You and your books are the reason why you torment yourself. Komli and I bear you no grudge. We are only grateful to you. It seems that sacrificing one's flesh does not always untie the bonds of the spirit, does it?"

"You are very wise and kind to others. Tell me, have you forgiven yourself for what you did for your mother and sister?" he asked suddenly.

"What do you mean?"

"You know what I mean."

"I think I have. Can't you tell how happy I am now?"

Rashid wondered if this beautiful, austere woman would ever let a man into her life. He wished he could tell her how lonely and impoverished he felt lately in that huge house of his where he lived by himself. He found himself wanting to go out less and less. Everyone he knew had done everything exciting, bought everything expensive twice over, and traveled to exotic places all over the world. When he curled up in his armchair with a book, he found himself wishing that armchair was by Roshni's rocking chair.

"Will you allow me to visit you from time to time if I bring you books?"

"You bought this place. It is yours even though I live here. You don't have to ask to visit me."

Darn it, Rashid thought, the woman refused to indicate if she would like him to visit.

"I love books," Roshni said suddenly, "I wouldn't mind learning about some of the things you read about, though I doubt if I'll understand anything."

Thank god for books and the written word, Rashid thought. It seemed to be the only bridge that connected the gaping differences in their lifestyle, although a little voice within him reminded him that it was the written word itself that had prevented the alliance between his nephew and Komli.

When the telephone was connected, Roshni looked at it with mixed feelings. Slowly but surely, modern amenities were creeping into her haven, modern amenities that were like the Wish Fulfilling Tree—the cooker had satisfied their need for food, but had brought meddling Tara in its wake; the clock had told her when to go to work and when to expect Komli, but before long it had started to quietly dictate precisely what she should be doing when. What would the telephone bring, she wondered.

She didn't have to wait long to find out that its shrill ring fragmented her peace of mind like a bolt of jagged lightning. At first, she had loved the telephone. It enabled her to talk to the two most precious people in her life. In time, she began to dislike the instrument a little because she found herself staring at it instead of reading a book; she found herself wondering when it would ring again so she could hear Rashid's warm, bass voice ask, 'Roshni?' What a magical sound that one word had become. She hated the black instrument because she never knew when it would ring again, morning, noon, or night. She was ashamed at the undignified way in which she scrambled to her feet to grab it; she was ashamed that she often hoped the voice at the other end was a male voice instead of her sister's.

She used to love dreaming dreams for her beloved sister. She used to thank Bhagvaan for creating dreams, sweet dreams, the ingenious device that nobody need know about, that could transport her anywhere, at any time. Now she could not stop dreaming dreams for herself as well; dreams she knew she had no business dreaming, knowing that the man in her dreams was simply being attentive out of a deep sense of debt, although, she had to admit, he looked more lost and lonely and needy each time she saw him.

The phone rang one Sunday afternoon. It was Rashid, wondering if Roshni would like to go to the zoo with him.

"Have you ever been to the zoo in Patna?"

"No."

"Would you like to? I'm going to be here for a few days. I'm free all day today."

"I saw animals all the time when I was young—cats, dogs, cows, mice . . ."

"I take it you saw tigers and lions and elephants and camels, too?"

"Komli and I saw them at the circus."

"Monkeys. Have you seen monkeys?"

"Yes, many times. And bears. Remember the guys who used to perform outside your house with their animals?"

"Yes. I used to love watching them when I was a child. Roshni, the zoo is a wonderful place to spend an afternoon. Don't you ever feel the need to go out?"

"I do go out when I feel the need to."

"Anywhere besides the library?" Rashid asked, a shade sarcastic.

"I go shopping for food and things."

"There's a world out there to see, Roshni. You did enjoy London, did you not?"

"Yes, very, very much!"

"How can you do something like that and then shut yourself up again in your room?"

"So you want to get me out of my room and show me how animals are shut up in cages?" she asked laughing.

"Yes! I can come and get you in half an hour. It's such a beautiful day. Please say yes, Roshni."

"Yes. I think I'll enjoy that." Roshni responded simply.

He was standing at the door, in exactly thirty minutes, with a handful of red roses that he had hand-picked from the very spot in his garden where he had first seen her. "They're from the garden where I first found you, smelling the roses," Rashid said as he handed her the flowers. "I will never forget it. I understand now why my gardener loves the flowers he tends." He searched into her soft, black eyes, hoping to detect a hint of understanding.

"They are beautiful. Thank you," Roshni said as she took the flowers from his hands. Their eyes met as their fingers touched. They were equally enthralled. "They smell so beautiful," Roshni said as she quickly bent down her head, thankful for the opportunity to bury her eyes into the flowers. She was petrified that they would betray something he must never find out.

Rashid was content to say nothing. He wished he could hold her, that she could return the embrace with equal fervor. But he was at a crossroad in his life when he was unsure of himself and of what constituted right and wrong. The time would come, he hoped, when he would at least be sure that Roshni was not just being gracious for his many acts of kindness; then he would openly admit to her that he was a far cry from the self-contained, perfect piece of humanity she thought he was.

It was at the zoo that Roshni realized why her sister and, now Rashid, felt that she lived in a prison. Other than reading and cooking, her lifestyle must seem no different than that of caged animals. She felt sorry for the animals. No wonder Komli wanted her to go places.

"Wow!" Roshni exclaimed when they came to the Polar bear in it's simulated Polar environment, fitted with huge slabs of ice and air-conditioning, "I've never seen a white bear before."

"It reminds me of you. Always in white. Come I want to show you something," he said suddenly as he led her to the aviary.

"See those beautiful parrots there? That's what you looked like in London."

"You know, when Komli first started school at Montessori, she used to talk about cave men and how they learned to use animal skin for warmth. Amazing how far we've come from simple hides to costumes and clothing for different people and for different occasions. Do you think Him-up-there . . ."

"Him who?"

"Him-up-there. It's Komli's word for all the gods of mankind. Do you think Him-up-there made us so drab because we were meant to make our own clothes?"

"Good question. Have you ever asked Him?"

"I wonder sometimes if He speaks a language. He never talks to us."

"If He were to make Himself accessible to answer our questions, we'd burn His ears to death, Roshni!" Rashid responded with a laugh.

He's supposed to be immortal!"

"I mean he'd have no ears left. Come to think of it, maybe He is deaf!"

"And dumb."

"Wow, I never thought I'd hear you talk like that! How did we get on the subject anyway?" Rashid asked.

"You called me a polar bear, living in the cold" she said, giggling.

"I don't think I said that! The zoo's good for you, though. You've laughed more today than I've ever seen you."

"You know something, when Komli first started school she used to feed me with all kinds of stories. Of all the things she said, what impressed me the most was that our world is divided into just three states of matter."

"Really! And they are?"

"Liquid, solid, and gas. According to her, everything changes from one state to another, again and again and again, depending on how hot or cold it gets."

"I thought Hindus believed that Karma (deeds) changed things, depending on how good or bad one is."

"You're right. Sometimes I think that it's all one and the same though; you can call it reincarnation, or transformation, or metamorphosis, or karma; it's all about change."

"We'll have to come to the zoo more often. I thought you knew very few words beyond yes and no! Do you want to know something?"

"Yes and no," she said, giving him a broad smile. He was left breathless. She had such a beautiful smile. Roshni continued, "I mean, the more I learn the more confused I get."

"Well, I want you to know that you just helped me understand what Father Joseph meant when he said, there is no new thing under the sun."

"What did he mean?" Roshni asked in confusion.

"What you just said; that it's all original, old stuff being recycled; all the laws, and all the prose and poetry and all the fiction and non-fiction you read are just the same old words being recycled to form different patterns. We have an amazing capacity to find more and more things to write about. So many darn words, so little comprehension!"

"I never thought I'd hear you use words like *darn*," Roshni exclaimed.

"I'm undergoing a major change, Roshni," Rashid said slowly, but dramatically, just to see Roshni laugh again. "Would you like to have an ice cream?"

"Yes, I need a break from talking. I thought we had come to look at animals."

And it was through little gestures, little conversations, a little warmth, and much laughter that their relationship evolved into something completely different from that first chilling moment when the illiterate beggar had looked up at the righteous judge.

It was around this time that Komli was introduced to her new room-mate, Margaret Miller-Smith. The first word that came to Komli's mind when she introduced herself to Margaret was 'grandmother'. She had to be in her late fifties, Komli thought. If she was any younger, cigarette smoking had aged her prematurely. The stiff curls that embraced her face were about the same nondescript gray as the cigarette puffs that she blew out with sophisticated confidence. Her eyes bulged out, somewhat like frog's eyes, except that they were watery and had little red rivulets criss-crossing around each icy blue pupil. Her nails looked like parrots' beaks. They were beautifully varnished, and always matched her clothes, Komli learned in time.

At first, Margaret seemed loving and protective. It was Margaret who decided how the furniture should be re-arranged, when the curtains should be drawn, what was a good time to eat, what was nutritious, and whom they should invite to their apartment, and when. Before long, Komli was trapped into a domineering mother-child relationship. Margaret misunderstood Komli's lack of knowledge of western ways for ignorance at large. During a pleasant conversation about their experiences in London, Komli had mentioned how much she had enjoyed going strawberry-picking in London.

"Oh, upper-class people never go strawberry picking," Margaret had informed her coolly. My surname, Miller-Smith, is double-barreled. People with double-barreled surnames are upper-class you know, she added condescendingly, as she puffed out a cloud of smoke to enhance the aura of mystery around her.

Double-barreled bullshit, Komli thought, but decided to keep her low-class opinions to herself. She walked into the haven of her bedroom, thinking sarcastically, so you upper-class, pompous prudes perm your hair and puff on your cigarette and paint your nails but never stoop to pick sweet strawberries gracing the bountiful pastures of Mother Earth!

Scott rescued Komli on many an occasion when together they were able to laugh off Komli's growing frustrations about sharing a room with insufferable Margaret.

"Do you know what she's brought into our apartment?" Komli asked Scott one evening

"A man?!"

"She would if she could cage one!" Komli said scathingly. "Try again."

"A Libyan."

"That's man."

"I'm not so sure."

"Stop being nasty, Scott. I hate it when you expatriates think all Libyans are animals, or inferior at best!"

"I know you do. I enjoy teasing you. Besides, when you get angry, I feel secure again that you're human and not some angel who will disappear on me some day. Have I told you, I think you're the most superior, sublime creature I've met, even though you go strawberry picking?"

She smiled, feeling some of her anger dissipate.

"One of these days I'll explode and you won't think I'm an angel!" Komli warned. She felt a little more calm as she continued, "Margaret's brought two caged canaries into the apartment. It wouldn't irk me at all if it wasn't for the fact that she keeps lecturing me about good manners and how I must ask her permission before I invite you or anyone to the apartment. And then, out of the blue, she just props up this cage in the sitting room we share! They start chirping at the crack of dawn and leave thousands of little bird seeds and shit and feathers floating everywhere. And of course if my pet, which she happens to think is you, would leave his feathers and food around in the sitting room we share, can you imagine what hell she would let loose?!" Scott had started laughing so loudly, Komli could barely hear herself. "What's so funny?" she asked.

"I just had visions of myself peeling off my clothes and running around your apartment with you and Margaret chasing after me. How come such wonderful things never happen to me? How come I can't drop my cigarette butts and beer cans wherever I please? Those caged creatures enjoy more privileges than I do!"

"Scott, I thought you'd sympathize with me for having to put up with this double-barreled woman with her double-barreled standards and triple-barreled high-handedness!"

"What can I do, Komli. My problem is that little canaries and little Margarets don't bother me when I'm around you. Everything you say turns into something magical. You've even wiped away some of my anger for the world, did you know that?" he asked suddenly. I've lived with it long enough." He held her gently by the face and searched deep into her eyes, wondering if she could ever return his feelings with the same intensity. "Do you care for me, just a little bit?"

"I do. In lots of little bits and lots of times. I'm just not ready for anything serious."

"I didn't ask, did I? I must have the patience of a saint! Do you want this bird out of the apartment?" he asked as an afterthought.

"Not really. I just feel kind of perversely angry that she can bring in what she likes without asking me, but feels she can throw all the tantrums she likes if creatures I like come to the apartment. How come I need her highness's permission?!"

"How come you can be so forthright with me and not with her?"

"Because you have a sense of humor and she doesn't!"

"Wanna know a secret? If she had men running after her like you have men running after you, she'd have no time for caged canaries."

"I don't have men running after me!"

"I guess I should be glad that you haven't noticed. Know what the problem is with our world?"

"Women, huh?"

"Guess again."

"Education."

"No."

"Men."

"No."

"Give up."

"Sex, honey, good old sex."

"Sex?!" Komli shrieked, "I thought that's what keeps us going."

"Exactly! But we don't allow it to keep us going, do we? You and I can't do it 'cause you're not ready yet; and Margaret's so ready, but there's no one around who wants to do it with her. So she lives vicariously by caging two love birds and trying to make sin and scandal out of everyone else's sex life. We're all so screwed up in the process, it's not even funny! Animals aren't as screwed up because if they don't get it, they move on and get it somewhere else."

"Then why don't you?" Komli said, without meaning to sound as rude as she did.

"I might have to if you keep pushing me away," Scott said, surprised that her jab had left quite a sting.

Slowly but surely, with or without the help of Scott, Komli was learning to iron out the big and little wrinkles in her life. Life was fraught with tremors for everyone in Libya it seemed; some were major and some were minor. But everyone seemed to survive. There was at least one story a week—someone was in prison for taking photographs of ruined cars; someone was flogged for selling 'flash', the code word for hard liquor; someone was asked to leave the country for dressing inappropriately, someone had disappeared; someone had reappeared. Komli had learned to follow Scott's advice and take life with a pinch of salt.

One Saturday, Komli, Scott, and a few other expatriates decided to walk to the famous Green Square down town to explore the quaint alleyways of the souq that had sprouted along its sides. The sights and smells and sounds of the souq never failed to intrigue the expatriate who had hitherto shopped only from malls containing big and little boxes, called stores, perfectly lined up one beside the other on slabs of spotless, ceramic tiles. The souq, on the other hand, had sprouted straight from the belly of Mother Earth it seemed. Many an expatriate strolled down the alleyways with a handkerchief around the mouth and nose to ward off the clouds of dust that preceded one wherever one went.

For the expatriate, the souq was not just a place to shop, but to sightsee as well. For it was only in this souq that they could see houses that seemed to have been there since the time of Abraham, if not Adam—old narrow rickety one or two storied houses with beautiful intricately latticed wooden windows. Sometimes no more than two people could walk abreast between two houses whose upper stories leaned precariously towards each other. The expatriates often stared and shook their heads in amazement, wondering how these ancient relics still held their ground. And the vendors and shopkeepers never seemed to worry that a house would some day collapse over them. Winding around the houses were stores that looked more like holes stashed with goodies that bore little or no relation to one another—copper pots and wooden boxes, jewelry and clothes and furniture and exotic perfumes and hand-woven rugs—making it an antique dealer's paradise.

As Komli was ambling down the souq, she suddenly spotted a man with two small mats in front of him. Sprawled on each mat was a mound of crystal-like pieces that she had never seen before. The crystals on one mound were a darkish brown; the other looked more like golden yellow tear-drops.

"Does anyone know what this man's selling?" Komli asked.

"Resin they chew on, I believe," Melissa replied.

"Someone told me they burn it in their homes."

"That's Frankincense and Myrrh," Scott said with quiet assurance.

"What?!" Komli asked, coming to a grinding halt.

"Frankincense and Myrrh," Scott repeated quietly.

"Frankincense and Myrrh?!"

"Uh-huh. You've heard of Frank . . . ."

"Of course, I've heard of Frankincense and Myrrh!" Komli exclaimed as though she was referring to diamonds and pearls. "I can still see Father Michael's sparkling eyes when he narrated the story of the birth of Christ. I guess he was so preoccupied with the sanctity of the occasion that he forgot to tell us heathens what Frankincense and Myrrh really were. All he wanted from us was that we spelled the words correctly." And, Komli thought to herself with some embarrassment, I was too interested in getting my gift of free milk to worry about the nature of more exotic gifts. "Scott," she continued, "is this really the Frankincense and Myrrh that the three wise men gave to Jesus?"

"The very same. The local people use it for incense burning and I believe they also put some in the hookah they smoke. It's supposed to aid digestion, or so at least I was told on one of my trips to Jeddah."

"Why did they give it to Jesus?"

"It was a precious commodity way back then. The resin only comes from trees that grow in Africa and Asia. The Egyptians used it for embalming and for medicinal purposes."

"Wow!" Komli exclaimed again, unable to digest the fact that what she thought had magically come and gone with the birth of Christ was still available in the twentieth century, right in front of her two feet. She was becoming more than fond of Scott, she realized. He was both knowledgeable and humble. Between his quiet but forthright ways and his humor and warm smile was a man who always seemed to be able to satisfy her appetite for learning. She wished she had spent more time with him in England. Maybe she would have appreciated the country better.

Komli noticed that the group had moved on. "Can you please wait for me, Scott. I'd like to buy some."

"What will you do with it?"

"It's Frankincense and Myrrh!" Komli said with a reverential regard Father Michael would have been proud of. "I'll keep some and I know at least two people I'd love to send it to." Komli stooped down on her knees and smiled at the old man selling his wares. He nodded at her in acknowledgement.

"Can I touch them?" Komli asked as she gesticulated with her hand, knowing that the man probably did not understand her. He nodded his head and smiled while she had a good old sensorial rummage. Komli's hand turned a powdery white. She smelled it and looked up excitedly at Scott. "Smell my hand Scott. It smells exactly like the church I went to."

Scott knelt down to smell her hand. "It does smell like church. I haven't been there for a long time," he said, holding on to her hand. He was inwardly thrilled to be with a creature so far removed from the women that had come and gone in his life. Again and again, he had been surprised to find that she derived pleasure in things he least expected would thrill women—dried up old wells in the desert, wizened faces of old men in the ancient village of Gadamis that had still to be introduced to electricity and plumbing, Bedouins in the desert, and now these mounds of resins from whom the rest of their group had walked away. What was her background, Scott wondered. She seemed knowledgeable and worldly in some ways and extremely naïve in others. How come she relished everything, like the starved, but behaved with the gentility of the schooled? He thought back on the day in Gadamis when everyone was petrified of the wild starving dog that had suddenly come yelping out of no where. What was it in Komli that had pacified the mongrel? What was their unspeakable bond? Maybe he would find out more about her some day. Maybe he wouldn't. All that mattered was that life in Tripoli was becoming very pleasurable. She was fast becoming the most refreshing thing he had encountered in a long time.

"Can I buy some?" Komli asked the street vendor. The old man understood the universal expression of interest in purchasing. He handed her two faded sheets of newspaper, suggesting that she help herself. When she had finished taking out what she wanted, he swaddled her two precious bundles with coarse brown string and handed them to her. She paid him and walked away with a heart singing with joy. Tripoli was so full of unexpected thrills, she thought—Roman ruins, sparkling Mediterranean, perfect temperature, ancient cities, wonderful Scott, and now she had found the priceless Frankincense and Myrrh, being sold with about as much abandon and enthusiasm as the unschooled women in India sold vegetables on the roadside! On mats that were equally tattered and torn. Her other treasure, Desiderata, had also come her way from a humble man she had mistaken for a tramp. In India, there were so many beggars that one had to simply ignore them or shoo them away like flies in order not to feel overwhelmed. Here in Tripoli, and in England, the tattered and torn did not form a part of every day life. In some strange way, they became her treasures, perhaps because they linked her to a childhood that was equally bedraggled, but innocent and untouched. She realized then that, ironically, it was the few glimpses of the humble and the meek in the desert and in the souq and on the sidewalks of London that had enriched her soul more than a hundred Harrods ever could. Happily, she savored the fragrances that weren't caged in expensive bottles, fragrances that were free for the world to whiff at will, if only one had the courage to remove one's handkerchief from one's nose. It was a happy Komli that walked beside Scott. She did not have a care in the world and two treasures to boot—a priceless one in her hand and a wonderful escort by her side.

"Who are the two privileged people who will get the Frankincense and Myrrh?" Scott asked.

"My friend, Tusneem, and Father Michael who taught me at Sunday school."

"He's going to be more than compensated for the free milk after all. Lucky man!"

"Does anyone need free milk in America? Or does everyone have three cars and four televisions and . . ."

"Two sailboats and one helicopter," Scott finished for her with a hearty laugh. "Will you come with me to America some day? I'll fly you myself."

"You have airplanes?" Komli asked in disbelief.

"No. But I can fly them."

"How? If you don't have any?"

"All you have to do is get a license, rent one, and push buttons. Will you fly with me?"

"Sure. I'll try anything once."

"Then will you live with me?"

"You're not proposing to me, I take it?"

"Not yet. But I just might, sweet thing, so don't go flying off with anyone else, will you?" Scott asked seriously.

Komli wondered casually if his family was anything like Mustapha's; what license they would require before he would be allowed to fly off with an alien to show her his religion, his country, and his culture.

It was the first of September. Komli decided that she had to avail herself of the opportunity to witness the grand celebrations of the anniversary of the first September Revolution which had taken place in Libya in 1969. She had learned from Scott that Gaddafi had led a bloodless coup to dethrone King Idris because in Gaddafi's eyes he was an imperialist puppet being supported by the west. Geoff had requested that the expatriates stay clear of the Green Square which was just a couple of miles away from the office. A huge military parade was to start from there, and he had warned everyone that the place would be packed with Libyan zealots, burning with revolutionary fervor.

Most of the expatriates decided to watch the parade from the terrace. Komli, however, wanted to be on the streets with the people. She had such fond memories of Independence Day parades in India. She remembered her college days when she and some friends got up at the crack of dawn to get a good view of the parade. The crowds were at least fifteen deep, she recalled, well in advance of parade time. She always loved listening to the National Anthem of India, and had always rejoiced with the crowds, and joined in the patriotic fervor. Her heart had always kept pace with the music to which the soldiers had marched in perfect unison.

Although living in Libya could be dangerous for some expatriates, Komli had realized that the expatriates tended to exaggerate many of the incidents. She had toed the line and nothing unpleasant had happened to her. In fact, life was getting better and better with each passing day. Yes, she would go to Libya's national celebration and witness it first-hand. Watching it from the balcony was for white wimps, she decided. She spotted a police officer and asked him when the parade would start.

"About one hour. From there," he replied pointing in the direction of the Green Square. Komli was disappointed that the streets were quieter than usual, devoid of an atmosphere of patriotic citizens waiting expectantly for something to stir their souls. She decided to keep walking. Maybe the atmosphere at the Green Square would be better. Within a half hour, Komli was at the Green Square. There were no mad mobs that Geoff had warned about, just people loitering around quietly. The streets were spotless, she noticed. She also saw that a special platform had been erected for whoever was going to be the Guest of Honor that day. A foreigner she bumped into said that rumor had it that Gaddafi was celebrating the anniversary in Benghazi. Komli ambled around, content to watch the crowds get thicker.

As imperceptibly as night creeps over twilight, more and more people had crept on to the streets until, Komli noticed suddenly, she could no longer see the street around her sandals. Wherever she looked, all she saw was countless pairs of shoes and sandals, in varying shades of black and brown. In body, if not in spirit, she had become a part of the people of Libya. Suddenly there was a lot of commotion. She looked up to see that policemen everywhere were waving their batons to clear the road for the guest of honor whose arrival seemed imminent. Much to Komli's chagrin, she was harshly herded to one corner where she was asked to remain with the few women who were attending the celebration. Komli felt relatively naked, because the women she was surrounded by were all in purdah, content to bare only their beautifully made-up eyes to the outside world. A few minutes later a car whizzed past her while the men in the crowd roared in unison; the women started trilling as loud as they could, to ward off any evil spirits that might be lurking around the VIP in the car. An immaculately dressed soldier stepped out of the car and climbed up to where the chair for the Guest of Honor was placed. It took Komli a couple of seconds to realize that the tall, proud soldier was no other than Gaddafi himself. She had seen several photographs of him in the office building. She was thrilled. So much for that foreigner saying Gaddafi was going to be in Benghazi! Thank goodness, she had chosen not to listen to the expatriates, she thought. Not only was she caught up in the fervor of the moment, she was but 30 feet away from Gaddafi who had her totally mesmerized. He was impeccably dressed in crisp khaki slacks and shirt that were separated by a broad, black leather belt. The belt was the only part of him that looked menacing. He had a shock of coarse, curly black hair that looked as stiff and proud as the rest of him. Nostrils flared with pride, he raised one hand to acknowledge his people. To Komli, he definitely looked more like a visionary than a mad man. Just then a small group of non-Libyan journalists with special badges were allowed to move directly in front of Gaddafi, to take photographs. Some of them started scribbling furiously in their notebooks.

In the grip of blind fascination, Komli decided to break loose and join the journalists. She had one thought in mind—she had to have a closer look at this leader the world claimed was mad. There was no way she could let such an opportunity slip by. Maybe he would let her shake his hands. Just as she was moving forward towards Gaddafi, the journalists stepped back. The parade had started and the first battalion of soldiers was about to salute Gaddafi. I must get over before that battalion does, was the only thought in Komli's mind as she made the mistake of running towards Gaddafi when the rest of the masses stood still, watching respectfully. The next instant, a heavy hand came down on her shoulder.

"Why you run straight to the stand?" the owner of the hand asked harshly as he thrust her backwards, wondering all the while what this chit of a girl was up to, committing a crime no sane man would commit, leave aside a female. He marched her all the way out of the crowds to a wall behind which lay the quaint, old alleyways of the souq where she had found some wonderful treasures not so long ago. But the shops were closed for the celebration; the souq was deserted. Komli stood against the wall as she was forced to stare at the security guard. She wondered if his sole duty was to make sure their beloved leader wasn't exposed to treacherous enemies of the revolution.

"I wanted to take a closer look at Gaddafi," she said timidly, having the presence of mind to smile at him in the hope that it would soften him a little. But he was made of stone, it seemed.

"Open your bag!" he ordered. Save me dear Bhagvaan, was all Komli could say to herself as she allowed the officer to delve inside her purse. In her bag was a book about Egypt. The Libyans hated the Egyptians for negotiating peace treaties with the Israelis. The bodyguard flicked through the pages without bothering to read a word. Would she be committed for being a spy, she wondered fearfully. No one in the world would know what happened to her, because no one knew where she was.

These people were also at war with neighboring Chad, and it was not so long ago that Tom Fitzgerald from her department had been turned back at the airport with wife and three children on their final exit. Reason? They wanted to question him about a joke he had made at his farewell party about seeing some of them in Chad. Obviously, poor Tom had incensed a Gaddafi fanatic who had informed Immigration who had in turn decided to hold him back for questioning. The harassed family had finally been allowed to depart the following evening, with three very irate children, a bitterly angry wife, and a harrowed husband whose sole concern was the safety of his wife and children.

She wondered who the Gaddafi fanatic or spy was in her department. Was it the guy who had offered to buy her some eggs because she had told him she couldn't find any. He had asked, no almost begged, that he deliver the eggs to her apartment over the weekend.

She had somehow managed to get out of it by saying she needed the eggs immediately and that she was going to be out the entire weekend. He rarely did any work, but no one ever seemed to say anything to him. Rumor had it that he was a Gaddafi spy. Oh God, Komli thought, these people are so messed up! She knew they could lock people behind bars for months on end, merely for taking photographs of abandoned cars in the desert, or for making innocent jokes. This body-guard could misinterpret her carrying a book on Egypt to mean just about anything. Save me, please, Bhagvaan, Komli prayed. I'll take cold, civilized England any time. Please get me out of this.

"What this book?" she heard the man ask.

"History book from my office library," Komli managed, trying not to look frightened. It was true; it was from the office library. She hoped the guard had the brains to realize that if the office permitted its existence in the library, it had to be a harmless, historical book.

"On Egypt, ha?! Where you from?"

"England," Komli said. After all, her contract was from England, and by now she had realized that the great colonizers of the world still impressed people more than insignificant little Indians like her.

"England?!" he asked in disbelief. "Wait here!" he commanded in a tone that would have paralyzed a brave soldier. He turned around to summon what looked like a senior officer. Just then, for a reason Komli never found out, the crowd in front of her came surging backwards towards her. Komli lunged forward. The prospect of being trampled to death by the masses seemed far more heavenly compared to prison in Tripoli. Although Komli felt her feet being trampled by what seemed like a wild herd of animals, she did not so much as wince. When all the trampling and jostling came to an end, Komli found that she had been thrust backwards into one of the alleyways of the souq. Should she make a dash, she wondered. The souq was deserted, it would be easy to spot her. For what seemed like an eternity, she stood transfixed, trying to look out of the corner of her eyes to see if she could spot the body-guard. She did; he was stuck among the crowd about fifteen feet away. Stealthily, she backed her way out into the deserted souq. She knew not to run; that would arouse suspicion. After a heart-thudding fifteen minutes, Komli managed to wind her way out onto the main street where the battalions were marching in full force. Silently, she walked on the pavement, thrilled that the spectators served as her shield. At last, she spotted her office building. It was on the opposite side of the street. This time, she was not going to risk crossing over. However, she had no intentions of waiting for the parade to end, just in case the body-guard found her again. Also, she knew the safe haven of her bedroom was all of sixty seconds away. When there was a large enough gap between two battalions, she asked a police officer if she could cross over. He offered to escort her.

Komli thanked him and fled to her apartment. There was nothing more precious than having a room and a key she decided as she flopped on her bed and said one more thank you to Bhagvaan for answering her prayers.

"Where the hell have you been?" Scott demanded in a tone Komli had never heard before.

"How did you get in? I thought I locked the door."

"Never mind. Do you know how worried I've been about you? You went down on your own to the Green Square, didn't you?"

"Yes." Komli replied sheepishly. In shame, she looked down at her feet and narrated what had happened. I don't think anyone in the world would be the worse off if I disappeared from the face of the earth," she added as if to justify her defiance.

Scott stared at her speechlessly for a while. "Do you really believe that, or do you just want to hear me say that you mean the world to me?"

"I don't know, Scott. All I know right now is that I'm so glad I'm back and that you're with me." She added with some humility, "For once, I agree with you expatriates; the Libyans are barbaric. It's been a long time since I begged and implored. I guess Him-up-there listened to me."

"Promise me, Komli, that you'll never do anything so foolish again. Have you any idea what happens in prisons in Tripoli? Not everything you hear about flogging and starving is exaggerated rumors. There's quite a bit of truth in all the stories that float in and out of our lives. I can't even begin to imagine what I would do if I heard you were whisked away by some illiterate officer. Do you realize that one just can't go to the police here and trace someone, like one can in other countries?"

"Yes I do, Scott. Believe me, I've learned my lesson. Never again will I go out alone, I promise." Realizing suddenly how truly fortunate she was, she exclaimed joyfully, "I'm free, Scott, I'm free! I'm the happiest girl in the world."

Rana, too, was learning the value of freedom. He knew he had to do something, however desperate, to get out of the rut he was in. With hindsight, he realized that his Arab boss hadn't mistreated him too much, that if he hadn't got caught drinking, he would have been in a great position to return home with a small fortune. Instead, he was stuck with an inhuman Korean boss who watched him like a hawk. Like cattle, he was shunted to his place of work in a truck with laborers of equal standing—no family in Saudi Arabia, no legal documents, no money, no regular showering facilities, and no incentive to wear clean clothes. He was herded back to his hole each evening with the same wretched people. The faces changed from time, but the stench, the back-breaking work, and the overall downcast spirit seemed to be set in concrete. Rana didn't even have the freedom to buy himself what he wanted to eat. So he ate to keep alive, slept the sound sleep of the exhausted, and woke up at the crack of dawn to repeat the cycle. He had little idea where he was transported on a day to day basis, and he cared even less.

It didn't take him long to realize that the only difference between the first prison and this so-called freedom was that the Korean made sure he ate so he could work. Death in the first prison might have been better, he thought from time to time.

"Get up! Dig!" the Korean hollered at him one afternoon when he found Rana doubled up in pain.

"I can't. My back's killing me."

"Then let it!" the Korean replied callously. "I have no use for cripples! Wonder who'll get you, the police, an angel, or a vulture!"

I really don't care, as long as you leave me alone, Rana thought, before he passed out.

Rana found himself being revived by a life force that has no life of its own—water, abundant splashes of it. The hand that cradled his neck was gentle. The eyes that looked into his were kindly and concerned and, as luck would have it, the face belonged to an Indian doctor.

The doctor had heard rumors about how illiterate laborers were treated in the Middle East. As soon as Rana realized that he could milk the gentleman for some sympathy, he spun out a sorry tale that transported him into the comforts of a hospitable Indian home.

"What should we do with him?" the doctor asked his wife. "He has no papers and no money and no idea how to get in touch with his boss. Judging from his state, he was probably so badly treated that he doesn't want to go back there."

"Do you know someone who knows someone who can do something for him? We just can't abandon the poor man," the wife replied with sympathy for her fellow countryman.

"Can we have him stay with us for a few days? I'll see what I can do."

Aatma,

> *You know how I bitch about my roommate. Well, I learned something very valuable yesterday. First thing in the morning, madam accused me of stealing her sapphire ring. Said she could not find it on the sink where she takes it out when (on the rare occasion) she does the dishes. It was also quite a rude shock to see this perfectly polished woman without all her polish. She looked nearer seventy as she walked out of her bedroom, hunchbacked and hacking out a cough that makes my stomach turn. Smoker's cough, Scott tells me. She looked pretty old and helpless. Far from the bossy puss in boots in her fine clothing and layers of makeup, armed to do battle with her talons and her cigarettes.*
>
> *While I can handle this snooty white woman bossing me around like I'm her little subservient pet, I could not handle being accused of stealing her ring. I had such nightmares about Margaret broadcasting the lie to the rest of the expatriates who I assumed would take her side of course that I ended up crying like an idiot, in the office of all places. Stephanie walked in just then. She's lovely and gentle and do you know what, when she heard why I was crying, instead of looking at me questioningly, she was horrified that Margaret could be so cruel to someone as nice as me! She said all the girls knew what a bitch Margaret was and even wondered how I could put up with her. But since I never complained and was always smiling, they figured I had some special ability to cope with people like her. Stephanie suggested*

I look in Margaret's bathroom and bedroom dresser. The ring was probably there. I told her I wouldn't dare go to her bedroom. Besides, even if I did find the ring there, she'd probably say I put it back there because I was caught. Well, Stephanie accompanied me to the apartment to find the ring. We found it on the sink in her bathroom. I realized then that all white people don't think all whites are superior. It not only brought me a lot closer to the girls, but also taught me that it was my cool, confident, invulnerable facade that kept these girls from asking me how I was coping with bossy Margaret. And I learned that gentle old Stephanie who wouldn't hurt a spider if it crawled all over her, is very strong indeed.

But that's not all. The girls started giving Margaret such a hard time that I now feel sorry for her! I came home last night to find her whispering to her birds. She does it all the time, but this time she hurried quickly into her room. They're birds of a feather, Fixit chirped, all alone in their world. While I have been gadding around with Scott and the other girls and focusing only on Margaret's bossy ways, I failed to notice that Margaret is never invited back anywhere a second time. Perhaps, the cloud of smoke is a fog behind which she likes to disappear. Trying to figure people out is far more confusing than trying to figure out our Gods. Scott says his first impression of me was that I was bold and brazen and tough; now that he's peeled off the crust, he thinks I'm an angel in disguise! Don't ask me what crust; he hasn't touched me! I love Scott. He helps me to see the world with four eyes and three hands, and he never feels sorry for me and let's me win. He makes me fight for every point.

I'm beginning to love Tripoli and all its people. Crazy Gaddafi's 'barren' desert is teaching me a lot about what we think countries and people have and what they really have. And I'm also so glad I have this room, and you, and the luxury to unfurl on my bed and indulge in my thoughts and memories. They are my real treasures. And Desiderata—'Listen to others, even the dull and ignorant; they too have their story'—stares back at me, again and again. It's the jewel on my wall. And who's to say who's dull and who's not? Margaret and Tara and the tramp and the Bedouin and the vendor of Frankincense and Myrrh have taught me that for every strand of pearl upon which we feast our eyes, there are a million dull oysters we ignore; pock-marked, dark, down-trodden shells that get shunted backwards and forwards depending on the force of the tide.

Thank goodness I have an R and R coming up. Tusneem wants me to visit her when her baby arrives.

I wonder what it would be like to have an R and R with Scott.

"Have you ever camped out in the desert?" Scott asked Komli one evening after work.

"I've never camped in my life," Komli replied. She almost added, except on the streets, but decided to leave it out.

"Some people in my department are camping out this weekend. Would you like to go?"

"Sounds like fun. What do I need to bring?"

"A tent, a hammer, a sleeping bag, a stove, a lamp, a . . . ."

"Are you telling me I have to go out and buy all that stuff here where I can't even buy salt and onions?!"

"Would you like to bring some chickens to bar-b-q, enough to feed about twelve people? I'll get the rest."

"And where do you propose to buy it? Don't tell me you're going on another business trip."

"Actually we have all the camping stuff we need. I was just kidding."

As luck would have it, the butcher by the office had fresh chickens on the eve of their camping expedition. Komli bought four, with quills in tact. The carcasses felt warm, even through the newspaper, but Komli had come a long way from that first shopping expedition when she had squirmed at the thought of handling dead fowl.

"Ugh!" one of the girls screamed the following afternoon when Komli opened the cooler with the chickens sitting on ice, "I'm not helping you clean that!"

"Me neither!"

"It's okay, I'll do it. Come hold them for me, Scott," Komli responded with a smile. She had lost count of the number of times she had cleaned chickens in the few months that she had been in Tripoli. Some grimaced and some grinned as Komli took the chickens to the shores of the Mediterranean, sat down cross-legged and matter-of-factly proceeded to wash out each chicken, single-handedly. Meticulously, she plucked out each quill before returning them to the chef.

"Here they are, all ready for the grill. Soft as a baby's bottom!"

"I'm not sure I can eat that chicken," Sheila said, screwing her face in disgust. Like Scott, Sheila was one of those who usually ate out of cans or in restaurants. "How can we expect illiterate butchers in this country to know anything about preserving chicken, when even the educated Libyans are so uncivilized! For mercy's sake, Komli, why didn't you get the ready broasted chicken?!"

"I thought the idea was to barbeque them right here. Broasted chicken also had feathers and quills once, you know!" Komli added calmly, although she felt the usual anger surge within her. Another supercilious remark from another arrogant white mouth, she thought to herself.

Scott twirled his moustache while he indulged in his own opinions about women— too squeamish to pluck the feathers off harmless chicks but brazen enough to pluck men's wallets in so many ingenious ways; preying in all its myriad forms was just another link in the chain that connected man to beast.

His eyes rested on Komli. What was this woman's secret, he wondered for the umpteenth time. He was convinced there was something unusual about her past. How could he draw her past out of her, when he himself was so cagey about his. About his grandfather who preferred to drown his memories in alcohol and gaze into the television with glazed eyes that seemed to absorb little. How could he share with decent, sane Komli that his hand had pulled the trigger that had killed innocent people? How could he tell her that he did not have the courage to defy his commander and scream *NO*? That he had quietly screamed inside ever since for being a coward, a meek lamb, a filthy pig with fungus not only on his body but about to overtake his brain as well. How could he tell her that in trying to put that hell behind him, his first journey through paradise was in the arms of different women, in different countries? That, all that was behind him; that all he wanted now was to spend his time with her. Komli's past, therefore, did not really matter to him, although it roused his curiosity every now and again. He decided to allow himself the luxury of staring at her. It cost him nothing to smell wild flowers, and it cost him nothing to stand back and watch this strange creature who had ripped off the chicken's skins, gutted the insides and had thought little of leaving behind the waste for the Mediterranean tide to sweep away whenever it felt like it. With such sweet simplicity, she had walked back, dangling two chickens at a time between her five precious fingers, like waiters dexterously dangling wine glasses from their stems.

The expatriates were, in the meanwhile, discussing man's gastronomic habits.

"Did anyone notice what was dangling outside the butcher's a few miles before we got here? The things these people eat. That was the grossest thing I've ever seen in my life!"

'Grossest' happened to be a camel's head. It's gullet looked like a six-foot pendulum swinging back and forth in the gentle breeze. Komli had wanted to stop to get a closer look, knowing that she would probably never have another opportunity to see a camel's gullet swinging from a shack in the desert. But Scott had denied her the pleasure, saying that they had to keep up with the group. Komli realized that this must have been the mysterious 'treat' Melissa had alluded to that first day when she had taken her shopping.

"Is it true, Scott," someone asked, "that Americans in Florida eat crocodile meat?"

"I believe so. It's one way of getting rid of parts we don't need for purses and shoes," he said coolly.

"Ugh! The things people do! And these Libyans serve goats' eyes as a delicacy and then go goat grabbing with their bare hands!"

Komli decided to intervene, "I'm assuming you mean they eat roasted goat with their bare hands; you made them sound like barbarians!"

"It's not very different, is it?"

"Eating with the hand can be very graceful," Komli said gently but firmly, as she thought back on Motapappasan and the thaal around which she had eaten once, not to mention the rest of her fellow countrymen, especially the poor, relishing simple meals with their bare hands.

"I know. It's not like I don't eat fruit and sandwiches with my hand. But to have gooey goats' eyes rolling around in the palms of my hand, ugh!" Sheila shuddered with closed eyes, as though she could feel the soft balls in her hands!

Are you vegetarian, Sheila?" Komli asked.

"No. Why?"

"Then, the way I see it, all you and I are really doing is condemning one another for preference of parts. Some eat breast and some eat brain, some eat feet and some eat liver and some eat absolutely everything. We Hindus shudder at the thought of hairy Ox tail swishing in your soup, and . . . ."

"We don't have hairy ox-tail swishing in our soup!"

"Ox-tail soup certainly conjures that image in my mind, just as you conjure gory images of eye-balls popping in and out of Arab mouths! They probably shudder at the thought of you pickling pig's feet for a delectable treat!" Komli said with a laugh.

"I guess you have a point," Sheila said with a half-smile. Komli was enjoying herself, so she carried on. "Do you know something, if a man eats meat, he is simply a carnivore; but if a tiger is let loose in India and eats man, he immediately becomes a creature to abhor and to ensnare at all costs! Cats are feline, cows are bovine, dogs are canine and we, made in the image of god I keep being told, are simply divine. So what do you think of those divine creatures who eat monkey's brains and devour dogs as the height of delicacy? Ask Scott. He talks about it all the time."

"Nobody eats dogs!" Sheila wailed in horror. She had two handsome bull dogs back home. She missed them terribly.

"They do in the Far East," Scott said matter-of-factly. If this diatribe of a verbal appetizer needed some garnish, he was more than willing to lend a hand. "Actually, I've tasted dog in my travel."

"You're lying! I think I'm going to throw up. What does it taste like?"

"Cat!" Scott managed with a straight face.

After everybody had stopped laughing, Komli continued in a deliberately sweet tone of voice to conceal her sarcasm, "We accept gifts from each other with our bare hands but when it comes to accepting god's gift of food, we think it uncivilized to eat that with our bare hands. So we eat with knives and forks. I think we should be civilized and wear gloves when we indulge in the other great gift from god . . . ."

"What's that?"

"Sex," Komli replied sweetly.

"You're being silly! Has she already been drinking, Scott?"

"Too little sex, if you ask me!" Geoff quipped.

Komli looked at Scott, hoping he'd have something sillier to add.

"Maybe that's why God chooses to be a holy ghost; he doesn't have to worry about what he eats or does with his flesh!" Scott obliged.

"That's sacrilege, Scott!" Melissa shrieked. "I think we all need to go on an R and R. Too much sun is bad for our brains!"

If laughter was the best medicine, Scott was the best dose Komli had had in a long time, she thought. "Where's the knife, Scott? Hold down the chickens and I'll quarter them. I promise not to nick off your finger. Trust me, I'm harmless with a knife."

"I know you are. It's your tongue I watch out for," Scott said, a shade more seriously than Komli realized.

In spite of the distasteful conversation, the barbeque dinner turned out to be perfect.

That night, everyone seemed content, sitting around the crackling fire, sipping coffee and listening to the Mediterranean's soft lullaby as it moved backwards and forwards like a devoted mother trying to lull its children to sleep—good night, enjoy the skies . . . good night, enjoy the stars . . . . good night, enjoy the sounds . . . . good night, enjoy the peace. There was not a color to be seen in the water. Indeed, it seemed that the sea had deliberately pulled a dark blanket over itself so man would be forced to gaze at the twinkling stars above.

During the wee hours of that morning, Komli found herself holding on to Scott for dear life. They were all fast asleep inside three tents when, out of the blue, they heard a pack of wild hyenas surround the tents. For once, Komli was also convinced that the ferocious creatures would tear down the tent and devour them all alive.

"Just keep quiet. They'll go away," Scott whispered, putting his arms around her. After what seemed forever, the howling died down. The hyenas gave up and went away. Komli lay awake long after, still holding on to Scott. It occurred to her that night that her life experiences were like different compartments in a train that had no destination. Where would she end up, she wondered. The prospect of stopping with Scott suddenly seemed very palatable.

It was only with hindsight that Komli wondered if the frenzied 'laughter' and angry barking of the hyenas was really a precursor of events to come, because the day that followed turned out to be as ugly as the preceding night had been beautiful. She would forget neither as long as she lived:

Everyone in the group was up early. After a chilly night, in more ways than one, everyone seemed content just to laze around and take it easy, happy in the knowledge that they had escaped the wild hyenas. Some were sipping coffee, some were taking advantage of the sun and tanning their bodies, while others were reading or reminiscing, simply content to have memories drift back and forth like the tide. It was Melissa who first shattered the peace by commenting on the newspaper article she was reading.

"Hey, has anyone read about the barbaric circumcision rites some women go through in parts of Africa and Asia? According to this article, 'women use broken glass or knives to excise the clitoris! It severs the nerves of orgasm so instead of being equal partners in sex, women think of themselves only as agents of procreation.'"

"That's disgusting!"

"That's not all. Listen to this, 'in some cases they remove the entire labia minora and much of the labia majora, whatever that means, and then they close up the woman with thorns, which her husband removes on the wedding night!'"

"Stop it, Melissa! I was chilled to the bone last night. I don't need it again!" Sheila exclaimed.

"Just think what those wretched women must go through!" Melissa continued, "Thank goodness for missionaries and people who venture out there to bring such barbaric customs to light! Otherwise most of these people would still be living like uncivilized cave men."

"It looks like some of them still are!"

Komli's Montessori education had left indelible memories of the wonderful timelines she had studied of the evolution of life. She had never forgotten the pictures of creatures great and small that had magically and mysteriously evolved from a microscopic spec in the water. Also embedded in her mind were wonderful images of the evolution of early man—hunting and fishing and learning to use fire. Mrs. Fletcher had shown great respect for humanity's forefathers who had labored and stumbled upon discoveries and inventions. They were the founding fathers of modern man, she used to say. Komli had developed a great fondness for those men who had little time to focus on anything but their fundamental needs. She remembered clearly those pictures of naked men, tearing apart animal flesh with their bare hands. It had never occurred to Komli to think of early man as wretched or uncivilized.

"Cave men were probably happier than people today. I don't think they were uncivilized," Komli said, without showing any signs of irritation, although her heart was beating faster than she could ever remember.

"Do you people in India circumcise women as well?" Melissa asked without meaning to be rude.

"Yes," Komli said quietly. *Brace yourself*, Fixit said to himself, as he felt the first tremors inside his mistress's body.

"Do they also just hack off the genitals?" Melissa continued.

"As a matter of fact, they don't." Either the blazing sun had got to Komli, or she had had more than an over-dose of derogatory remarks Melissa handed down from her self-appointed seat on the highest pedestal in the animal kingdom. At least that's the way Komli perceived Melissa. Komli decided on impulse to push her off that pedestal. Komli was also sick of her own lack of courage. As Fixit sometimes said when they were alone in their bedroom, *all you do is snigger along with the expatriates when they make derisive comments about the local people, and then complain in writing to your sister in India. Don't you have the guts to give them a piece of your mind? You know you would if it happened to be Tusneem!*

"As far as I know, circumcision means to cut around. Do you agree, Melissa?" Komli asked.

"Pretty much. I know they cut around the foreskin on the penis, but female circumcision sounds pretty horrific from what I've just read!"

"So do you agree that circumcision is the removal of something our Creator blessed us with?" Komli persisted.

"Yes. How do they circumcise women in India?"

"I was circumcised when I was a child, but have been too embarrassed until now to talk about it. All I know is that my genitals were not hacked off. I loved a man once, and actually enjoyed sex with him." Komli had anticipated the shocked silence, so she continued after hesitating for a fraction of a second to summon up more courage, "You've just helped me realize, Melissa, that I am circumcised in more ways than one. I was born with two hands, but some barbarians in Calcutta circumcised one."

"Whatever for?!" Melissa exclaimed in horror.

"Control. All circumcision is done for control. I haven't finished. I was also circumcised by my mother, by a Catholic priest, and by several teachers and professors along the way."

"What do you mean?"

"Each one told me different stories of how the world was created and what I must believe and what I must not believe, thereby circumcising my ability to think for myself, as the Creator intended. I ate with my bare hand and loved it, until I went to England where I learned that it is considered uncouth to eat with one's hands. So I follow in your footsteps, Melissa, hoping you will perceive me to be as civilized as you believe you are!"

"I'm sorry, Komli. I did not mean anything personally . . ."

"I know you didn't, but I'd like to finish. To be honest with you, I'd much rather lose a part of my clitoris and my virginity, and live life, than just sit on that mighty high pedestal of yours and laugh at those you and your forefathers once conquered and colonized! I'll say this much for you though, Melissa, you have the courage to fart in public. Your unkind opinions of foreigners are just like stinking farts you have the guts to air in public, and I am sick of its odor. Tell me, why do you think the right way to eat is with the fork in your left hand?"

"Because I'm a proud, ambidextrous Brit!" Melissa said angrily, wondering if this Komli in a deceptively simple, flimsy white robe was the same docile Komli who had cried in the office the other day because someone had accused her of theft.

Komli put up her right hand and added, as she wiggled her fingers in front of Melissa, "As far as I am concerned, this is the best fork of all, but that's the opinion of a WOG, and I know it doesn't count. Strange thing is, Americans eat with the fork in their right hand, and they think that's the right way of course. Do you know why?"

"No. You've jumped on my mighty high pedestal; why don't you tell me!"

"Because you yourself are circumcised intellectually. You just don't know because you're so busy circumcising others. Snip, snip, snip," Komli said vehemently, using her index and middle finger to snip at the air, "from the time we're born, our parents, our teachers and our society circumcise our minds—pink is for girls and blue is for boys; this is how you cut your hair, and this is how you don't; this is how you sit and eat; and this is how you don't. And you go through life circumcised, unable to have an affair with another culture, much less an orgasm of the mind!"

"And what are these wonderful orgasms of the mind, pray tell?" Melissa asked sarcastically while the rest maintained a stony silence, not knowing how to react.

"Seeing poetry in the innocent Bedouin sipping coffee under the stars. The tragedy for you is that you are blind to his poetry because in him you see only the uncouth. So of course you would snigger that his cup had no handles . . . ."

"And I take it you would have an orgasm because his cup had no handles!" Melissa retorted, managing to get a chuckle out of Geoff.

Komli refused to let their argument end with a snigger and a titter. More angry than before, she continued, "If you saw Muslims pray, you would fail to see any beauty in their actions because they don't sit quietly on benches or kneel down with folded hands and pray like you do in church."

"How do you know?" Melissa screamed. She was livid herself that Komli was making such high-handed assumptions.

"Because you're always making fun of their beautiful call to prayer. I've just never had the guts until now to say something. That's all you do, make fun of anything that's foreign to you. To be honest with you, you're good and very funny most of the time. We're always sniggering and sniveling at your jokes. But when I saw you the other day at your house sale, I was horrified at what you did when that poor Ethiopian guy walked in."

"I didn't do anything to him!"

"Of course not! But you were so darn uncomfortable . . ."

"How do you know how I felt?"

"It was pretty obvious, the way you dashed into your kitchen and brought out the air freshener as soon as he left! Did you even stop to marvel at his innocence, his fascination for the foreign goods you were selling? Did you so much as glance at his beautiful Muslim head-dress? Of course not! You were too busy worrying about the germs he might be spreading! So as soon as he left, you started spraying air freshener all over your house, getting rid of whatever it was you thought he polluted your house with! What do you think you cleansed yourself of? His innocence? His humility? His lack of sophistication? I wanted to scream then, but the coward in me did not. Do you know how he would treat you if you visited him? Like a queen. The sad thing is that you think you're the sparkling jewel, when in reality the only sparkle you have is in your scathing wit and in your wonderful ability to mimic people. Did you ever think to penetrate his soul?"

"No, but I am sure you saw the light. Enlighten me!" Melissa jabbed back, feeling hurt, angry and shocked herself at Komli's uncalled for meanness.

"As far as I am concerned, the only creatures who are pure and uncircumcised are those who don't read and write—the Bedouins and the bushmen, and the hunters and gatherers, which includes of course the birds and the bees and all those who live instinctively, as perhaps we were meant to."

"We were not meant to live instinctively! God gave us a brain, to think, and a tongue to use tastefully . . ."

"Oh yeah? How come we don't practice what we preach?! Maybe tongues were just meant for taste buds!"

"Then I suggest you curb that wild tongue of yours and cut out the crap!"

"Speaking of crap, have you watched a bird shit? It just opens up its rear end, deposits its waste with reckless abandon and flies away, instinctively knowing that it has far from despoiled the earth because a worm or mother earth or something in the food chain needs its shit. And I have yet to find bird shit that stinks! But as for us, we hack down trees and whatever else our little hearts desire, to make toilet paper and wrapping paper and writing paper and even diapers to preserve our shit and our stench! Good thing, come to think of it, because who in the food chain would want our shit anyway? I wonder what will kill us first, lack of oxygen or overdose of paper!"

You're playing with words, babbling senselessly, if you ask me," Melissa retorted.

"I think it's time you both stopped babbling senselessly!" Stephanie said quietly, but Komli was unstoppable.

"Once we've satisfied our fundamental needs for food and shelter, don't all civilized human beings just play with words? Here's some more babble—Catholics believe that they will not go to heaven unless they are baptized with water, holy water that is the origin of all life. Makes a lot of sense to me since life began in water anyway."

"Not everybody believes that life started in water!" Melissa managed to get in.

"I know! But you believe in baptism with water. I don't know of any religion that does not use water for purification. Strange thing is though that you think that those who use water instead of toilet paper to wash their asses are uncouth!"

"They are!"

"They're not! Civilized man uses paper for two things—to wipe his ass and polish his intellect. I bet his ass is cleaner than his brain! We've created thousands of ingenious words and so-called laws and truths with which we brainwash and control others. Civilization is just another synonym for circumcision and, if you ask me, I think circumcision of the body has caused far less pain than circumcision of the mind."

"If we white people are so arrogant and pompous and shitty, God alone knows why you choose to suffer our company!"

I didn't say all white people are arrogant and pompous! The only difference between you and me is that I'm still searching for answers which, as you just claimed, perhaps God alone knows, although you seem to think you know them, too!"

"No, Komli! I know I don't have all the answers. It's you who thinks you have all the answers! We do have one thing in common though—we both fart in public! I don't think the Bedouins have all the answers, and you don't think we Brits do either. Why don't you go live with the birds and the bees?!"

"I wish I could! Their lifestyle is probably healthier than ours," Komli said, a shade quieter. She had come full circle to the time when she had lived with the birds and the beasts. Life had been tough then. She was now also aware of everyone staring at her in bewilderment for having caused such a stink. She realized she had angered and saddened a group of people with whom she had so much fun. They had done everything to help her enjoy a country whose people refused to have anything to do with her outside of work. She wondered if the expatriates would ever feel comfortable with her again. Even Scott who had come to her rescue yesterday, was rendered speechless. Deflated, spent and stricken, she walked out towards the sea shore, even though she knew that she would find little solace in its stoic sighs.

"Phew!" Geoff let out, "I'm getting in the water! I've never heard so much verbal diarrhea in my life. That kettle's obviously been simmering for a long time!" Komli's whistle had been too shrill; the steam too hot. Best left untouched, seemed to be the unspoken consensus, as one by one everyone went into the water.

Fixit wished he could spring out of the restricting walls of Komli's body and dive into the water with the rest of them—and stay there forever. The stones she had cast were so much more hurtful than the stones the Libyan children had cast not so long ago. What had happened to the sweet girl on the streets, he asked himself; to the humble creature with whom he thought he would enter the kingdom of heaven? Baffled and saddened, he shriveled up like a dried old prune.

The road from the streets of Calcutta to the shores of Tripoli had been long and winding. Komli had stomached many ups and downs. She had endured before. She would endure now, she told herself, although it seemed that all she had left in her stomach was an iron lining that felt cold and empty.

Scott had not joined the others in the water. He was a little concerned about Komli. He recalled how much she had wanted to go talk to the Bedouins; not so long ago she had ventured out into the Green Square and barely escaped the clutches of a police officer. There was no telling how far out she would venture this time. He watched her until she turned into a tiny speck on the horizon.

"Geoff, I'll be back soon. I can barely see Komli. I'm going to try and calm her down."

Komli was still walking when Scott finally caught up with her. He walked beside her, not saying a word. When she stopped to gaze at the horizon, Scott did likewise.

"I'm sorry," she said simply after staring intently into the sea as though she was searching for something."

"So am I. I realize now that at times it must be quite hard for you to decide whose side to take, the Libyan's or ours; after all, although you're an expatriate, your culture is closer to Libya's, isn't it?"

"In some ways. I don't know. I've never been to their homes. I don't hate you all, Scott. Not even Melissa, actually. For some reason, she got to me today. My sister always said, be careful what you say; you can't take words back. I guess it's too late now."

"There's a snarling, snapping, howling creature in all of us, Komli. Some choose to howl quietly; some employ lawyers, and some do it themselves. Maybe a lucky few go through life without ever feeling the need to howl," Scott said quietly.

Komli had calmed down and seemed somewhat remorseful and receptive. Sensing that he had an opportunity to find out more about her, he decided to question her further. "Melissa should never have talked about circumcision the way she did. What do you know about female circumcision?"

"Very little," Komli replied, not really feeling like bringing up the subject again.

"I, too, happen to be circumcised, Komli. Many boys are in America. For hygienic purposes, I was told, although there is an international movement now trying to prove otherwise."

"You mean people in the west know something about circumcision?"

"Oh yes. There's a whole web-site on it. I became more interested in it when I was in Egypt a couple of years ago. On one of the walls of an Egyptian tomb, I saw an engraving showing a boy's wrists being held down by a man, while a priest was circumcising him. I decided then to find out more about it."

"What did you find out?"

"It's fairly widespread, but no one knows exactly how or where it originated. The Arabs, Africans, Mongols and Indians are people that come to mind. I don't think it started out as a hygienic practice though. According to one theory, it was a blood offering to the gods, to remain immortal. Another theory claimed that it ensured longevity and reincarnation! There was also something about sacrificing a part for the welfare of the whole. The Jews believe it's a covenant between God and Abraham."

"Did you come across anything about female circumcision?" Komli asked, showing more interest suddenly.

"Yes. It, too, is widely practiced, not just in Asia and Africa, but also in Australia, South America, and parts of Europe. In Egypt alone, about seventy-five percent of all Muslim and Coptic Christians are circumcised."

"You're kidding me!"

"If I can recall correctly, it's not mandated by any religion, and, yet, it's a cultural practice that has been passed from mother to daughter for centuries."

"It's hard to believe that in this day and age people still do such things."

"You know something," Scott exclaimed as he recalled another piece of information, "the encyclopedia also said that in India, Hindus are not normally circumcised. How come you are? You're Hindu."

As always, Komli couldn't help but admire him for being more knowledgeable than she expected. It had certainly never occurred to her to read up about circumcision. "Did the encyclopedia refer to any sexual implications at all?" she asked.

"Not that I can remember. There was something about cancer of the penis being non-existent among Jews who were circumcised at an early age. Were you given any explanations at all?"

He was so matter-of-fact about the whole subject that Komli realized she didn't have to be ashamed of something over which she had had no control. "I was circumcised when I was about seven, I think. Not for immortality or longevity or good health, but for good old money. Sounds awful doesn't it? Actually it wasn't. Until I was about seven, my mother, sister, and I were in the clutches of a horrific, underground begging industry in Calcutta. The big bosses hacked off the lower half of this stump when I was new-born . . ."

"Why?!" Scott managed hoarsely.

"Wouldn't you feel sorry for a mother with a maimed infant and give her alms?" Scott wanted to yell, *NO, I would never indulge a beggar*, but he chose to say nothing, so Komli continued, "Well, when I was little, a wealthy Muslim mother offered to give us everything money could buy, if I was circumcised instead of her daughter. My sister accepted the offer in order to save my mother who was very sick at the time." Seeing Scott's horrified expression, she added calmly, "It's okay, it was fate." The last thing she wanted was his pity or, worse still, somebody pointing a finger at her dear sister, the one human being she knew she could count on no matter what she said or did.

"No, it was not fucking fate!" Scott said angrily. That's the trouble with you passive people, you just sit back and lick your bleeding wounds and call it fate and resign yourself to it. Just a few minutes ago, you fought with all your guts, and now you quietly tell me that the hacking off of your arm and circumcision were all a part of fate? It's not okay to sit back calmly; it's not okay that no one in your family fought for . . . ."

"Oh yeah? So you're telling me fucking fate did not send you and all the men in your family to war? You chose to go yourself? You killed willingly, and now you are so much happier than we passive people who quietly accept our fate? You mean you have no wounds to lick? That there is no fury and frustration in you? That it's okay to remain angry and allow your pain to get fossilized, while we passive people calmly allow it to drain out of our system by accepting it as our fate?"

Scott stared at her for a few seconds before he said, "How tough is it for you to do battle single-handedly?"

"That's a good pun. With whom?"

"The world, it seems to me. You're quite a fighter, but it's a thankless task, isn't it?"

"I didn't know it was a thankless task. I didn't even know I could be such a horrendous fighter. I love life and I love people; they fascinate me. I don't know what gets into me sometimes. Would you believe me if I told you I was a real sweet beggar girl?"

"You were never a beggar, Komli. You were a mere shadow. All children have to be shadows first while adults bask in the sunlight. That's why we sound like our parents. It wasn't your choice to beg, and it seems like it wasn't your sister's either. You know something else?"

"You're very chatty today!"

"Amazing how a little heat can transform one! I was going to say, the beggars and the homeless are purified again and again by the elements—the rain and snow and wind, while the affluent and the educated sit on their butts, watching television and punching keys on computers . . ."

"I used to love watching heaven in all its glory paint the skies at sunrise and sunset, but most of all I used to love getting drenched in the rain. Only difference was that at that time just my body needed to get cleansed. I didn't realize how spiritually pure I was back then."

"You're not such a bad egg, you know. A little hard-boiled perhaps!" Scott dared with a gentle smile.

"And you're certainly not one of those who closes windows to the natural world. If anything, you seem to have your eyes open all the time, and your mouth shut. I could never even imagine a foreigner knowing as much as you know about circumcision."

"And who is the foreigner if circumcision is universal?" Scott asked. Komli simply shrugged her shoulders, so Scott continued, "Did your sister or you ever find out why Muslim women are circumcised?"

"Not really. Keeps women from getting wild in bed, is what Roshni was told. So here I am Scott," Komli said with the first glimmer of a smile, "A part of myself, sacrificed for the preservation of the body and sharpening of the mind! Out of rags, into school and college, emerging with a tongue that definitely needs to be circumcised! Still think I'm an angel?"

"I'm not so sure." He stared at her for a few moments before asking, "What is worse, Komli, the memories of the physical wounds or the mental anguish?"

"Both recede in time. Especially if you keep busy," she replied without much emotion. "What is worse for you, Scott?

He stared at her through eyes blurred with tears. Was that the reason for his anger, he asked himself, that he hadn't kept busy enough while he tried to fight off memories of bodies brutally disemboweled by the weapons he had used. Pretending not to notice his tears, Komli said astutely, "It seems to me that you have iced your suffering with a thick coating of guilt, which makes it a far heavier burden to carry than the suffering of the innocent. How old were you when you went to war?"

"How does it matter?" he answered, still re-hashing some of the horrors in his mind.

Ever thought that you, too, were a mere shadow while your commander was in the sunlight? Snap out of it, Scott. There will always be greater and lesser persons than yourself."

"I've heard that before."

"Somehow I'm not surprised! It's from *Desiderata*."

"That scroll on your wall?"

"Yes. We have to focus on our good memories, you know. I've been very happy here in Tripoli. I'm sorry I ruined the weekend for everyone."

"You don't have to apologize to me. If anything you've taught me again and again that it's possible to soar on clipped wings; to find beauty in places I would not have thought I'd find any. You have so much to be proud of, Komli," he added as he tilted her chin up towards his face. "The irony is that civilized man looks up to the biggest circumcisers of all—our priests and our politicians and our historians. They dress their thoughts and ideas with words as we do our bodies with clothes because there's so much that cannot be revealed!"

"Flesh or truth?" Komli asked with a smile.

"Both, I guess. Do you know anyone who's not circumcised?"

"Not really, although my sister comes close. She's unschooled and pure, even though she reads a lot. She's too pure, though. I wish she would live her life."

"Do you know what, little one? I, for one, am thankful for scholars and teachers and inventors. Without them, you and I would still be hunting and gathering in our respective continents, and I would never have met you. How about a good dip in the holy waters of this gorgeous sea? We could both do with some cooling and cleansing," Scott said as he dragged her into the Mediterranean.

While they were enjoying the water, Scott said playfully, "I'm beginning to believe every grain of sand in the desert contains a secret in a language we don't understand. Those who walk the sands bare feet learn many truths, although in the end the truth scorches their feet."

"Whatever! It's great not having to think at all," Komli replied as she immersed herself in the water for the umpteenth time.

"You are so beautiful," Scott exclaimed a few minutes later as he fished her out of the water and carried her to the beach in his arms. Komli was glad she was soaking wet, because when he held her in his arms and gazed into the depths of her being, all she could think of was that somehow it did not seem right, after all the insults she had hurled, that Scott should find out that she was dripping in her groins as well; that unlike water it was a more gelatinous state of matter; that she was ready to be taken. But Scott knew she was dripping with desire; her fire had seared through his clothing as his had penetrated through hers. If this paradise was anywhere out of Gaddafi's jurisdiction, Scott would have taken her there and then.

Take me inside the water, Komli was about to beg when Scott shattered the moment by snapping, "Stay calm, Komli. Let me do all the talking. I see some Libyans heading our way." Komli turned around to see a group of teenage Libyans walk menacingly towards them. She could see their lecherous eyes slowly strip her of the drenched, flimsy voil robe that revealed every outline of her slender, curvaceous body. She crossed her hands over her breasts; her nipples were as hard as peanuts. Leading the group was an older Libyan with a baton in his hand. Unlike the teenagers who were viewing her with obvious relish, he was disgusted to see an attractive, young Indian sell herself shamelessly to a white infidel.

The teenagers had watched Scott and Komli for a while, before they decided to summon a more elderly Libyan. White men corrupted the non-white, the young Libyans had learned again and again. Here was an opportunity for some drama in their otherwise uneventful lives.

"Is he a policeman?" Komli asked nervously.

"No! He's just another brainwashed, fucking, frustrated bastard who has nothing better to do. If you weren't with me I'd tear his guts apart.

"Scott, please calm down. We can't do battle with a mob!"

"Your name?" the officer asked Scott harshly.

"Scott Douglas."

"American?"

"Yes." You may as well have said, *devil*, you bastard, Scott thought angrily.

"Where you work?"

"Libyan Oil Company."

"Your name?" the officer asked pointing his baton at Komli.

"Komli Seth."

"Married?"

"No."

"From India?"

"Yes."

"Speak Arabic"

"No."

"Work here?"

"Yes."

"Where?"

"We work together, we . . . ." Scott intervened, but was rudely cut short.

"Keep quiet! Where you work?" the officer repeated, looking at Komli.

"At Libyan Oil Company."

"What you doing with this American?"

"We came in a big group from our office. I can take you to them," Komli offered.

"Show me your papers!" he demanded of Scott.

"They are in my car."

"Where is your car?"

"It is further down there, where my colleagues from office are," Scott said pointing in the said direction.

"Why you touch this woman?"

"I . . . . she was . . . . I was trying to comfort her."

"You lie! Why you allow him to touch you?" the officer asked Komli.

"I fell and hurt my hand, he was . . . ."

"You also lie! Come with me, you two."

"Can we get our papers from the car?" Scott asked, hoping he could solicit some help on the way.

"No! Come with me, now." At this point they were completely surrounded by the mob. Although neither Scott nor Komli understood a word of what was being said, it was quite obvious from all the giggling and sniggering that the teenagers hadn't had so much fun in a while.

Melissa, too, had wandered off by herself to cool down. It was she who had noticed Scott's white face bobbing a good ten inches above a throng of what seemed like Libyan hooligans. She stared for a moment, whirled around and ran to her group. "Geoff," she yelled, "hurry, quick! I think Scott's in trouble."

Fortunately, Geoff knew more than anyone else how to deal with the local people. He also knew a spattering of Arabic. He talked with the elderly Libyan at length, patting him on the shoulder, and smiling from time to time. Subtly, he let a fifty pound bill fall out of his pocket. The Libyan picked it up. Geoff pretended not to notice, while he continued to plead their case, "I promise you, sir, this will never happen again. I agree with you, Americans should not touch Indian women. I apologize."

"You no go out with him! Understand?!" The officer ordered, looking at Komli.

"I understand," Komli said meekly. She was ready to agree to anything, as long as this lunatic of a man was willing to let Scott go.

"And you, leave her alone, you understand?" he ordered Scott.

"Yes, sir." Scott said, praying he would some day have the opportunity to confront him on another battlefield—he would happily mash his balls and his empty skull and everything else on him to mincemeat! And this time he would harbor no guilt feelings later!

The Libyan asked the mob to leave. Reluctantly, they dismantled, wishing the drama could have continued for a while longer.

As soon as they approached the campsite, Geoff pounced on Scott and Komli, "Now do you two fucking morons understand why I said you must not venture out on your own?! This is the second time you've been in trouble, Scott! Believe me, you're lucky Melissa saw your bloody, thick skull above the crowd. There's no telling what that illiterate, fucking mob would have done to you!"

A humble Komli went up to Melissa. "Thank you, Melissa. I'm also very sorry about this morning."

"Don't be. I like people who speak their minds. It's my pleasure to save expatriates. I'll always stand by them," Melissa replied, without a trace of sarcasm. She knew Komli was smart enough to get her message.

When Geoff had calmed down, he took Scott and Komli aside. He was still angry with them for having been foolish enough to walk off on their own, but relieved at the same time that he had been able to save two, decent, innocent people, although he was not quite sure what to make of Komli any more. "Look, you two, if you're interested in each other's safety, you better not be seen alone together, not even in the office! As you know, there are spies everywhere in this country. You never know who will report who and, before you know it, one of you will be behind bars! And by the way, don't think you got out of this scot-free, you bastard. You owe me a hundred pounds, a few dinners and drinks forever for my sharp wits!" Geoff said, giving Scott a warm thump on his shoulders.

Komli looked at the love birds as she timidly entered her own cage of an apartment that evening. There was a part of her that wanted to leave Tripoli immediately. But there was another part of her that wanted to be with Scott, even though she had been warned to stay away from him. She was so shaken by what the Libyans had subjected them to that for a couple of days she felt nothing but a sense of relief that Scott and she had got out of it without being physically hurt in any way. The reality of the rumors about expatriates being harassed and imprisoned for no rhyme or reason had at last hit home.

Komli regretted having erupted like a raging volcano. She wondered if the expatriates would view her as she did Melissa. After all, as Melissa had been so quick to point out, they were both arrogant women, just on different sides of the same fence. The more she thought about it, the less inclined she felt to socialize with the expatriates. She realized all she would do is end up ruining their evenings, because they would not be able to laugh and joke freely any more if she were around.

It took her a couple of nights before she finally found the courage to write to her sister.

Dear Roshni,

I know the contents of this letter will bother you. So let me say I'm sorry before I start. I have to confess that I made a total ass of myself the other day. It all started because Melissa made some mean comments about barbaric circumcision rites in third world countries and I just flew off the handle. I went so far as to say that their ass is cleaner than their brain because they use toilet paper for one end and paper filled with crap to polish the other!

When Scott tried to calm me down, I had a mob of Libyans tell me that because I was Indian, I should not defile myself by associating with a white man! The world is so screwed up, Roshni. Everywhere I go I find people designating others as untouchables! Mustapha couldn't touch me unless I converted, the Brits think no one can touch them, period. Tusneem thinks all animals are untouchable, at least before she prays, and these brainwashed Libyans think I should not be touched by the white devil, Scott, who is in actual fact the closest I've ever come to an angel ever since I left India. Between the senseless Libyans and all the insults I hurled out, I doubt if I'll ever see Scott again. I feel like Shakespeare's Caliban who said, "You taught me language, and my profit on't is, I know how to curse." It seems that's all I have got out of my passion for books—to curse and condemn the ways of the world! With words I rode a heartless see-saw, caring little how Melissa came crashing down, as long as I got a free ride up! And when the see-saw finally brought me hurtling down, all I could hear in its thud was—you're an arrogant bitch whose brain's full of crap, too!

Am staring at the line in Desiderata that says, avoid loud and aggressive persons, they are vexations to the spirit. So here I am, in this hole of a bedroom, steering clear of the expatriates out of shame and embarrassment, and too scared to talk to a Libyan in case he turns out to be a spy who wants to put me behind bars for touching a white man!

The silver lining in the dark, gray clouds is that in another few months, (as soon as I pay off my debts), I'll be back again with the most precious person I know—my sister.

With all my love,

I can't think of any other way to sign this letter but as your little Komli sprouting sharp thorns.

P.S. Tusneem just phoned to say she's had a daughter. She doesn't know, but I've just decided to take an R and R. I'll see her baby and get out of here for a while. I'll phone you as soon as I return.

It was while Komli had been talking to Tusneem on the telephone that she suddenly felt the need to go away to some forsaken mountain somewhere, just to think and to be alone. Somewhere far away from her cage of a room where she sat in the evenings, hoping that Scott would come around. She mentioned him to no one, and no one ventured information voluntarily. Scott had decided to stay away from her, more for her safety than his, knowing that the office was ridden with religious spies and political spies and social spies; spies who had nothing better to do than to get cheap thrills out of ratting on those who dared to defy Gaddafi's laws.

Although Komli did not know it, the silence she had imposed upon herself was perfect preparation for her next R and R. It took a few days for personnel to sort out the paper work related to her exit and re-entry permits.

"Komli?!" Tusneem shrieked with delight as they embraced, "You made it for my little one's Chuttee (6th day). What a wonderful surprise!"

"Can't match the surprise you gave me when you had Roshni come over for your wedding," Komli responded.

"Did I mention to you on the phone that the baby gets named today?"

"Yes."

"Have you come here specially for the Chuttee ceremony?"

"Yes and no. I'm on one of my R and Rs, but I decided to time it so I could be here with you first. I'm sure it's going to be a grand occasion. Tomorrow morning I leave for Scotland. I'm going camping."

"On your own?"

"No, with some friends from Tripoli," Komli lied. "Can I see the baby, where is she?"

"My mother-in-law's bathing her. You'll see her in a minute. She's beautiful, Komli."

"What are you going to name her?"

"That happens tonight. I don't get to know her name until after the ceremony."

"What do you mean, you don't get to know her name? Who chooses the name, her father?"

"Yes and no. Bawasahib, our spiritual father, chooses her name. As soon as the baby was born, my father-in-law sent a cable informing Bawasahib of the sex of the child. I believe Bawasahib chooses the name from the Koran."

"So your father-in-law already knows the name?"

"No. He hands the cable to the aunt who's going to name the baby. You'll see for yourself this evening. I'm so excited you made it, Komli." Komli knew better than ever before not to react to something that did not make sense to her.

"Are you alright? How come you're still in bed?"

"It's customary for the mother to stay in bed for forty days. Not everyone can afford the luxury any more, but my mother-in-law insists. She thinks the rest is vital for all the hard years of motherhood that lie ahead. Besides, she asked me the other day what could be better from an infant's perspective than to have a pampered, calm, content, well-fed mother whose breasts produce the most delicious, the most pure, the most nutritious food in the world?" Tusneem said, trying to mimic her mother-in-law.

"Too bad my neighbor's mother-in-law never saw mammary glands that way when Devi had her first child! So we're both on a kind of an R and R!" The baby was brought in just then. "You two can chat to your hearts' content Tusneem's mother-in-law said warmly, "but remember, Tusneem, babies can sense that your attention is divided, so no talking while you nurse her."

"She's full of old-fashioned notions, Komli, but she means well," Tusneem said as soon as her mother-in-law left the room.

Komli held the baby tenderly. She was beautiful, like her mother. She was happy for her friend. She gave Tusneem a broad smile. A smile that she hoped would hide the sense of emptiness that had engulfed her suddenly, knowing that the baby had placed yet another barrier between their friendship. Gone were the days, thought Komli, when she could whisk her friend away to a movie or for lunch so they could chat for hours on end.

"You can't leave tomorrow, Komli!" Tusneem exclaimed suddenly. "We have the Akheeka ceremony tomorrow. You have to stay for that."

"What's Akheeka?"

"That's when the baby's hair is shaved off."

"I can't stay, Tusneem. My ticket's booked and I have friends who will be waiting for me, but at least I'll be here tonight. Forgiven?"

"Of course! I can't tell you how thrilled I am that you're here for Chuttee at least. Thank you, Komli."

"What time do I have to be back for tonight's ceremony? I might go out for a bit while you're resting."

"Do you expect me to rest while you're here for just one day?"

"Not normally. But you've just had a baby!"

"I'm fine. But just in case you lull me to sleep, be back here around six. The naming ceremony starts at a precise time given by the priest. I'm not sure what it is though."

"Which one of your aunts gets to name the baby?"

"The faiji, baby's father's sister, always names the baby. Do you remember my sister-in-law, Durriya?"

"Is she the pretty, tall sister who dyed her hair with henna during your wedding?"

"Yes."

That evening Komli decided to be a quiet spectator for a change, and found that she thoroughly enjoyed herself.

The guests started arriving around six. Chuttee turned out to be an evening of much anticipation and gaiety. Family members and guests alike whiled away the time trying to guess what the baby's name would be. Everyone knew that the radiant mother who had to stay in bed the whole time was noting down who had guessed which name because she had a prize for the one who guessed right.

Durriya arrived in a beautiful, leaf green orna ghagra that she had designed specially for the occasion. In her hand she was carrying an elegant lace-covered wicker basket that contained a beautiful, white, lace dress and a pair of gold bangles for the baby.

At the precise time prescribed by the priest, Durriya sat down on a pillow on the carpet. Tusneem lovingly handed her baby to Durriya who proceeded to change the infant into the new dress she had brought in her basket. She slipped the bangles on to the baby's wrists and then proceeded to pray, first into her right ear and then into her left. In the room there was pin drop silence. The moment was on hand. Durriya would now whisper the name, first into the baby's right ear and then into the left. Tusneem's eyes glowed with pride as she watched her little bundle. She smiled graciously at Durriya when she got up and walked over to her.

"Farida," she whispered into Tusneem's ears as she handed the baby to her.

"Farida," Tusneem announced joyously to the guests. She handed Durriya an elegantly wrapped gift which Durriya would not open until she returned home, as was customary. The next few minutes were drowned in simultaneous cheers of Mubarak (congratulations), and claims for the prize from the person who had guessed the name. Shortly thereafter, all the guests were whisked away to another room for dinner, while mother and child were left in peace and quiet.

When all the guests had departed, Komli came in to chat with Tusneem for a while.

"Farida's a beautiful name. Do you like it?"

"Of course. It's my baby's name!" Tusneem replied, wondering how one could dislike one's baby's name.

"Are you telling me you had no clue as to what your own baby's name would be?"

'That's right. Nowadays some couples request a particular name if they so desire, but Abbas and I decided to leave it to Bawasahib. I was named the same way. Your little mind's ticking away. I can see it, Komli."

"Actually, I loved the ceremony. I'm just not so sure I would like someone else to name my child." Although that would be better than losing one's baby, Komli thought with some self-pity.

Tusneem chose not to comment. She couldn't quite put her finger on it, but she knew this Komli was not the same Komli that had left England. There was something Komli was holding back.

"Is something the matter, Komli? You're not your usual bubbly self you know."

"Drilling in the desert for whatever it is one is after can have that effect on people, they say; that's why expatriates get R and R time," Komli said with a smile, having quickly decided that a new-born mother should not be burdened with the aches and pains of a friend. "Supposing the baby was given a name you didn't like, what would you do, Tusneem?"

"I just haven't thought about it, Komli. It's been this way in our family for generations. It's hard to explain, but when you have a baby it seems that there's more than just milk that comes oozing out of one's glands. Those nurturing instincts are not just satisfied with providing nourishment. I want to secure my little one with blessings and cushion her with ceremonies. You'll understand one day, Komli, I know you will." Tusneem squeezed Komli's hand, wishing one day soon she, too, would be blessed with the joys of motherhood.

"I'd make a terrible mother. I just don't have your patience and grace!"

"That's the most uncharacteristic thing you've ever said, Komli. Are you planning to stay in Tripoli much longer? It's having a strange effect on you!"

"In a few months, I hope to be in India."

"I miss India, Komli, especially all my cousins. We had so much fun together. You know how you've always questioned me about our customs and ceremonies. It's all I have to cling on to here in England, the few people in my family and our customs. Without them I'd be lost. You're lucky! It seems you've made lots of friends in Tripoli."

"Not one of them can touch you, Tusneem."

"All kinds of interesting things happen to you."

"They sure do!"

"You sure you can't stay for the Akheeka? Just stay for the ceremony, Komli. It takes place first thing in the morning. You don't have to stay for the celebration, which comprises of feeding the guests, of course!"

"And if I say yes, what else will you coax me to stay for?"

Nothing happens for a few years after Chuttee and Akheeka, except that I'll have Farida's little ears pierced in the next few weeks. That's not a ceremony, though. It's just easier to pierce the ears when they're infants, because they can't pull on their ear-rings and hurt themselves."

"What if she wants to have her bellybutton or her nose pierced instead? Can't you wait for her to have a say in the matter?"

"I don't think I need to answer that. That's a silly question!" Tusneem declared confidently.

"It's not really a silly question, Tusneem. Think about it. You'll be inflicting pain on your little one, without her consent."

"For a few seconds, maybe. But after that she'll enjoy wearing earrings for the rest of her life."

"How do you know she will? I don't have my ears pierced and I've never yearned for earrings."

"To each his own," Tusneem said quietly. She loved Komli too much to say anything injurious about her hapless infancy on the streets of Calcutta, an infancy that seemed to have robbed her of some of the desires of normal girls.

"What's the next ceremony about?"

"Around seven we . . . . "

"Tusneem! You're not going to have Farida circumcised, are you?!"

"Abbas and I have already discussed that. No, Komli, that's a custom we're definitely giving up."

"So what else happens at seven?"

"If this little one finishes reading all thirty chapters of the Quran, we have a celebration called Aameen."

"So will Farida have to suffer through the Mullasahib you did when you were young?"

"Komli, motherhood sprouts tender shoots from the very seeds that our parents embed in us throughout our lives. I'm a product of my mother. I have some tenacious little roots that I did not even know existed until now. I just thought I'd mention it so you'd understand me a little better. I need friends like you in this cold country. I hope you'll never abandon me and my ways for all your other more worldly friends."

Komli hugged Tusneem as tightly as she could before she replied, "And here I was worrying that perhaps little Farida would come between our friendship!"

"Is that why you've seemed a little pensive all day?"

"I didn't know I had been that way. If I was, I feel much better now. You need to get rested. I'll see you in the morning."

"You didn't answer my question. Will you stay for Akheeka and then leave?"

"To see your little Farida bald?"

"Akheeka is like a baptism; it's very important for us. A goat is sacrificed while her hair is being shaved."

"Around what time will it all end?"

"Noon, I imagine."

"Tusneem, I can't change my train ticket. I hope you don't mind."

"I do. But I also understand," Tusneem responded with a smile. "Thank you for being here today, Komli. I'll never forget it."

"Me neither. Goodnight."

After bidding her friend goodbye, Komli acquired a small tent, a few related necessities, and a train ticket for Inverness which she had heard was the gateway to the Scottish highlands. With her world on her back, she set off to find a small, flat piece of earth she could call her own for a couple of days at least.

It was with a twinge of sadness that Komli boarded the train for Scotland. She realized that while Tusneem had carried her tenacious roots with her across the Atlantic, hers were scattered somewhere on the streets of Calcutta, roots that had never sprouted well enough on the asphalt to cling on to anything. With little baggage, she had uprooted herself from India, harshly reprimanded the expatriate society as though she knew it all and was now on her way to camp out on some deserted spot where she hoped all roots would be submerged underground so she could shy away, for a few days at least, from society that suggested to her, again and again, that one cannot survive happily without roots, customs, and tradition.

Some time later that afternoon, Komli finally found a clear spot by a stream where she felt she could set up tent. Unlike Tripoli where the bare sands and the ageing palm trees never seemed to change colors, it seemed that all of nature had dressed up for some grand occasion. In the cold, clear water were reflected the mustard yellows, the flaming oranges, the brilliant reds and maroons, the limes and greens of grass and heather and trees that greeted her with quiet surprise, as though they were not used to footsteps creeping in on them. She saw a mountain in the background, lightly dusted at its peak with snow that had trickled further down the mountain in random rivulets. To Komli, it looked more like a bearded father-figure shielding his untouched valley from the outside world. Komli took a deep breath and exhaled as she stared into the silent serenity of her surroundings. Nothing moved. She didn't either. She took another deep breath as she felt every muscle in her body relax. Slowly she sat herself down on a clump of grass.

She did not know for how long she gorged on the silence before she asked herself the question: why was so much of creation so silent? The sun, the stars, the sand, the sky, why did they not speak? She doubted if they were really deaf and dumb; they had their seasons and cycles, so they must follow divine order. Was there something in their majestic silence that man's puny brain could never fathom? She wondered if there was a subversive dialogue going on between the roots of flowers and trees. How does one know that the rain is not their tears, the sunshine their smile? Could autumn be nature's burst of inspiration? Spring its orgasm? Do orgasms have to last just a few seconds? Maybe nature does pay heed to the messages in the whirls and swirls of leaves, in the crashing waves, and in the phases of the moon. How does one know that the full moon is not nature's Christmas? The crescent its broken dreams or the stars its fourth of July? That wrinkled sand dunes aren't wizened remnants of all knowledge? God alone knows, Melissa had said the other day. Perhaps that was the good old one truth that Plato had been smitten by—God alone knows!

Komli closed her eyes and reveled in the deep reverence she felt for the silent stoicism with which nature accepted its relentless seasons and cycles. Perhaps, there was something after all in the cold silence of the Brits that she had yet to fathom, she admitted reluctantly. She felt humbled and at one suddenly with her surroundings, neither inferior nor superior. It was at that moment that she realized that there was little in her that was not in nature and little in nature that was not in her; that their seasons and cycles were mere reflections of one another—she could not think of a single thing that nature experienced that she had not experienced herself—famines and floods, spring and summer . . . they had manifested themselves in her at some point in her life. She felt sure life had more cycles in store for her. Her eyes were closed shut. She could not see the clouds that drifted above her. Just as the clouds could not see the thoughts that drifted in and out of her mind.

It was while she was lying down with her eyes closed that it occurred to her that the genius of the Creator of the universe was not reflected so much in the complexity of His creation, as it was in the simplicity of His demand. The SIMPLICITY, she repeated to herself, as though she was struck by a bolt of lightning. She opened her eyes for a few seconds to truly absorb what had just occurred to her. Follow my UNWRITTEN LAWS is all He seemed to have asked of the elements and the countless creatures that had emerged from water and from the bowels of the earth. Amazingly enough, she thought, other than man, all of creation simply obeyed unwritten laws, for which man had at least one fancy name—fate. Unwritten laws that nobody questioned, much less fought other than man. She was transported back to the age of the mighty dinosaurs. They had come and gone, seeking to leave behind nothing but their bones for posterity, or for mother nature to recycle for the unwritten laws of the food chain, until of course mighty man came along and strung the bones into garlands that grace natural history museums the world over.

Suddenly, a panorama of creatures paraded through her mind: birds soared contentedly to the skies and swooped gracefully down into the sea knowing that the heavens was theirs alone. They never seemed to feel the need to delve deeper into the bottom of the ocean for treasures that were not in the air. A small fish stared at her from the cold, clear stream. Forget me not, it seemed to say, for I don't care that heaven is for the birds alone; I am equally content weaving in and out of the magic of my domain. The waves of the ocean came next, dancing tirelessly to the music of the seashore, caring little about high tides and low tides knowing that they would always come and go. Industrious little ants went about building their colonies, quite happy to simply work their lives away. Butterflies and bees flitted and fluttered their gossamer wings, flirting with freshly-blossomed flowers. The humble mole peeked out, resigned to the fact that his lot is to burrow in the dark. Crocodiles and alligators, basking in the sun's glory, bared their teeth as they passed her by without batting so much as an eyelid, not quite understanding the need to be in constant motion. Leaves turned colors and allowed the wind to blow them where it willed. Not one of them ever opened a book to learn customs and manners. And the mighty mountain and tranquil trees stared back at her stoically, suggesting that they, too, graciously accepted that their lot was to simply stand tall and keep an eye on the pageantry of life, knowing that night would draw its curtain time and time again to enable the sun to introduce a new act; that roads and rivers and rootless creatures may change their course, their destiny was to stare and to store the secrets of the universe; secrets stored in the mighty caverns of silence:

Silence that did not have man's ingenious ability to change truths into
   lies and lies into truths—
Silence that cleansed all nature by quietly creeping in and adorning her
   with new seasons—
Silence with which monks and meditators cleansed themselves, too—
Silence with which man's countless Gods counteract man's endless
   babble—
Silence with which man's countless Gods protect man.

Enthralled by mighty silence, Komli reminisced about her few encounters with silence. The vicious mosquitoes on the streets of Calcutta had first introduced her to silence as it crept up on her like a stealthy cat while the rest of Calcutta was asleep. She recalled how she had looked at her mother, breathing peacefully beside her, on a mattress of concrete. What a heavenly blessing was sleep. Perhaps the only time her mother was at peace, she reflected with hindsight. Then there was the wonderful silence when Roshni and she had read books until the wee hours of the morning, devouring words and ideas like two starved children who needed nothing else to feast upon. Too bad she would never know the blessings of the silent companionship of a grandfather, but at least she had had a glimpse of Motapappasan; at least he had smiled at her, and graciously passed her rotlees when she had wanted more. Then there was the silence of prayer, but it was always a pregnant silence, a silence filled with hope that her prayers would be answered. There were the ecstatic moments of silence that had come with love; when there had been no need for words. But this silence, amidst the mountains, was the most sublime of all, Komli thought.

She opened her eyes and held her breath, wondering if this is how a chrysalis feels, wrapped in silken silence, hanging out there until it is time to face the world again, transformed into something with wings. It did not occur to Komli to use the moment to pray to her god and to ask for peace, or for freedom. Instead, she exhaled and thanked Him-up-there for covering her so gently with a blanket of heavenly peace. Perhaps, for a few fleeting moments in eternity, she had experienced Nirvana. Maybe it was not Nirvana. What did it matter, she thought, what name it was given; she had experienced something special. Maybe she had momentarily turned into the cripple in the Wish Fulfilling Tree. The cripple who had forgotten to ask and found true happiness. Or bliss. Another name. She could give it her own name, just like the names man had given to all these trees and leaves and mountain in front of her, that she could not identify or classify. Classify! Classify! Classify!

So immersed was she in her thoughts that she hadn't noticed that the sun had turned into a flaming red ball. Time had lost all meaning. She had not eaten all day, but with reverential regard for its mistress's state of mind, her stomach had not so much as rumbled or growled. Komli continued to sit and stare, reveling in the myriad pinks and purples and gold the setting sun had slashed at random on a sky that had been a cloudless blue but a few moments ago.

She shifted gears all of a sudden and reflected upon her first informal introduction to the mighty sun. Ma used to call it Surya, the mighty God who rode on chariots of fire. A few years later, in school, she had had her first formal introduction to the sun. It was a flaming star, 93 million miles away, she had been told; any closer, earth would burn down to ashes; any further away, earth would freeze. 93 million miles away was just perfect! And to honor the sun, they had performed a play called A Touch of Gold. Tonya had played the part of King Midas. She had learned a lot from discussing that play. The children had decided that the only gold Midas needed was the golden rays of the sun because without its rays there would be no plants or water and, therefore, no life on earth. She wondered if she herself was a mere manifestation of the sun's rays—a miniscule creature that could not survive without warmth and love and laughter that she had become accustomed to.

And as she gazed at the resplendent sky bathing in the sun's fast-diminishing rays, she wondered if all truth lay in the silence of the sun's rays; if, indeed, truth was synonymous with life and beauty and was, therefore, as iridescent as the bubble of life; truths that appeared and disappeared with the whims of the sun's rays. *Truth is beauty, beauty truth, that's all ye need to know in this life.* Over the years, Komli had tried to understand those famous words, but had never succeeded. Satiated with beauty, she felt that at long last she had grasped the elusive bubble, if only for a moment, before it burst and disappeared into thin air.

Before long, Komli was enveloped in a shroud of darkness. She decided it was time for her to stop thinking, to stop seeking, and to feed her starved body. By the time she had figured out how to light her stove and had finished a piping hot soup and bread, it had turned quite cold outside. She decided to zip herself inside her tent. Fortunately, her tent had a small screen, through which she could gaze at the stars. Maybe the sun's rays wasn't the only truth after all, she decided, a little tired and confused. Maybe the sun set every day to silently suggest that one must remove oneself from it's light in order to see the other stars. How gracefully it had disappeared over the horizon and with what glory it would rise again. No bickering, no clamoring about it being the only source of truth and light. Yes, we could not survive without the mighty sun, she thought, but the mighty sun chose to reign in silence. Its rays, its sunbeams, its rainbows that appeared and disappeared never said a word either.

She rested her eyes and finally drifted off into another world of silence. Her last thoughts were about the nocturnal creatures outside. She could hardly believe how dramatically the silence had been transformed to an orchestra of a million creatures serenading to the glory of a pitch-black night. She wished Scott was with her, so she could hold his hand and revel together in the wonders of nature. Mustapha and Ma and her unborn child and Zenub floated in and out of her dreams that night as though to assure her that they were out there somewhere, watching after her, even though they had turned into a state of matter that could not converse with her.

Komli awoke the following morning, perfectly content in the knowledge that the experiences awaiting her would never match the silent affair she had had with mother nature the day before. She was content to hike and climb and read; even mingle with the other tourists she saw from time to time. She wondered if they would find the treasures in silence that she had found. When she saw young couples holding hands, she wondered if she would ever find the treasures she had lost twice in her life—Mustapha and Scott.

The third day, Komli decided to satisfy her need to communicate. She bought a notebook and whiled away the time writing when she pleased and chewing on her pencil, or her thoughts, or a blade of grass, if she so desired. She used the stump of a tree as desk. Coarse lilac heather served as both chair and bed, depending on her needs from moment to moment.

"Want to read a strange letter I received from my sister?" Roshni asked Rashid while they were having tea together. "Tripoli's having a strange effect on her. I wish she would return to India." The letter read :

Dear Roshni,

I'm having a fabulous R and R. I have not spoken to a single soul in three days. I feel cleansed by silence. I am at peace with the world. Strictly, I should not be writing to you right now. I should be soaking in silence, knowing that it's a rare luxury, but being a creature of contradictions, I am also overwhelmed by the need to communicate.

Roshni, although I can see little from where I am, magical silence has instilled in me a strong, strong sense of the spirit of all creation hovering around me. It has taken me all these years to be bowled over by the simple fact that has been glaring at me all my life—that other than man, no one needs paper and pencil and clothing.

I have become a part and parcel of educated, or not so educated, little people besotted by trying to make my two-pice contribution about truth. I have come to the wondrous conclusion, Roshni, that all of mankind's beliefs are nothing but one gigantic homogenized bubble boiling in the cauldron of myth. A cauldron that contains heaven and hell and Hindu and heathen and hundreds of other magical and mysterious words and ideas and stories that we chuck in from time to time, like cackling witches spicing up the broth! Take for instance the wonderful stories Ma told us about Ram and Sita and Hanuman. Are they true? I'd like to think so. But do you think the rest of the world believes in our Monkey God who saved Ram? And do we ourselves not take the water to wine stuff with a pinch of salt? The parting of the Red Sea with tongue in cheek? So many stories, so many beliefs, resulting in so many fights between Hindus and Muslims, Muslims

*and Jews, Jews and Gentiles . . . . how long would I have to sit here if
I had to list them all?*

*And the stories could be such fun, if only we would stop using
them to wield power. Slaves and women were forbidden to read for the
same old reason—so their masters could control them! Treated like
moles, to be kept in the dark. Remember I said to Mustapha's folks
that it's not people but our Gods who confuse us? Well, I was wrong.
It's not our Gods, but the written word that has us all baffled. Next
time you see Rashid, ask him if he can think of a single God or prophet
who wrote down anything. I cannot see a single written word on the
leaves of trees, on the blades of grass or the specs of sand on which I
am sitting, or on the gentle breeze that comes and goes to remind me
that it, too exists. And they are all so much at peace, Roshni, so much
at peace. Not a single word in the mighty rays of the sun or in the
droplets of water. And Mrs. Fletcher said sunlight and water and
plants are what enable us to live. I want to scream it out. But what
good would that do? Someone would come along and clap me behind
bars for being crazy. And nature would not so much as turn a leaf!*

*I wonder what it thinks of us. Do you think all nature is our
audience, watching our tragedies and our comedies, our mysteries
and our soap operas? Is that why thunder claps and the wind whistles,
why lightning bolts and trees give standing ovations, because with
words and costumes fantasmagalorific (I decided to make up a word
myself) we put up such spectacularly, ingenious shows?*

I know there is such a thing as war and peace,

*but is there such a thing as 'Vietnam' and 'Versailles', or are they
mere words?*

I know there is an almighty Creator,

but is there such a thing as 'Bhagvaan' or 'God', or are they mere words?

I know there is land and there is water,

*but is there such a thing as 'Scotland' and 'Red Sea', or are they
mere words?*

I know there are the haughty and the humble,

*but is there such a thing as 'kings' and 'subjects', or are they
mere words?*

I know there are the oppressors and the oppressed,

*but is there such a thing as 'master' and 'slave', or are they mere
words?*

I know there is love and there is hatred,

*but is there such a thing as 'marriage' and 'divorce', or are they
mere words?*

I know there is such a thing as seasons and cycles,

but is there such a thing as 'life' and 'death', or are they mere words?

I know there are such things as flowers and weeds,

but is there such a thing as 'civilized' and 'uncivilized', or are they mere words?

I know there is such a thing as pride and prejudice,

But is there such a thing as 'inferior' or 'superior', or are they mere words?

I know the earth revolves around the sun,

But is there such a thing as 'Gregorian' or 'Hegira', or are they mere words?

I think there are seasons and cycles, linked and locked to land and water and fire and air. The rest is mere words, Roshni.

The innocence of the unschooled is a priceless gem that has no written value. I think the purest people of all are the Bedouins and the bushmen and the beggars of the world; those that live on the fringes of a literate society that cannot see how it has been dwarfed by circumcision of the mind. I wish everyone could live on the streets during the early years of their lives, or maybe later would be even better—so they can appreciate that all man really needs is food and love and shelter—those fundamental needs that Mrs. Fletcher went on and on about.

I am at peace now and back in love with the world. To end with the biggest paradox of all—write fast! And don't worry about me. I'll survive Tripoli, but, believe me, I'm leaving as soon as I can.

With all my love,

Komli.

Rashid set down the letter on the table and smiled mysteriously for a few seconds before he commented, "It is a strange letter. But I think it has some grain of truth."

"Do you agree with her?!" Roshni asked in disbelief.

"In some ways. Unfortunately, that grain of truth is buried so deep, deep down under modern civilization, it can never be unearthed."

"So are you admitting we don't need written words?"

"I am saying I understand what Komli is saying. But I also know that it's airy fairy, romanticized rambling. Man can survive in nature's jungle without the written word. In our urban jungles, we cannot."

"I'm getting worried about my sister, Rashid . . . ."

"She'll be fine. It would do her well though if she found a man and settled down to food, shelter, love, and raising children. She will have no time for idle chatter."

"Oh, I didn't know that was the secret to becoming sensible!"

An unwritten secret, Rashid thought to himself. A secret perhaps the caveman understood better than modern man. If he were to go back in time, would there have been any problems asking for Roshni's hand in marriage, he asked himself. There was no marriage then, he reminded himself. Asking for just her hand, her companionship, her body, her soul, her everything would have been no problem at all—sheer bliss! But now everything he was, everything he had learned tormented him. You can't marry a Hindu and you can never, never, never, ask her to convert, bearing in mind how nobly she had reacted when Sakina had asked that Komli convert. And you can't live with her in sin. SIN. Three little letters the caveman must have known little about. He was trying so hard to have just a platonic relationship with her. But the starved animal in him had begun to stir. He could not, he must not allow it to control him. He was a learned man, not a caveman.

"You seem to be far away," Roshni commented.

"Thousands of years away, yes, when peoples' minds and bodies had little clutter."

"I don't know much about those times. Tell me something about it."

Rashid was tempted to make up a story about a man and a woman who loved freely, but realized he might weaken as he narrated the tale. "I have to leave now," he said abruptly. "Another time perhaps."

It was in a semi ecstatic state of mind that Komli returned to Tripoli.

To her surprise, she was welcomed back warmly. Even Melissa made an effort to make her feel better.

"You know Komli, she said to her one day in office, even if we were all white, we would still find something to quibble about, like our height, or our hair, or our brains, who knows. Man is a beast who loves to fight. I miss fighting with you, especially over scrabble. Will you come over tonight? We're playing scrabble at my place."

"I would love that," Komli said humbly but genuinely. Although Komli did not know it, like a volcano that leaves behind fertile soil in the wake of an eruption, she had left behind some arable soil on which new perspectives and better understanding had awakened in some expatriates. Graciously, she began to accept a few invitations. In her heart of hearts, she could not help but hope that Scott would reappear. But Scott seemed to have disappeared completely. She had grown to love him so dearly that she did not dare ask anyone about him, lest they guessed how she felt.

My dear Komli with thorns,

I hope you are feeling better by the time this letter reaches you. Please phone me as soon as you return from your R and R. I am very worried about you. I am so glad you are thinking of returning to India soon. I don't know how much money you owe, but there might be enough in the bank here to help you. Remember, it's your money. That way, you don't have to stay in Tripoli a minute longer.

I kind of agree with some of the things you said in your letter. But, dearest sister, is it worth giving your piece of mind to someone just so you lose your own peace of mind? You taught me to read and look how well I have learned to use those homophones or puns or whatever they are! I can see you smiling!

The end of your letter got me thinking seriously about people and flowers. I think there are four kinds of people/flowers. Those that are beautiful, but also have thorns, like you; those that have no blossom, only thorns, like Rana; those that have no thorns and only blossoms, like me, but boring, huh, and those that have no thorns and no blossoms—like the poor weeds, the beggars, that everyone tries to get rid of. If I had a choice to pick one, I would pick you every single time. Who knows, thorns may contain a lot of goodness, just like the poison from snakes! I learned that recently from a book. Thank goodness for books. I love to read and think and get baffled. And thank goodness for the telephone. At least I can talk to you once a week. But here's one reason why I don't like the telephone so much— you don't write as much any more.

Please, please think of returning as soon as you can. Take care, with all my love,

Roshni

Komli folded the letter and closed her eyes. Writing letters, making phone calls, playing scrabble once in a while, going out to dinner, contained her from time to time. But, every time she returned from an outing, she felt Scott's absence even more acutely. She could do most things mechanically, which left her mind free to think about him more and more. One evening, she took out a piece of paper and started scribbling :

I do not peel carrots any more when I peel carrots, I peel away the thin façade of my every day existence, my blotches, my blemishes, and feel my inner self—how I have been peeled by others and how I have peeled others myself. No, I do not open and close doors when I open and close doors, I go in and out of my past, to those who opened and closed doors for me, and to those for whom I would like to open and close doors myself. No, I do not ride in cars and trains when I ride in cars and trains, I fly to America to find your hand; I fly to Ma to hold me close; I fly to things sublime, things that have no words, no rhyme. You touched my heart, you saw my past, you eased my pain, will you ever come back to take my hand? I miss you so much. If Him-up-there were to grant me one wish right now, I would wish that you were standing by the door, staring at me, just so I can tell you how much I love you . . .

She looked up at the door just then, to try and picture how wonderful it would be to have Scott standing there. Somehow, her being managed to survive the shock when she realized that she wasn't hallucinating, that Scott was actually standing there, in a beautiful lemon shirt, content to quietly stare at her.

"How . . . . who . . . . when . . . ."

"Margaret let me in. She said you were in your bedroom. May I come in?"

She sat up in bed and simply stared at him, heart thudding.

"I've missed you so much, Scott. Where have you been?"

He took her in his arms and simply crushed her. For how long, neither knew nor cared. When he finally let go of her, he tilted up her face and said, "I was so scared some demented Libyan spy would hurt you that I stayed away from you. I went away on business trips so I didn't have to torture myself because I couldn't see you. Then when I found out that you had gone away yourself, I was petrified that I would never see you again. You know what gave me hope that you would return?"

"What?"

"Desiderata, hanging on your wall. I knew you would come back for that."

"You mean you've been coming in and out of my room?"

"From time to time. After Margaret and I finished making love!"

"You . . . ."

"A poor joke I admit. You wouldn't believe that, would you?"

"Anything's possible."

"I believed that once, Komli, that anything's possible. I didn't believe I would ever hear myself say that I could not live without a woman. I cannot live without you, Komli. I love you so much. I've decided I'm going back to America . . . ."

"When?"

"I can't tell you how wonderful it feels to see the dismay on your face, sweet thing! When am I going back? I'm not sure. As soon as possible. I guess the good thing about working here is that it helped me realize that America is truly a land of freedom and liberty, compared to this hell hole where illiterate bastards tell me who I can go out with! Komli," he pleaded, "I'm not asking you to marry me. Not yet. Will you please just come to the States after I send you all the goddamn papers you will need to come as a tourist? Just live with me for a while, in heavenly freedom. Then you can decide if you want to spend the rest of your life with me. I already know what I want, but I'd like you to have more time to decide. Will you?"

Komli buried her head in his chest and whispered, "I would love to, Scott. I guess everything that happened to us is a blessing in disguise. It helped me realized how much you mean to me. I love you so much. Life seemed pointless without you. I was thinking of returning to India myself, but I think I can survive here without you, for a while, now that I know you love me, too."

"Did you ever doubt it?!"

"When you disappeared on me, I wondered. How long will this paper work take?"

"A few weeks I imagine."

"Would you like something to eat?"

"I'm starving, but if you feel differently, I'll be able to wait until we're married, or out of here at least!" Scott replied, looking at her intently.

Komli stared at him for a few seconds, eyes aglow with desire. Quietly she turned around, closed the door and came back where she was, "Did Adam and Eve have pen and paper and priests in paradise?"

"I believe not," he said, twirling his moustache while wondering what strange ideas were running through her mind.

"Then they were not married by our standards, were they?"

"I guess not."

"So by our standards they lived in sin? Right?"

"If you say so."

"If they can sin, can't we, Scott?" she asked, surprising him with her intensity. "As long as the Libyan angels don't find out," she added, half joking, half serious.

"Where did you go for your R and R ?"

"The Scottish highlands."

"It must have worked some wonderful magic on you. Let's not worry about what is sinful, Komli. There are enough nuns and priest who worry and pray for the rest of mankind. Did you know I was ready to devour you at the beach that day?"

"Yes! What happened to that animal?" Komli teased, wondering when Scott would start undressing her.

But Scott seemed in no hurry. He caressed her hair and looked lovingly at the treasure that was about to become his. When Komli started unbuttoning his shirt single-handedly, he didn't come to her help either. If it took them all night to consummate their beautiful relationship, so much the better, he decided. Although he had realized what an alluring figure she had when he had seen her soaked to the skin on that fateful day at the beach, when he undressed her finally, all he could do was to stare at her breathlessly. This woman who had been twice butchered was simply beautiful and, what was more, burning for him in every fiber of her being. He suckled at her breasts like a hungry, newborn child. He was glad now that he had been unable to take her at the beach that afternoon. He would much rather initiate a physical relationship with his beloved Komli by first savoring every inch of her body. Slowly. Tenderly. Reverently. The man in the animal was suddenly overwhelmed by a deep sense of gratitude that circumcision had saved this beautiful woman from the streets, from wild, ever-lusting men. What had he done to deserve her, he wondered with humility. The soldier in him who understood so well what physical pain was about smothered her with kisses, and petted her, and licked her in all the places he knew she had been wounded—to heal her wounds or to satisfy his passions, he did not know. She writhed, and moaned, and groaned. "Take me, Scott," she begged, but he refused to be rushed. When he himself could no longer keep away from becoming one in body and spirit, united by a raging fire that could no longer be contained, their *agony* turned into ecstasy. Sweaty, spent, and satisfied, she snuggled under his arms and fell asleep while he smoked cigarettes His mother often bragged to his father that it was women who contained and nourished the world. He felt he now had some grasp not only of what his mother had meant, but also of how sacred was God's gift of the fire that could be ignited between man and woman.

"What will I do without you, Scott?" Komli whispered when she stirred again. "I don't think I can live here without you. I feel so whole and powerful and complete."

"I was thinking on the same lines," Scott said as he drew her closer and kissed her on the side of her forehead. "Here's a promise, unless you decide otherwise, I will never be parted from you after you join me in America."

"Why can't we just live in this room for the rest of our lives. All we need in here is some plants, and it would be our paradise, wouldn't it?" Komli asked.

"And our prison, judging from what happened at the beach, sweet thing. Tell me more about the paradise and pen and paper that you mentioned earlier."

"I've been thinking a lot about it ever since I went to Scotland."

"Really? And what did the mountains reveal? I take it it's different from the toilet paper theory?" Scott asked in jest.

"I don't know what it is about you. If Melissa had said that I would probably blow up again!" Komli said with a laugh.

"I can tell you what it is about me," Scott said cheekily, "It also begins with a P. I have it and Melissa doesn't!"

"That's disgusting, and crude! You don't believe that, do you?"

"No. But I do believe you're the most teaseable person I've met. Tell me, what did you find out about Adam and Eve and pen and paper when you went into hiding? I promise to listen seriously."

"I think the written word is the root of all our problems!" Komli said dramatically and stopped.

"Is that all the mountain revealed to you? I figured that out on my first day at school. I was only five!"

"That's one of the reasons I love you, Scott. You never brag about all the things you know."

"Most of it is trivial bullshit, as I am sure you already know. Is that all the mountain revealed to you?" he asked again.

"No. I'm waiting for you to respond. Do you agree or disagree?"

"Let's see. I can think of an instance where a woman sued her husband for his infidelity. She got so fed up of waiting for long drawn out legal proceedings that one fine day she just hacked off his penis. It hurts just to think about it. I think I'll go with lengthy, written documents any day!"

"I thought you were going to listen seriously!"

"This did happen in America. It's the first thing that came to my mind. So why are you anti written word all of a sudden?"

"When I was having my affair, so to speak, with nature, it occurred to me that other than man, no creatures need pen and paper to live or die or to emigrate somewhere else. And then I thought of Paradise and Adam . . ."

"And good old God, I hope, for taking a spare rib and turning it into the best meal known to man!"

"Thank you! So He created this delectable thing called Eve. Didn't God ask Adam and Eve to stay away from the Tree of Knowledge?"

"I believe so."

"That's what I can't get out of my mind! I think what God wanted is the exact opposite of what we've become—busy woodpeckers who simply cannot stop furiously drilling hieroglyphics on the tree of knowledge!"

"You mean, that He meant that we should stay away from trees and not make toilet paper, or any kind of paper whatsoever?"

"Yes!"

"Some of us don't need paper and pencil to drill, it seems!"

"Are you talking about making love, or me prattling?"

"You have the benefit of the doubt, my little woodpecker!"

"Seriously, Scott, think about it for a minute. God, whoever He is, sends us messengers and prophets from time to time, right?"

"Like Mohammed and Jesus?"

"Yes. Both of them were humble, unschooled, and neither of them wrote down a single word! Neither did famous sages like Socrates and Confucius and Buddha. Their disciples went about writing down everything they heard. I think the real truth lies in silence, in the intangible. As soon as we write it down, it is open to different interpretations, and a million quibbles!"

"So are you suggesting we burn all books? I've told you before, I can live on wine, women, and cigarettes!"

"It's too late now. We've acquired such a taste for reading."

"If you ask me, other than lawyers and priests and politicians, no one will be too upset. Books have often been banned and burned, you know."

"What I can't seem to get out of my head is the fact that I can't think of a single prophet or God who ever wrote down anything. There's got to be a reason! And I think the reason is that Allah, Bhagvaan, Jesus and all our Gods must have known about the danger of the written . . ."

"How can they if they're all illiterate?!"

"I didn't say they were illiterate! I said they just didn't write down anything. By the way, smart one, your cigarettes are also wrapped in paper. Another evil use of the tree!"

"Perhaps I'll switch over to pipes. Except that pipes are also carved from trees! I'm doomed, Komli. I refuse to give up toilet paper or cigarettes! What time is it by the way?"

Neither had realized that it was well past midnight.

"Do you think Margaret will tell someone you've been here all evening?"

"She's lonesome, honey, not evil. Do you think you can make us a sandwich? Don't need a recipe book for that, do you?"

"Why all the sarcasm, Scott? You just don't think we can survive without the written word, do you?"

"Right now, I am the happiest man in the world. The only thing I can't survive without is you. Come to think of it, Adam was quite content with his woman and his Paradise. It was his woman who first prodded man into temptation. Somehow, there's always a woman behind everything!"

"And do you know what else, Adam and Eve didn't have in Paradise?"

"I can hardly wait to hear."

"No clothes. There were no clothes and no written words in Paradise, because in the pure state man did not need clothes or written words. Therefore, the only creatures on earth today who go against nature are human beings, because they are the only ones with clothes and written words!"

"If I agree with all your theories, will you fix me a sandwich? I need to get some sleep. I have a very busy day ahead of me tomorrow. Guess why?"

"Why?"

"Getting all my paper work sorted out so I can leave this place! Then I have to look forward to getting more paper work sorted out in America so you can join me! I hate to admit it, Komli, but I think you have a point. Impractical, but valid. And do you know what's just occurred to me?"

"Dare I ask?"

"Humpty Dumpty is another name for Adam and Eve. They had a great fall! And all the king's angels and all the king's devils could not put Humpty Dumpty together again!"

"That's all I was trying to get out of you! Let's go see what we can find in the kitchen."

"I have one more thing to add, even though it may cost me my sandwich."

"What?"

I think the Gods and prophets refrained from putting down anything in writing because they could foretell that in the hands of woman words would turn into a tower of babble, babble, babble!" Scott said, eyes twinkling delightfully.

"You're darn right! And, I bet, the rest of creation laughs at us fumbling for truth in books when the truth is out there—silent, invisible, and intangible! I'll have you know, I maintained stone silence for three whole days!"

"Did you have a choice?"

"Yes!"

"Did you miss me?"

"As a matter of fact, I did. But not because I needed someone to babble to!"

"Do I still get a sandwich?"

"Why not? Although I wonder if it's written down somewhere that woman must fend or man?"

"It is," Scott teased, "in all the religious books of the world."

Aatma,

> *Scott is back! I'm the happiest girl in the world.*
> *LOVE IS ALL THAT MATTERS!*
> *Such a short, sweet entry but I know that it contains all the truths*
> *of the world.*

ೞೲ

CHAPTER 6

PRIME

Komli's spirits soared as the plane surfaced above thick, white clouds that finally drew a curtain over the rippled sand dunes of Tripoli. Mechanically, like a seasoned air traveler, she downed the juices and meals that were served. This time, she decided to sit back with headphones and closed eyes. She could think of nothing better than having soft music serenade the panorama of colorful memories that flitted in and out of her mind. She felt extremely fortunate to have experienced, and survived, the many contradictions of Libya. She looked down at her hand luggage. In it were her two, most precious possessions—*Desiderata,* and Frankincense and Myrrh—both acquired inexpensively from street vendors she had known but for fleeting moments in her life.

She thought fondly of Margaret who had surprised her with a farewell party, and had given her a framed picture of her birds. The card had brought a warm smile to her face. It had said, 'Whether you like it or not, we're all birds of a feather, fluttering for freedom with about as much brains as my little birds. Now that you're walking out of the zoo, keep flying girl, but stay in touch!' She would definitely stay in touch, Komli resolved. She already missed each and every one of the expatriates.

As for Melissa, as usual, she had been the cause of much laughter, especially when she had handed Komli her farewell present. Melissa had insisted that Komli read her note out aloud. It had said, 'Komli, the darn stores were empty, as usual, so I had to import these for you, all the way from England. Thought they might come in handy at your next stop—I hear there is a water shortage in Maryland. I'll miss you! Take care, Melissa.' Everyone had doubled up with laughter as they watched Komli unwrap a six-pack bundle of toilet paper. That had been one of the glaring differences between the expatriates and the Libyans, Komli reminisced. One knew how to laugh; the other rarely did, not in office at least. The expatriates trusted one another, while the poor Libyans were too scared to trust anyone.

No, she would never forget the beautiful and the ugly experiences that were already being homogenized into one, enthralling, indelible memory. Memories of the ancient and the modern sights and sounds that had enriched her beyond measure, even though they ad done little to untangle the many confused strands in the ever-broadening horizon of er mind.

Komli and Tusneem greeted each other with warm embraces and loud squeals of delight.

"I'm so thrilled you could make it!" Komli exclaimed as she ran towards Tusneem who was waiting for her at Heathrow airport in London.

"As though anything would stop me, especially since you're just transiting for a few hours!"

"Thank you, Tusneem. I know mothers have different priorities. I just wasn't sure if you would be able to leave Farida. How is she, and Abbas?"

"Everybody's fine. How come you didn't plan to stay for a few days with me?"

"I couldn't bear to, Tusneem. I haven't seen Scott for an eternity, it seems," Komli replied honestly.

"That bad, huh?"

"He almost came to meet me in London, but decided against it when he realized I only had a four-hour stopover."

"You should have convinced him to come."

"One of these days you'll meet him. Let's go and have coffee somewhere."

"Would you rather come home for a couple of hours?"

"I'd rather have your undivided attention at the airport. Do you mind?"

"Not at all. I could do with a break from domestic chores."

"Good!" Komli responded, making a note of the fact that Tusneem had avoided meeting Komli's eyes when she had said that. She would find out in time what those burdensome domestic duties were. But first, she wanted to enjoy being with the soulmate who had been so far removed from all that she had been through.

"Wow!" Tusneem said enviously after Komli had talked at length about some of her experiences in Tripoli. "How come you never mentioned all this when we talked on the telephone?"

"We were warned that the phones might be tapped. You have no idea how much I truly appreciate my freedom, now that I'm out of Tripoli. I got lucky a couple of times, as you now know, and you wouldn't believe the paper work involved in my being able to finally leave that country. As soon as you hand in your resignation, they take your passport and hold on to it until you are cleared of any and all obligations you might have to the company and to the country."

"Like what?"

"Car loan, apartment check, security clearance, boring stuff like that. You know, when I saw you last, on my way to Scotland, I was pretty down and lonesome. I didn't have the heart to tell you how much I envied your full life with your husband and Farida. What's this about wanting a break from home?"

"I'm happy most of the time. It's just that Abbas and my in-laws think my place is at home with little Farida. I love being at home with her, but I often wish I could get out and meet people other than Bohras. It seems such a long time ago since you and I were romping around having the time of our lives. I can't quite come to terms with the fact that I am here in London and my life revolves around domestic chores, going to the mosque and meeting Bohras. It's even more depressing because my mother-in-law has got me involved in trying to help confused, rebellious Bohra teenagers who've been born and brought up here and are unable to deal with the two extreme cultures they've been exposed to."

"So what would you do if you had my freedom to do whatever you want to do?"

"Take Abbas and Farida to Tripoli. Meet people from all over the world. Play scrabble, entertain, take some risks, escape by the skin of my teeth. Sounds so exciting, Komli. Freedom seems to follow you like a shadow."

"Like a shadow, yes, but shadows are not real; they're intangible at best. Mothers with children don't survive Tripoli that long, believe me, Tusneem. You're romanticizing my experiences. I don't think you really understand how relieved I am to be out of there. I will always think back fondly of Tripoli, now that I am out of there. I might be getting married one of these days, Tusneem. I would have bet anything that a love marriage and motherhood would make you delirious with joy. Do I need to know something about marriage and having babies that has obviously escaped me?"

"No, and I'm not that miserable!" Tusneem managed with a laugh. Pappa and Mamma did everything to enlighten and to educate me, but when I wanted to become an air stewardess, they couldn't bear to let go of the strings it seemed. So they sent me to one of our priests for permission. I was told that stewardesses have to serve alcohol, that as a good Muslim I could not so much as consider such a profession. So here I am, cooking, cleaning, and changing diapers, while you're out there, able to experience life in mysterious exotic places."

"You know millions of women would give anything to be in your shoes."

"But isn't it alright to get depressed sometimes with my little circle of life that I cannot see expanding in any way? And, by the way, it was when I suggested enrolling Farida in a Montessori school that has a long waiting list, that Abbas' parents intervened saying that it's because of liberated schools like that that some of our young Bohra girls in London are facing identity crises. I want Farida to have the best of both worlds. I don't want her to grow up in London as though she was still living in India! Most of all, I don't want her to learn like I did—passively, in front of a desk, listening to sermons on the mount day in and day out. Sometimes, I still do. I want her to learn actively, like you did, Komli, like you have been all your life!"

"Can't you talk to Abbas?"

"He just thinks I'm going through post-natal depression. That Farida's too young anyway for us to be worrying about her schooling."

"Maybe he's right. Sounds like you two need to get out by yourselves for a while."

"I think you're right. I'm sure things will work out."

"I know they will, Tusneem. If they don't, you can always assert yourself a little bit. You're a mother! I'm sure your in-laws will hate me for this, but Farida is not their child. You make the decisions about her future, not her grandparents! And have confidence in our instincts. I think children were meant to be raised with one's instincts and emotions."

"That would go down well with my in-laws!"

"Tusneem, do you truly appreciate why I'm free to travel around?" Komli asked suddenly.

"Because you're gutsy and can make decisions for yourself."

"No!" Komli said, suppressing a scream only because she was at a restaurant. "I'm here because your mother was gutsy. Not necessarily right, perhaps, but gutsy. Be her daughter, Tusneem, follow your heart. You must!"

Tusneem squeezed Komli's hand, "Thanks," she said simply, "I feel better already. Maybe I needed someone to tell me it's okay to rebel."

"Then all you need to do is look up to your mother." Komli decided to change the subject. Although she had kept in touch with Tusneem from Tripoli, she had never mentioned anything about Roshni and Rashid meeting from time to time. Now that she could see Tusneem's every expression and movement, Komli decided to carefully broach the subject. "How's your father, by the way? How is he coping on his own?"

"He sounds alright every time I talk to him. He's thinking of buying a house in Patna. Do you know he visits your sister from time to time?"

"Does that bother you?"

"No. Has Roshni mentioned anything?" Tusneem asked, looking straight into Komli's eyes.

"I know she likes him a lot. Wouldn't it be wonderful if they were to be married?"

"You think they're in love?!" Tusneem asked, hoping the question would camouflage what felt like a bolt of lightning splitting her body. That was so presumptuous of Komli, she thought with some irritation. Her parents had done everything to lift them off the gutter. She could not see her father replacing her mother. And if he did, surely her noble father would find someone of equal stature, Tusneem found herself thinking.

That did not sit well with Tusneem, Komli realized with a twinge of sadness. "A penny for your thoughts, Tusneem," she asked casually.

"I was just thinking about the irony of both you and Roshni choosing non-Hindus for companions. Is that just a coincidence, or did it happen because you have all the freedom?"

"How about good old fate? Don't you believe in it at all?"

"You mean I was fated for domestic drudgery and you for a life of freedom?"

"Perhaps. Our lives are not over yet. I long to be in your shoes, rooted to custom and tradition and husband and child. I'm tired of drifting and searching for truth. The penny drops from time to time, but, before I know it, it's gone, until some other penny drops and disappears again. Scott says my brain must be a criss-crossed bowl of spaghetti!"

"What new strand of truth are you chewing on now?" Tusneem asked with a smil
Like Komli, she, too, was relieved that they had dropped the Rashid-Roshni topic.

"Silence."

"As in not talking?"

"As in nature and, yes, as in saying little and allowing Farida to discover her ow
God through the use of all her senses."

"You'll definitely have to practice silence when you see my in-laws next!"

"We used to sing a song at Montessori. Want to hear it?"

"Why not?"

"Tabulah Rasa, Tabulah Rasa, that's how I came, that's how I came, to see the worl
with my eyes, to touch the moon with my hands, to smell the rose with my nose, to feel a
life with my heart, to taste all things with my tongue, you are you and I am I."

"What's Tabulah Rasa?"

"Latin for clean slate. We don't look at children as clean slates, do we? More like ou
miniatures who must use their five virgin senses like we use our half-dead ones, seein
and hearing and smelling only what we want them to; touching little but that which i
encrusted with shining, modern technology!"

"I don't think that's really true, Komli!"

"I know it isn't. What I'm saying is that as scary as it sounds, you have to allov
Farida to think for herself. You often envy me for being able to assert myself. Give tha
ability to your child then. Who knows, she may taste God in a mango, see Him in the dar
and light sides of Rembrandt's self-portrait, hear Him when you sing to her, smell Hir
when she's suckling at your breasts, touch Him when you touch her . . . ."

"So much for custom and tradition that you yearned for but a minute ago!" Tusneen
said, shaking her head and smiling at the same time.

"Told you my findings were like bubbles, didn't I?"

"I'm assuming Scott isn't just a bubble! Tell me something about him."

Before the girls knew it, it was time to say goodbye.

"I need a promise from you before I leave, Tusneem. You'll come to India at shor
notice if I decide to get married."

"I wouldn't miss it for the world!"

"Promise?"

"Promise."

The plane was circling New York city. The Statue of Liberty seemed to be smilin
reassuringly at Komli when her heart started fluttering. She wondered suddenly if Scot
would be there to meet her. She couldn't help but remember how he had failed her wher
she had first landed in Tripoli. After all, he had enticed her to both countries and, lik
Tripoli, other than Scott she knew not a soul in America.

She sailed out of immigration and customs. To her utter dismay, Scott was no where
to be found. No one stared at her this time as she strained her neck to find him. It seemed

hat no one noticed her. After about ten minutes, Komli started rummaging through her wallet for Scott's phone number.

Suddenly there was a tap on her shoulder. The voice had a distinctly Libyan accent "Miss Komli Seth?" it asked. Komli reeled around to find Scott standing behind her. He lifted her up as though she were a child.

"You didn't hide from me deliberately did you, Scott?"

"No, sweetheart. I couldn't have stayed away from you if someone had paid me. Damn traffic! I should've known better. When I saw you looking so lost, I couldn't resist playing the Libyan who met you in Tripoli. If I remember correctly, you were thrilled then hat somebody knew you at least!"

"I'll get back at you someday, Scott!"

"Actually, I'm the one getting back at you—you gave me several heart attacks in Tripoli, or have you forgotten already?"

"It's so good to know that someone in the world knows me," Komli squealed as she returned his tight hug.

"Loves you, you mean, and can't bear to be without you. God, Komli, I can hardly believe you're here. I can touch you and hold you and no one's going to clamp us behind bars. No one gives a shit! Do you know how good that feels?"

Komli nodded her head as Scott escorted her out to his car.

"Where are we going?"

"My spirit tells me I should take you to the Statue of Liberty. Get a photographer to film us while we make love and send the photographs to Gaddafi!"

"Be serious, Scott, where . . ."

We're going to a hotel around the corner. When we're tired of each other, we'll make plans to fly home to my parents. Is that okay with you?"

"Whatever you say. I'm at your mercy!"

"Hi honey! I've heard so much about you from Scott that I feel I know you already. How was your flight, honey?" The second honey was meant for Scott, Komli realized, so she allowed him to answer, while she took the time to assess Scott's parents. Judging by the way she treated her son, she seemed warm and loving with no airs and graces.

"I made some cookies for you. Help yourself," she said with a broad smile.

Scott's Dad seemed more quiet. "Hello, pleased to meet you," was about all he managed.

"Do you think you can take some simple living for a change?" Scott asked Komli later that afternoon "No sight seeing, no running around, do some laundry, some gardening, some grocery shopping, and some cooking, so you can get the feel of how we simple folks live."

"I think I can handle that. Your mum's a doll. I'm so relieved she's not some sophisticated executive!"

"Did you hear that, Mom?" Scott shouted so Mom could hear in the kitchen. "Komli' glad you're not polished and spiffed up like your dining table!"

"I didn't say that!"

"Don't mind him, honey. I'm used to his jokes." She came out of the kitchen an continued, "Here's a secret to keeping them men happy: feed 'em, keep their clothes clea and let 'em think you can't do without them. You'll soon learn that in reality they can't d without you. Just don't ever tell 'em honey!" She smiled warmly at Komli as she wen about laying the table.

"America is truly a land of milk and honey," Komli said after a few days with Scott family and friends. "Everyone drinks gallons of milk and everyone calls everyone honey I wish I could bring myself to call everyone honey. I wouldn't have to remember so man names."

"So how do the people compare to others you've known?"

"All that smiling and chatting wherever you go is as refreshing as spring flower after an icy dose of the inscrutable Brits, and a chilling, thrilling dose of Libya and its poo unhappy people! It seems no one here has any hang-ups about being God's chose people."

"That's because we know we're God's chosen people," Scott quipped. "By the way Komli," Scott said seriously, "America is truly my land of milk and honey, now that you'r here. I'm so happy."

Aatma,

The most impressive sightseeing we've done so far has everything to do with the work of water without seeing any water itself. It was stupendous. Scott took me to see the underground Luray Caverns in Virginia. I went crazy looking at the underground stalactites and stalagmites. They would not be there if it wasn't for the fact that for millions of years artist Water has been patiently drip, drip, dropping little droplets of water through earth's cracks and crevices. It seems that the little droplets of water carry miniscule speclets of chemicals which get left behind as the water carries on regardless. The speclets that arise from the floor are the stalagmites. And because they sit on the floor so much, they're fat! The others dangle for dear life from the roof. They're the stalactites and they're skinnier, of course, because their life's probably more stressful.

And to shut me up once and for all, we flew to Arizona to see the Grand Canyon. It did shut me up! 'Grand' is not a good enough superlative for this canyon! And again, artist Water, whom man calls river Colorado, carved this canyon, patiently chiseling away an inch or two every millennium, who knows! Staring into the gigantic, gaping hole sure did whet my appetite for silence. I saw history fossilized in its walls and understood at last what Mrs. Fletcher meant by fossils being man's first books. Strangely enough, this history, too, is devoid of the written or spoken word! All my mighty opinions, and all my book knowledge paled into insignificance as I stared into the stomach of the canyon, unable to grasp a single bubble of truth.

I felt shivers going down my spine when Scott took me to see the Hoover dam which was built to control the mighty Colorado river. I got a creepy feeling there that the river was patiently biding its time. That it would burst with anger one day, like prisoners at the Bastille.

I had a scary dream that night that I had been turned into a hard-bound book that, together with all the other books in the world, was violently flung into the stomach of the Grand Canon by young, white, male Hitlers dressed in shiny, black, skin tight leather suits; young brutes who wanted to propagate their own oral truth. The pages of all the trillions of books fluttered in frenzy making it sound as if someone was having a mighty laugh that resounded the world over. Suddenly, the silenced Colorado river burst through its restricting walls and swept away man's gargantuan efforts with one, sweeping stroke. The books screamed in terror as they were swept hither and thither by a furious current that had at last been unleashed. Millions of years passed by before I found Mustapha, turned into a miniscule, fossilized, skinny, brown line of concrete. I woke up to find myself shaking—I guess from the force of the powerful currents in the water.

When I told Scott about my dream, he handed me a glass of orange juice and said calmly, 'I think the river is the greatest circumciser of all.' For a change, he spent the next few minutes babbling about our holy river Ganges, baptism, and ablution, and finally suggested that perhaps the holy trinity of life is the Father, the red hot sun, and holy water because they are the only three things whose appearance and disappearance man cannot control. I think Scott's right because if our Creator or sun or holy water came to live with us permanently, we would trap them and clone them, and bounce them up and down like a yo yo on the stock market. I'm pretty sure Him-up-there prefers to control the yo-yo all by Himself! Can we make it rain? Can we flick on a switch for the sun to shine? Can we make Him appear? I made the mistake of asking Scott if we can make God come. He laughed and laughed and laughed and said I could try, but he didn't think I would succeed. In America you come when you reach a climax in bed! So many words, so many fascinating meanings. All the better to laugh with, the wolf would have said to Little Red Riding Hood.

I think I will definitely hang on to the story Ma used to tell us about the sun god, Surya, riding on his magnificent, golden chariot drawn by seven white horses. It may not be a myth after all! It's all connected in some rigmarole way. Sun makes water; truth is in the silence of gaping canyons circumcised by water. There is truth everywhere, only the truth is silent, for us to find out for ourselves; not preached from the books of priests and politicians.

"We haven't done much lately, what've you been writing about?"

"Catching up on some of the things we've seen and discussed. It'll be fun reading it in my rocking chair days."

"*Our* rocking chair days, I hope. So what've you filled the pages with?"

"Water."

Scott's mother walked in just then. "Hey, Mom, do you think water is the greatest circumciser of all?"

"Circumciser?"

"Sharpener. What is most important in our lives? Is it the father, the sun, the holy ghost, or holy water?"

"Water may be the greatest circumciser of earth, but love is the greatest circumciser of man. You'll understand better when you have children."

"You mean I've turned you into the beautiful person you are, Mom?"

"Don't forget the gray hair, and the fat, and the wrinkles . . ."

"And the twinkle in your eyes."

"I worry most for those who have no one to love."

And it was then that Komli realized that it was not cowardice, but love, that had compelled Roshni to make the decision she had made all those years ago; that perhaps she was yet to truly understand Roshni's selfless love that had taken them through the many meandering alleyways of life.

One stormy night while it was thundering and raining outside, Komli declared to Scott that she was going to apply for a job. "Both Mom and Dad work and I know you will start soon, too. I find it very embarrassing being treated like a royal, penniless guest."

"You've only been here a few weeks, Komli. Give yourself a little more time, then we'll think about it. Besides, I doubt if you'll be able to work here unless you have a social security number and a work permit."

"Start work, get work permit later, worked in England. It may work here, too. There's no harm in trying. The school round the corner needs teacher's aides. No experience necessary, the ad says. I'm going to phone them."

"Good luck! Although I'd rather you didn't."

It turned out that the headmistress was desperate. Start immediately, will get permit later, seemed to have worked once again for Komli.

Komli loved working with the children. She had her mother's gift for being a natural story teller. The more far-fetched the story, the more eagerly the children listened to her. And she had so many stories to tell. So many distant lands to transport them to. After lunch, she joined in their games, and taught them some simple ones that she had played once with sticks and stones.

The lunches the children ate had Komli truly baffled. The trash can appeared to be the fullest thing after lunch—bursting at its seams with boxes and bottles and straws and cups and spoons and forks and napkins and wrappers and plastic. Whatever happened to a tin lunch-box with a sandwich, some vegetables, and a piece of fruit for after? Did mothers never cook in America, Komli wondered, but dispelled the idea immediately, knowing how Scott's mother cooked hearty meals after she came home from work. And there was always a pie, or cookies, or ice cream for dessert. And whatever happened to the great sustainer of life? Did the children in America never drink water? There was more colored water on the tables than she had seen during the Holi festival in India. She decided, like all things modern, Oscar Meyers' discoveries about nutrition had yet to reach third world countries.

"What do you think of all the paper and plastic that's trashed in America?" Komli asked Scott one evening.

"Just be thankful there are no written truths on them! It's harmless paper, Komli! When are you going to get rid of your obsession with paper?"

"If I were to start a business in America, I would definitely get into the printing business. You throw away most of your mail without even reading it; there's more plastic and paper than there is food in the lunches the kids eat. The printing business has got to be the biggest money-maker in America!"

"Perhaps we should start a business printing on toilet paper. Everyone in America uses toilet paper! What a way to promote literacy! Should I stop looking for a job? We could start our own printing business!!"

"Why do you always turn everything I say into a joke?"

"Why not? I thought silence is the only thing to revere."

"You're not always that funny, you know!" Komli said, a little piqued.

Scott held her in his arms and added, "You know, I only make fun of those I love. And so I only make fun of you and my mother. Tell me, how is school, other than over-packaged lunches?"

"Wonderful. I love the children."

"Don't have to deal with Margarets and Melissas, do you?"

"That's not why I love children!"

"I wasn't suggesting that! You're quite edgy little one. Anything the matter?"

"No."

"A little homesick, maybe?"

"I guess," Komli agreed, not quite realizing herself that her isolation from everything eastern was hard on her sometimes. It hadn't taken her long to realize that both Scott and she were outsiders in America. Average Americans seemed to know little about foreign cultures, and soldiers like Scott. She felt like an oddity in the windows of store. Passersby stopped to look, but always moved on. She missed not having a female soulmate. Although she had enjoyed Halloween and Thanksgiving and Scott's friend and family, she could not truly relate to the customs and traditions of Americans. She wondered if she could ever get truly enthused about them. She herself often felt like the passer-by who was curious and stopped to look, but was not interested enough to make it her own. She wished she could participate in ceremonies and traditions with the enthusiasm of Tara Bahen or the Rashids or the Johnsons or Scott's family. Like the gritty grains of sand in a desert storm, different customs and traditions whirled around her, taunting her because she had none she observed with a passion. Although she understood why Roshni had raised her in a near-isolated cell, now, more than ever before, she longed for that one treasure that had eluded her—having a large family seeped in culture and tradition. There were times when she seemed to know exactly what was right and what was wrong. But the knowledge she had acquired, the opinion she had, failed to fill her need to belong. She seemed to be going around in circles of confusion. As much as she scoffed at the written word, she knew deep down in her heart that without the written word she would never have seen so many wonders, met so many interesting people. She had scoffed at meaningless traditions and religious fanaticism, but she realized now that it didn't matter if the source or reasons for customs and ceremonies had been lost to time; just like it didn't matter why children ran in and out of one's home; what mattered was that there was camaraderie and culture and tradition, for they were the silken threads that formed the unique patterns that bonded hearts and homes and countries. It's not that great being completely free, she thought. For what can one embrace when one is completely free? The wind and the waves? She no longer wanted to walk aimlessly around the world. She wanted to soar, like the birds. For which she needed the spirit; the spirit that comes with love, hard work, and being wanted. She could see the wind-blown frenzied trees outside. They seemed to be attempting frantically to uproot themselves, while she suddenly craved roots, the shackle of entwining arms, and a little one for whom she could build a nest criss-crossed with culture and tradition.

"You sure your teacher's not beating up on you?" Scott asked, trying to raise her spirits a little.

"Hell, no! If anything, kids and parents beat up on teachers, it seems. In India, we wouldn't dare talk back to our teachers; everyone idolizes teachers!"

"Ooooh! That would be considered extremely sacrilegious in America! Keeping one's mouth shut does not necessarily mean one idolizes the teacher, I hope you know."

"Here the poor teachers seem humble and always on the defensive, like someone's waiting to gobble them alive!"

"We call those gobblers lawyers. Unfortunately, it's one of our favorite pastimes, together with eat, drink, and be merry for tomorrow we diet or have lipo-suction."

"I thought you loved your country!" Komli said with a giggle.

"I love you, too. Neither happen to be perfect, though."

"Thank you very much! You led me to believe I was perfect!"

"Perfect for my needs is different from being perfect," Scott said as he pulled her close to him, happy to see that she was in better spirits again.

"Hey, Komli, I've been meaning to ask you; would you like to help my cousin, Cindy? She is looking for someone to watch her ten year old son for a few hours after school. She'll pay you, of course."

"I'd love to do something for your family! But I wouldn't dream of taking money from her. Everyone's been more than kind and loving. My sister helps out her neighbor. I think they end up paying each other in spirit and companionship . . ."

"Well, sweet thing, you figure out what part of my cousin you want. She's one of those busy, efficient executives who has more money than time. You two can sort it out, I'm sure."

After school, Komli found herself taking a bus to cousin Cindy's home to watch her son, Brandon. All she did for about a week was watch Brandon. Neither said a single word. Brandon did not know the meaning of making polite conversation. It seemed he preferred to hold a one-way conversation with the television. Komli found herself wandering around the family room that had no family. Ironically, it was the deathly silence around Brandon that first burst Komli's grand notions about the magic of silence. Children don't need stone silence to welcome them when they come home from school, her heart cried. She remembered how Roshni had always greeted her with love and laughter and hugs and a hearty, home-made snack. What lofty ideas she had nurtured about silence up on the Scottish highlands, she thought wryly. Silence was quite a double-edged sword, she realized, as she saw school children come tumbling out of buses, key rings sadly dangling from their wrists. She wondered how many, in reality, were holding keys to the kingdom of silently wailing walls welcoming them home to cold kitchens and still rocking chairs; how many homes were like Brandon's, devoid of the sounds of a warm parent or grandparents—only a cold television silently enticing them to come turn it on—*in turn I will turn you on, too, my child, with so much shit and violence and crap that one day you, too, will turn on your shit and crap and violence and amaze adults with what you can do all by yourself!*

Too much silence could drive one crazy, Komli decided, as she observed Brandon. What truths was silence teaching him, she wondered. That strawberries pop out from tarts in microwaves, and popcorn from bags? That meats in the refrigerator are not the only cold cuts in the house, and that juices too can be frozen, like his heart? That fruits only come rolled up in flat, reincarnated sheets? That marriage comes with separation? Mothers come on weekdays and, if one is lucky, fathers on weekends? That marriage is a worthless bond on paper, like the worthless, arduous, meaningless papers he had to produce for school? That papers are meant for crunching into balls for the trash can? That the only book worth

opening is the television guide? That television is man's salvation from loneliness? E-mail
the answer to companionship? That modern technology programs parents to push buttons
on ovens and buttons on coffee-makers, and buttons on bread machines, so when the clock
strikes six, Mom walks in from work, coffee is brewing, bread is baked, and dinner is ready.
Did no one think to push the buttons inside his heart because he seemed so content pulling
every which way on the joystick? Were rocking chairs obsolete because no one rocked,
everyone rushed? Knitting needles and knuckles might just as well be used as weapons
since no one knits or knows how to knead dough for bread, she thought cynically.

After a few days of uncomfortable silences drowned by the sounds of violence that
erupted from the television, Komli discovered some board games. Judging from the dust
that had collected on them, they had obviously not been used for some time. At first she
played by herself, taking it in turns to be her own opponent.

"Want to play Monopoly?" Brandon asked her one afternoon.

"I'd love to," Komli replied, relieved to know that the boy could talk! Board games
and companionship finally opened the gates to Brandon's soul. Before long, the two
spent most afternoons playing games and fighting to win.

'What happened to your hand?" Brandon asked one afternoon.

"A mean man cut it off when I was young," Komli said matter-of-factly.

"Why?"

"Do you know why kids kill kids in school?

"Because they're crazy."

"This man, too, was crazy, I guess!"

"Did you get any money for it?"

"No! Would money give me back my hand?"

"How come you're not angry about it?"

"Ooh! It's a good thing you didn't know me earlier. I used to get angry a lot. All it did
was make other people angry, too. It's more fun to find things to laugh about, although
you know something, I'm angry that you spend so much time alone, in front of the
television. Do you get angry?"

"Sometimes."

"Because your Mom and Dad don't spend enough time with you?" Komli asked,
knowing full well that Brandon may be too young to realize what made him angry.

"I guess. What's your Dad like?"

"I don't know."

"Neither do I."

Neither did Jesus, Komli wanted to say, but decided she might get into trouble for
that. Instead she said, "You know you're so lucky that you have a mother who wants to
make all this money, so you can have good clothes and expensive shoes and games and
all that stuff. When I was your age, the only things I had were books and board games, no
television, no Nintendo, not even Mickey Ds!"

"You're lying!"

"I'm not."

"What did you do with your spare time?"

"Listen to stories. Want to hear one about a mole and a crippled boy?"

"Not if it's sad."

"Sad is only something you feel sad about. I feel happy when I hear it. You tell me how you feel after I finish. Okay?"

"I guess."

"Once upon a time there was a boy with beautiful, silky, gold hair. He spent all day sitting in a wheelchair because he was born without legs and arms. When he saw people run and swim and play basketball and strum the guitar and draw fantastic pictures and write exciting stories, he was terribly, terribly saddened that his lot was to sit and stare. One day he saw a creature he had never seen before in his garden. It looked a little bit like a rat. But it wasn't. It was a confused, black-brown mole who had accidentally surfaced from underneath the earth where he belonged.

'Do you like our earth?' the boy asked the mole.

'Oh yes!' Replied the mole, 'It's my home and I have so much work to do each day. I burrow and eat and play with my family and friends and sniff the wonderful smells of my world. Yes, I love the earth. Do you?' he asked the boy.

'No!' the boy replied angrily, 'I can't do all the things you do because I have no arms and legs. I can only sit in this stupid wheelchair and watch the world go by!'

'And what do you see?' the mole asked eagerly.

'I see the birds fly and I want to fly. I see fish swim and I want to swim. I see boys and girls play games and I want to play. I see television and movies and . . . .

'Wait, wait, wait!' the mole interrupted with great excitement. 'You're going too fast for me. Tell me about these birds. What do they look like? What's flying? I can only take in one thing at a time.'

'Haven't you ever seen a bird?' the boy asked in amazement.

'Nope! I cannot see. It seems that you can spend a life time marveling at the wonders of your world. I bump into earthworms and ants sometimes, but they never stop to talk to me. You are so kind. You've actually taken the time to talk to me. Will you tell me about some of the things you see every day?'

'Like what?' the boy asked.

'The bird.' Describe the bird to me. Does it look a bit like me? Does it have four legs? Can it see . . .'

'Wait! Wait!' the boy exclaimed, laughing. You're asking too many questions. Let me tell you about the bird, one thing at a time.'

And so the boy described the bird to a mole who knew nothing about wings, and feathers and flying and colors of eggs that birds lay. The mole was so thrilled with his image of the bird that he pleaded with the boy to tell him about something else he saw. And that was the beginning of a wonderful friendship that developed between the blind mole and the crippled boy."

"So who am I?" Brandon asked with eyes screwed up suspiciously, "the mole or the cripple?"

Komli was delighted that he had thought about it. "Neither!" she said calmly. "If anything, you're so much luckier than the mole or the boy. You use all your senses and limbs so efficiently. I would say you're ambidextrous because you can eat popcorn with one hand and push buttons on the remote control with the other. You can see because you watch television; I wasn't sure at first if you could talk, but now I know you can; you rush to the microwave when the popcorn is burning, so I know you can smell, and walk. And your taste buds are working obviously because I know you enjoy snacks and sodas. So what made you think you might be a mole? Because you never go outside, right? I was referring to moles and cripples in India. They are not as lucky as you are."

"I thought I was the cripple because I just sit around watching T.V.

"You mean television. Why do you abbreviate words? Are you in a rush to go somewhere?"

"Not really. My mother does all the rushing. I wish she would just sit down sometimes."

"And I wish you would just get up sometimes. Want to go out and play?"

"Are you trying to be the one-handed cripple?"

"You could look at it that way. I don't see myself as a cripple. I can draw, cook, write, play tennis, badminton, and many other games. Do you like any ball games?"

"Soccer. Will you play with me?!" Brandon's eyes had lit up for the first time.

"I love soccer. We call it football in India. I used to play it a lot!"

Not only did she know something about soccer, she had decent ball skills, too, Brandon discovered. And she was a tough cookie. She refused to play soccer unless he did his homework; she refused to bake cookies unless he helped; sometimes he had to weed the yard before they played. It was Scott who had suggested that Brandon work in the garden, knowing that Brandon's mother would love that.

Scott loved gardening himself. He dropped by from time to time. Under his guidance Komli and Brandon started a miniature hot house. What a wonderful mother you would make, Scott thought one afternoon as he watched Komli and Brandon delight in the seeds that had sprouted in the hot house.

In time, the tentacles of loneliness began to loosen its grip on the souls of the two playmates. Not only that, the extra money helped Komli feel much better about being able to give Scott's parents something towards her living expenses. They did not make a great fuss about it at all. If Scott was happy, they were happy to treat her as their guest. On the other hand, if she felt uncomfortable, they understood, and graciously accepted the groceries she bought from time to time. Life was so simple and straightforward for Scott's parents, Komli thought. Go to work, cook, clean, watch television, and spend Saturdays laboring in the garden. Sundays were reserved for church and for the rest of the family. Add well-traveled soldier to the recipe, and you get Scott, she thought—not a hero for history books; just a wonderful guy with the kind of head, heart, humor, and humility she could live with for the rest of her life.

"Am I forgiven?" Komli asked sheepishly when Scott finally found her shivering in their backyard.

"I'm sorry myself, sweet thing. I can't believe I flew off the handle on Christmas day, of all days! Do you forgive me?"

"Only if you explain why you've been so mad with me. All I said is that you should have told me I was going to be showered with presents. It's embarrassing being at the receiving end without having anything to give."

"Promise you won't get angry if I tell you the whole truth and nothing but the truth?"

"Promise. That's how I like it anyway."

"You're always so darn critical about peoples' ways! But because there's a grain of truth in some of the things you say, and most of all because I love you, I don't ignore your words. Do you remember what you told me when we went to buy my cousin a wedding present?"

"Yes. That presents are gifts that should come from the heart. That one should not put up a list in some store, asking what one wants. It's so unromantic!"

"But practical. That way, you don't get fifteen sets of wine glasses!"

"And you don't get beautiful surprises either."

"Thank you! That's exactly why I flew off the handle. One minute you want to be romantic and idealistic, and the next, you want me to tell you in advance what Christmas presents you were getting!"

"That's not what I meant, you know that, Scott!"

"Do you know how much my family slaved to make your first Christmas magical? To give you a beautiful surprise? Do you realize how Mom and even Dad and all my cousins and aunts scurried around last night after you went to bed, just so you would wake up to the magic that we experienced as children?"

"It was more than magical, Scott. I've spent the last hour writing to my sister and Tusneem telling them how wonderful you've all been. That I wish children all around the world could witness the magic of Christmas. I wonder if you'll ever realize how deeply rich I feel at times like this because my rootlessness has allowed me such wonderful glimpses inside mosques, and temples and churches."

"I wonder how much our Gods bicker about who has the better celebrations and who builds better houses of worship."

"You're beginning to sound like me! Seriously, Scott, was it so wrong on my part to be embarrassed that I had nothing to give your wonderful family?"

"Mom and Dad were more than thrilled with the Frankincense and Myrrh you gave them."

"I can't believe you convinced me that Christmas is only for children. I got you nothing, Scott! How can I help but feel bad?!"

"Don't worry sweet thing, I know exactly what you can give me. So what was your favorite present?"

"Guess."

"Gloves and spade?"

"Try again."

"Pearl necklace?"

"No. The Giving Tree. I've already read it three times, and told Tusneem she must ge
it for Farida. What a simple, yet profound book!"

"I knew you'd like it. Goes to prove that I pay attention to all your ramblings abou
trees and toilet paper."

"Well, The Giving Tree's got me even more convinced that trees are our very specia
gifts from Him-up-there. I wonder if there is some wonderfully symbolic reason why Jesu
was a carpenter working with wood?" Komli asked hungrily.

"It's a good thing we don't have all the answers. You'd have nothing to talk about.

"We would become serene, like trees! Do you think trees know that without bearin
the cross man cannot experience true joy?"

"Trees are deaf and dumb, honey; they don't know a darn thing. We're all trees of
kind—rooted to earth's trials and tribulations but aspiring to heaven. A woman once tol
me that one has to be crucified in order to be resurrected."

"You should start writing, Scott!"

"About what, the confusion you've brought to my logical, thinking mind? Hold o
a second; I have something to show you." Scott went into his mother's bedroom an
brought out a Celtic cross he had given her once. "Read what it says on the back. I thin
you'll like it."

Komli turned the cross around and read out the words :

> *This Celtic tree cross brings together two of the most ancient
> symbols, each uniting pairs of opposites.*
> *The tree unites material earth with the spiritual heavens.*
> *The cross unites the masculine trunk with the horizontal feminine
> branches which bear protective leaves and nourishing fruit.*
> *The tree is highly significant in the Bible with, first,*
> *The tree of life (earthly paradise and its seductive fruits) and, second,*
> *The tree of knowledge of good and evil (the spiritual paradise,*
> *the other reality, reached through the pursuit of Sapientia, wisdom.)*
> *The tree by the annual renewal of foliage promises life's continuity.*
> *The cross, by the resurrection, promises death's defeat.*

Komli was left speechless. She read the words again and again, while Scott watche
her lovingly.

"Should have got you one for Christmas."

"Can one buy it?" Komli asked, thrilled at the prospect of adding the cross to he
other two treasures.

"We'll see. I bought that in Annapolis, several years ago."

"You've become awfully quiet. What's the matter?"

"I'm bonding with the tree! Ma used to tell us stories about our Banyan tree in Calcutta. The mountain in Scotland set me on the right track, Scott, I'm convinced. Maybe the tree is the Creator Himself, do you think?"

"No, I don't think so! I don't think any God in His right mind would allow man to turn Him into toilet paper! Even if He came down to suffer and to save mankind!"

"I clean forgot that! Well, anyway, I still believe that the tree is meant for fruit and fragrance and shade and shelter. Trees, air, water, fire—all of them give and give and give, while we take and take and take. If man is raped, he sues and creates a stink until he is compensated. What does nature do when it is raped and pillaged?

"This might shut you up forever but I can't resist asking you, sweet thing, if you remember where Buddha attained enlightenment?"

"Oh, my God! It was under the Bodhi tree!"

"Without pen or paper. Of course, you've been on the right track! Why do you think I love you so much?"

"And I love you 'cause you're like the tree yourself. Those invisible roots are pretty deep! I think you're the cleverest man in the world, Scott!"

"And the luckiest and the horniest. Let's play trunk and branch for a while, shall we?"

"At this time of the day?! What will your Mom think?"

"That her son's no different from his father!" Scott said with a grin. Here's a joke that might bring you back to earth : "What do priests and Christmas trees have in common?"

"They stand and pray all day?"

"Their balls are just for decoration! Mine aren't!"

"One minute I think you're deep, and the next you go behaving like an animal."

"And I know you think that's the best way to live life—try a little bit of everything!"

Roshni, Roshni, Roshni,

It's two in the morning. The whole world around me is asleep. One of the most spectacular things is happening right before my eyes. It started this afternoon while I was with Brandon. It is so spectacular that I started crying when I first saw it and that confused him when he found me in his garden, shivering, but feeling oh so wonderfully warm inside! I promise you, if it's the last thing I do, I'll make sure you see it. In six-sided glory Bhagvaan, Allah, Surya, Jesus, Zeus and the Holy Ghost or holy water or holy whoever came down to earth in spectacular silence as I watched in speechless wonder. No, I'm not hallucinating! You know the little pieces of soft, white cotton-candy we loved to pick at and savor as it melted in our mouths? That is exactly what it looked like as it came falling down from the sky! Only, it wasn't rain, although it tasted like cold water instead of sugar when it melted in my mouth. The four letter word for it is SNOW. At first, this snow just disappeared into the stomach of the street and the grass and the branches of trees and everything it landed upon. After a while, though, something even more magical happened. Everything wondrous snow touched slowly but surely turned into spotless, sparkling white ghosts, be they swings, chairs, picnic tables, statues, gardens, power lines, absolutely everything. As far as my eyes could see, snow had robbed nature of all its colors—like an angel that had decided to spread a clean, white bed-sheet over the world and sprinkle it with a wordless hush. There were no birds, no squirrels, no cars, no sounds, whatsoever! It seemed as if snow contained the purified spirit of man's ancestors, silently blessing sinful streets, for even the hardened, black asphalt was baptized with this white magic! And so was I. I felt as fresh and pure as Tusneem probably did when she came out of her mosque on the tenth of Mohorrem. The sun, too, had disappeared, to make way for yet another kind of light that was completely different, but equally dazzling. And as though this were not enough magic, when the sun finally came out, its rays made the snow clad trees sparkle like sleeves of white lace studded with diamonds. And the trees themselves, with their filigreed, white arms, looked like radiant brides without a blush, graciously accepting that although their colorful youth had slipped away, more joyous times were ahead, when they would ripen and yield fruit.

It's the first time I really noticed the limbs of trees, Roshni. You know limbs on trees do not stretch out straight like a man-made yard stick. The limbs kind of dip down and curve back up again to the heavens—like the outstretched arms of beggars willing to graciously accept whatever comes their way. The more I really see trees, the more I love them.

Brandon took me to a neighborhood park that was filled with children rejoicing in the snow. Believe it or not Roshni, this snow is like a dough of white flour and water. You can do all kinds of things with it (except bake it). As crazy as this may sound to you, when Scott came to pick me up that afternoon, Brandon, Scott and I rolled three big balls out of this dough, large, larger and largest, and made a man. We gave him prunes for eyes, a carrot for nose, and two sticks for arms. I tell you, when Brandon draped a scarf around his neck and put a hat on his head, he looked real. And he was bigger than Scott!

I just had to hug him. Scott took lots of pictures. Will send you some. While I was hugging the snowman, I said cockily to Scott that as cold as this snowman was, it did not make me feel that my brown-ness was defiling his white world. Just then a bright, red cardinal flew down out of nowhere. Scott took one look at the bird and replied, "That's 'cause the snowman has no blood, sweet thing! If it did, it would be melting in your arms!"

We Hindus have so many Gods and Goddesses, Roshni. Snow has to be a God of good blessings. And like many blessings in disguise, some perceive snow to be nothing but a curse and a hindrance to their life style. You're not going to guess, so I'm going to tell you, the first one to desecrate the sanctity of snow was man! I was horrified when I first saw monstrous yellow trucks come and simultaneously a-salt it and shove it to the side, turning pure, white, gentle snow into horrendous, little mountains of blackened mush. The blackened mush looked like magnanimous God's confused, saintly spirit slumped over, mourning at man's inability to stand still and enjoy the Sabbath He had sent us for free. Not being quite so saintly or quiet, I felt like screaming at the yellow monsters—stop salting, stop shoveling the snow to the sides, you horrors! But these yellow monsters are deaf and dumb machines, so they would not hear me anyway. Besides, according to Scott, working people heave a sigh of relief as soon as the hardened black streets re-appear again. That way everyone can go speeding down the roads again, to the more familiar sounds of shrieking sirens and screeching cars, as though black were heaven and white were hell. I'm sure Scott's joking, but he says some people have another four-letter word for snow—they call it SHIT!

So much for your suggestion to see the world and seek the truth, Roshni! I'm getting more and more confused with each passing day! If God chooses to send us water, magically turned into snow, to baptize the earth, why the hell do we have to remove it, I simply cannot understand. We go through life using water for ablution and for baptism as though it's our only ticket to heaven! We know, of course, that water's our only ticket to life itself. Everywhere, I hear talk about civil rights and political rights and educational rights and human rights, but I've yet to hear something about the rights of water and earth and air which we damn and assault and pollute. The only difference is that man has insurance policies against the ravages of nature, while nature silently stomachs the salt and the asphalt and the oil spills and the concrete walls that restrict its flow. If you ask me, nature passively accepts the blows for a while and then, when it can stomach no more, it retaliates with fires and floods and famines. We perceive them only as natural disasters, never as natural retaliation.

We never think of our roads as blackened agents of death and degradation. And when snow silently signals us to slow down a little, we just call it white shit, wipe it off, and go screeching down the streets, relieved to see hardened black streets overpower pure white snow. What a reflection of our priorities! We cannot see, Roshni, we cannot see. We're blind as bats; we think that snow is shit and shit is crap; that cow manure stinks and real manure comes in 80 pound plastic bags! And we have the gall to consider ourselves landlords of the earth.

I am writing to you again after a half hour break. Scott's mother was wondering what I was doing out here at four in the morning. When I told her I had never seen snow in my life and how much I was enjoying it, she stopped to chat with me for a few minutes. She said her husband, who rarely says anything, loves the snow, and that the only thing his children were allowed to do in Pennsylvania where they grew up, was to play in it. We never shoveled the snow on our farm, she said. Dad thought it was a time for building fires and baking bread and playing board games, for looking at photographs and telling stories around the hearth. Sometimes other families would drop by for pot luck (eat whatever whoever brings). She said that was the only time Dad had no problems if his children decided to hibernate like polar bears, or to do nothing except stretch and sigh from time to time. What a nice idea! She said he is an old fashioned man who dreams about the old days. When she left, she asked me to remind her to show me a poem he had once written about snow.

And now here I am thinking, why couldn't we have had snow when we were begging in Calcutta? We never did have to go to work. It would have been perfect. We could have built fires; Ma could have reminisced and told us stories. Oh Calcutta, city of joy and city of sorrow, but not destined to be city of snow. Start saving Roshni. I'm going to make sure some day you and I see snow fall somewhere— even if we have to climb up to the Everest!

But remember what Scott told me, Roshni, snow is not blessed with blood like you and I are. You were meant to show your warmth. You were not meant to be icy! According to Mom, when it gets very cold, soft beautiful snow also turns icy and that can be dangerous, that's when people go slipping and falling and breaking more than just repairable bones. Don't know what I love more—silence or communicating.

With all my love,

Komli.

P.S. The following is Dad's poem. Amazing isn't it how quiet people can capture the endless drift of the talkative in 46 words. Well, at least Scott's Dad and I think alike about something. I'd never have known if it wasn't for the poem! Neither would I have thought that there was a poet lurking under the glazed eyes and beer bottle!

S-ENTIALLY SNOW

Sacred, sublime, sparkling snow
Selflessly sanctifying sinful streets
Spectacularly spellbound
Sans stealing
Sans shooting
Sans speeding
Sans sirens.

Streets simply silent,
Simply stoic,
Singularly sane,
Singularly serene.

Stop salting!
Stop shoveling! Stir souls! Surge Spirits!
Stretch, stare, smell,
Sigh, search, soar.
Savor celestial snow's
Sovereign Sabbath.

Quite a poem. I guess I'll never underestimate the far-away look of an old man with a cigarette dangling from his lips and a beer bottle from his hands!

Roshni smiled and savored Komli's letter which she had already read three times at east in the last two days. With the fervor of a mother carefully putting away her beloved child's freshly dried laundry, Roshni folded the letter and gently pressed it down as she aid it on top of the pile of all her sister's other letters. These letters had become her treasures; treasures that she had learned to share with Rashid; treasures that made Rashid envious because although he talked to his daughter all the time, he knew that what Komli gave to her sister through her letters was a priceless part of her soul. A soul that rolled and stumbled and staggered but gave completely of herself.

"Roshni, why don't you ask Komli when she is bringing the smaller snowman t
India. Tell her we won't crush him with our warmth!" Rashid added, making Roshni smil
her rare, shy smile.

"I think I'll put it to her exactly that way! I can just picture her laughing. I've bee
thinking about it myself, Rashid. I'm dying to meet this Scott."

"Do you think she'll marry him?"

"I don't know. Education and travel have done strange things to her mind. One da
she thinks God is the sun, then she thinks He is the hot silent air in some gaping hole, an
now He seems to have turned to snow! I think I'll phone her tonight."

Rana was amply compensated with money and gold for the years of groveling i
Saudi Arabia. Just when he was thinking of returning home to India, however, he hear
from an equally nifty friend that the United States was another land of opportunities, bu
that, unlike the Middle East, everyone in America was treated equally. To America, t
America illegally went the pig; from whence he traveled home again, home again, jigget
jig, happy in the knowledge that he could travel back and forth while he was slowly bu
surely climbing up the golden ladder of material wealth.

Rana had heard about the Statue of Liberty, but not that the statue was indeed
woman. All the women he knew had been subservient to men in one way or another, and in
the Middle-East they even stayed behind purdah. What was the matter with this mos
powerful country in the world, he wondered cynically. But not for long. Happily he accepte
what liberty doled out to him in the next few years—a green card, a social security card, a
master card, with all of which he became master once again of his own destiny. The Statu
of Liberty meant business, he discovered. She would not allow him to trample willy nilly or
anyone. When he went to India, therefore, the pig was able to appreciate its people, it
customs and its foods with a sensibility previously unknown to him.

But, as the saying goes, once a pig, always a pig. And the pig in him almost jumped ou
of its skin one morning at the supermarket when he heard an American gentleman ask the
one-handed Indian girl in front of him, "Did you remember the cottage cheese, Komli?"
There could not possibly be two Komlis in the world with a stump for left hand. Rana wa
used to thinking with the speed of lightning. He knew he had to react immediately because
nine times out of ten, people simply disappeared in cars in America, never to be seen again

"Excuse me, madam, I heard the gentleman call out your name. Do you have a siste
by the name of Roshni?"

"Yes!" Komli replied with a smile, delighted that here in Maryland, so far away from
India, was a man who knew her sister. He looked vaguely familiar, but it did not even occur
to Komli to go as far back as her childhood in Calcutta. "Are you from Patna?"

"Yes, yes. Is Roshni still in Patna?"

"Yes. How did you meet her?"

"At one of my relations' house," Rana answered vaguely.

"You mean Devi and Mohan?"

"I have so many relatives, I'm not sure," Rana replied cautiously. "Look I am going to India in a few days, would you like me to take something back for her? I'd be delighted to."

"Oh! Thank you. I'd love to send her a couple of books. What is your name?"

"Pradip Shah. Why don't you give me your phone number. I've parked my car in the handicapped parking so I need to rush out."

"I'm not so sure you should have given him your phone number, Komli," Scott said as soon as Rana was out of sight. There was something about him that I did not like, specially when he admitted to his car being parked in the handicapped area."

"You Americans are so privacy conscious! What can he do to us, Scott?"

"Nothing! He better not! I'm going with you if you decide to give him some books to take back."

"Mr. Shah?" Roshni asked with a smile that instantly turned into a look of horror. She tried not to reel with fear, as she realized that the Pradip Shah who had phoned her to say he had a package for her from her sister was actually the animal from her past, reincarnated into something that looked like a beast in gentleman's guise.

"Roshni!" he said smoothly, as he stared in awe at a woman he would have sworn was an untouched virgin had he himself not abused her all those years ago. "May I come in?" he asked, just for the pleasure of making it known that she really had no choice; he was already inside.

"What is it you want?" Roshni managed to ask, as she held on to the wall to prevent her from staggering any further.

Rana stared at her for a long time before he answered her. "I want many things. Strangely enough, what I want more than anything else is to know how the chichree I once knew slipped out of my fingers and turned into this beautiful woman?" When Roshni said nothing, he added menacingly, "If you choose to remain quiet, I swear I will drag you outside and tell all your neighbors what you were once."

"And what will you do if I tell you the truth?"

Rana was born with natural instincts about human psychology. He decided to take a gamble, "I won't hurt Komli or the people who helped you. Otherwise I will."

"You know them?"

"Yes. Just remember, you never got away with lies in the past. Don't try it now. I have ways of finding things out, just like I found you, even though it took me all these years."

"You told me you had a package from Komli. Where did you meet Komli? Are you living in . . ."

"You do the answering. I'll do the questioning," Rana interrupted harshly. His mind was working the whole time that it took a petrified Roshni to spill out her story. It seemed to Rana that the woman was a little remorseful about what she had done to her sister. He would make her feel worse. He figured, the worse she felt, the easier it would be to extort money out of her. "So," he remarked smoothly, "the big sister is not such an angel after all. Sacrifices little sister for her own comforts, huh!"

"That's not true!"

"And the family who pays you, they still live in that palace in Calcutta?"

"I don't know."

"You do know!" Rana screamed. "I can always tell when you're lying! Can you get i touch with them?"

"Why?"

"In America, a man can get millions of dollars for suing someone for the kind of thin that family did to your sister."

"They didn't do anything. I let them!"

"Shut up! I can hurt your sister if you don't listen to me," Rana threatened, hopin that Roshni would fall for the lie. "I want you to pick up this phone and call them."

"I don't know their number." Roshni lied, hoping that way she could somehow avoi involving Rashid.

"You know their name. What is it?" he asked, wringing her arm.

"Rashid Khan."

"After I get the number from directory enquiry you will phone this Rashid Khan an tell him that unless he comes here with ten lakhs ($2 million) by tomorrow sometime, I wi publicly broadcast what his wife did to your sister. I know they will pay any price, to avoi the shame it will bring to their family!" Rana said complacently, as he lit a cigarette. It wa difficult for Roshni to tell if the beast's hands shook from nerves, or from excitement at th prospect of making a couple of million!

"Rashid?"

"Yes. What a nice surprise, Roshni! To what do I owe the honor of a phone call?"

"My husband is here. He wants to talk to you." Rashid could tell from Roshni' tremulous voice that something was wrong.

Rana quickly grabbed the telephone from her. "Mr. Khan?" he asked.

"Yes. And you are?"

"Roshni's long lost husband. Don't ask any questions. Here's what I would like you to do. By tomorrow afternoon bring me ten lakhs in cash. If not, I will tell your whole community and the entire city of Calcutta how you exploited an innocent girl. I am going back to America shortly. If you don't comply, I will also bring a law suit on your head from America!"

"I will bring you fifteen lakhs, on one condition, that you do not touch the lady by your side. I know she is not your wife. If I find out that you have so much as laid a finge on her, I will not pay you a penny. Do you understand?"

"And why are you so interested in her honor? Rana asked, as little bristles of suspicio began to surface.

"I'll bring you the cash, without question. You follow my directions, without question. Is that understood?" Rashid barked.

"Yes, sir!" Rana replied, happy in the knowledge that in India he could still make a quick buck without the help of lawyers.

Within a couple of hours Rashid was on a plane bound for Patna. There was nothing he could do now but bide his time. He thanked Allah that he did not have to worry about Zenub or Tusneem at this time. He had made a few telephone calls, filled his briefcase with all the hundred-rupee bundles it could hold and here he was, grateful that the roller coaster of emotions he was undergoing was under the control of a tightly fastened seat belt. He knew he was capable of doing anything, fair or foul, to face the biggest challenge of his life, and to save the woman he had grown to love so dearly. Rana had given him 24 hours. He would deliver well before that.

Rashid closed his eyes and tried to rest. Ironic, he thought, that someone vile from Roshni's past had to jolt him into the realization that nothing but Roshni mattered to him any more. The wounds from Zenub passing away had healed. That space in his heart would always be hers. But his heart had made room for companionship. Time had re-arranged the room and made space for more love. If two helpless beggars could show the courage they had, how could he hide behind the laws of religion and society, he asked himself. The Koran, the Bhagavadgita, the Bible—he had read them all. Each one was a masterpiece! Perhaps they were all inspired, piece by piece, by the same Master, but through different hands, different languages, different lands, reaching different souls. How wonderfully they had inspired man, he thought. He realized that in one life time no one could zoom around the world and catch even a glimpse of all the fantastic mosques and temples and cathedrals and customs and ceremonies religions continue to inspire. But the temple in his heart spoke a different language now. Did he have the courage to proclaim to the world that he loved a Hindu. The world was too indifferent; it didn't care. Did he have the courage to proclaim to his family, to his beloved daughter, that he loved Roshni?

Rashid realized that the wisdom that is given freely with the coming of age and blossoming of love is more powerful and more precious than the zillion laws that are pressed into hard bound books; cold laws that could never rejoice or grieve with the joys and sorrows he had witnessed in courts. Just as imperceptibly as the hair on his temples had turned to gray, so also he seemed to have acquired the ability to see the myriad shades of gray in the previously black and white compartments into which he had meticulously separated the deeds of man. At long last, he had begun to wonder about the course of action his wife had taken in the name of love. Suddenly, he wasn't so sure how he should have judged her. He wondered how Allah the beneficent and the merciful had judged her. He would never find out. It was to this gray area that he wanted to retire now, to a simple, small home with a non-judgmental woman who exuded nothing but peace and purity.

He could never renounce Islam. His religion meant too much to him. And her religion means as much to her, he remembered. Although she was an unschooled woman, she had had the courage all those years ago to ask why her sister should convert if his nephew wasn't willing to convert for her sake. Maybe Abdul was right. Maybe this would never have come to pass if Hindus were never allowed to enter Muslim homes; if beggars were never allowed to be educated. But Abdul was uneducated. And Rashid could not deny in his heart of hearts that he was thrilled that the seed that had been planted all those years ago had sprouted into something beautiful, even though the world may think otherwise.

"Mr. Khan?!"

"With the money. Where is Roshni?"

"In the bedroom. Give me the money, and you can see her."

"The deal was that I make sure you haven't touched her."

"You act smart with me and I'll shoot you!"

"I expected you to have a gun. You have the right to bear arms in America, don't you? But when you walk out of here," Rashid said with a calm he did not feel, "you will find police officers waiting outside for you. You see, people like me are not just loaded with money, we have lots of strings, too, that we can pull. The police will not touch you if you cooperate with me." Sensing the change in attitude the word 'police' had brought about, Rashid walked into the bedroom to make sure Roshni was alright.

"That's the evil man from Calcutta, Rashid. Please don't let him take me away," distraught Roshni begged.

"I promise you he won't. Come with me."

"Now can I have the money?" Rana asked as soon as Rashid came out.

"Sit down," Rashid said to Rana, "I need to ask you a few questions before I hand you the money."

"Make it quick!"

"Tell me, why is the human flesh so important to you, young man?" Rashid did not remember his name and neither did he care to. 'Young man' was about all the respect he could accord this hunk of inhuman greed sitting in front of him. "In this country, Hindus and Muslims have massacred each other by the thousands, and I hear in America at least one innocent human being is shot every day! In fact, people everywhere are killing people in the name of religion or race or land or money. So what makes you think you have a case against my family?"

"In America you can make a case out of anything."

"So I hear. Uncle Sam has a wife called Aunty Sue," Rashid said flippantly.

"All I know is that in America I can sue . . ."

"But we're not in America. And if your God or mine wanted us to spend our lives suing each other, we would somehow have been able to sue Him for all the havoc He . . ."

"I'm not here to argue with you or to listen to your philosophy. Just give me the briefcase, and I promise never to bother you again."

"I will give you all the money in a minute."

'Money!' The magical words brought back a glint to Rana's eyes, as he calmed down again. A minute was not that long to wait. He had waited a life time to make a quick million.

Rashid decided another approach. "Personally, I think human flesh is priceless. But you're so fortunate you live in the United States," he said calmly. "People there seem to now exactly what price to pay for different parts of the body and mind. Is it true that a woman was awarded a huge sum for an accidental coffee spill that burnt her?"

"Yes."

"And you want ten lakhs for what my family did to this lady's sister, is that correct?"

"And another five lakhs for not touching this lady," Rana reminded Rashid coolly, trying not to salivate at the mouth.

"Here is the money," Rashid said as he dangled the briefcase in mid-air, "but before you take it, will you tell me what price you are prepared to pay for an amputated arm?"

"What do you mean?"

"You know what I mean, you bastard! You amputated Komli's arm when she was newborn! Everyone in India knows about the evil begging industry. Shame on people like me that we know, but do nothing about it!"

"I did not amputate her arm!" Rana screamed.

"Neither did my wife circumcise Komli. But both of you took Komli to someone to remove a part of her body," Rashid said, feeling a new stab of pain because he had to drag his beloved wife through the same cesspool.

"What proof do you have?"

"Ah, those oft-repeated words, 'what proof do you have'. I wonder if anyone goes through life without asking at least once in his life-time, 'Show me where it is written'. We must document, document, document," Rashid said, pounding his fist on the table. "To the extent that we are now blinded to the world outside of papers."

"You didn't answer my question, what proof do you have?" Rana asked.

Rashid turned to Roshni and continued, "You see what I mean? We hear but do not listen; we see but seem to have lost our vision; we smell foul play but are helpless if there is no written proof."

"So give me the money and I will leave."

"I have as much proof against you as you have against my wife. You've threatened me with an American law suit. I suggest you go back and do that, while I bring a lawsuit against you from here."

"If you give me the money, I won't have to bring a law suit . . ."

"Civilized man rummages through mountains of law-suits, and meaningless treaties. If you're lucky, your case will come up for trial in a year. Jury selection should be easy, considering we're neither white nor black. We'll both have to dig up reams of papers, if we can; drag each other through mud and slime. For all I know, the earth quakes because of the masses of paper we force down its body, even though it was created for the sole purpose of supporting life. Maybe your law suit will turn into another one of those year-long soap operas that will mesmerize the east and the west, in the courts, and on the television, and in all the newspapers and even on the internet, if we get lucky. The best soap operas are those that mesmerize us for months and months. My daughter will cringe and suffer, but it seems the world cares little about the suffering of children if they have a choice between that and a good old scandal. And if all twelve jurors can't come to a unanimous verdict, it will be called a mistrial, and we can start all over again. And do you know what else, if you get lucky you'll make a few more million if someone asks you to write a book! I take it you can read and write!" Rashid added sarcastically.

Rana realized he had dug his own grave; Rashid had two weapons he did not have—money and education. "Sir, I am not really interested in courts and battles. I am telling you if you hand me the money, I will never bother you again." Seeing that Rashid was staring straight through him, as if he were a piece of stone, Rana tried to soften him a little, "I need the money to straighten my papers for U.S. citizenship. If you hand me the money, I will never bother you again."

"And I am asking you to tell me what price you will pay for half an arm!" Rashid insisted, lowering his voice a little. "Wrongs cannot be righted by a sum of money. The awarding of money is like a cancer that feeds on itself and multiplies. I will go to prison before I pay you a single penny!"

Rana knew he had one more plea left. "You promised me you would give me 5 lakhs if I did not touch Roshni. I did not, sir."

"You filthy beast!" Rashid roared. There was no seat belt to strap him down this time. He stood up, trembling a little, and lunged out his fist with all the superhuman strength he could muster. He had never struck a human being in his life. "For years you abused both her body and her mind. I'm amazed she's still the saint that she is!" He fished out a hundred rupee note from his pocket and thrust it at Rana, "Buy yourself a train ticket and get out of here. If I so much as see your shadow, I swear you will be behind bars! Get out! Now!" The wrath of a noble human being was something new to Rana. All he knew was that it was time for him to get out.

"What about the police?"

"What about them?"

"Will they get me?"

"No," Rashid said, feeling a little sorry suddenly for Rana who looked more like a lonely, wild dog howling in the wilderness he had created for himself. "They are in plain clothes. If you walk out of here quietly, they will not so much as question you." Rashid wondered if there was any dormant, decent chord in this base man, as he quietly added, "Money and papers will make you legal, but only people, other people, can bring you happiness. Do you have anyone in America?"

"No, sir."

Rashid took out a bundle of hundred rupee notes and handed it to him, saying "This is not to bribe you or to buy you legal papers. Treat it as alms being given to a mendicant in the hope that Allah will forgive me for the sins I have committed."

"What is a mendicant?"

"A beggar. It seems to me that we are all beggars at some point in our lives; if we're not begging for money, we're begging for jobs, or for mercy, or justice, or honor, or understanding, or peace, or the greatest gift of all, love," he ended, looking Roshni straight in the eye. And, I would like to say one more thing before you leave. I have ıffered for my sins. I have a right to keep them to myself. Some stains are best left ntouched by human scavengers who think nothing of picking them apart until they're own to the bare bones. I doubt if such scavengers ever find peace. The Gods of our ıorld want us to spread the word, not the dirty word."

Rana walked out into the world feeling a little out of sorts with himself. He had not et come to grips with the fact that Rashid had actually struck a human chord in his ıeart. Women and money had only stirred his passions and whetted his appetite for ıore. Artfully, he had managed to steer clear of written laws and punishments. But he ıas tired of living like an underground mole. He was tired of the company he kept. He ıad never known the meaning of going home to someone he loved. He walked to the ırst restaurant he found and ordered a cup of tea. He sipped it slowly as he stared into is past. Not one of his limbs had been severed for all the wrong he had done. Was his ıunishment this void that he felt? This realization that he had absolutely nothing to go o or to look forward to? That the poverty of loneliness was far greater than material ıoverty? That perhaps spiritual punishment was far worse than the physical horrors he ıad perpetrated.

"One mistake I made all those years ago has caused you so much trouble. I'm so orry, Rashid."

"If that's the only mistake you've made in your life, you should consider yourself xtremely fortunate, Roshni! Although I'm not so sure that even that was a mistake on our part. May I have a cup of tea, please?" he asked.

"Yes. But first I must pray and give thanks to Ganesh. He removed a big obstacle oday."

Rashid watched her go up to a little corner in the room. The Ganesh he had helped her ıurchase all those years ago was still there, together with several other deities she had ıcquired since then.

He saw her open a small, wooden box. Using the index finger of her right hand, she ılaced some kumkum (red powder) in the middle of her forehead. Carefully, she lit the oil ın a paisley-shaped, earthen container before she placed it in front of Ganesh. She took a ıip of water from a metal container and then sprinkled some around her. Not a sound was o be heard. Reverently, she lifted a small dish containing some marigolds and bay leaves ınd coconut and offered it to her deities. Next, she lit a stick of incense and waved it in ront of the gods. Gently, she tinkled a plain, brass bell and placed it back on the table. Quietly, with eyes shut, she proceeded to pray. When she was done, she placed a small ıiece of coconut in her mouth and walked back to Rashid. She looked so saintly, Rashid hought. She may have prayed to idols, performed rites that were very different from what ıe did before he prayed, but he felt utterly connected to her in spirit.

"Will you come with me to the kitchen while I make tea? She asked simply.

"I've never seen a Hindu pray before. It was very moving."

"Komli told me she was very moved when she saw your people pray once."

"How come I never heard you chant the mystic word, *OM*?"

"I always start my prayers by meditating with that word. I just chose to say it ver quietly today since I had an audience."

"What does it mean?"

"Ma used to say that OM contains everything in the universe—the Creator and a time, past, present, and future. It's hard to understand, isn't it?"

"I'll have to think about it. Why did you put the red powder on your forehead? thought only married women do that."

"So did I, until Devi, my neighbor, told me differently. She's my guru in many way The red color is to remind us of the power of our holy trinity—Brahma, Vishnu, and Shiv. Brahma creates, Vishnu preserves, and Shiva destroys. I know all three were present i this room today," she added as an after-thought. We put it between our brows because is considered to be the seat of wisdom and concentration."

"How come I've never seen it on you before?"

"Widows don't wear it, and since I pretend to be one, I make sure I remove it when go out."

"Why did you light the lamp and burn the incense? There was something else yo burned, although I couldn't tell what it was."

"That was camphor. It's all symbolic, I'm told. By lighting the lamp, I dispel ignoranc so my mind can be illumined with light and I can become one with God. Water, as you mus know, is for purification. The flowers symbolize my soul as I offer it to the gods. Th incense is the fragrance of god's love, and the camphor is the burning of my own ego."

"And the ringing of the bell? Was that to awaken the Gods?"

"No," Roshni said with a smile, "the Gods are always awake. The bell is supposed t ring out all other sounds, so I can concentrate on prayer."

Rashid felt humbled as he sipped on his tea.

"You're very quiet. I hope you are not bashing my Gods in your head, like you di that first day you brought me here."

"With or without the ability to write, our Gods bless us with the gift of being able t read each other's minds at least! I'm sorry about that. It was unforgivable on my part. Ca you guess what I'm thinking right now?"

"That my puja (prayer) is really no different from your namaaz (prayer), I hope."

"I know now that it isn't. It seems that all our Gods' job is to watch and listen quietly while we go about creating customs and ceremonies and condemning one another. Te me, Roshni," Rashid stated quietly, "If you were in some kind of great dilemma and yo had three choices, to whom would you listen—to your elders, to what was written i books, or to your heart? I respect your wisdom more than you realize," he added humbly

Roshni wanted to say heart but something urged her to say, "I always listened t Ma."

"You know that I love you dearly, don't you?" Rashid blurted out suddenly.

"You have your family to think of!" Roshni said, taking a few steps backwards.

"It's our elders and our books that frighten me, Roshni. And then I think of people like Gandhi and Abraham Lincoln, and Martin Luther King. Had they not fought age old customs and laws, we would still have untouchables in India; women would still not be allowed to go to school and the world would still have slavery. And look at the other side. We just had Rana bragging about freedom in America. If the gun laws were changed in America, fewer people would get killed. So you see, laws have to be changed from time to time. I want to spend the rest of my life with you, Roshni."

"That's impossible. I'm not worthy of you or your family."

"Now you've made me angry, Roshni! Do you know anything about the Lotus flower in which I see pictures of your Gods?"

"A little. Why?"

"I read that the lotus blossoms from the muck and mire at the bottom of a pond. You are such a lotus. You must see yourself that way, not as someone dirty! Love does not see the past or the future, or color, caste, or creed!" He held her firmly by the shoulders as he continued gently, "I love you, Roshni. I felt something for you the first time I saw you in the garden, stooping down to smell our flowers. You know, I never once went to the garden to smell those flowers. They were there for decoration and for the maali to tend to. In the courts where I worked, I smelled many fragrances in many people, but none as beautiful as you. Zenub, too, was beautiful. I loved her dearly."

"That is why you cannot love me; to honor your wife."

"I didn't ask to love you, Roshni. Just as I didn't ask for the thousand other blessings Allah showered me with. You believe in reincarnation don't you?"

"Yes. But you Muslims don't."

"There are several ways to look at reincarnation. Every new season is a reincarnation. Every time something profound touches a human being, he goes through a metamorphosis of the spirit. Of the aatma. I believe love and marriage are forever. If you get divorced, that's a cycle of your life that's over, because after divorce you are no longer the person you once were. You change, or are reincarnated into something else. A part of me died with Zenub. So, you can look at me as a spiritually reincarnated human being. And it is this other soul that is in front of you. Does it make some sense, Roshni?" he asked, desperately hoping that she would be able to convince him that it was alright to run a red light.

"Some sense, yes. But we also have to be careful what we say and do, because through our actions we can cause so many spiritual deaths that we are not even aware of. Until I met you, the men in my life had caused a part of me to die many, many deaths. Do you think they were aware of the deaths I died? What if loving me kills something precious in your daughter? Can you live with that?"

"I Love you, Roshni. What can I do?"

"You didn't answer my question—can you live with hurting Tusneem?"

"She is as precious to me as Komli is to you. It's our two girls who've brought us together. If we're too careful about what we say and do, we may never revive the spirit that dies so many premature deaths. That, too, is a tragedy, isn't it?"

"And what would your wife think, as she looks down on two recycled remnants, one a piece of silk and the other a rag, trying to patch up?" Roshni asked seriously, although she could not help smiling a Mona Lisa smile. "Remember that nun who said silk and rag don't go together?"

"And since when have the Mother Christinas of this world become authorities on what goes together? You know it was Zenub who insisted that I come and visit you from time to time to make sure you were alright. Maybe she knew in her last days that we were meant to spend a part of our lives together. To whom must I beg for an answer?"

"Beg? You? Never! You can never be anything but noble. You even handled Rana so nobly!"

"I could say to you that I'll become a Hindu, but I would be false to myself. Islam is too wonderful a religion and too deeply entrenched in my being. I will never give it up. I do not want to give it up. Neither do I want you to convert for my sake. I want you as you are. I can live with your Ganesh and Vishnu, if you can live with my Allah."

"The destitute never have problems with Gods," Roshni said simply. "If it weren't for all the different gods of the world, we beggars would not have survived Calcutta."

"And you are so wise, my dearest Roshni. I don't want a ceremony; I don't want any people around. All I want is a piece of paper that says you're mine."

Roshni started laughing. "A piece of paper!" Between you and Komli, this paper business is getting confusing. One minute, I hear that paper is evil; next minute, it's all one needs!"

"I could spend the rest of my life with you, without pen or paper. But the reason we need papers is so we can see the world together."

"You know what Komli taught me again and again. There are three states of matter that keep changing, not just depending on the temperature, but sometimes depending on what it combines with. You and I have changed, but we cannot combine," Roshni said with calm finality.

"Do you love me, Roshni? Tell me you do."

"I've come across those precious three words in many, many books. But you know what, I've never said them. Love is about how one feels inside. So I'll tell you how I feel inside and then you, mighty judge, decide if what I feel for you is an *I love you,* okay?" Roshni was relaxed and smiling, while Rashid listened intently. "Lately, every time I sit down to read, I have to read each paragraph at least three times because I keep seeing this face with caterpillar eyebrows and black-rimmed glasses sliding down a proud, parrot nose. I think of him for I don't know how long, before I go back to the beginning of the paragraph because I've forgotten what it said. Sometimes this happens many times. Then I stare at the door, for I don't know how long, and wonder when that beautiful moment will come when my heart starts thudding all because of a gentle knock on the door. If it's my neighbor, Devi, I pretend not to be disappointed. If it's this man with caterpillar eyebrows and long, slender hands dangling helplessly beside him, I pray he won't hear my heart pounding like crazy. And I often want to lay his head between my breasts and comfort him ecause I sense his loneliness. I knew he was gentle and loving the first day I saw him in is garden. And I envied his wife for having such a man to have and to hold for all of her fe. I savor every second I spend with him, every word he utters, every gesture he makes, ke the precious pennies that once came my way. I think about him, and think about him, nd think about him. Is this an *I love you?"*

"No! It's an *I'm crazy about you!"* Rashid exclaimed. He took her in his arms and rushed her. After a while, he felt a wet spot on his chest. "Why are you crying, Roshni?" e asked, a little bewildered.

"I am so happy! I wish I could die now. That way we won't have to worry about sin r scandal, and I don't think there will be another moment in my life when I will be so appy again. I never knew until now what it must feel like to be held by a good man who ares so much. I cannot allow you to come any closer to me. I know it will not be right for ou."

Rashid tightened his grasp. People thought he knew so much. In reality, he was arning again and again that there was so much that passed before his very eyes, of hich he knew so little. He had been able to let go of Zenub, of Abdul, of Tusneem, his ociety. But Roshni refused to let go of the building blocks of their respective past. This woman, from the sewers of Calcutta, this woman who craved and deserved all the love he elt for her, had the nobility to say a superhuman 'no', that it simply cannot be.

"You will allow me to come visit you, won't you?" Rashid asked fearfully.

"If you don't visit me, the beautiful flower that has blossomed in my heart will shrivel. t will be hard for me," she confessed simply.

Komli loved watching Scott work in his parent's garden. If he had a passion, surely it ad to be gardening, she decided. He stood still sometimes, it seemed forever, while he ourished thirsty plants with water from the hose. In some ways, he reminded her of the ohnsons. They, too, had taken great pride in their garden. Although Komli was very xcited about the good news she had to convey, she decided to be patient and enjoy cott at his best—tending lovingly to his parents' garden. When he finally set down the ose and came up to her, she said casually, "It's seems such a shame that people who can fford homes in India have maalis to tend their garden. You get a lot out of gardening, lon't you, Scott?"

"I don't work in the yard as much as I once used to. It's not a bad place to get lost in. ⁄ly grandfather always claimed that the more slowly one lives and the more rustic the nvironment in which one lives, the richer is the soil in which one can till ones passions."

Komli wondered if gardening was Scott's therapy to whatever horrors of war he was unning away from. She wished Roshni had a garden to tend. She knew her sister would nake a loving, wonderful gardener. She remembered how Mrs. Johnson used to talk to her blants. She had claimed that plants thrive on loving conversations. "How come you never alk to the flowers, Scott? I know some people who do."

"They talk to me, all the time. Remember, I prefer listening?"

"Dare I ask what secrets they reveal?"

"Same as the mountains and grand canyons," he responded with a smile.

"Why do you clip and prune the bushes? Why can't you just let them grow as natu intended?"

"Some prefer them wild. My parents like to clip and prune them to perfection," Sco replied, wondering if she was thinking of their discussion on the shores of th Mediterranean. Until now, he had certainly never looked at gardening that way. He realize that civilizations themselves were gardens that were constantly being cut and prune "Come and help me weed this patch," he asked, throwing her a pair of gloves. "How weeding coming with Brandon?"

"We're both getting better at it, thanks to you."

"Good! Start digging here, will you. The sooner we finish, the quicker we can go and have a sandwich. That's the other good thing about gardening—food always taste better after I've worked out here."

Over the months Scott had helped Komli deal with the slugs and worms that sh unearthed from time to time. "I wish my friend Tusneem could see me now, Scott," Kom said as she dangled a worm in front of her eyes. "You know she has a great fear for thes creatures."

"Why?!"

"When she was young, she was told that if she was wicked, the worms would gnav at her body when she was buried!"

"Amazing, isn't it, how people make up job descriptions for God's mute, harmles creatures! As far as I know, this poor, humble worm's sole purpose in life is to burrow an wiggle and loosen the soil, so water can reach the roots of plants, so plants can make foo for us. Can you imagine what man would do if he were assigned the important task of th earthworm?"

"He certainly wouldn't let anyone trample upon him, that's for sure!"

"I think I would much prefer worms gnawing at me when I'm dead and unfeeling, tha have my butt spanked by those priests!"

"You mean you got spanked in school?" Komli asked with a hearty laugh.

"All the time!" Those priests didn't take the time to warn us about after life. If ther was punishment to be meted out, it was given there and then! Maybe it was their onl opportunity to grab a butt!"

"I thought spanking was not allowed in schools here?" Komli said, rollicking wit laughter.

"Sure was allowed during my time!"

"Are we almost done, Scott? I have some good and bad news to give you . . . ."

"What's the bad news?" Scott asked quickly, wondering if she had decided to leav for India."

"You know that hunch you had about Mr. Shah? You were right! The guy turned ou to be the very guy who had abused my sister when she was young."

"Is your sister alright?"

"Yes. I also spoke to Rashid who assured me that she was safe. I still feel shaky, cott, to think he came over here to collect books for Roshni. Makes me shudder!"

"That takes care of you going anywhere on your own. Pays not to be so trusting, oesn't it?"

"He can't do anything to me, Scott. I'm sure he knows better. This is not India!"

"He's not going to do anything to you, believe me. What else did your sister say?"

"Now she's all worried about me because I work at a school. She thinks I'm going to et shot down, if not by Rana, then by some kid at the school!"

"What did you tell her?"

"That there are two Americas in America; the one you see on television and read bout in newspapers, and the one you don't hear or read about. That I live in the second America—amongst wonderful people who are very safe."

"I'm not so sure about the safety part any more. There are all kinds of lunatics arrying guns."

"Guess what Roshni had to say about that?"

"What?"

"How come the man who played holy Moses in the *Ten Commandments* is going around talking like he really is some Moses giving out commandments about the right to ave guns."

"That's one way of looking at him, I guess," Scott said with a laugh. "Do you really want to know why he goes around thinking he's Moses?"

"Why?"

"Because he's obsessed by the written word. Remember what you once said about rue prophets never writing down anything themselves?"

"You remember? I'm flattered!"

"In their infinite wisdom, the prophets must have known that sooner or later people would take written laws to the extreme, like our rifle association maniacs who insist that everyone has the right to bear arms, because so it has been written! If only they could eel the tragedies of innocent victims," Scott added softly as he rested his right foot on he hoe he was using and pondered the unknown tragedies of families victimized by combat. "Remember, you said once that no one other than man uses pen, paper, and clothing?"

"Yes."

"You can add guns to that list. Do you ever wonder, Komli, if God really made us in his image?"

Komli decided to change the subject. She wanted Scott in a good mood. "My sister was also wondering when I was returning to India and if you would come with me. By the way, she refers to you as the little snowman!"

"Is that the bad news? Are you leaving me, Komli?"

"No! The bad news was about Rana. I have a small piece of good news."

"Are you going to tell me you'll marry me? We could have a garden just like this, an 27 children scampering around in the yard. That would be paradise!"

"I'm old fashioned, Scott. I'm waiting for you to propose to me."

Scott went down on his knees and took Komli's hand, "This is the oldest of ol fashioned ways that I know. Will you marry me, Komli?" he asked earnestly.

"Yes, my dearest Scott, I would like nothing more in the world than to spend the res of my life with you."

"Thank you, dear God!" was all Scott could utter as he swept her in his arms.

"Come, let's go tell Mom and Dad!" he said at last.

"I told you I had a little piece of good news."

"Can I be so lucky? There's more?"

"The first of our 27 children is due in about as many weeks?"

"What?! Can you repeat that in plain English?"

"I got myself a do-it-yourself pregnancy test. Are they supposed to be one hundre percent correct?"

"They better be! Oh, Komli, you've made me the happiest man in the world. Let's g tell Mom and Dad."

"How do you think they'll react?"

"They'll probably spank the hell out of you for getting pregnant before gettin married!"

"Don't tell them, Scott. I don't want to upset them."

"First things first, sweet thing, I have to ask them for their blessings."

Komli felt a tight knot in her stomach. Hai Bhagvaan, don't let history repeat itsel she prayed.

"You go in and talk to your parents, Scott. I'll stay out here."

"You'll do nothing of the sort!"

"But supposing your parents don't want you to marry me; they can't say anything i front of me, Scott!"

"So you think my parents are heartless and dumb! You and I share a bedroom a night. They know I'm crazy about you, but you think they'll object to us gettin married?!"

"They could. They might be hoping that things would just fizzle out between us. happens you know."

"Well, let's go in and find out, so you don't torture yourself any further. Torture's no good for a growing baby! Hold on a second," he said, stopping suddenly and getting al serious again; "I love you, Komli. Nothing and no one will stop me from spending the res of my life with you. I just wish you had done the pregnancy test with me."

"I wanted to surprise you, Scott; see the thrilled look on your face."

"Was it worth it?"

"Yes. I'll never forget it. Too bad we never get to see our own expressions. Was i worth staying up all night and decorating the Christmas tree for me?"

"Yes, sweet thing, every flipping, yawning minute!" As they walked inside, hand in hand, Scott remarked, "By the way, after our baby's born, you're going to work and I'm staying at home."

"Why?"

"Would you like our children to think like you do?!"

"No," Komli conceded uncharacteristically.

"A meek no is the last thing I expected! What's going on in that little head of yours?"

"Shouldn't I be a little concerned? How would we raise our children, Scott? It's one thing for my head to be a spaghetti junction, but if we don't want our children to grow up all confused and wild there's really no way out of clipping and pruning them is there?"

"Let's see," Scott said as he joined the palms of his hands together and looked up to the sky, "I would pray to Him-up-there several times a day and ask him to bless me with wisdom. My prayer would go something like this :

How do I raise our child, dear God?
Hindu, Christian, Muslim or Jew
Or simply just a believer in You?
Tell me, dear God, which way should he face
When he prays to you for wisdom and grace?
North or south or east or west?
And what, dear God, would be the best—
To pray in Sanskrit, Latin, or plain old English?
We want to go to heaven when we finish.
How's that for a prayer?" Scott asked with a grin.

"Good. Carry on," Komli asked, delighted with the way he was clowning around.

"You can contribute, you know. It's your baby, too!"

"Okay. Let's see . . . ." Komli shut her eyes and thought for a few moments. Here's what I'd ask :

Would you mind if she sits or kneels or stands?
And where oh where should she place her hands?
When should she fast and when should she eat?
And what is the truth about fair and foul meat?
And when she sneezes, dear God, or Allah or whatever you are,
Should we say God Bless You, or Alhumdolillah?!
How's that?" Komli asked, quite pleased with herself. "Your turn to end it."

"What's Alhumdolillah?" Scott asked.

"Why do you say, God bless you, when you sneeze?"

"Something to do with the soul, but I'm not sure."

"Muslims give praise to Allah when they sneeze. I just wasn't sure what you and I should say when our little one sneezes. Do you have any more lines?"

"Let me think—

While I hold on tight to my parental reign
Should I go ahead and circumcise his brain?
No matter where he lives or schools
Please help me, God, to make good rules
And make sure my rules are never abused
So, unlike my wife, he's never confused!
Amen."

"How did you make up all that?" Komli asked shrieking with laughter.

"You inspire all kinds of crazy poems in me."

"Do you write them down?"

"Sometimes."

"Can I read them?"

"After we're married."

"Why?"

"You may change your mind about marrying me! Tell me, is your sister as cris crossed as you?"

"I don't know. Would you know what's going through the mind of a nun?"

"Sex, probably!"

"That's all you men think of!"

"You would, too, if you could see women through my eyes!"

"Thank God I don't. I'd hate to become a passionate lesbian!"

"Let's go inside. I know you'll behave in front of Mom and Dad!"

"What if your parents object? My sister might love you, but that does not mean she would necessarily be happy that I marry a white man."

"That doesn't sound like you . . . ."

"You didn't answer my question. How will your folks react to a mixed marriage," she asked, emphasizing the last two words.

"Not as well, perhaps, as they would to a beautiful white swan, but it's neither here nor there, is it?"

"You mean their permission's irrelevant? You wouldn't have to get approval from your Church?"

"I could if I wanted. As liberal as you might think we are here in America, I highly doubt that the Church will be thrilled that you are both non-baptized and Hindu! So what's going on in that little head of yours? Your brow has more furrows than college lined paper!"

"In America, marriage and divorce seem like a private matter between two people."

"Not always, but isn't that how it should be?"

"It makes sense. But in India we have to obtain permissions and receive blessings. Sometimes, women have to pay horrific dowries!"

"That's not such a bad idea you know. Would your sister pay me a handsome dowry to marry you?"

"Actually, I would be much more expensive to get rid of, since I only have one hand and am not a fair-skinned beauty!" Komli said, with her head cocked cheekily to one side.

"So does your sister have a couple of million? I'll take you exactly as you are." He stared at her lovingly before he added seriously, "I'll love and cherish you in sickness and in health."

"And if my sister has no money?"

"You'll be left on the shelf. A shelf in my bedroom though, so I can gaze at you while you collect dust. Dust wouldn't show on you, would it?"

"That's why I love you. You're so honest."

"Is that the only reason why you love me?"

"I shouldn't answer stupid questions, but I'm going to." She went up close to him, put her arm on his shoulder, looked straight up at him and said, "I love you because you make me laugh, and because you have a wonderful heart, and I think you would have no problems living like a Bedouin or a cave man. You wouldn't totally freak out if we ate with our hands and had no toilet paper."

"I could go down in the Guinness book of Records for being loved for the strangest reasons, but I think we should keep it a secret between us, sweet thing. Don't know what my family would think if they knew you and I are like two animals that care little for customs and tradition."

Komli became pensive suddenly. She felt tired and confused. Perhaps she was part animal, she thought. An animal that cared for little other than the fundamental needs of man. Had street life circumcised her need for culture and tradition? Did she herself scoff at others because grapes were sour?

"I was just kidding, sweet thing. I love you for reasons very similar. I think the only difference is that I also love you for knowing so little and making me feel like I know it all!"

"Why do you call me 'sweet thing'?"

"Does it bother you?"

"No. I'm just curious."

"I've been traveling around the world, running away from human beings. I wouldn't touch you with a barge pole if I thought you were human!"

"So I'm just a thing?!"

"I think you're Dumpty who relentlessly tempts Humpty to use water instead of toilet paper; to worship silence instead of Jesus, and who talks non-stop while dangling her apples!"

"And when do you propose to take a bite?" she asked laughing.

"Right now sounds like a good idea," Scott responded, undoing her shirt buttons.

"You know what Margaret warned me about when I was in Tripoli?"

"What, pray tell?"

"Guys like you. She said you were like dogs, always in heat!!"

"My, my, Margaret was more knowledgeable about men than I thought! She couldn't possibly have been as lonely as I imagined! Can I ask you for something impossible?" Scott asked putting on a real serious face.

"What?"

"Stop talking until I'm out of heat!"

"I thought we were going in to talk to your parents."

When Scott's parents heard what they knew was inevitable, his mother simply sai
"We love you both dearly, and we're delighted. Komli, I sensed your loneliness durin
our family gatherings at Thanksgiving and Christmas. Scott may feel the same way whe
he goes to India. You do realize you will have to do more giving and taking than Dad an
I had to do?"

"I'm not so sure about that!" Dad said, with a spark that suddenly decided to igni
itself.

"I never thought of it that way. I just know that I would be happy spending the re
of my life with Scott, Mom," Komli said simply, wondering if this was the beginning of th
end.

"Mom, I understand what you're saying" Scott said matter-of-factly. "Famil
gatherings happen just a few times a year. Komli and I will deal with them and, hopefull
enrich ourselves a little even though one of us may not feel completely at home." Sco
loved his mother dearly, and understood her concerns. He held her hands as he continue
"Here's something I've never told you, Mom. Pardon the pun, but I know you had grav
concerns for me when I went overseas to fight people of a foreign culture. I left behind
part of my soul there, with the enemies. We became soulmates in horror. If enemies ca
become soulmates, surely there's more hope for Komli and me. We love each other!"

"I just want you both to make sure you know what you're getting into. We love yo
both, and you certainly have our blessings."

"Thank you, Mom and Dad!" Komli responded with relief. "It's hard for me to dige
how easy you made it for us. In India, there would be permissions to seek and dowries t
pay."

"Our church can be pretty strict, too, but times are changing," Mom replied, withou
revealing which times she preferred.

"Komli and I are going to spend the rest of the day at the zoo. Don't count on us fo
dinner," Scott announced. He turned round to Komli and said, "How would you like t
make plans among the birds and the bees?"

"I would love that, Scott."

As they were getting dressed to leave, Scott asked Komli when she had last been t
a zoo.

"You know I'll never forget the man who gave me a ticket to go to the zoo in Calcutta
That was my first and only time." Using some euphemisms, she added with a smile, "W
hadn't started living like regular human beings then, so what I remember most vividly i
how deftly I got my hand between bars to snitch out carrots and peanuts from the cages

"I'm going to grab a cup of coffee. I'll meet you in the garage," Scott responded
happy to have an excuse to turn his back on Komli. Their child would never suffer hunge

angs, he swore, as he poured himself a cup of coffee with a hand that was not quite as teady as usual.

"The baggage I carry bothers you, Scott, doesn't it?" Komli asked astutely. "I'll try ot to go there again."

Scott squeezed her hand. "I can handle that. Just don't ever go quiet on me."

"I'll remember that! Are you scared of what Mom said about give and take?"

"No. When you truly love someone, and I'm just beginning to realize this, sweet hing, all the giving feels like taking and all the taking feels like giving."

"Feel like taking some of my morning sickness? Komli asked with a warm smile.

"I haven't even thought of that! Are you feeling sick?"

"No. But when I do feel nauseous, I'm happy. It tells me my baby's still in there omewhere. I can't wait for it to start kicking!"

"By the way, do you have your birth certificate with you, Komli?"

"That's a dumb question, Scott! I'm sorry I have to go back to my past, but do you eally expect street litter to have birth certificates?!

"Don't refer to yourself like that!" Scott said angrily. How the hell did you get to ingland and to Libya.?"

"Oh I have some kind of an affidavit that father Michael got for me years ago. Will hat do?"

"I hope so."

"So what happens if one doesn't have a birth certificate?" Komli asked

"We'll cross that hurdle when we have to."

"What hurdle?"

"I should have known I'd have to answer a barrage of questions! I'm not quite sure vhat papers we'll need for you to live here permanently as my wife. But to explain things nore clearly, let's start with our little one to come. In a manner of speaking, life doesn't egin when a baby is conceived. Life begins only after you obtain the birth certificate for he baby. If you don't have one, you may as well forget about your baby. It doesn't exist!"

"Really!" Komli retorted sarcastically, "You just dump it?"

"Children can't go to school if they don't have a birth certificate. And if you have a irth certificate and die, but don't get another piece of paper called a death certificate hen, guess what, you're not dead! You can't get buried, you can't get cremated, and you ontinue to get mail."

"What happens in between? That was a pretty big leap from one extreme to the other!"

"Here comes the zoo. What great timing! In between you go bunny hopping from age to cage . . . ."

"So do your animals in cages also have birth certificates?"

"I've never bothered to find out. But I bet the news-making pandas and new-born abies in the zoo do! You know what, we even have dolls that have birth certificates!"

"Get out of here, you're lying!"

"I am not. Ask my sister about Cabbage Patch dolls."

"Tell me more about the bunny hopping from cage to cage. That sounded like fun

"I'm glad you think that way! Where was I?"

"What happens between birth and death."

"One usually gets sick from time to time, right?"

"Right."

"If you're sick and you don't have a paper called an insurance policy, you may as well get yourself healed by positive thinking, 'cause most doctor's won't touch you, an I forgot to tell you, schools won't touch you if doctors don't touch you because you als have to have an inoculation certificate in order to go to school. And if you want to g places and don't have a paper called a driver's license, you may as well walk; you won be able to drive. You could use public transport, but as you've already learned, publ transport does not come to you, you have to go to it. And to go to it, you have to buy car and to be able to buy a car you have to have an insurance policy and money and t have money you have to go to work and to be able to work you have to have a soci security card, and you can't buy a house without most of the above. And I forgot t mention gold card, silver card, platinum card and you, my dear, will need a green car before you receive the honor of becoming naturalized . . . ."

"Now I know what they mean about people in love sounding like each other! You' already babbling, Scott! And if you expect me to get overwhelmed by that, let me tell yo that I probably dealt with as much or more paper work in college, and when I got ready t go to England. When does the bunny hopping from cage to cage happen?"

"As soon as you cut off the umbilical chord and put the baby in clothes."

"Ugh, Scott! You're depressing me! What's got into you suddenly? I thought w were happily going to discuss marriage plans."

"We will. But we men happen to be the practical kind. My mind is buzzing wit thoughts of all the mountains of paper work ahead of us. Don't worry; we'll deal with it.

"I don't think I'm the one who's worrying."

"I'm not either. I just want you to get my drift, so you're prepared. As soon as th baby gets out of the womb, it gets caged in a crib, and as soon as its up on its two feet starts bunny hopping.—caged in school, caged in church, caged in college, caged i professions which in turn are caged by conceited little capitalized BAs and MAs tha dictate how big or small a prison one can afford. We're caged on wheels and within wall and by numbers and alphabets on clocks and cards, countless cards! And the more card we acquire, the more cages we acquire—more and more and bigger and better cages."

"So what can one do in America without paper?"

"Have sex and live on the streets. But you can't have babies, remember, unless yo want them to live on the streets, too."

"What am I supposed to get from this drift? That you're scared of marriage and wha it entails?"

"No. You're my wife-to-be. I'm just thinking out loud."

"Will you feel better if I tell you I can't think of anyone better to be imprisoned with?!"

"Neither can I," Scott said with his usual warm smile. Hand in hand, they strolled inside the zoo.

"You know what," Komli said to Scott as she played let's-see-who-blinks-first with a well-groomed, black baboon, "It's hard to believe that I had to travel all the way from India to London to Tripoli to America to look into the face of a baboon to realize that in order to be really free, one has to be like him, without social, intellectual, or material baggage!"

"The one big difference between this baboon and us is that at least he knows he's caged. We don't!"

"What do you think is better, Scott, being caged and fed, or being free but starved?"

"Ooooh, I don't know."

"Look at him peering at us, Scott. What do you think he's thinking?"

"That if he had fore limbs, like man, he would never chain anyone behind bars. He would write songs and strum the guitar and paint and create . . . ."

"If I were to unchain myself and walk out of my clothes, I would be slapped behind another cage, wouldn't I?" Komli interjected.

"I'm afraid so! It's frightening to think what would happen to us if someone came along and set us free of our paper leashes. Our lives would come to a stand still. Would we be able to survive as the so-called illiterate and uncivilized survive?"

"Let's go eat lunch, Scott. Your brain's over-working, in the zoo of all places! Your mother was right, it's hard for men to handle two things at the same time."

"Such as?"

"Becoming husband and father."

Aatma,

Roshni's so excited for me, but deep, deep down in my heart I wish older sister would be married first, like it should be. Tusneem's also coming to the wedding. There again, I feel this sadness because I know she thinks my sister's not good enough for her father. It was written all over her face. Just the fact that she feels that way hurts! I don't think Scott's right about us going from prison to prison, but we do put people in compartments, don't we? My sister's good in compartment B, but not if she tries to move to compartment A. I think Tusneem was also shocked that I'm pregnant. Thank goodness for the telephone—I'm glad I didn't have to see her expression.

I should be thinking about my little one. I'm so excited! Do wisdom and good sense come with motherhood? I sure will need it! It's been almost two years since I left India, to broaden my horizon . . . I wish I could claim that I was returning home with a silver platter of truths. At least I tried. I hated the silence of the Brits, and then when I encountered it on the mountains and at the Grand Canyon, I thought almighty silence itself was truth. And then I met Brandon. His silence shattered that idea. At Christmas time I thought God was the giving tree itself, but Scott quickly dispelled that idea. I thought perhaps He was pure, white snow. That didn't last long either. Is God a simple nomad wandering around the world? But then, I've just returned from the zoo, why would God want to be drab old man when he could be spotted, or striped, or draped with glorious feathers? Why would He want to deal with color or caste or creed, when He could be in all flowers? When He could have wings or fins or whatever His heart desires? Or is that what it is? He has a heart, and we're made in his image because we have the heart to laugh and cry like no other creature does! I don't know. I don't know. I don't know is all I'm returning with, Aatma! Although this much I do understand now, thanks to the baboon—

> *I understand why the Garden of Eden was without brick homes—*
> *In the garden of Eden, there were no homeless.*
> *I understand why birds and bees don't read or write or calculate—*
> *Among them there are no paupers, priests or presidents.*
> *All of them soar.*
> *I understand why fish or fowl don't go to school—*
> *Ignorance is bliss is all they know they need to know.*
> *I understand why fruit comes without fins or feathers or feet—*
> *They were not meant to travel; they were meant to be fragrant*
> *and free for plucking.*
> *I understand why there were no pens or papers in Paradise—*
> *Pens and papers make prisons and Paradise lost.*
> *I understand, Oh I understand*
> *Why the earth quakes and the volcano erupts*
> *Why lightning strikes and the thunder bolts*
> *Why the river floods and the wind howls*
> *Why the trees sway and the grass quivers*
> *Because mighty man with his mighty brain*
> *Never did get the unwritten lessons*
> *Of freedom and ignorance and bliss*
> *that were taught in the Garden of Eden.*
> *I know I will have no time for senseless talk after the baby's born.*
> *I pray it will be healthy. That's all I want. I can't wait to see Roshni.*

"If you're not too busy, Mom, will you help me in the yard for a little while. You know how I hate weeding by myself!" Scott asked his mother one afternoon while Komli was with Brandon.

"Sure, honey. Maybe we can have sandwiches and coffee outside after we're done. 's such a beautiful day."

It was while they were having coffee and sandwiches that Scott decided to take the direct approach. "Come on, Mom, I want you to spill it out. I know you've given Komli and me your blessings to get married. What's bothering you? I don't have to be married to you to know you, Mom!" Scott said with a smile. Although war and travel had set some barriers between them, Scott knew they loved each other unconditionally. But she behaved sometimes as though she had lost both her husband and her son to alien wars and foreign cultures.

"All a mother wants for her children is for them to be happy. Sometimes, I wish that you had been to India first before you decided to marry Komli. And sometimes I wonder 'you'll ever come back again. You never really came back from war, son. Neither did your dad. I wonder what marriage to Komli will do to you. Don't get me wrong, I love Komli. We really warmed up to each other one night when I came out to find her writing to her sister while she was watching the snow fall."

"She enjoyed talking to you herself. She told me."

"She's very sweet and simple."

"She's not actually, Mom. She's as flaky as the snow and can be quite icy at times. All know is that I love her dearly."

"And I love you dearly. Just be careful, son. Even though we don't talk much, and you keep going overseas, it's so good to have you back. What if you die of a little mosquito bite or something in India?!"

Scott doubled up with laughter. "Komli's sister phoned her the other day and asked what if Komli dies of a little bullet in school?"

"Those things don't happen all the time!"

"If you have to go, you have to go, Mom. It's the first thing they told me in school, to make sure I didn't wet my pants. And it sure as hell was what Dad and I thought of in the trenches! I'm going to go Mom, but I promise I'm going to come back. Do you know, in some ways I've never really left home, Mom. I still hate chicken . . ."

"You used to beg Granddad to take you into his chicken pens to feed 'em."

"That's exactly why I developed such a hatred for the filthy, cackling creatures! And my favorite meal still is your ham and cabbage. Wait till you tell Komli you put nothing in it but salt and pepper and a ton of water!"

"Why?"

"She says some real nasty things about bland, old British cooking."

"You're making that up. I can't ever imagine her being nasty!"

"You just continue to think of her that way, Mom. Maybe she'll start living up to your expectations! And I still love gardening. So you see, Mom, you don't have that much to worry about. Although I've wandered far and wide I've returned intact—I still love wine, women, except that that's narrowed down to one, cigarettes, your ham and cabbage and gardening." Mother and son looked at each warmly and smiled while Scott continued, "You teach Komli to cook when we visit you over weekends. We'll try not to kill you with her spices when you visit us. Think about it this way, Mom: Komli's the only way yc have any hopes of getting grandchildren!"

"She's pregnant, isn't she son?"

"You never cease to amaze me, Mom! How did you know?"

"Let's just say a little snowflake landed on me while Komli ran in and out of th bathroom the other day."

"I take it that's going to stop after she's had the baby, Mom?" Scott asked.

"My worldly son!" she exclaimed, as tears of laughter rolled down her cheeks, "Onc you have babies, you never stop going in and out of bathrooms!"

"I'm so excited, Mom!"

"Are we done with the weeding?"

"I love you, Mom."

"And I love you and Komli."

"Want to go for a ride?"

"Where to?"

"You need to start knitting, Mom. Some clickety click on the rocking chair would b music to my ears!"

"I guess you'll never cease to amaze me either!"

"I told you I haven't changed, Mom. I'm still your old fashioned son!"

"I'm going in to give Dad the good news."

"Take it easy, Mom, otherwise he'll think it's you who's expecting!"

No, he hasn't changed after all, Mom thought as she went in to tell her husband tha they would be grandparents soon.

"When will you come back, Komli?" Brandon asked in dismay when he heard tha she was going away to India."

"I'll be gone for about eight weeks. You know your uncle Scott and I are gettin married. So I'll be back soon," Komli replied cheerfully, although she could sense tha Brandon was more than disappointed that she was leaving. "I'm going to miss you Brandon."

Brandon knew he would miss her, too, but he did not say so. "Will you come back i the afternoons when you return?"

"I would love to. I'm going to have a baby, Brandon. Perhaps we could arrange fo you to come round to us so you can help me." A younger child might have been thrille with the prospect, but Brandon didn't look very enthused. She had become both hi outdoor and indoor playmate. Just when he had started to enjoy life outside televisior she was leaving. The prospect of going back to watching television by himself suddenl seemed very distasteful.

Komli felt sorry for him because she understood herself how lonesome life could b without family. Thank goodness Scott wanted lots of children, she thought. The though of a small house with little ones scampering around thrilled her. She promised Brando e would be back as soon as she could. Just before leaving, she handed him a parting resent.

Brandon ripped the paper. It was a book entitled Mind Boggling Puzzles. "I think ou'll be good at it, Brandon. Let's see how many you can solve while I am gone."

"Thank you, Komli, I'll miss you."

Komli hugged him before they parted company.

"I'll weed the yard while you're gone. So when you come back it'll be your turn!" he houted as Komli waved goodbye.

ᏟᏃᏅ

CHAPTER 7

REINCARNATION

"What if you absolutely hate India? It's one thing seeing great, romanticized film like *Gandhi,* it's another thing to actually . . . ."

"I'm old enough to form my own opinions," Scott assured her with a smile.

The airport at Calcutta felt more oppressive, sticky, hot and humid to Komli than it di to Scott who was too preoccupied attuning his senses to the different smells, sights, an sounds.

Roshni was waiting impatiently outside customs. Rashid was also there, to keep he from turning into a nervous wreck, he confessed later. To welcome her sister and prospectiv brother-in-law, Roshni had two garlands of bright golden-yellow marigolds. But no garland could reflect the welcoming smile and tears of joy that burst loose when Roshni spotte her sister emerging out of customs. Scott wore his garland well. Komli's was sandwiche and crushed between the tight hugs and embraces from Roshni and Tusneem.

"What are you doing here?!" Komli screamed when she saw Tusneem.

"We decided to come early so we could spend some time with Pappa. So how ar you? We're all so excited for you!"

After calm was finally restored, two chauffeur-driven cars transported the families t Park Hotel located in the heart of Calcutta's shopping area.

"Get rested," Rashid had advised before departing, "you have a train journey ahea of you tomorrow evening. We all go to Patna."

"How come we're not staying with Tusneem?" Komli asked Roshni as soon as Scot went to take a shower."

"Rashid no longer has a house in Calcutta. He sold it. They're staying with thei relations. Rashid only has a small place in Patna now, where Scott will be staying as yo know."

"Has the priest given us a date for the wedding? I'm sorry we've had to rush things Scott needs to get back to get my immigration papers sorted out."

"I understand. You're getting married in a week from today, next Thursday, at nin minutes past seven, to be precise. That's the time the priest gave. How's the little on

292

oing?" Roshni asked, looking at her sister's stomach. She wasn't showing at all. That as a good thing. The last thing she wanted was a disapproving priest chanting the arital rites with a scowl on his face! That would not be a good omen, Roshni thought. As ard as she tried to think positively about the pregnancy, a little voice kept reminding her bout the doctor who had said all those years ago that Komli might not survive another regnancy.

"Good. I feel wonderful. You look worried, Roshni! Aren't you happy for me?"

"What a foolish thing to say, Komli! I guess I'm just not used to so many things appening so quickly. I can hardly believe you're back in India, leave aside getting arried. I don't even know where to begin asking you questions."

"You know everything there is to know. I haven't kept any secrets from you. What bout yourself? You look so calm and radiant. My heart tells me something is happening etween you and Rashid. You would be so good for one another. Is there, Roshni? A eny-tiny little spark somewhere?"

"There sure is a teeny-tiny little spark, Miss Nosy. I enjoy his visits and, thanks to ou, I can even discuss books with him sometimes. We're as good friends as you and usneem."

"You're not a very good liar, Roshni. There's more color on your face than I've ever een! I'll get to the bottom of it sooner or later. Tell me about Devi and her family. Nothing o hide there I'm sure.

When Scott came out of the shower, he realized the two sisters needed to be by hemselves. "I'm going to have a beer and then I'm going to take a walk." he announced.

"Scott, you cannot go for a walk on your own. The people on the streets will cling on o you like leeches because white is synonymous with wealth."

She hadn't used the word *beggars*, Scott noted. Is that what she did, he wondered.

"Do people carry guns here?" Scott asked.

"No!"

'Do policemen here pick up foreigners for spying or defiling its people?"

"We're not in Tripoli!" Komli exclaimed.

"No suppression of movement, no random violence. Whatever makes you think I'll e unsafe, Komli? Besides, I'm kinda disappointed we just have one day in Calcutta. I ave to make the most of it."

"It's not like we'll never come back again. We only have six days to get ourselves neasured and suited and booted for the wedding. You can't get out of it now, Scott!"

"Neither can you."

"Just don't go too far, Scott. If you get lost, grab a cab and ask him to bring you back o Park Hotel."

"Yes, Mother Hen, I won't stray, I promise," Scott replied with a reassuring smile.

Scott wasn't devoured alive, but he returned to the hotel faster than he had anticipated. _eave me alone, he wanted to scream at the beggars who thought nothing of clinging to is hands and tugging at his pockets in the hope that he would spare them some pennies.

Don't touch me, you filthy creatures, you're disgusting, he wanted to yell. He was gl;
Komli wasn't with him. Being repelled by the wretched beggars was more difficult
handle than he had imagined. Within an hour Scott was back at the hotel again, badly
need of another beer. Komli had left him a note saying she was out shopping.

After the ladies had shopped a little, Komli asked Tusneem if they could see t¶
house where she had grown up.

"It's sold, Komli. You can't go in," Tusneem replied.

"Let's just go see it from the outside."

"Why?!"

"I just feel like it," Komli said mysteriously, knowing that her friend had no clue th
it was right outside her house that she had spent the first few years of her life.

While Tusneem chatted nostalgically about her house, Komli stared at i
surroundings. Like the parting of the Red Sea, everything she had seen and done in th
last few years receded in her mind. She was transported back to where she had started li╞
The cracks and crevices on the concrete were still there, only some had become larger.
was the home of the hunters and gatherers, seeking a pittance from the hunters ar
gatherers of knowledge and wealth. Sure enough, another beggar had happily filled th
space. Komli stared at the woman. Dare she assume the role of the knowledgeable ar
wealthy and give alms, she asked herself. The little child inside her urged her on.

"How much money do you have, Roshni? I only have dollars on me."

"Five one-hundred rupee notes and some change," Roshni replied, knowing exact╞
what her sister was thinking.

"Can I have it? I'll return it later."

Komli folded the five notes again and again, until they looked like one small chit ¢
paper. She walked up to the ragged woman and said, "This is for you. Pray that Bhagvaa
will bless my baby."

"Oh, bless you Ma, bless you, bless you and your baby," the woman wailed as sh
tried to absorb the shock of what had just fallen from the hand of what could only be a
angel in disguise; no human being ever gave a beggar five hundred rupees.

"It's not good to encourage beggars. We'll never get rid of them if we continue t
indulge in them," Tusneem remarked casually.

Komli was unable to respond immediately. She was thinking; 'you fasted, Tusneem
but knew there would be a feast laid out for you at the end of the day, and perhaps i
heaven, too; that woman fasts and remains in hell, day in and day out.' When Kom
finally did respond, she said with quiet confidence, "A tramp in London taught me onc
that good memories make people do good things. Who knows what she will do fc
someone some day, now that she can believe in little miracles."

When Scott stepped inside Roshni's simple apartment in Patna, he understood fc
the first time why, unlike most women he had known, Komli rarely wanted to shop.

emed she had grown up with nothing but books, board games, and a deck of cards. He
nderstood better what Komli meant about Brandon having too many material things and
ot enough warmth. In the few days he saw the two sisters together, he realized what
nvaluable gifts they had given to each other—laughter and conversation and
ompanionship in a space no larger than his mother's kitchen. What an economical and
marvelous way to raise a child, he mused. And no wonder she was so enamored by the
arden; they had never had a garden. He understood why she was content to look, and
alk away without souvenirs. He made a mental note of the invisible writing on the stark,
white walls of this humble abode, and in the warm, sparkling, eyes of her beautiful sister,
ne *nun*.

"Do you ever wonder what life would have been like for Komli had she married
Mustapha?" Rashid asked his daughter one evening.

"That's a strange question to ask on the eve of her wedding to another man. So many
hings have happened since then. I can't say I've ever sat down to think about it seriously.
Why do you ask?"

"She's so different from you. I just wondered how she would have fitted into our
amily."

"Komli's the type who can fit anywhere, east, west, middle-east . . ."

"She's traveled a little, but I'm not so sure that she felt at home where she went,
judging from some of the things Roshni has shared with me."

"Does Roshni confide in you about Komli?" Tusneem asked, showing some surprise.

"Sometimes."

"Like what?"

"Sounds like she can be very opinionated at times. I believe she upset a few people
n Libya."

"Sounds like Komli, the opinionated part. She can be very blunt, I know, but I've
earned a lot from her."

"Such as?"

"Have the courage to be honest. To think for yourself. She makes me think about the
hings I do. Roshni seems much quieter. Is she as feisty as her sister?"

"No, not at all. She's very peaceful to be around."

"Do you see her often, now that you live in Patna?"

"I drop by from time to time," Rashid replied, trying to sound casual.

"You seem to have abandoned everything that was a part of our past. What will you
o if you fall in love with her, Pappa?"

"Rashid was so taken aback by the question, he looked like a child caught red-
anded by the principal herself.

"I'm sorry," Tusneem continued. "That's the kind of question Komli would ask,
matter-of-factly, like all things are possible. I don't know if it's her, or living in England,
hat prompted me to ask such a stupid question. No one could replace Mamma, I know."

"The two people with whom everything was meaningful are no longer in my life. I[t] a blessing for me that Komli is such a good friend of yours. Perhaps you will be able [to] understand that Roshni's quiet, non-judgmental ways satisfy some need in me. Does th[is] bother you?"

"It would have, a few years ago."

"Why not now?"

"When I was a child, I viewed you only as my father. You could do no wrong. In m[y] eyes, you can still do no wrong, Pappa. But marriage and living in England have change[d] some of my perceptions. I would be dumb and insensitive if they did not. I think I hav[e] only recently begun to truly understand the meaning of loneliness and the need f[or] companionship."

"A lot of parents take it for granted that their children are happy once they are marri[ed] and have children of their own. Are you happy, Tusneem?"

"I am . . ." Tusneem said with some hesitation.

"But?"

"I had it too good as a child, Pappa. I couldn't have asked for better anything– parents, family, schooling, traditions. Everything falls a little short as a result. I can nev[er] give little Farida the things you and our family gave me."

"Such as?"

"Sunday gatherings; birthday gatherings; Eid gatherings. Remember how after Ramad[an] all the children dressed up in new clothes and went from door to door getting Eidee (gif[ts] from all our aunts and uncles? I used to love comparing our Eidees. I could hardly wait [to] visit aunt Amena then. She used to have this miniature bottle of sherbet for each one of u[s.] I can hardly believe now that we had servants accompanying us and carrying our good[ie] bags for us! How can I ever create such treasured memories for Farida?"

"If you shower her with love, all things are possible," Rashid replied vaguely, althoug[h] in his heart of hearts he knew exactly why there was a void in her daughter's heart.

"She will never have a father like you, Pappa."

"Anything wrong with that?"

"I love Abbas, but he grew up in England, as you know. I wish he was a little les[s] mixed up. I've been to his office parties. He tries so hard to be like the British people wit[h] whom he spends eight hours every day. But he never will be. Sometimes on weekends, h[e] attends our community functions, but I know he's not all there either. I don't have th[e] heart to tell him that he's a watered down Bohra, swinging from east to west all the time[.] The good news is that little Farida is working wonders with him."

"You will, too. Be patient. Your mother and I didn't see eye to eye about many thing[s] but we loved each other more with each passing year."

"It bothers me that you sold our beautiful home; that you hardly see our family[.] People like Aunt Sakina are treasures."

"I thought you were always scared of her. And have you forgotten how you complaine[d] about all the family and community obligations we had?"

"I was scared of Aunt Sakina as a child, just like I was of Mullasahib. But now, I miss
ot having aunts and uncles and cousins around. I was so secure as a child. God forbid,
ıt if something were to happen to Abbas or me, Farida would have no loving aunts and
ıcles and cousins to go to in England. Just her grandparents. It's scary, Pappa. I took so
any treasures for granted. If I could have all of you around Farida, I would take that in a
eartbeat."

With elbows on table, and hands clasped under their chins, father and daughter
oked at each other lovingly and respectfully.

"Would you prefer to come and live here in India?" Rashid asked, wondering if his
aughter was less happy than he realized.

"Abbas wouldn't, and I love him too much to expect him to. Besides, he's Pakistani,
ɔ he can't live in India, even if he wants to, can he?"

"I'm afraid not. I wonder when Hindus and Muslims will at least begin to feel some
armth for one another?"

"Can't say you and I haven't taken great strides forward, can we?" Tusneem asked
ith a smile.

"Is that what you yearn for the most in England, our family ties?"

"Yes. Hundreds of little things we did together. Even things I dreaded, I now miss."

"Like?"

"Going to the mosque at five in the morning for Khudba and then breaking our fast
ith khujoor (dates) seems pretty special now."

"My! Have you changed! We used to turn hoarse trying to wake you up!"

"But I now understand, Pappa, how the ordeal of waking up and praying made the
hajoor so much sweeter."

"You'll make Farida a wonderful mother," Rashid said, eyes shining with pride.

"And I wish I could meet people outside our community, like Komli does."

"She's very special to you, isn't she?"

"Yes. That's why I understand why Roshni must be special, too."

"And you're more special to me than Roshni," Rashid said with a lump in his throat.
Thank you for being honest with me. That's one of the hardest things to do, I know."

"So is understanding others. It's amazing what children and distance do for
nderstanding."

"Let's go see if my grand-daughter is awake," Rashid said lovingly. He wished more
eople could see the world as his daughter did—from across the ocean, and sometimes
hrough the eyes of a starved beggar.

After a hectic two days of shopping and getting fitted, Rashid said to Scott, "Tomorrow
am going to visit a retired, faithful, old servant. Would you like to accompany me, Scott?
Jur villages can be very tranquil and picturesque, quite a contrast to our throbbing cities.
think you might enjoy it. Besides, I think it would be good for the groom and bride to be
eparated for a while!" Scott accepted the invitation enthusiastically.

It was while they were driving that Rashid prepared him for their visit. "Abdul, t servant we are visiting, is illiterate and very old-fashioned. If you were Hindu, I would n dare take you to visit him. For many like him, the partition of India has only served to f the flame of senseless prejudices between Muslims and Hindus."

"We're no different in America. Martin Luther King's dream has yet to become a tr reality."

The only car that ever stopped in Abdul's village was Rashid's. The cloud of dust unpaved roads had heralded Rashid's arrival long before Rashid could actually see h servant's thatched, mud hut. Abdul and his grandchildren were always there to greet hir This time, however, Abdul greeted him from his khat (bed) that had sat under the shade an old mango tree for as long as anyone could remember.

"My legs don't permit me to walk much any more, Sahib," Abdul said simply.

"I thought Zenub Memsahib introduced you to letter-writing. How come you haven informed me? Do you need to see a doctor?"

"It won't be long before I go to my Doctor, for good. I'll never be sick enough to g to city doctors and be tied up by tubes dangling from hospital beds, Sahib!" Abd replied without any signs of loss of spirit. He had visited Zenub Memsahib in hospit and had resolved right there that if his Allah ever willed that he should turn into vegetable, he would stay close to the earth, in his village, with his own family.

Rashid patted Abdul fondly on the shoulder as he introduced him to Scott. Abdu simply nodded his head and acknowledged the white man. Rashid could see that his dea servant's health had deteriorated considerably. His breathing sounded raspy and painfu Abdul had not only refused to see a doctor, but also no one in his family had insiste either. Everyone accepted that it was just a matter of time before the head of their househo would die. A plot of land had long been chosen for his burial. In the meantime, it wa Abdul's prerogative to sit outside and gaze at his land and indulge in whatever it was h wanted to indulge in. He had toiled for years in order to provide food and shelter for hi family. It was their time now to tend to his needs, whatever they may be. Therefore, just a if it were another season in nature, his wife catered lovingly to his every need, and hi grandchildren happily tended to his plot of land and to the goats and chicken that ra around freely. No one begrudged him the luxury to sit and stare; instinctively everyon seemed to know that it was his by right.

So Abdul had simply turned his head in the direction of the car when hi grandchildren came scurrying up to him with the news that his Sahib had come to visit He was calm and serene and at peace. Sahib must have heard that it was time for him t go, Abdul said to himself. He had, therefore, come to pay his last respects, even thoug he would not actually admit it. What was there to say? It wasn't as if death spared th privileged. The only difference was that the privileged fought it, the under-privilege accepted it.

"Scott has never seen an Indian village, Abdul. Do you think your grandchildren ca show him around while you and I chat?"

Since when have you allowed me the luxury of making decisions, Sahib?" Abdul asked cheekily. "I'm too old now for you to go making changes on me!" he added with feigned irritation. "All you have to do is tell me what you want. It has always been my privilege to serve you. Authoritatively, Abdul summoned his grandchildren and ordered them to take their honored guest around the village. "I don't ask my children when I want something. I just tell them! The way it's always been."

"And who is this giant of a white man?" Abdul asked as soon as Scott was out of sight.

"He's from America. He's staying with me for a few days."

Abdul nodded his head. His breath was short. He would not waste words on unnecessary questions about a passerby whom he knew he would never meet again. "How are you, Sahib? Is everything alright?"

"Yes. I can truly say that I feel as peaceful and content as you seem to be, Abdul."

"Then you must be happy now, Sahib."

"I am. Are you in pain, Abdul? Are you sure you won't see a doctor?"

"Do you see anything wrong with me?"

"No," Rashid said with a smile. "Is there anything you need?"

"No, Sahib. I just wanted to see you one more time. It seems Allah has granted my wish. You always know the right thing to do. I am glad you came. The rest of my family is with me. My father always used to say that the prayers of those who are about to depart are answered." Rashid was tempted to kneel before his servant and ask for his blessings. But he knew that would embarrass Abdul. So he sat by his side and joked instead.

"You're a strong man, Abdul. I wouldn't be surprised if you live to be a hundred!"

"I think I'll have a better view from up there," Abdul said, looking up to the sky. No one in my village saw man land on the moon, and I still think you're being fooled by some white lie, Sahib. And if man lands on Mars, as you keep telling me he might, I want to see it for myself, from up there!"

I'm sure you'll make a very entertaining companion for Allah, Rashid thought to himself as he looked lovingly at his servant.

"You might not enjoy watching us from up there, Abdul. It would be like watching a horror film."

"You keep telling me about the horrible things you read in the papers. But the reality of my life has been so different. I've seen a grand life in your household and I'm blessed with a big family in this village. You never know, Sahib, I might just enjoy a horror film. Films and stories are not for real, after all."

Abdul's wife came in just then with two cups of tea. The two made little conversation while they blew into the piping hot tea and sipped it from time to time. "Abdul, do you mind if I lie down here and take a nap before Scott returns?"

"Sahib, if you shock me with questions one more time, I'll die before my time! What happened to my Sahib who just did what he had to do? Is it that white man's influence?"

"Maybe!" Rashid said with a hearty laugh, "I'm going to take a nap, Abdul. Wake m
up when the white man returns," he declared like a master.

"We're taking a nap," Abdul shouted to his wife. "Wake us up when the white ma
returns." Rashid looked at his servant quizzically. He couldn't help but wonder if he w
really that much better off than Abdul staring happily at his pasture and his goats and h
grandchildren, and a devoted wife, while he bided his time until the forces of natu
silenced him.

Scott returned to find master and servant peacefully sleeping under the shade of t
mango tree. Their bodies were not cushioned on mattresses, but on khats made out o
coarse, jute rope that was tautly woven around flattened, wooden frames standing o
upright logs that served as wobbly legs.

"You cannot leave yet, Sahib," Abdul protested when Rashid got up to leave. "A
soon as my wife saw you, she cut up a chicken. You can leave as soon as it is cooked.

When the chicken was ready and it was time for them to bid each other farewel
Abdul placed his right hand on his master's head. "Something tells me you are ve
content. I hope whatever it is that brings you peace, you continue to have for the rest o
your life." Rashid's eyes welled up with tears as he bade farewell to his faithful servan

"Would it be alright to leave some money for his children?" Scott asked Rashid a
they were leaving.

"It would, but I suggest that you don't." As they climbed into the car, Rashi
continued, "Why taint their innocence with money? They give from their hearts, withou
expecting anything in return. If you give them money, they might start expecting more o
of visitors next time. Didn't you like them as they are?"

"Very much," Scott replied. And I like you very much, too, he thought to himself as h
studied Rashid's profile.

"Those that have less tend to give more freely. This is the beauty of our villages,
Rashid continued as they drove home with the pungent aroma of a heavily spiced chicke
curry. "When you were in Tripoli, did you go out into the Libyan Desert?"

"Many times."

"So you must have noticed the isolated shrub, or oasis, among the sand dunes?"

"Yes."

"I look at modern society as one huge desert, with few pockets here and there o
selfless people who give readily from the little they have because they are both free an
carefree. They are the treasures we must preserve, Scott. I don't want you to feel guilty
but have you any idea how valuable that chicken was for Abdul's family? They probabl
cannot afford to eat any meat, much less chicken, but a few times a year."

"Is chicken more expensive here than beef?"

"Absolutely."

"It seems that all people living on the fringes of what we call civilized society are wis
and untouched. It was the same way with the Bedouins in Tripoli, and with our nativ
Americans. For some reason we always succeed in weeding them out."

Rashid looked at Scott holding the pot of chicken over a gray-brown rag on his lap. hope you don't mind holding the pot. I know it would spill if we left it in the boot! I ways leave with some vegetables or fruit from them. I think they did something extra pecial because you were with me."

"It did feel strange, but wonderful, being treated like a Greek God!" Scott said with a nile. "Of course, I don't mind holding the pot. To be honest with you, if we had some read on us, I'd probably try it. It smells good, and I'm hungry!"

"Maybe we'll get some bread on the way. What did you think of the village?"

"It was extremely charming, although I think I would have enjoyed it more had I not pt gathering disciples! I'm sure I'll make the local news!"

"You already have! It's spread by word of mouth. By now, I'm sure every household ready knows that their village was invaded by an alien, white god! They'll thrive on the xcitement for months!"

"I'll thrive on it for a while myself. Thank you, Rashid." They drove on for a while efore Scott observed, "It seems that Abdul has reached that point in his life for which you id I fight all kinds of battles; he has his wife and family and his abode, he is surrounded by reen pastures, and he commands the respect of the villagers. Are you sure he's illiterate?"

"That's the word my teachers used for those who cannot read and write. How would ou describe him?"

"I'm not sure. Sage, without toys?"

"Toys?"

"It seems that we simply play with more toys, questionable or otherwise, before we each his stage of contentment. And we end up being confused and cantankerous along ie way because we have too much to deal with. Komli once told me that most American iings were like jewelry. Attractive, but not necessary."

"Sometimes the two sisters seem so alike, although at other times I could swear they veren't real sisters."

"Was Abdul ever confused or cantankerous?"

"Cantankerous, yes! Confused? No! How can you be confused if you listen implicitly your forefathers and to your masters and never read a book in between?"

"What did Abdul get cantankerous about?"

"Women's liberation, western influences, treating non-Muslims as humans."

"Ooh! I am guilty on two counts. How come I was treated so well? I have a wonderful melling curry here to prove it?!"

"Put that one down to senility!"

"So, do you believe that only Muslims go to heaven and the rest of us to hell?" Scott sked.

I know Abdul does. All the reading I've done has left me confused. What about you? Do you believe in heaven and hell?"

"Oh yes! I just keep losing track of their addresses. This much I do know; any time 've come close to heaven or hell, I've been firmly planted on my own two feet, not

whizzing around in cars and planes. That's what struck me again and again as I walke
around the village—everyone seemed rooted to earth, literally; no one wears shoes. B
the way, the women who carried water from the wells had beautiful figures."

"I don't know if you want to mention that to Komli!"

"These people never leave paradise. I wonder if they know that."

"You're not telling me you would be content living in such a village, are you"
Rashid asked.

"Probably not. I would thirst for the toys that I've gotten used to."

"You would. Going back to Komli on an ox-cart would take a few weeks! Do y￼
know, Scott, Abdul refuses to believe that man has landed on the moon. He insists that
not a part of Allah's divine plan!"

"And who's to say which passion is loftier in God's eyes, to look out for the earthwor
or to go to the moon!" Scott remarked, pleasantly surprising Rashid with his sensitivi
for the lowlier creatures of god. "Too bad I can't bring Komli back here. I know she wou
love the village."

"What makes you think you can't bring her back here?"

"She's Hindu."

"I think you'll find that most villagers who are so close to nature have little time f￼
the kind of hatred cities breed in people. Abdul's an exception, and of a different generatio
They treat their plot of land as God's land. People can come and go as they wish. Fortunate
or unfortunately, few people do because they prefer the cities."

The two looked out and enjoyed the tranquil scenery, although, like city-bred peopl
they were happy in the knowledge that their car was whizzing by at a pace all the better f
being quickly reunited with their loved ones.

Although Devi accepted that times were changing, she could not help but think ￼
her now loving Tara Ma. How would she react, she kept wondering, if she saw her and he
husband sitting stiffly at a round table at the most expensive restaurant in Patna, wi
Muslims for hosts. But there was no way she could decline Rashid's invitation. It was th
eve of Komli's wedding.

"Where are you two going for dinner today?" Tara asked astutely of her son an
daughter-in-law, "I've never seen you look so agitated before, Devi."

"Oh! My boss has invited us for dinner," Mohan lied, "I might be getting a promotion.

Both Mohan and Devi had decided that they would spare their mother-in-law th
shock of what was going on in their neighbors' lives. It was bad enough that the younge
one was marrying a foreigner, and that she was expecting a baby already; the older on
seemed to have a Muslim lover! Devi had told him that was not true, but the man i
Mohan found it hard to believe it was not so.

Both Devi and Mohan were dreading the evening.

"Mohan and I don't know how to eat with knives and forks," Devi had told Komli
hoping that they would be excused from going.

"Neither can I, but if I had two hands I sure would try!" Komli replied. "Besides, we're not taking no for an answer. Here's a promise, Devi; if you still feel uncomfortable after half an hour, you and Mohan can leave. Besides, if I see you flutter your beautiful, big, almond eyes at Scott, I might ask you to leave myself!"

Dinner turned out to be an extremely pleasant affair. Scott turned out to be far from a frightening alien. He seemed so human, and Rashid such a gentleman. If anything, Mohan and Devi were more confused by Abbas. They knew he had been brought up in England. But he seemed neither Indian nor foreigner. Unlike the others, he looked a little bored and seemed to drift off from time to time.

Between the one million questions a genuinely interested Scott had for them, and the warmth and concern both Roshni and Komli had displayed, the evening had actually ended a little too quickly for Devi and Mohan. When Devi returned home that evening, she wondered why her mother-in-law had so many nasty things to say about the modern world. If these were the kind of non-Hindus that lived in this fourth, doomed, Kali yuga, the world couldn't be such a bad place after all, Devi thought.

She tossed and turned in bed that night. There was so much to reflect upon. She looked forward to the wedding the next day. Although she understood why there would be only a handful of people at the ceremony, she knew it would be strange, having no family from the groom's side, and only Roshni from Komli's side. What mattered was that something wonderful was about to happen to her unusual, but wonderful neighbors whom she had grown to love like they were her own family. She had never seen them look so happy before. As far as Devi was concerned, a woman lived for the day she got married.

Devi remembered how on the eve of her wedding she had sat demurely in her bedroom, with a paste of haldi (Turmeric) plastered on her face and hands and legs. It was supposed to be good for the skin, she had been told. She had been too nervous to speak to anyone. Her mind had jostled with the countless pieces of the yet-to-be-seen jigsaw puzzle that was to become her husband in the next twenty-four hours. She had not even seen his face. Would he be handsome? Would he be pockmarked? Would he have an aquiline nose? She did not like aquiline noses. Would he be kind? Would he be a monster? Would he be gentle on their first night? Would he simply take her and rape her? Would he . . . . would he . . . . would he . . . She had lucked out. Mohan had turned out to be a good husband. The loan her father had taken to pay her dowry had been worth it.

Her mind wandered lovingly to Komli. She and Tusneem had kept them entertained during much of the evening. Neither Mohan nor she had felt out of place for a moment. If anything, everyone had treated them like guests of honor, and as for the gentle, white giant, he had seemed so intrigued and interested in them.

She had found the conversation about numbers quite interesting. She would have to ask her mother-in-law if she could throw any more light on it. It had all started with Tusneem asking Komli if she knew that mothers carried babies in their womb for 40 weeks.

"I thought it was nine months. Does it translate to 40 weeks?"

"Yes. I just find it very interesting that the number is forty."

"Why?" Rashid had asked.

"Because forty is such a recurring number in our lives, Pappa. After Farida was bor
I had to sit in bed for forty days, and we mourned Mamma's death for 40 days."

"And your mother asked you to shave your pubic hair every 40 days, didn't she
Komli had whispered to Tusneem. But Devi had heard. She had hoped Mohan hadn
That would have embarrassed him.

"Didn't Moses wander in the desert for 40 years, Scott?" Tusneem had asked.

"So I believe. So did Noah, in the ark."

"They floated for 40 years?!"

"No. Forty days."

"And you know what, Tusneem, Father Michael said Moses and his people a
Manna for forty days!" Komli had added.

"I'm sure there are other things, too, Pappa. Can you think of anything else?"

"I think prophet Mohammed was 40 when angel Gabriel first appeared to him, an
zakat, our religious tax, is 2½ percent or one fortieth."

"Did Jesus die at 40 by any chance?" Komli asked.

"I don't think so, but we observe Lent for forty days," Scott had said. Devi had like
the way he kept twirling his moustache.

"Devi, is the number forty auspicious in any way for Hindus?"

"I can't think of anything. I'll have to ask my mother-in-law."

"I'm not sure where all this is leading, but if it helps you, Tusneem, some crimes
Saudi Arabia are punishable with 40 lashes," Rashid had added with a laugh.

"The Egyptian rites for embalming took 40 days."

"And life begins at forty for men . . . ."

"And goes downhill at forty for others!"

"I've always liked food for thought, once my belly is full, Tusneem. What are yc
trying to get at?" Komli had asked with a smile.

"Nothing. I'm just fascinated that 40 is such an auspicious number."

"So is three," Komli said suddenly. "Our holy trinity is Brahma, Vishnu and Shiv
and Scott's is Father, Son and the Holy Ghost. Come on Devi, help me. What did Tar
Bahen teach you?"

"I can't think of anything," Devi had said shyly

"Tell us about Shiva's trident. What's that for?"

"Oh, that depicts Satyam, Shivam, and Sundaram. They are the three great aims c
Hindu thought—truth, auspiciousness, and beauty. It is also supposed to remind us c
the three qualities in man, purity, passion and inertia."

"And tomorrow you will go around the fire three times," Roshni had added with
sparkle in her eyes. She could hardly wait for the moment. "Mohan, why don't you te
Scott and Komli what to expect at their wedding. You and Devi are the only one's wh
know something about a Hindu wedding ceremony."

"As you have already mentioned, Agni, the God of fire, has to be present at the edding. It represents power and light. On one side of the fire, there will be a container of ater, for purification. On the other side, there will be a stone. You had to mount it, Devi, dn't you?" her husband had asked of her. "What was that for?"

"The stone symbolizes the strength of the bond of marriage. After that, we took the ven steps without which a wedding cannot be completed. The seven steps are for food, rength, fidelity, comfort . . . . help me," she had asked demurely of her husband, "what e the other three for?"

"Welfare of cattle, which we no longer have, so she's forgotten of course. The sixth ep is for the welfare of the couple's life together and the last one is for fulfilling religious ties. After that, the priest will ask you to pray to Agni. Then you have to sip the water wash away impurities and start a clean life." Devi had been proud of her husband. He ad not forgotten the significance of the sacred rites.

At that point there had been a lull in the conversation. Komli had beckoned one of e waiters. As requested, he had returned with a sheet of paper and some pencils. Komli ad ripped the paper into eight slips and handed them to the four couples. "Will you do mething for me, please," she had asked. "On this chit of paper will you write down in ne word from whom or from what you have learned the most."

"One word?" Tusneem had asked in disbelief. "I'd like to see you go first, Komli!"

"Okay," Komli had responded. "But I'm not going to show you what I write. After e're all done, we'll jumble them up and see if we can guess who's written what." eeing the puzzled look on everyone's faces, Komli had added, "It's not a test, you now. You can write anything you want! Grass, for all I care. Just one word. How hard an that be?"

Komli had thought for maybe five seconds before she had written down her word, olded her chit of paper and tossed it to the middle of the table.

The eight words had been—

Travel
Love
Komli
Roshni
Trenches
Streets
Marriage
Children

Rashid had asked Komli the purpose of the exercise, which had turned out to be ery entertaining, judging from the laughter and arguments that had resulted from rying to guess who had written which word. Most of them had seemed nterchangeable.

"Two years ago, this dear sister of mine booted me out of India," Komli began, as s
nodded her head in Roshni's direction, "so I could find out something about foreign wa
and real truths. Like those lottery machines on television, my mind kept bouncing c
answers that were always replaced in time by other answers. When we started delvii
into the hidden meaning in numbers, I suddenly wondered what it is that we truly lea
from. What it is that I must teach my little one to come, bearing in mind that we all seem
play with fire and water and words and numbers." Komli had paused for breath. No o
had said anything, so she had continued, "I find it very curious that no one mentione
religion, or book, or school or teacher."

"So have you come up with a final truth, Komli? What will you teach your child? W
you allow her no books?" Rashid had been quick to ask.

"Of course I will. Books are for education, for getting jobs. Our prophets nev
wandered around with books and briefcases and 9 to 5 jobs, did they?"

"I think not," Rashid had said, staring at her intently. "Maybe there is no truth. On
understanding."

"I think the real truth is out there somewhere in the wilderness. It never change
Only our babble does. And with it, so do we. Most of my precious lessons in life can
from little people. Big people actually, only we view them as little because they are not ri
or book learned. And sometimes they are book-learned, but do not appear to be."

"So what will you teach your child, if anything?" Tusneem had asked in jest.

"To love and look and listen and discover her own truth, if that's okay with Scott
Komli had replied without hesitation.

"I take it then that from time to time you're actually going to practice silence?" Sco
had asked as bride-and-groom-to-be had exchanged warm smiles. Devi's heart had misse
a beat. They had looked so much in love with one another.

As Roshni gazed lovingly at the radiant bride, she thanked Bhagvaan for allowin
her dream to materialize before her very eyes: the shimmering pallau of Komli's red an
gold sari was tied to Scott's silken, white kurta. Scott looked strange. He was wearing
white izaar and knee-length kurta over which he had a short, shimmering brocade ve
that ended at his waist. On his head he had a gold turban with a white feather in the cente
Normally, the white feather would have a gold brooch under it, studded with preciou
stones. But Komli had insisted that neither Scott nor she were interested in conformin
for the sake of conforming. If they had no jewelry, they had no jewelry; it was alrigh
Komli would have had no jewelry either, if it weren't for the fact that Tusneem had insiste
she wear the gold and diamond earrings she had purchased for her. She had made sur
they were clip-on ear-rings, knowing that Komli did not have pierced ears. The bride an
groom looked perfect for each other, as they circled around the fire. Komli walked demurel
behind her chosen life-partner, in bondage as it were, as was deemed appropriate. He
head was bent down, and her face almost completely hidden by the sari that hung we
below her forehead.

Scott took careful, small steps, to make sure nothing would undo the knot that had at
st been tied. Slowly, they walked around the fire three times, bodily apart, but united in
irit; ecstatic in the knowledge that they were united not just by the knot in their clothes,
d by the marital rites being chanted by the priest, but also by the precious secret secure
her womb. She wondered how many brides were pregnant when they were getting
arried. There was something very special about taking her child as well around the fire.
ire seemed to be perfect preparation for the future—marriage and children have to be
ucibles for heating souls at high temperatures, she decided. The priest recited the
cient marital rites in Sanskrit. Neither groom nor bride understood the passages. Neither
d they know the exact reason for going three times around the fire. What was important
as the sentiments it generated.

Komli thought all marriage ceremonies were beautiful, especially for the emotions
ey aroused. However, going around fire itself seemed so much more significant and
mbolic. According to one story at least, earth itself had evolved from a ball of fire. So
ad their child. Yes, both husband and wife were mesmerized by the wild dance being
erformed by God Agni himself, and by the mystical chanting of the priests. Like blood
rculating in one's veins, their thoughts criss-crossed feverishly, carrying similar prayers
nd passions, throbbing and pulsating through the heart :

Hai Bhagvaan, let me be good to my husband;
Let me be consumed in her flames, be they love, anger, or confusion;
Agni, melt us into one;
Let us kindle and crackle forever;
Grant us understanding;
Let me be a good father;
Let me be a good mother
I love her
I love him
Bless her
Bless him
Thank you
Thank you
Bless us with a large family
Lots of love and laughter
Grant us long-lasting ties
Shield us from bumps and bruises
Let us send down deep roots
We must see and seek
Grant us love, learning and laughter;
No more rolling; we must lay down roots;
With our head and heart

With humor and humility.
Fate is deaf and dumb and blind, who knows where it will take us
I love her
I love him

And on and on and on and again and again they prayed and dreamed the univers
dreams of couples about to be pronounced man and wife.

After they had taken the seven steps and sipped the water, the priest pointed to tl
sky and asked Scott to look at the Pole Star. "You must be as unmoving and constant
your love as that star," he had said solemnly. And to Komli he had pointed to tl
constellation of the Great Bear. "They are the seven sages of Indian astronomy; they a
always seen together in the skies, as you will always be seen from now on, together
marriage.

Within a few months of going around the wild flames that had ignited his marriag
Scott found himself staring in disbelief at the same wild flames that now engulfed Komli
body. She had not survived child birth. How blind and heartless was this mighty God
fire, he thought. Did He not know that the dance He was performing on Komli's funer
pyre of sandalwood and oil, was the very same dance He had performed during the
wedding? Did the fiery bed of wood have any idea how much the woman it cradled ha
revered all trees? The chants of the mourners fanned Agni's flames. The more they crie
the better He danced it seemed. The mighty God looked like a Bharat Natyam dancer—H
lower body swayed gracefully while every once in a while His hands darted out in shar
jagged movements; flames that had not so long ago leapt and soared; that had seeme
wild and erotic and joyous as they had celebrated their union, now looked like swor
swishing and jostling, deliriously devouring the wife he had known but for a few second
in eternity.

"Fire and water are assigned the task of changing matter from one state to another
Komli had stated just before she had died. "After I am cremated, take my ashes to our hol
river Ganga, so I can go back from one state to another. We're made from the fire betwee
man and woman, and cushioned and cradled in a bed of water, until we're ready to face tl
larger womb that Him-up-there prepares using a recipe that has never been written down–
some dust, some fire, some water and some wind."

While Komli was being consumed by Agni, and Scott by the tears that gushed dow
his cheeks in silent profusion, Scott reflected on her last days. She had been a fighter fro
beginning to end. And in the end, it was he who had succumbed to her wishes.

"Baptize our little one in the Holy Ganga," she had requested simply.

"Forgive me, Komli, but the water of the Ganges is supposed to be the most pollute
water in the world. How can our little one survive those germs?" he had asked.

"Same way as we survive germs everywhere, by becoming immune and desensitize
If children like Brandon can survive day-care centers and loneliness as well as he did, ou

ild will survive the Ganga," Komli had said with a certainty granted perhaps to souls ady for take off. "The Ganga can never pollute her body as much as man will pollute her ain. And man also pollutes the water with his sins and his spills. Don't be scared of the ttle germs, Scott. Water is a purifier," she had added, fighting to the last.

Komli herself had never been baptized, never performed ablution before praying, and r the first few years of her life she had bathed only when the heavens sent her water in e form of rain. Was that the reason why she had such a deep-seated reverence for water, cott had wondered as he had squeezed her hand and promised that he would baptize eir little one in the Ganges.

For a long, long while, Scott simply stood at the banks of the river Ganges with aughter and urn in his arms. He was mesmerized by the pathetic mass of humanity verently trying to cleanse itself, oblivious of the germs around them. When he saw them nerge, spiritually transformed and momentarily tranquil, he felt a twinge of empathy for llowman. Man was not that bad after all; trying so hard to cleanse himself. He stared at e masses. Would they get out of the water, run around being human, and then come ack again to get cleansed? They did that in churches, too, he thought kindly. Go to the onfession box, drop off sins, go back out, sin some more, and then come back in again. good cyclic exercise to prevent oneself from meandering too far away from the narrow ath. As the waters of the Ganges rippled in little and large circles, many a circle whirled rough his mind: 28 days and the moon would be where it started; 365 days and the earth ould be where it started; a few million seconds and man was back where he started, from ust to dust, or ashes to ashes, or whatever name man chose for the speck. Yes, Komli had een right; she had been his oh-so-short-lived, iridescent bubble, now turned to ashes. low would he live without her, he wondered. The burden of the infant in his arms seemed nbearably heavy.

Quickly, he immersed himself in the water, hoping that some of the pain would drown. le stayed down there for as long as he could. Fearlessly, he let his tears mingle with the erms in the water. He realized this was not half as bad as the fungus and lice that had fested his body while he had inflicted wounds on others, in the name of patriotism and reedom. The agnostic in him that had often wondered if there was such a thing as God nd reincarnation, realized suddenly that the materials for reincarnation were all in this vater; the great life force that baptizes and purifies and purges and quenches and egurgitates recycled flesh and blood and fire and ice and sins and sorrow and urine and aliva and hope and prayers for yet another ripple called life.

Scott had saved some of Komli's ashes to take with him to America. Suddenly, Komli's simple words came back to him: that all of earth and all its creatures were connected; at there were only three states of matter, constantly undergoing change. He delved into is pocket, opened the little box and scattered the rest of her ashes in the wind. He was onvinced that the reincarnated remnants of his love would drift to him somehow, some ay—maybe they would nurture a rose that he would hand to his daughter; maybe they

would drift to the ocean in which they would swim, or waft in the air that they mu
breathe, who knows, who knows . . . . Scott had a bottle in his pocket. In it he had slipp
a hand-written note of his favorite lines from the poet, W. B. Yeats. It said, *We must fi*
some place upon the Tree of Life high enough for the passion that is exaltation and j
the wings that are always on fire. He threw the bottle into the water, along with Koml
ashes. Maybe his daughter would find the bottle some day.

Strangely enough, he felt a little lighter. He had let go of the ashes and, with it, son
of his pain. He would devote himself to his daughter, he resolved. He would try and sho
her the world through Komli's eyes; expose her to as many iridescent bubbles as I
could. The first ripples of his life had been happy ripples. At mid-point, through one of h
cycles, he had evolved into a cynic. He had now become a father who felt a humb
oneness with his child and the elements. One had purified, and one had purged.

Yes, she would peel potatoes and climb trees and skin her knees. No, she would n
have all her meals at Mickey Ds!

Just before they parted company, Roshni handed Scott a letter. She said simply,
found this tucked inside Komli's pillow slip." The letter said :

> *My dearest Scott,*
>
> *I love you so much. And I miss you even more. Roshni tells me you*
> *will be here soon. I told her not to get you too worried, but I guess you*
> *are. Waiting for you now is the toughest thing I've done in my life.*
> *Feels strange, saying 'in my life'. Judging from all the whispering*
> *that goes on between doctor and Roshni, I'm not sure how much more*
> *time life will grant me. Believe me, I will fight to the very last to see you*
> *and, if I get lucky, to spend some years with you and our baby. Can we*
> *name our baby Joy? Tusneem once said that children live up to the*
> *names that we give them. Joy can be a girl's or a boy's name. I think*
> *we're going to have a girl.*
>
> *I'm trying to think positive. I will survive. I don't want to go*
> *quiet on you. But just in case divine order has a different mind set, I*
> *want you to know that all I know is that I love you and that you made*
> *me the happiest girl in the world. I have all the time in the world to*
> *stare at these white walls and think and think and think and all I*
> *can think of is that I love you and I want to live, and that I'm not*
> *ready to abandon either you or the little one inside me. I feel so*
> *angry with Him up there. That saying must be true, once a beggar,*
> *always a beggar. I'm begging Him for life. He better not short change*
> *me! Our little one just kicked me, like I'm not supposed to get angry*
> *or ungrateful!*

Roshni spends almost all day with me. As much as I love it, I am glad to be alone so I can think of you. And write to you. Don't ever stop smiling, Scott. You have such a beautiful smile. Did you know your eyes always crinkle up and smile when you smile? Always. And your soft green eyes, they are like the soft green leaves of trees that sway gently with the breeze. You always smiled, even when I huffed and puffed and blew houses down! I can see you smiling right now! I miss you so much. All the huffing and puffing was of no use. Like the wind, must I dissipate and disappear? Will I be allowed to reappear?

All my huffing and puffing with Roshni was of no use either. It's so obvious how much she and Rashid love one another. A platonic relationship is all she wants from him. Or so she says. I don't believe her! I asked her one day if they had ever made love. She almost screamed at me, but not quite. 'Nuns don't do it,' she said, 'and I don't either. I don't need a lover. I can't tell you how wonderful it is to have a father, a brother, an uncle, a friend, all rolled into one. Try to understand me, she pleaded. Sex does not make the world go around, not for me,' she said with such finality, that I don't bug her any more about Rashid. Although deep down inside I know they're missing out on something beautiful. To each his own, I guess.

Hi, I'm back again. Must have dozed off. Don't even know what day it is. Roshni tells me you're arriving on Friday. I can't wait. But I will. I must. The doctor says the baby may arrive before you're here. But I'm going to try and hold on. I want you to be here. I want us to experience the miracle of birth together.

Scott, remember the funny prayer you and I made up about how we'll raise our baby? I don't mind if you raise her Hindu, Muslim, Christian, Jew or Jain. They're all the same. The words are different. I hope you will forgive me if it turns out that I was not tough enough to live through child-birth, even though you and I were once in the toughest profession of all—soldier and beggar. I think they are the only people who don't live in society's myriad cages. I know that the last thing you will want is for our child to live amongst soldiers or beggars. So you'll have to cage her in customs and tradition, so she can belong, so she does not become a wanderer. The day you give her a birth certificate is the day you will circumcise her, for that is the day when you will impose the Gregorian calendar on her, or the Hegira or the Chinese. Whatever. We cannot dream of using nature's calendar. It is without numbers or alphabets. Poor illiterate nature! No, I mean abounding illiterate nature. The day our baby opens a book, she will be circumcised again. Circumcision of the mind is a small price to pay in order to prevent her from growing wild. Man has little patience for weeds. You have no choice but to clip her and prune her. But I am at peace because I know she will be in the hands of the best gardener in the world. Sunshine and water have already been taken care of. So all you have to worry about is the fertilizer—sprinkle her with lots of love 'n laughter.

Make sure she has a passion, even if it's just for socks! She must have passion and compassion—both stem from the heart.

And like a blossom, let her stand and stop and stare into the majestic beauty of silence. But don't let her stop and stare at screens and push buttons all day.

Tell Mom to teach Joy how to make bread. I loved watching Mom screw up her face and exclaim, shit, when her bread did not rise. Cold, expressionless bread machines cannot do that. Bake bread with our little Joy. And tell Mom to tell Joy stories, so she can cuddle up to her and go to sleep on her lap. Televisions can't smile back or stroke children's hair. I can still feel Ma stroking my hair to ease my hunger pangs. I didn't know then, but it helped a lot. Speaking of hunger pangs, make sure she has some; they're good for the body and the soul.

Make sure Joy uses both her hands. Not because I had only one, but because as I lie here in bed thinking of your beautiful country, I'm convinced that children who grow up kneading bread and planting tomatoes, painting and playing an instrument, praying and walking hand in hand with their families will never defile those precious hands by pulling a trigger. I'm not so sure about the un-held hands that go through life feeling and touching nothing but cold keys, so many cold keys.

How is my dearest Brandon? Tell him I love him dearly. We were birds of a feather. I wonder which starvation is worse during childhood—of the stomach, or of the soul? Please look after him, Scott. He needs uncles like you, not e-mails and internets. He's over-nourished with junk, but starved otherwise. Please try to take out the demons in his mind; otherwise, they may turn into bullets and go boom, boom, boom for no rhyme or reason.

Let our little one know that there is as much freedom in the tree's rootedness as there is in man's wanderings. Let her learn and experience any and everything she wants to, so she can be lush and healthy and bare her beautiful branches to anyone who cares to seek shelter. Let her also be everything else in nature—a cloud, a breeze, a blossom, the wind, the storm, the bubbling brook and the mighty wave, crashing and frothing and lashing, if she has to. There is nothing in nature that is not in man and nothing in man that is not in nature, for what is the wind but our very desires buffeting around? What is fire but our very passions kindled and rekindled? And what is water but our tears and sweat disappearing and reappearing? And what is the earth but our very being—a weathered crucible for the wind, the fire, and the water? If there is something that man has that nature does not, it's that big fat EGO that ends with a big bubble of an O! The ego that leads us to believe that the world was specially created for us! The ego that drives cows crazy because we think we can turn herbivores into carnivores! Make sure there is a fire raging in her heart, not just cold ashes that are the leftovers of a body and mind fatigued by too much learning and too much working. I once heard an American say on television that we were intellectually arrogant. Do you agree, Scott?

Do you know when I began to truly appreciate the vibrant colors of nature? When I saw you turning the dark brown soil in your garden. I realized then how truly fantastic is the turning of nature's colors— from rich earthy brown to countless greens to the myriad colors of Holi to snow white, cushioned always by blue seas and blue skies. Always. I had no choice but to live on asphalt when I was young. Strangely enough, we choose asphalt even when we do have a choice. Please, don't let our little one be blinded by asphalt. Please don't allow her to become a slave to sheet-rock walls and hunks of metal.

I once heard that tigers come out of jungles to eat man when man has hunted down all the animals the tiger relies on for food because that is when the balance in nature is broken. We'll be doing the same thing, Scott, if we abandon our child in the daycare jungle without parental nourishment. Something might snap and break the inner balance in our little one. Who knows what such a child will prey upon to satisfy her hunger pangs. Take Tusneem and me, for instance. I know she will never pull a trigger in her life. She is too well balanced— she was well nurtured and always worked with her head and heart and hands. Me? Who can tell! You know better than anyone else how unstable I was, and am even now—I am not even allowed to stand up, lest I fall!

Roshni was with me for a few hours. She looks very worried. It's a good thing there's no mirror here. Had some terrible cramps last night. I think baby and I can hang on another day. We must. We will. Roshni said you'll be here tomorrow.

Hi Scott,

In a matter of hours you'll be here. I am so full of energy today. With one sharp kick the little one inside me has at long last solved the greatest puzzle for me: God comes to us in the form of children! Don't laugh, Scott. Listen. Over the centuries, man has worshipped the sun, the moon, the wind, and water, the tree, fire, who knows what else. But as soon as he understood it to be a mere work of science, he dropped them as objects of worship. We just don't worship what we master, do we? And since man has always been the master of children, since he has always manipulated children it has never occurred to him to worship the child. No wonder adults listen less and less to God; when have we ever listened to children?! And yet, we hear again and again that we must be like children to enter the kingdom of heaven!

Oh, I can think of so many, many ways in which God and children are alike. If you ask me, life for the Child-up-there is one big Halloween, so He can parade in countless colors and costumes and trick and treat us all our lives! Hide and seek has got to be His favorite pass-time. And think of all the other things, Scott, that children love that God does, too—children love to play in water and sand, and I don't need to go into that again, I know.

Do children have any sense of justice? And economics? Does God?

Do children love blowing bubbles? You and I know without a doubt that god loves blowing bubbles; not just in the ocean and in the skies, but also in the water that turned to bubbling wine! I can just see Him with a gigantic straw in His mouth. And is there a child that doesn't enjoy a straw?

Children have a wonderful imagination and they love to color. And if God didn't, how the hell did we get sunsets and sunrises and rainbows and rainforests and elephants and earthworms, and leopards . . . you can come up with some yourself.

Let's see, don't all children love the gory and the horrific? If God didn't, we wouldn't have famines and floods and burning lava erupting from volcanoes.

Is God logical minded? Are children?

I know at least one God that suffered for the sins of mankind. Maybe that's why so many children suffer as well. They're just paving the way for their parents! And when they turn into adults and start sinning, they'll have children themselves to save them, too. Thank god for divine order! No wonder large families with lots of children are blessed and wholesome and hearty. Sharing the cross must make the burden lighter.

God loves us no matter what we do. Don't little children love us blindly, too, no matter what we put them through?

Don't children bring adults together? Doesn't God?

And does a baby come into the world with language? Has god ever written a single word?

And can a child force us to do anything? Does God?

Does a child need ink to think? Does God?

Make sure Joy understands that she does not need ink to think. I like that!

I know you will view this letter as ungodly babble, but I also know you will be smiling. That smile always killed me, Scott. Wish you were here. At least, I hunted for the truth. And the little that I gathered is oh so precious—you and Roshni and Tusneem and Devi and the little one inside. You were my treasures, my truths.

I was born Hindu; I almost converted to Islam. I got married to a Christian and would have happily followed him to church, but, alas, somewhere along the line of duty he turned into an agnostic. The agnostic who is the most giving and the least bigoted. I might leave all of you and turn to ashes wafting in the water, blowing in the wind, but even if your five senses tell you I'm gone, look for me, Scott. Remember, it's all a game of hide and seek. It's all about change. Change is the only constant. No, it's not. I will always love you. I shall wait for the minutes to tick away before you return, before I deliver our child. I love you.

Komli's energy had been converted to Joy. Scott had been there to witness the miracle of birth. He had never let go of her hand for a single moment. His respect for the inner strength of women had quadrupled. Komli had been so delirious that the baby was perfect, although several weeks premature. She had counted her fingers and her toes. She had two eyes, two hands, two nostrils, two, lips, two ears, two feet, and a little heart that was ticking away. What more could she have asked for?

The baby was so small that she had fitted in the palm of Scott's hand. He swore he would never take Joy for granted. Joy had come after so much hard labor and with so much sacrifice. His heart had pounded with grief when Komli had breathed her last. "I'm so happy, Scott, because I know you'll take good care of her," she had said, clutching on to his hand.

"I will. I promise," he had managed.

"In your country, you can give a child so much."

"I know."

"I know no one will butcher her."

"No one will. I promise you," Scott had said, unable to control his tears any longer.

"I love you, Scott."

"I love you, Komli." She had looked so peaceful, as though she was happy that sh had at long last been able to consummate her capricious affair with silence.

He would take Joy back to his family. He would try and give her everything Komli ha assumed he could give her.

He had been glad that Tusneem had come back to indulge Komli's last wishe Tusneem had prayed in each of the baby's ears before she had whispered *JOY* into ther as though Komli was willing her little one to be joyful. Tusneem had sobbed in his arm "She was my mentor and my mendicant, willing to share everything that dropped in h bowl!"

Even if there was no truth in God being a child, he would treat Joy as his God. I would listen to her and play with her and respect her and try never to impose h preconceived ideas upon her.

"Thank you, Komli, for Joy. I love you," he had whispered as he had kissed her on th forehead and bade her farewell. How could a woman who had rarely played with boug toys, who wanted to save the tree and wipe her ass with water, and who had refused shovel the snow, survive the 21st century, a little voice inside him had asked.

When Scott boarded the plane for America, linked and locked to his seat and to h child and to his memories, he found himself beginning to think like Komli:

> Fire and Water
> Beauty and truth
> Earth and Wind
> Life and death
> Given to us for nothing
> Taken from us for nothing
> Deaf and dumb creatures all
> Carved without pen or paper
> Man's priceless playmates on planet earth.
> The rest is mere words.

CℑБО   CℑБО

Edwards Brothers, Inc.
Thorofare, NJ USA
May 10, 2011